❧ J.H.Project ❧

The day before the day after

II

Complete Edition

Title | The day before the day after II - *Complete Edition*

Author | J. H. Project

Cover art | Atelier Grafico

Editing | Vittoria Serena Dalton

Translated by | Stefania Castellaneta

ISBN-13 | 978-1546637493

ISBN-10 | 1546637494

Official Site: www.jhprojectbooks.com
E-mail: jay.acca@yahoo.it

Dedicated to my readers: some will love you for what you are and others will hate you for the same reason... get used to it.

J. H. Project

Prologue

Fear filled the car. Maria could feel it slide along her neck and tighten its grip, as if to strangle her.

The jeep proceeded quickly along the road. The sound of the sea at the bottom of the cliff where the long road led to the witness protection safehouse, seemed as if it was trying to relieve their tension.

Antonio's hand tightened around hers. His firm grip was trying to give her courage and Maria sensed that her husband was feeling the same emotions as she was.

Not even the presence of the unmarked police cars surrounding them, full of plain-clothes officers ready to do whatever it took to protect them, was able to calm their nerves and the worries which were troubling them.

"We'll be at the new safe-house in a few minutes. The hearing is tomorrow and then this nightmare will be over at last," Antonio said, trying to reassure her.

Maria turned around. Their only son was sleeping peacefully, lying on the seat back.

She let go of her husband's hand to adjust the blanket tenderly on the little boy's shoulders. He was just thirteen years old, far too young to be involved in a maelstrom like this. But Antonio was right, everything would be over soon.

She turned forward again and took the comforting hand of the man she loved in hers. "Antonio, my sweet love, you don't need to reassure me. I'm not afraid. I knew what your work was and what you fought for even before we got married, that's why I chose you."

"I'm putting you in danger, Maria, in danger while I fight against an ailing and corrupt system that will never be eliminated."

Maria smiled as she caressed his cheek. "You have always been a loving husband and an exemplary father. Thanks to you Nickolas has grown up with important values, and what you're doing will serve as an example for everyone, what you're doing is really wonderful", she soothed him.

Antonio looked at her lovingly, grateful for the affectionate and comforting words. Maria had always been like this. She had always found the right words to infuse courage and hope in him.

"I want to make a difference." he exclaimed encouraged, "and I hope that Nick will join me in this when he grows up."

They sped along the road to safety. Fear was beginning to loosen its grip. Maria was beginning to feel she was safe. It was just an immense flash of light. Maria saw it erase the world in a heartbeat. Then came the thunder like the roar of a dragon. The car was swept away like a dead leaf carried by the storm.

An explosion? She wondered confused.

The car was now rolling disastrously down the cliff, heading into the icy sea with no possibility of rescue.

She lifted a hand to her temple and felt a warm liquid under her fingers. She was bleeding.

The jeep crashed into the dark waves with a terrible thud.

She managed to look toward her husband. He would certainly save them; he always had a way to survive any tragedy.

But he was lolling on the seat like a puppet, trapped by the seat belt. His eyes were slightly shut, staring into space.

She screamed in desperation. Her husband was dead.

The sea water flooded into the vehicle. She screamed again terrified, crying for help.

She tried to free herself from the seat belt and realized with horror that it was stuck.

Squirming under the sash that was trapping her, her sole thought was the only love she had left: Nickolas, her precious only son.

Two small cold hands grabbed her shoulder.

Nick was crying as he pulled at the seatbelt with all his strength in a desperate attempt to release her.

The jeep was plunging deeper and deeper into the waves. The water was rising inside the vehicle; now Maria could breathe only by lifting her face as high as possible.

With a desperate gesture, she tried to break the window. She made a sign to Nick to do the same. Her only desire was to be able to save him at least, but he kept pulling the seatbelt.

He was trying with all his might to save his mother, with his father's dead body there, a few inches from him.

Maria stretched upwards to breathe, but there was no more air in the car. There was no more air in her lungs. The sea was swallowing them up. Their end had come. She shut her eyes tight, frantic and overpowered by the inevitable fate that awaited them.

It was impossible to cry underwater, but if she could have, she would have shed all the tears she had.

Nick's slender arms slid around her neck.

Whatever happens a mother's hug will calm you and console you, Maria used to say when Nick needed comforting.

Nick was in need of comfort in that moment too, but ironically he was the one comforting her. His was the simple gesture, brimming with love, of a son who had been tossed into bloody games by a life which was too big for him to face.

Suddenly the car window exploded into a thousand pieces. A strong hand in a black glove grabbed Maria by the collar of her shirt. The woman felt herself being tugged over and over again, but she didn't move.

Maria seized the hand and pushed it to Nick's. She didn't know if this was enough for F to understand that she was trapped, that there was no way nor time to save her, but she hoped it was sufficient.

And it was. F's hand quickly took Nick by the scruff of his neck and pulled him vigorously out of the jeep.

The boy kicked around in the waves, opening his mouth shouting and weeping as he was dragged away.

Mary looked at her little one, her last great love, as he was snatched from death.

She blessed the hands of agent F that had seized her son to take him to safety and as she died a smile crossed her face.

1.

When you see it from the *Four Seasons* - the tallest skyscraper in the city – Miami is a magnificent spectacle. Or at least it would be, if Nick had the time to stop and contemplate the panorama.

But he's too busy pursuing a well-built and bare-chested guy with very short blond hair. He has a backpack on his shoulders and under his right arm, all tattooed black, he's holding tightly onto the painting he has just stolen from his client's suite.

The thief is giving him a run for his money. He keeps escaping him and, as if that wasn't enough, he's destroying everything he finds in his way. And a luxury hotel has plenty of furnishings, furniture, mirrors to smash into pieces.

"Stop! You're under arrest!" Nick yells as he tries to dodge the first of the long row of gazebos that separates the pool from the garden.

The boy escapes him, scarpers between the sun-chairs and stops on the other side of the pool.

He stops in front of him with his gun drawn. The other looks at him in silence, as he rests the painting on the ground. They stare at one another, without saying a word. It is all too tranquil.

The investigator tries to understand what the boy has in mind. His body and face are covered with scars.

"Nick, I'm here," gasps Benjamin breathing hard as he points his weapon at the thief and with the other hand dries the sweat from his forehead.

The blond man moves his hands towards the backpack, and pulls out a golden Beretta 98FS.

He takes a step forward. "Stop! Don't move!"

Slowly, he tries to get closer to the boy. He too knows that there's no way out of this. There's no way to leave the hotel without running into hotel security. But strangely the thief smiles and looks him straight in the eye, then as if he wants to incite him, provocatively caresses his face with the weapon.

Benjamin quivers and screams: "Make one more move and I'll shoot you! Don't move!"

And a barely perceptible movement by the boy is enough for Benjamin to pull the trigger. He is so cold-blooded that he doesn't even blink.

The bullet whizzes very fast towards the boy's left arm, thumps against his hand and severs the little finger.

Gun and amputated finger fly a few meters away.

Blood squirts onto the paving around the pool and draws a pink halo in the water which has a pungent smell of chlorine. The boy lifts his wounded hand and looks at it, totally motionless. No groan or grimace of pain distorts his face. He slowly raises his head, looking back and forth from Nick to Benjamin who are cautiously approaching him. A sarcastic smile appears on his face and with a fake disappointed tone he asks: "Is this the best you can do, old man? Amputate my finger?"

His Russian accent is strong and irritating.

Ben opens his eyes wide, surprised and angry. "Old?"

He turns to Nick with an incredulous expression. "He called me *old* ?"

"Ben, please!"

The thief smiles, as if the river of blood flowing from his body wasn't his. The two detectives look at him in disbelief. With incredible speed, he grabs another gun from the backpack on his shoulders and shoots twice.

As precise as those of a professional hit-man, the bullets he fires hit both detectives dead center in the chest. They fall to the ground like rag dolls and lie there motionless.

There's some writing on the barrel of the Russian Vladimir's gun: *smile and wait for flash*!

Satisfied, he slips the weapon into his jeans, picks up his finger and puts it in his pocket, and it's only when he picks up the painting from the ground that he realizes he's also bleeding from his left leg: Nick had hit him.

There is so much blood on the ground now that a good part of the water in the swimming pool is turning into various shades of red.

He looks towards the two unconscious detectives again and no expression of pain for the amputated finger and the injured leg shows on his face. He turns his back on the place of the shoot-out and parachutes himself into the night, toward that escape route that the two detectives had not even taken into consideration.

Nick, lying on the ground, opens his burned white shirt and looks at the bullet embedded in his bulletproof vest. "Dammit! It burns!"

Still in pain, he touches his earpiece and in a loud but distressed voice he says: "Veronica?"

From the other end of the earpiece you can hear the roar of the motorbike and the woman's voice. "I'm ready!"

"He has just jumped from the skyscraper."

"Without the painting and without the parachute, I hope."

"He's armed, be careful. Will is going to give you the coordinates, we're on our way."

"I'm off!"

Nick turns to Benjamin, who has been silent the whole time trying to take off his bulletproof vest and get up from the ground, but without success.

"Are you alright?" he asks him. Ben looks at him annoyed and complains: "I'm getting married in two weeks! No, I'm not alright!"

***

Koki, a nice-looking Japanese guy, is leaning on his bike, a black Kawasaki Ninja ZX-10R, a hat covering his long black hair and a huge smile on his lips. He's looking at the Cuban girl passing by on the sidewalk. "Hey, hot chick! Do you want to be arrested by any chance?"

The girl stops intrigued and asks him: "Arrested? For what?"

"For going around with *bombs* like that?" he remarks, pointing at her generous breasts, and starts laughing amused thinking he has just cracked a really witty joke. Instead of laughing, the girl slaps him hard and says a couple of swearwords in Spanish, then walks away indignant. Still surprised by her unexpected act, he sees Vladimir approaching him, getting rid of the parachute. He's bare-chested, covered in blood with an injured leg, his left hand missing the little finger, his gun sticking out from one side of his jeans, the amputated finger from the other.

Koki bursts out laughing, pointing at his beat up brother, while Vladimir in his rough and rude way asks him: "What the fuck are you laughing at?"

"They gave you a good going over," he continues sniggering, "Tell me they're still alive, I beg you."

"Yes unfortunately! How much time have I got left?" he enquires, referring to his wounds.

"Before your body has the good sense to pass out? Judging by the wounds, I'd say about half an hour."

"That'll be enough! Here..."

He hands him the painting marked with blood, takes the finger from his pocket and puts it in the cooler under the seat of the bike, closes it and gets on the bike. "I'm driving!"

The noise of another motorcycle traveling at a great speed can be heard in the distance. The Japanese man turns to the road, adjusts his hat with a smile on his face and remarks: "Ducati 999, my friend Xena is arriving."

Vladimir just growls as Koki gets on back to back with him, waiting for Veronica's arrival.

She has been pursuing them for months now, hoping to capture them, with no success to date. In the meantime, from the agency headquarters Will is following Veronica with the satellite tracker.

"Veronica, in ten seconds the tra-traffic light straight in front of you will turn red, you're not going to ma-aake it, DAS."

"I can make it, I can make it!"

"Turn right, there is a shortcut aaan..."

"No! I can make it Will!"

The white bike tears along the road. She doesn't want to lose sight of them, knowing that with just a couple of seconds of distraction they'll disappear again without a trace until the next robbery. She's getting closer and closer to the two thieves who have just passed the traffic light, when suddenly the light changes and turns red. Veronica brakes quickly, with the risk of flipping over. "Dammit, Will! It's not ten seconds yet!"

"Someone has a-a-altered the operation of the traffic lights! Frff", Will justifies himself, upset. Veronica, agitated, turns quickly to the left passing between the skyscrapers.

"I can see them," says Will, "At the next one turn tt-t-to..."

"Will!" she yells annoyed, not knowing where to turn.

"T-to the left."

She turns the corner and is once again on the main street, right behind the two thieves. The blood from Vladimir's wounds is dripping on the road. She exchanges a challenging glance with Koki, then takes her trusted boomerang from the belt of her white jumpsuit and throws it with all her strength towards Koki, who avoids it with great skill.

He smiles at her satisfied, clutching the painting between his hands. Veronica, though, suddenly raises her hand. The Japanese realizes at that moment what is about to happen, but it's too late. The weapon comes back and the next moment it hits his hat, tearing it off his head.

"You're not laughing any more, huh?" screams the woman as she catches the boomerang. Koki smiles.

"Will you stop messing with the detective, once and for all?" barks Vladimir, and more than a question it sounds like an order. "Knock her flat! I have a finger to sew back on."

Koki takes some small Japanese four-pointed nails from one of the leather pockets on his bike and smiles as he shows them to Veronica, who immediately realizes what he's about to do.

"No! You wretch!"

"What? What's haaappening, Veronica?" Will shouts.

But Veronica doesn't have time to explain. Koki throws the nails on the ground and in a moment the front tire of Veronica's bike rips open. It's difficult to stay on the road and avoid colliding with other cars. She tries a final move: she lifts the bike up and drives it on the rear tire only.

Unfortunately a second nail pierces this wheel too and the woman ends abruptly on the ground, sliding on the asphalt for meters with the risk of being run over by the oncoming cars.

Veronica keeps sliding along the road as several vehicles collide in an attempt to avoid her bike. In the midst of all that chaos, Nick arrives in his black BMW X6 and stops in the middle of the road shielding Veronica from the crashing cars. The two thieves are already far away by now.

Nick, worried, is the first to get out of the SUV. "Veronica, how are you? Are you hurt?"

"No, I'm fine, I'm fine! They're getting away!" she shouts angrily, looking toward the thieves on the run.

"It doesn't matter, let me see" he orders. He kneels beside her. Seeing her white helmet split in two, he checks her head, while Benjamin stops the cars showing his badge. They are both still wearing the shirts burned by the bullets from the shoot-out with Vladimir.

"Nick, I'm fine. It's them you have to worry about!"

"Veronica, stop it. You're bleeding." He checks her injured leg, but she is not happy that the thieves have got away again. She lowers her eyes, annoyed.

Will, concerned, continues to call them through the ear-piece from the base. "Gu-gu-guys, da-daamit! Can you hear me?"

"Yes, Will, I can hear you."

"*Yes, Will?*" he repeats, annoyed, "Tha-that's it? I waaas dyy-ying here alone, no one ever tells me aaanything, I am a-a-always the last one to know wwhhat's ha-happening."

Nick reassures him: "Yes, she's alright."

"*She's alright?* I to-to-told you I lost the thieves, I can't s-s-see them anymore!"

Nick smiles embarrassed, he hadn't understood. "Don't worry, Will, what's important is that we're all okay. We have to clean up the road, Mr. Michael's suite and collect the evidence inside it."

"I'll de-de-deal with it. I'll w-w-wait for you at the base."

Veronica is downcast, lost in thought. She looks angrily at her smashed bike, pulls her black hair into a pony tail and then shakes her head.

"Veronica?" begins Nick, trying to console her, "We'll catch them. It's not your fault."

"I was so close! That Japanese one was looking at me and challenging me! It was some kind of game for him! Damn him!"

"He was not challenging you, but what you represent. You must not confuse the two things, do you understand?"

"I know, I know!"

13

"Come here", he says to her, smiling. He knows her competitive and proud nature. He holds out his hand, helping her to get back on her feet.

"You should have followed them," she keeps complaining in a low voice.

"What's the second rule of our team?"

"Nobody is left behind."

"And if he is?"

Veronica smiles and says: *"We go back and get him."*

"There is no success without a team, keep it in mind, always."

"I know", she smiles again, and shows him her boomerang, where some black hair has been caught. "At least now we have DNA."

"You were really good."

Meanwhile, the chaos around them gets worse. The chase has caused several accidents, the road is blocked and car horns are honking. The journalists will be here soon. On the other side of the road, Benjamin is dragging Veronica's damaged bike with one hand and with the other is talking on his cell in an edgy tone. "My dear, I'm in the middle of a..." he stops, making a puzzled face, "What? Wedding hat? But it's a dog, for God's sake! No, I don't hate Naomi, but it's absurd for me to go up to New York just for... Hello? Hello, Katherine?"

He hangs up, turns to Nick and Veronica who are looking at him intrigued, and barks furiously: "I need to hit someone!"

***

In a room on the eighth floor of the *Watchtower*, Nick, Patrick and Will are watching Benjamin through the two-way mirror. The poor wretch that ended up in Benjamin's hands and being interrogated is a boy of twenty with a criminal record and a face which is far from reassuring. There's just a rectangular table and two chairs in the room.

"We've traced where the anonymous call we received came from and it came from your sleazy stinking apartment! Can you explain that, Sam?"

The boy looks at him with a couldn't-care-less air as he rocks to and fro on the chair and looks at the man's burnt shirt without replying.

"Can you answer me, please?"

"*Please?*" he repeats, laughing at him. "Do you think that I'll answer your question just because you ask nicely?"

"Oh no, I certainly hope not", replies Benjamin, happy. He goes to him in a threatening way and kicks the chair making him fall to the ground.

"I don't know anything", claims Sam, far from scared, spitting on the floor in a disgusting way.

"No? You don't know anything, eh? Well, if I can't have the information by asking politely, let's try another way!" He grabs him by the hair, lifting him from the floor and throwing him against the wall. He begins to punch him furiously in the stomach as he insults him.

In the next room, the others watch what's happening, surprised.

"I've never been married, but... shouldn't the bridegroom be in a euphoric and generally happy state of mind?" Patrick comments casually.

"Maybe it's o-only the fi-first time you get ma-married."

Patrick nods. "The third time must be somewhat stressful."

Nick is bewildered. "I'd better step in or he runs the risk of killing him. Is this the way to behave? I don't like this violence." He's about to open the door and exit the small room, when Patrick stops him. "No, wait a moment. He has to let off steam in some way."

"Not with him and not like that. In the United States of America *this* is called abuse of power!"

Nick is about to leave the room again, when between kicks and punches he hears the suspect scream. "*I'll talk, I'll talk!* Alright, for fuck's sa... Stop it, please!"

Nick stops, closes the door and goes to the two-way mirror.

"I decide when to stop!" replies Benjamin.

"I received an anonymous phone call. I would have had a thousand dollars in my bank account if I called you and warned you about the robbery."

"You expect me to believe that an anonymous phone call asked you to make an anonymous phone call to us? Have I got *idiot* written on my forehead by any chance?" he yells, punching him in the face again.

Patrick has been watching Sam the whole time, his hands, his eyes, the facial movement. He's not listening to his words, but his body. "He's lying about the thousand dollars", he decides.

"Are you sure?" asks Nick.

"Have I ever been wrong?"

Nick shakes his head and smiles. His was a stupid question.

"Okay, okay. They gave me four thousand, four thousand! But the rest is true, I swear, I swear on my mother, my poor sick mother!"

Benjamin clenches his teeth and comments: "Your mother died four years ago." Then lands another punch for the lie he just told.

"But she really was sick!"

"Tell me about the anonymous call, what voice was it? Male or female?"

"Male! With a foreign accent, Russian maybe, I don't know."

"Any background noise? Ships, railways, airports..."

"I... I don't know! I don't remember!"

Benjamin smiles in a sadistic way, raises his fist, eager to start hitting him again. "Let me refresh your memory!"

With a worried frown, Patrick turns to Nick: "Go and stop him, the boy is telling the truth."

It's not going to be easy to calm Ben. Nick looks at him for a moment and says: "Will, you go."

Will shudders. "W-why me? Frfff, I don't ghyti..." he stammers, until he becomes incomprehensible as he rocks nervously on his usual faded red chair.

Patrick smiles and reassures him: "You know how to calm him. Your method is foolproof and unique."

"Frrrf!" complains Will and, after adding further indecipherable words, he gets up and goes out of the room with a long face.

Nick sits down on the red chair in front of the computer, and starts to watch the security videos of the suite that has just been robbed. "Look here, during the chase the thief runs along the corridor and looks straight into the camera, with his face

16

uncovered and a defiant expression, as if he were doing it on purpose."

"I think he's under the influence of some drug", says Patrick, "Both when Ben shot his finger off his hand, and when you shot him, he didn't even blink, his face didn't show even the minimum sign of pain."

"They stole a Medusa painting", Nick thinks aloud as he cleans his burned shirt, "It's unique, invaluable, and the anonymous phone call was made by a man with a Russian accent."

"You think it has to do with Boris, don't you?" guesses Patrick.

"Either him or his brother. We'll have the blood tested as well as the fingerprints and the hair that Veronica managed to get. If he's got a record, we'll nail him."

In the next room, meanwhile, Will is trying to deter Benjamin from his murderous instinct against Sam. He jumps on his back, but considering that Ben is well-built and Will is short and not athletic at all, it ends up with Ben beating Sam with Will on his shoulders.

2.

In the meantime – From Mina's diary

Miami is without doubt the favorite destination for people who love excess, pleasure and entertainment. Sun, palm trees, crystal clear sea, colorful and full of life by day and even more so at night. You're never bored here. It's full of wacky and quirky characters from all over the world, young girls on roller skates, boys showing off their pecs, everyone here looks like a model. Spanish is the second most widely spoken language here.

Downtown is very modern, it's all tall skyscrapers lit up with bright colors. This city is certainly one of a kind.

And right here, in the midst of these fabulous skyscrapers, stands *Watchtower & Co.*, Florida's most exclusive detective agency. It's a very tall modern building, in mirrored glass with the huge *Watchtower* sign watching over the city from the top floor.

Ah, I almost forgot, my name is Mina Gallina, I'm nineteen, and I've been living in Miami for two months.

I'd never been further than Naples in my whole life but now I even find myself in another continent, and needless to say I'm really delighted to be in this wonderful city!

Miami is a far cry from how it is described in some American movies, full of thieves, murderers, criminals, and dodgy people in the streets who go around with guns and other weapons day and night. On the contrary, it is very well organized as far as law and order are concerned. It's normal to find criminals here too, and I know this because I hear about it on television or from Nickolas' team, but tourists like us who aren't aware of the environment, feel perfectly safe and comfortable thanks to the police patrols that go around at all hours of the day and night.

I'm just back from the beach, and I'm trying to climb the stairs leading to the *Watchtower*. I say *I'm trying* because it's not easy to get through all the journalists who storm the agency every day in the hope of obtaining an interview with Nick and his colleagues. They're tireless, lying in wait for hours under the tower; they push and shove, insults fly at times, and when I go past them all hell lets

18

loose. I might seem annoyed and outraged from the way I describe this whole situation, but it's not like that at all. I feel like a VIP every time I go in and out of this building. The journalists know me by now and when they see me in the street they even say hi. I love all this!

With great difficulty I manage to climb the stairs and reach the huge glass door, forcing myself to ignore absurd questions such as: *are Patrick Sword and Nickolas Ortega Torres really friends or as rumor has it, are they trying to hide their competition from the media? Is Veronica Banderas homosexual? Where is William Smith? We never see him, has he been fired?* Italian journalism used to amaze me, but I see that baloney is alive and well here as well.

The modern-style steps lead into a large well-lit waiting room, with comfortable sofas and side tables. The door of this glass building is always wide open to everyone, except journalists. Nick wants people to know that he and his detectives are always available, at any time of the day or night, to help anyone in need. And I have to say that people have appreciated this initiative very much.

In the room there are no doors or stairs leading to the upper floors, there is only a huge bullet-proof elevator in the center of it. I walk up to the scanner and look into the red light, the door opens, I walk in, and it leaves. I don't push any button. Even if I wanted to stop on the fourth floor, for example, the elevator wouldn't stop. All other floors are strictly off-limits to me, since I am not part of the investigation team. Every time I get into the elevator, I am amazed at how fast it reaches the top floor of the skyscraper, you feel like you're at the funfair.

On the other hand, I'm in despair. Everything is a mirror here, and this promptly reminds me that while everyone in Miami has a beautiful golden tan, I've been trying for months to obtain the same result and all I can manage is a maddening blotchy red: I have the awful white shape of my swimsuit and sunburn of various hues. And yet I am of Neapolitan origin, so one would expect that I would become incredibly tanned and not end up in this state.

The door opens and the first thing I see is the huge circular white and orange counter on which there are three computers, at least five telephones, two monitors and lots of newspapers, papers and pencils scattered everywhere. Usually, it's the secretary, a forty year old African-American called America, who's there waiting for me, with a serious face and eyes underneath her thousand black braids, always ready to criticize and scold, but strangely she's not there right now.

I go around the counter to see what's written on the blackboard hanging on the wall. Under my name there are usually not many commitments like the others have, thank goodness. Maybe it's because my only commitment is Jas.

I've almost reached the board when I see Franklin - Benjamin's younger son - lying on the ground, motionless.

I run to him. "Franklin! Oh my God!"

I turn him over slowly, his eyes are closed and I'm not certain I can hear him breathing.

"Franklin! Can you hear me, little one?"

I begin to tremble, I don't know what to do, I can't call for help, my voice won't come out of my mouth, and I hold him tight in my arms caressing his brown skin. "Help... Can anyone hear me? America... America", I call with a tiny voice. I grope for the telephone on the counter to call an ambulance. I don't know what's happening. I can't understand why Franklin is lying unconscious on the ground. Suddenly from the end of one of the three corridors I hear America's voice screaming annoyed: "Franklin! Get up right this minute before I kick your black ass!"

"What?" I ask, confused.

Franklin opens his eyes immediately and gives me a huge smile. "Technically *black ass* would be a racist insult, but I don't think it has the same meaning when a black woman says it", he remarks and cheerfully gets up from the ground as if nothing had happened, while my heart is still pounding from the fright.

"Are you crazy? I was about to have a heart attack, Franklin!"

"The same thing happened to his chemistry teacher today, when she went into the classroom she found him on the ground with his throat cut!" retorts America.

"That's not the right definition", he corrects her, "Because by heart attack we mean the necrosis of a tissue due to an ischemia, whereas she had a blackout, that is, a momentary loss of her senses or loss of consciousness, which we can't be sure was caused by me."

I don't know exactly what he has just said, but it all sounds so intelligent. America gives him a dirty look and answers the phone on the circular counter, while Franklin smiles at me again, looking at me with his sweet dark eyes. I can't be angry with him, especially knowing that he's only six years old and is very much in need of a female presence near him. I kneel to fix the black braids falling over his eyes.

"You fell for it, didn't you? Was I good?"

"Yes, but usually, when people make jokes, it should make you laugh."

"I'm laughing", he announces. Clearly he doesn't understand where the problem is. "Wasn't I good?"

"Yes, you were very good", I smile at his naivety. "Didn't you see how scared I was?"

"Do you think mom would have liked it?"

I recall the enormous stern black woman Franklin speaks to every once in a while on Skype. "Well, let's say that she's not the type for this kind of thing, but I fell for it hook, line and sinker."

"Franklin!" America interrupts us, "Have you already chosen which faculty at university you're going to enroll in?'" she asks, as if it were a normal thing. Which faculty? At six years of age? Is that legal?

"No."

"Then see that you do before your mother turns up and yells at you during the video call!"

"Okay, America", he says with a smile on his lips. He runs towards the living room.

I hear America complaining loudly: "Damn journalists! I'm going to make a private call", she looks at the security monitors for a moment and then turns back to me: "Ross is on his way with the groceries, get him to sign these papers and tell him that I forgot to add peanut butter to the list, and to go and get it as soon as possible before Will has a fit. I have no desire to listen to his hysterics!"

"But Ross hates me, I don't know if..."

"*I don't know if, I don't know if*", she repeats in a mocking tone, "Stop being afraid of that skinny little fairy and show some balls for once!" She leaves with a determined step and heads towards the living room.

I don't like being treated like this. I don't like the language they use here in America, sometimes all you hear are profanities and gratuitous insults. Fuming, I go behind the counter. Ross gets on my nerves, not because he's gay, and not even because he's black - I am not a racist, not me! It's because he enjoys humiliating people, saying how perfect he is and how everyone else is nothing. I have never heard him pay a compliment to a woman. He's nasty. He snorts and criticizes as if everyone else were the last shit on earth. From the video surveillance cameras, I can see Ross is already in the elevator and I get the creeps.

Today his hair is dyed green, matching his pants. The elevator door opens and he gets out carrying the grocery bags as if he'd just been to do some shopping.

"Good morning, Ross", I greet him coldly. He looks around, disoriented. "Ahaaaa, yes, hello *M,* nice dress you have, it looks like the towel from the john."

It has only taken him a second to offend me; it's a new record.

"How come it's you here to meet me?" he asks still looking around, "Where are all the people that really matter around here?"

He's so irritating when he speaks. It's too quick and he makes faces. I prefer to say nothing, he can go to hell. He leaves the bags on the ground and starts to walk two fingers on the counter as if they were a little live man. I look at him with raised eyebrows trying to understand what the hell he is doing.

"The journalists downstairs assailed me thinking I was a detective, isn't that incredible?" he begins to laugh happily, sounding like an excited young girl. I don't reply. I just want him to sign the papers and leave as soon as possible.

"Well then, little *M?* Are you trying to steal big *A*'s place?" he continues, obviously referring to America, and he makes that obnoxious face again and gesticulates. The green streak in his hair swings back and forth as well.

I grunt again and say: "America said you have to sign this sheet and go and get peanut butter. She forgot to write it on your list."

"Aha, and did she say this before or after you tied her up, gagged her, killed her and abandoned her in some dark alley in Brooklyn?"

"Brooklyn? In Florida?"

He nods and looks at me warily. It's pointless for me to keep talking. What he's saying is absurd. I turn to the other side and look at the board to see what time I have to go and pick up Jas, ignoring him completely, but unfortunately I see him approaching me again, walking his fingers on the counter.

How annoying!

"You know, unlike you, a petty bourgeois without any hope or plans for the future, I have the path of my upward growth very clearly mapped out in mind. Now I do grocery shopping for *W*, tomorrow I will clean the counter for *A*, the day after tomorrow I will wash *V*'s cars and engines, perhaps I'll do *B*'s dog, but in the end I'll become Nick's partner! And when I say *partner*, I mean in every way, if you know what I mean", he says and starts to laugh like a lunatic, even pretending to be embarrassed. What's more, I don't understand why instead of saying the names in full he only uses the initials A, B, C, so I get lost and I don't even know what he's talking about.

I hear the elevator door open behind me, and I see them: Ben with the singed white shirt and his gray hair all disheveled, Veronica with her head and one leg bandaged and Will, who is visibly upset, mutters to himself as he drags his inseparable torn red chair behind him. What the heck has happened? They all look stunned and shattered except for Patrick who enters the room all nice and elegant and with a smile on his face.

"Good morning", I greet them with raised eyebrows. They simply raise a hand, all except Veronica, of course, who ignores me. I move away from the counter and sit on a padded bench.

"*Oh Good Heavens*", shouts Ross, looking at them terrified, "The goddess of good taste will arrive and put you all to death, you cannot go around looking like this! Come on, guys, you're making me look bad, there are journalists downstairs!"

His voice rises to a shriek and he talks non-stop.

They don't even give him a glance. They lean on the counter, terribly tired. Nick is the last one to come out of the elevator, still wearing the burnt shirt and holding a black bag. Ross suddenly pulls himself together, sits down next to me, crosses his legs and with a childlike voice he greets Nick with a wave of his hand: "Hi Niki!"

It's a pitiful scene. Nick just nods at him. I don't know if he even he remembers him. "Where's America?" he asks.

"I'm here, I'm here!" you can hear her bored voice coming from the corridor. "And with me I also have five files full of your personal and working life disasters."

She throws them on the counter and goes behind it. The guys look at each other forlorn. Will is the only one who, while waiting for what the woman has to say, also starts to tidy up pencils, pens and papers on the counter. America looks at him bewildered raising an eyebrow, while I move to the end of the bench away from Ross.

"Let's start with work," she says in opening the first file. "Just today, you have destroyed almost half of the unsuspecting Mr. Michael George's suite."

"Wow," exclaims Ross and jumps to his feet, "George Michael is here? Yes?"

They all turn towards him annoyed. He sits down again, casually crossing his legs like a young lady.

America resumes talking: "As I was saying, as well as coloring the hotel pool with blood and breaking furnishings, furniture, mirrors and windows to pieces all the way from the suite to the foyer, you let the thief get away, fleeing with a painting of inestimable value."

Ben and Nick make eye contact without commenting.

"Veronica's fall and the nails scattered on the road have caused other car accidents, then there's the bike that was destroyed, and it comes to a total of..."

"No, no, no, no", Ben interrupts her, quickly closing the file in front of her nose to prevent her from saying the cost, "We'll get to the numbers later."

"You've been chasing these two thieves for months. If you don't want more numbers, the time has come to catch them, instead of playing chase on the streets of Miami."

The guys grimace and look at each other as if to say *if only it were so easy*. Patrick is the only one who, as usual, stands back leaning on the wall behind them listening to it all without commenting. He's so fascinating. This quiet, mysterious way of his drives me wild.

America turns to Ben again, opening another file. "Your son Franklin nearly scared his chemistry teacher to death by pulling a tasteless prank on her. The lady is now in hospital for some check-ups."

"It can't be that serious."

I think he said it to lighten the situation, but immediately after he becomes serious and with a tone just as serious he asks: "Does his mother know?"

"Choco hasn't been told about it yet, she's performing in Washington right now, and I think she's playing Carmen."

"Good! And the other two?"

"As far as your son Pavarotti is concerned and the door he demolished last week, I wanted to let you know that even though the damage has been paid for, Pavarotti can no longer set foot in the shopping center."

Ben shakes his head while the others, bored, wait for their turn.

"Today, instead, he broke two glasses in the kitchen. He claims they provoked him", she says with a strange grimace, "I know he's thirteen and he's coming into full puberty, but I think that a good spanking every so often wouldn't go astray."

"First of all I'm going to talk to him and ask him why the glasses bothered him, it may well be that he gives me a sensible answer."

America looks at him as if to say *you're delusional.* "If you wish to speak to the glasses as well, they're in the garbage", she says sarcastically.

"You're very kind, but there's no need. Instead, what's happening with the older daughter?"

"Benjamina is still weeping; she's been weeping since yesterday evening."

"Has she left him, at least?"

"No."

"Her mother won't be happy at all."

25

Ben sits on the bench between me and Ross; after greeting me he starts to read and sign the papers that America has given him. She turns to Veronica, opens another file and says: "Your father called from Spain, your brother Jose is fine, it was just an appendectomy, he'll be discharged from hospital the day after tomorrow, so you can stop afflicting everyone."

"*Gracias Dio!*" she cradles the cross hanging on the chain around her neck and looks upwards, saying something in Spanish, a prayer maybe or a thanksgiving to God, I don't know.

Will, who is still tidying things on the counter with one hand, pats her on her shoulder. "Ee-e-everything we-we-went well, see?"

"Yes, but it didn't go so well for you. Your parents want a video call with you during the week. As far as I could understand they want to meet your girlfriend", America tells him and then closes the file and adds, "Nonexistent and the reason you moved to Miami so you could be with her."

She looks at him as you would naturally look at someone who talks bullshit. Will goes all red in the face, and as usual he starts to say incomprehensible things, scratching his head and his beard in embarrassment. "Wh-what?! Frf. Wh-wh-wh-what will I do?" he asks Veronica stammering.

"I'm not sure. For your parents I'm now your ex-girlfriend so I can't help you anymore," says Veronica, giving him a pat on the back, "Why don't you ask America to be your new pretend girlfriend?" She smiles as she says it and opens a newspaper she finds on the counter.

America gives her a filthy look. "I don't want to be part of this general scam. You're thirty-one now, show some balls and tell them the truth, you'd be better off."

Will says nothing. He grabs his red chair and drags it along the corridor with a nervous gait, uttering weird things until he disappears into his room.

"Now to you, boss", continues America addressing Nick and she opens the file, "Jas's ex-psychologist filed a complaint this morning, that's the third that she's managed to get rid of in order of time. It's for moral damages and slander against her, discrediting her as a professional in her work. She has to appear in court on the twenty second, but you already know the drill."

26

Yeah, that's right, we really need a twenty-two here, *leave, flee!*

America continues: "As for the state exam, and for having taken blood samples and administered drugs without a proper degree at Jackson Memorial Hospital, Ben has managed to arrange a settlement. Until September, Jas must work her butt off cleaning every corner of the hospital from top to bottom, as well as having to pay the modest sum of..."

"No, no, no, no", exclaims Ben. He gets up suddenly from the bench and rushes to the counter taking the file out of her hands again. "We'll get to the numbers later."

The woman just scowls, pulling back her long black braids and continues: "And another thing, the most important: tell Jas to feed that poor fish every so often! It's turning into a piranha; you can clearly see a bite on the little plastic house inside the fish tank! I'd tell her myself but even if we live in the same building, we never manage to meet."

After her monologue, everyone remains silent for a few seconds, but no one is particularly shocked by America's words. The good thing about the wonderful state I'm living in is that trouble with justice seem to be an everyday occurrence, therefore nobody cares about Jas's daily screw-ups any longer.

"Has she come out of her room for at least two minutes today?" Nick asks me, turning towards me.

"Yes, yes she has."

It's clear he's expecting a useless platitude from me, dammit!

"She went out when I accompanied her to the psychologist", I add. As I thought, Nick doesn't seem to be at all buoyed by this news.

"She also went out for her morning cappuccino as soon as she woke up, at two-thirty in the afternoon", America points out.

In the meantime Ben turns to Nick, saying, "Well, I'll deal with the complaint later, there'll be no need to go to court. I'm going to take a shower now and speak to Franklin, see you later guys." He's about to head towards the bedrooms when America stops him. "Oh, Ben."

"Yes?"

"Your future young lady wife left a list of the things to do before the wedding", she says, waving a pink sheet. I can smell the strawberry perfume all the way over here. Ben doesn't seem too enthusiastic and grabs the list, but America holds onto it tightly and says with a snigger: "Do you want me to give you a hand choosing the shoes for the dog?" and goes off annoyed.

America sighs. "Jas is onto her fourth psychologist, Ben onto the third wife, is there anyone who collects stamps or shoes like normal people do?"

"I collect stamps too!" Ben shouts from the corridor.

"It would have been better if you'd stuck to those!"

I try not to laugh. America gets back to work putting the files down and giving some papers to Nick to sign. Nobody cares about Jas and what she did any longer. Ross is still sitting next to me, participating in the whole discussion nodding his head and making faces as if he were part of the group, although in reality nobody cares two hoots about him. I don't understand why he doesn't leave, once and for all.

"Jas doesn't need a psychologist, she needs an exorcist!" you can hear Veronica's annoyed voice as she reads the newspaper and grumbles to herself.

"Ah look, I fully agree with you on this, my dear *V*, she's totally and monstrously mentally unbalanced, that one!" exclaims Ross.

Veronica looks at him for a few seconds and then, even more irritated, she asks him: "Who are you?"

"I'm Ross, *W's* shopping boy". When he says *W* he also shows it with his fingers. She looks at him and doesn't understand, so Ross sits back on the bench, disappointed.

Veronica goes back to talking about Jas: "The few times she does come out of her room she just insults us and creates disasters. We spend more money buying news about her so she doesn't end up on the scandal tabloids than for the damage we do on the job", she says indignant and throws the newspaper on the counter. "Sooner or later someone will speak, sooner or later she'll get into such trouble that it will be impossible to cover it up, and the journalists will make a meal of us! And this is the last thing we need right now!"

With Veronica it's always the same story. When Pavarotti makes trouble and destroys things she says nothing, but if Jas does something, it's immediately a controversy. I detest her.

Nick's face turns gloomy. "I have no intention of discussing this matter with you," he says, and from the tone of his voice it's not difficult to understand that it's best to leave him alone. Patrick is no longer leaning on the wall and this is not a good sign.

She continues to needle him: "Of course you won't, because you know I'm right! I know she went through a difficult time after what happened, and I'm sorry, but this doesn't mean that because of her psychological state and *your* feelings of guilt, the whole team should have to put up with it."

"Veronica, that's enough! I said that I do not intend to discuss this with you! Jas is my family, she's the most important person for me here, and if someone is not happy with my attitude towards her, then they can leave! And this applies to everyone!"

Total silence descends on the room. Nick is red in the face and terribly angry. Veronica with bright eyes and a sad face goes toward the third corridor that leads to the offices. I don't understand why she insists on bad-mouthing Jas if she knows that she'll get the usual tirade.

You can cut the tension in the room with a knife. America just tightens her lips and continues to do her job without interfering, while Ross sits there with a shocked look on his face and talks without emitting a sound. He's like a silent movie. The calmest of the lot, as usual, is Patrick. He looks at us with his hands in his pockets and doesn't show any kind of emotion. With great calm and elegance he approaches Nick saying: "Shall we go?"

I know it's my turn now, and in fact Nick turns toward me. "Come on Mina, let's go to the living room."

He speaks to me in a gentle way with no trace of the anger he showed with Veronica. I get up, and I see Ross get up as well. He smiles and claps his hands, I don't understand. America looks at him from under her black braids. "Not you! Go buy the peanut butter. Quickly, get going!"

Ross leaves at a run, sending little kisses to Nick behind his back. Apparently his mood changes in a second and at least he has lightened up the situation a little.

We go into the corridor to the right with the white tiles, the one that leads to the relaxation area. In the center of the living room there is a very large round table, perfect for at least twelve people;

little Franklin is sitting at it doing his homework on the laptop open in front of him. He looks at us for a moment then gets back to it.

We sit at some distance from him, facing the panoramic window with the breathtaking view. I am afraid of Nick's questions, I can't seem to learn how to lie, it's difficult, you can read on my face that I'm lying, I'm not convincing. With Nick, more or less, I can manage, I can divert certain questions, but not with Patrick. He reads inside me, he makes me nervous and I'm even afraid to move in case I make a gesture that could give me away and I give him to understand what I'm desperately wanting to hide from him.

Jas does nothing but teach me body language, but it doesn't help me much if my eyes and the terrified expression on my face betray me. I sit down. I have Nick on one side, his shirt has a burnt smell; and on the other side I have Patrick, carefully sitting at a safe distance. Physical contact with him is almost impossible. He quietly smiles at me. He looks like an angel with that blond hair and those green eyes, but underneath it all I know it is only a trap to mesmerize me and make me crumble.

"I wanted to talk to you about Jas", begins Nick.

"Really?" I ask, clearly ironic. It is obvious that he wants to speak to me about her. She's the only thing we have in common.

He smiles and continues: "It's exactly four months today since Borak escaped from the surveillance of my colleagues and Jas was..." he stops. He fixes a spot on the table and seems to be lost in another dimension. Perhaps he has remembered what condition she was in when he found her that terrible evening.

Patrick glances at him for a moment and noticing his long silence he continues to speak in his place: "Four months ago she was diagnosed with PTSD. After an event of this kind a loss of memory is normal, the mind tends to protect itself from bad memories. Nick is worried because, despite all our efforts, her memory has not returned yet and we still don't know exactly what happened that evening", he explains to me and waits for Nick to say something, but he remains silent looking at the empty spot on the table.

"Nick?" he calls him, suddenly waking him up from the trance-like state he's in. After staring at us confused for a moment, he continues. "Yes. She is behaving differently, she sleeps till late, she has left the training sessions, never comes out of her room. In four months she hasn't bonded with anyone of the team, she has become too wary."

He looks me straight in the eyes, waiting for my opinion on what he has just said. I blanch. I swallow the saliva that I don't have and stammering I explain to him: "Eh, no, she's well, you know how she is, she doesn't like socializing, but she's fine", I don't know how complete the sentence, *I've choked, dammit!*

I continue: "There's nothing new about Jas not wanting to bond with anyone. After three years of school she didn't even know who her classmates were. She's is... like this. And she sleeps till late because she's tired."

"Tired of what? Of doing nothing?"

Actually, Nick has a point. I don't know what else to say or how to justify her.

"I don't know what to do anymore."

He's so sad that my heart aches, I feel like weeping, why on earth am I so sensitive?

"Why don't you look at the positives? She hasn't been drinking for months and..." I don't know what else to say, I really don't know what other positive side I can find in the midst of this heap of lies, "And then I haven't heard you argue in months, this is a good thing, isn't it?"

"Yes."

"Then why that depressed tone?"

"Because she has suffered a serious shock. Every change in personality, even if it's positive, is actually negative, believe me."

I don't think I have understood correctly.

"The more I look at her, the more I speak with her, the more I realize... that she is present with her absence!"

I still don't understand.

"Then the fact that she refuses to cooperate and get help from a psychologist makes me understand how much she's suffering! And I'm not able to help her. What does she say to you?"

"Nick", I sigh deeply, "I am her best friend. I am sworn to silence."

He looks at me raising his eyebrows. I've actually learned many big words since I've been here. The only problem is that I don't know if I put them in the right context.

"Can you at least tell her..."

"No, I won't speak on your behalf, if you want to say something to her, do it, but don't drag me into it, I will not act as a go-between."

"She listens to you."

"It's really not like that. And besides, even if it was, I don't think it right to do so behind her back, no. You tell her, she listens to you too."

"But not like she listens to you."

"That's not true", I can't believe it. I'm convincing Nick that Jas listens to him more than she does me. If they'd told me that a few months ago, I would have died laughing.

"Is it possible that she doesn't want to remember, that she's afraid?"

I literally go into a panic, again. "Well, I", I begin to stammer nervously, "No, it's like Patrick said before, that, that she is hiding, the memory."

"Protecting, her mind is protecting her, you mean", he corrects me, smiling cunningly. I become even redder in the face than I already am from sunburn. "Yes, yes, protecting. The mind, is... protecting her", I correct myself, before Nick notices my Freudian slip.

"Don't worry, my friend", Patrick reassures him, "The memory will unlock on its own, we only have to wait for the right moment. What do you think, Mina, when will the right time be?"

I don't know what to say, I am terribly uncomfortable and I would like to sink under the table. Nick doesn't understand the question or why he asked me. Unexpectedly the door of the lounge opens abruptly.

"Guys, let's go!" yells Ben breathing hard, "There has been an explosion at the airport!"

I feel scared and relieved at the same time. I stopped breathing at the word *explosion*, but immediately after, the fact that the attention moved away from me lets me breathe again.

Nick quickly gets up from the chair, while little Franklin, who for the entire time was on the other side of the table studying without saying a word, makes himself heard to explain to us: "Explosion: it is a sudden and violent release of mechanical, chemical, or nuclear energy, normally with the production of gas at very high temperature and pressure."

Ben pretends not to hear his Wikipedia-like explanation and with a hard tone he rebukes him: "I'll talk with you later, young man! I'm tired of your constant jokes!"

In response, Franklin exclaims: "I love you, papa!"

And at that, from stern father Ben turns into a cuddly teddy bear. "I love you too, son."

"Mina, come on!" Nick calls me. We all go to the hall, where America quickly distributes a stack of sheets to each one of us while in the other hand she is holding a clean ironed shirt for Nick. I feel sorry for him, he didn't even have time to change and already he has to run out for another job.

"What was it? A terrorist attack, a fanatic, an accident?" asks Nick, reading one of the sheets while America quickly helps him put on the clean shirt.

"We don't know anything yet, that's why they called us", replies Ben walking past him holding a bag in his hands.

"You can leave from the main entrance, guys", the woman informs them. "All the journalists disappeared in a second."

"When does the session with the psychologist end?" Nick turns to me, how does he think of multiple things at the same time?

"In an hour or so."

"She'll have already finished by now, sending the psychologist to the psychologist!" America comments ironic, walking to the elevator with the others.

"This time it will be different," says Nick with conviction, "I chose her personally. Great professional, military education, curriculum to rival the very best, she's tough, she won't be broken easily."

All of us but Nick look at each other smiling with our eyes, while the elevator door closes.

And so my interrogation on Jas was interrupted by an explosion at the airport. I would like to say I'm glad, but I really don't think it's appropriate, so I'll say nothing. It is the first time in many months that I hear talk of such a thing. A bomb: perhaps Miami is not as safe as I thought.

3.

In the meantime, Miami hospital – From Jas's diary

Upset, she gets up from the swivel chair sending it slamming against the window of the fifth floor of the hospital, and galloping like a runway horse, she goes out into the corridor screaming: "That's enough! You'll hear from my lawyer!"

I remain lying on the couch - really uncomfortable, among other things - and I don't understand what the devil has got into her. We were chatting so happily until a few seconds ago. The only thing I can do is get up and leave this empty room. The corridor is deserted, on this floor there are only the offices of doctors and psychologists, even crazier than their patients, it would seem.

I reach the elevator and descend to the third floor. Even before the cabin stops I can hear noises, yelling and fuss, but it's only when the door opens that I know I was wrong; it's more than that. A constant coming and going of people with burns and serious injuries all over their bodies and cries of hysterical women asking for help. Some speak German, others Chinese, I don't really understand what is happening and, to tell the truth, I really don't want to find out.

I try to blend into the crowd to get to the hospital pharmacy as soon as possible, the only really interesting place in here.

A nurse is busy soothing an elderly woman who does nothing but repeat: "His throat was cut! Awful boy and his bad jokes! Bad jokes!"

I take advantage of their distraction to steal a white coat lying on the counter and I put in on to disguise myself better. I stop at the door of the pharmacy and as soon as I see that the path is clear, I sneak inside and close the door behind me.

I feel as cunning as a fox, if it weren't for one small detail: a girl of about six years, with pink pajamas and a shaved head, is sitting on the chair in the middle of the room. She's clutching a big yellow toy cat, she has blue rings under her eyes and she's extremely pale. She looks like something out of a horror movie.

For a few seconds we look at each other without saying anything. Then she's the one who greets me first: "Hello, I'm Diana", she says with a strong English accent, dangling her legs and looking at me with curiosity. I look around. Maybe there's still someone in the room. As soon as I'm sure that we are alone, I simply ignore her. Without saying anything, I start looking on the shelves full of various drugs, a magnificent sight. While I snoop around, the girl asks me: "What's your name?"

I ignore her, just trying to find what I came for as soon as possible.

"What's your name?"

I continue to ignore her.

"What's your name?" she insists.

I ignore her, but apparently, she has no intention of ignoring me.

"What's..."

"Little girl! That's enough! I heard you, I'm not deaf!"

"I know you heard, but I thought that maybe you didn't understand the question."

Piss off!

I quickly read the name on the tag of my coat and I lie: "I'm Arizona Jackson. Satisfied, now?"

I turn toward the huge shelves again. I don't know where to look any more; they change things around every week in here. Again I hear the little girl's irritating voice: "What are you looking for?"

"A medicine."

"Who for?"

"A patient."

"And what has he got?"

"A disease."

"And where is the patient?"

Holy Mother of God!

She's sitting there with the yellow cat in her arms and she scrutinizes me, how annoying.

"And what about you? What the heck are you doing here?"

"Here in this room or here in the hospital?"

"You're a big ball breaker, has anyone ever told you that?"

36

"No." She swings her legs and studies me. "I'm in the hospital because I have cancer, and I'm in this room because I'm waiting for my friend Arizona Jackson. She has to get a blood sample."

Great! Among all the coats I could have stolen, I take her friend's!

"I must have a name-sake; the world is full of name-sakes."

"I knew you weren't Arizona. She has short, curly black hair. Yours instead is long, straight and blond. I used to have long hair like that, but it was brown. You know, I'm scared when they take blood, it hurts and I cry, I don't like needles, they hurt me."

I take no notice of her, also because – at last! - I find what I was looking for amongst all the multicolored medicines.

"Does Arizona know you're here?" she asks with suspicion.

"No, and I don't want her to", I say looking at her serious and threatening, hoping to frighten her.

"What are you willing to do for my silence?"

Apparently it didn't work. Of course, she's already dying, what does she care about my threats?

She strokes her yellow toy and looks at me with a wily air.

"Are you blackmailing me, little girl?"

"Yes" she says confidently without batting an eyelid. I look at her incredulous. On the table next to her I see all the equipment ready for the blood sample. I have an idea. "What do you say we do this: I'll take a super painless blood sample and you keep your mouth shut!"

She crosses her arms and looks at me doubtfully. This whole situation is starting to exasperate me.

"Who'll guarantee me that it will be painless?"

"And who can guarantee me that you'll keep your mouth closed?"

She spreads her lips into a smile and holds out her hand. Her skin is so white, and she is so thin. I take the tourniquet and tie it around her arm - she's skin and bone - to stop the blood flow. It disturbs me to sink such a big needle into such a tiny arm. I put the disinfectant on the cotton pad, disinfect the part of the vein that is most visible and pick up the needle.

"I like you."

"I don't blame you."

She smiles scratching her bald head with the other hand. "What did you say your name was?" she asks me.

"Arizona."

She smiles again at my reply, without moving her eyes away from my face while I draw her blood.

"How can you spend your days in here? I'd get bored to death", I say.

She looks at me in a strange way and only afterwards do I realize that this is perhaps exactly what she's trying to avoid doing in here: die.

"My parents come and see me every day, we moved here from London, you know? And sometimes, when I'm really sick, my mom sleeps in the room with me. And if mom isn't there, I talk to Jesus."

"Wow."

"Do you talk with Jesus?"

"But of course! Just yesterday we became friends on Facebook."

Diana looks at me with her mouth open; I smile, I didn't think she even knows what Facebook is.

"It will be my birthday in August, I'll have a big party and the black man will come and visit me."

"Wow."

"Yes, he'll come to see me and I'll be happy and my cat will be happy as well, won't we Yellow Cat?" she speaks to him as if it were a real cat, "You know that it's not easy to win the friendship of a cat and that the cat doesn't ask, it just takes". She's talking so much she hasn't even noticed that I have already taken her blood. I put the cotton pad with the disinfectant on the spot where I drew her blood, loosening the tourniquet and putting things back on the table.

"So, was it painless, or not?"

"Yes", she smiles amazed looking at the needle on the table. I hear the door slam suddenly and an angry voice shouting: "Jas! I can't believe it! Get out of this room immediately! I wonder where you get the nerve to reappear in this hospital without calling first and without your formal apology to me!"

I turn toward the doorway and who do I see? The head of the hospital, a fifty year old black woman who does nothing but yell at me every time she sees me. The only problem is that she's too good, and when she rebukes me she's not believable, she reminds me of Mina.

"Hey, chief, what brings you here?"

"This is my hospital! What are *you* doing here?" she says almost crying and with a despairing tone.

"I have come to visit the carcinogenic little girl who can't wait to be taken away by Nightmare."

"The black man, not Nightmare", the little one corrects me, "Hello, Arizona!"

"You're Arizona?" I exclaim, surprised by this discovery. And to think that Diana knew I wasn't Arizona from the color and cut of the hair. The fact that the chief has black skin and must be thirty years older than me was not a clue!

"Oh Holy merciful God! You took her blood! You took her blood?" she repeats horrified, "Haven't you learned your lesson? Are you a repeat offender or what? Do you want me to be fired? You don't have the schooling, you don't have a degree in medicine, you didn't do an internship and you have no medical specialization to be able to take a blood sample from a patient! It is strictly forbidden!" she says almost crying and walking around the table.

"She was better than you, I didn't feel any pain."

"Listen to the voice of innocence", I propose.

"Diana, next time you must wait for me, got it? You can't just let anyone you meet take your blood."

"You were taking forever."

"You're right, I'm sorry, all hell broke loose out there and I was unable to get to you earlier. Now go back to your floor, alright? I'll come and see you later."

"Okay."

The chief turns to me with quite a different expression. "And you! What am I to do with you? You'll drive me mad! Mad!"

She doesn't talk to me with the same sweet tone she used with the little girl, only because I have all my hair on my head! It's not fair!

"And why are you wearing my coat?!"

"I was cold."

Diana says goodbye and leaves, hugging the yellow cat in her hands. Arizona instead takes a huge yellow bag and starts to quickly put packs of needles and other first aid accessories into it. She seems to be more worried and anxious than usual.

"Why are you putting all those bandages and medicines in your bag? And why are you upset? Where are you going?"

"Will you mind your own business please?" she asks me grumpily, looking for something on the shelves.

"No, I want to mind your business." I place myself in front of the cabinet and look at her with curiosity. "What happened?"

She continues to ignore me.

"What happened?"

She throws the medicines in the bag and pretends to not see or hear me.

"What happened?"

"*Stop it!*"

Okay, we're done with the pretending. She turns to me looking angry and worried. "There was a terrible explosion at the airport and they need medical back-up, apparently there are many people injured and I'm short on staff, I'm devastated!"

"I'll come with you", I propose. It seems to me like a sensible solution.

"Forget it!"

Clearly she doesn't think it's so sensible. She puts the huge bag on her shoulders and leaves the hospital pharmacy without even ordering me to get out. I run after her, while she walks nervously among the wounded and the crowd to reach the elevator.

"Wait! Listen, I know everything that there is to know in circumstances like this. I can be of help, really."

"I know your help. I risked being reported thanks to your help! Do you really want to help me?"

"Yes, I do!"

"Then leave, please!"

The elevator door closes and, as we reach the ground floor, we hear some lovely music in the background.

"Why are you being like this? I don't understand."

"Why? Forgetting about your shameful history? I need serious and qualified help. There are people out there that are suffering and who need us, it's a big responsibility, because if we make just one mistake, they lose their life!" she says still with a desperate voice, "You, on the other hand, are a spoilt little girl who goes around creating problems for me taking blood samples from patients and all the rest! And no degree!"

I snort. It's always the same things. I've been hearing them for months now, "You're forgetting that I passed the written test in medicine."

"You passed it because you cheated! And you even posed as an intern! The only reason I covered for you is because I didn't want to end up in front of the medical board, I'll have you know! I hope that the punishment at least will make you straighten up a little!"

"What punishment?"

"Your lawyer didn't tell you?"

"No, he didn't. And I didn't cheat!" No one believes me anyway. "I can go with you as a civilian, that way it will be legal." She has stopped listening to me again, but I insist: "There are three types of injured. The very serious: meaning the ones who risk dying, they're unconscious, they have difficulty breathing or aren't breathing at all, have turned blue or have serious hemorrhages."

The elevator door opens and she gets out with the bag in hand, ignoring me. She goes over to Pamela, the blond with short hair who always runs behind her holding the medical records. I join in their run towards the unknown.

"I got everything", Pamela informs her, "There's four of you and you have only one ambulance available. Hi Jas."

"What?"

"Hey, Pam, how's it going?" I return the greeting.

"I'm sorry. It's just that two ambulances are out of action and the others..."

"Pamela, stop. Talking. Now. Stop talking now because the more you speak, the more I'll be sorry that I've come to work in this hospital! How can we work like this, how? No ambulances? It's the most important vehicle! I'll go mad! I'll go mad! And you!" she says, turning to Tim, a Chinese guy who works in the hospital laboratory, "What are you doing here?"

41

"I need to get out of the lab once in a while, I feel lonely."

"Tim!" she rebukes him.

"Okay, okay, I'm going," he says, and takes off at a run, while Arizona keeps complaining about the ambulances and other things I'm not listening to, I'm not interested in her whining.

"Then there are the seriously injured", I exclaim, resuming my lesson on first aid, "Those who, even if they're in very bad shape, don't risk dying, such as: head trauma, multiple fractures, spinal injuries..."

"Will you stop promoting yourself unnecessarily?" the chief reproaches me.

"No."

"But she's good", Pamela intercedes, "She might be useful. What school did you go to?"

"She didn't!" Arizona replies on my behalf.

"For your information I studied with *my grandmother* and this means that I am as prepared in the same way, if not better, than the wimpy interns I see over there."

They look towards the exit, where the only ambulance is waiting for them with the door open and three scared interns: a girl with long dark hair, a guy with dark hair and a chubby black guy. They're talking to each other, nervously biting their fingernails.

Just looking at them you can see they're real losers! Where do they think they're going?

The chief's expression is one of incredible disappointment, she stands there with a slack jaw, not knowing if she should cry or kick their asses. It's all too funny.

"My grandmother always said that, if you want to assess the wounded correctly, it's essential to remain calm and think clearly. This step is very important because the fate of the injured depends on what is decided. And I wouldn't want those people over there to even put a band-aid on me!"

Pamela looks at them shaking her head, while the chief exclaims: "You're right."

"Yes?" I'm taken aback for a moment, "I meant, yes! Of course I'm right!"

"Remember when I told you to stay away from my patients, Jas?"

"No."

"Pretend I never said it."

"Said what?"

"The third group?"

"Huh?" I still don't understand her.

"The third group of injured?" she urges me on.

"The slightly wounded, they're the ones with simple fractures, slight traumas, in short, light wounds."

She remains silent for a moment. I on the other hand feel like handing her a tissue, she looks a wreck.

She points a finger at me and says, "You're coming with us, you'll go with our cowardly interns as a civilian, something which is neither illegal nor immoral."

And what did I say earlier?

"You'll triage the injured with them, making sure you provide us with accurate information, both to us and the other first aid operators."

"Cool!"

She takes me by the shoulders with both hands and with a serious and at the same time scared face she says: "Under no circumstance must you touch the injured, is that clear? You'll just observe and report."

"Sir, yes sir!" I exclaim standing like a soldier and making Pamela laugh, while the chief, after and enormous deep sigh, rushes towards the three terrified interns. "Come on, come on, wake up guys, we are going to save lives, let's be cheerful, come on!"

Pamela remains at the hospital and I climb aboard the ambulance with the three very pale-looking losers. The chief throws a gray jacket with phosphorescent stripes onto my knees telling me to put it on. The doors close, the sirens of the ambulance start, and I feel so... I feel so... full of adrenaline!

My heart pounds inside my chest and I can't wait to get to the scene of the explosion.

Pity that grandma can't see me, she would be proud of me! I'm going to save lives!

***

43

Terrorist attack at Miami's international airport! An explosion in the baggage arrival area created havoc not half an hour ago. The exact number of victims is as yet unknown. The first interventions speak of around seventy dead and an unknown number of wounded.

The President of the United States has ordered an increase in security measures in all airports and railway stations! That's all for now from your Olivia Fox!

We listen to the radio all the way and look at each other in silence. The ambulance stops, at last, and I am curious to see if the apocalypse is really waiting for us out there or if it's just one of the many news items pumped up by the media.

Unfortunately, there are no windows in here. And the only glass is the porthole of the rear door, but it's darkened. I can't see anything, but to make up for that, I can now hear everything very well: deafening sounds of sirens, helicopters flying above our heads, moans, cries and noises of all kinds.

Next to me, one of wimpy interns - the chubby black boy - is clutching the first aid bag tight in his hands and breathing as if he's about to give birth. We're all wearing ridiculous uniforms, gray with phosphorescent strips, and huge black bags with the first aid kit inside. The chief gives us the final instructions: "Remember! Even if you're overcome by the anxiety to rescue the injured, try to also think about what is happening around you! You will avoid endangering other people, yourselves included!"

Finally she opens the door of the ambulance and outside I see... chaos!

Smoke fills the sky, two helicopters are flying around the airport in flames and what is happening on the runway is incredible. On the ground hundreds of stretchers next to one another and on them wounded people are moaning, some shouting in pain. The rescuers run from one side of the airport to the other, some with the emergency kit in hand, some with blankets. And the sickly smell of blood lingers in the air. For a few seconds we are all silent.

"Jas! Talk to no one, touch nothing, you're not here, is that clear?"

"Jawohl!" I say like an obedient soldier, when it occurs to me: "But? Wait, what did you bring me here for if I can't do anything?"

"I'm wondering that myself!" she replies angry and turns toward the terrified interns, "Brenda, Brendon! And the bags?"

While Arizona is amazed at how they could forget the first aid bags inside the ambulance, I am amazed at something else altogether. "Brenda and Brendon? Seriously?!" I start laughing out loud, "And where's Dylan and Kelly?" I continue to laugh even though the deafening noise of the sirens covers my voice. This is too funny, but the two protagonists of *Beverly Hills* look at me all serious, as if they don't understand what I'm talking about. Arizona looks at me shocked. "Do you really think you should be laughing right now? Shame on you!"

I prefer not to answer.

Meanwhile she orders me: "Walk, observe and report to me and only me, what Bren..." she corrects herself immediately to avoid another outburst of laughter from me: "Things that my interns will not be capable of reporting to me."

"Yes, yes, I understand."

Thanks to a plastic ID pass which shows us as members of the hospital, the policemen at the airport gate let us in. You can smell the smoke even here, two hundred meters away or maybe more, I don't know. I walk among the many stands full of first aid kits located every twenty meters or so and I don't know exactly what to do and where to turn. The wounded are either being looked after already or are lying on stretchers simply because they're in shock from what happened.

I'm distracted for just a couple of seconds and already I can't see the chief or the interns any more. I look around and I don't know where to put myself. In spite of the chaos, the sirens, the smoke and gut-wrenching screams, everyone knows exactly where to go and what to do; instead, I feel out of place and almost in the way, since the rescuers, running all over the place, keep bumping into me.

I was convinced that once I got here, I would have bandaged, cut, sewn up, helped someone, and instead after not even a minute I'm already useless. I don't want to stand here like an idiot, so I approach a dark-haired guy with his shirt all torn and burned, holding his hands to his chest and looking like he needs help. I don't even have the time to ask him what's wrong before I'm rudely and quickly shoved to the side by two paramedics who take him away on a stretcher.

Darn it!

As I look around I see the loser interns, even they have found their own role in all this mess, helping the injured drink and consoling terrified children. But not me.

After more than ten minutes of useless attempts to help someone, of being shoved and ignored by everyone, I'm sick of it and decide to leave.

I am really disappointed, I was sure I'd be able to do more than just be in people's way. I so wanted to do something different from the usual routine.

I decide to go across to the other side of the airport, the one that is not in flames. Perhaps I'll find somewhere I can make myself a cappuccino, at least I know how to make that properly, and wait for the chief to call me to go back to the hospital. My mission is over even before it started, that's for sure, like everything else, when it comes to that.

On the other side of the airport I notice the yellow tape of the police. I don't understand the meaning of all this, the explosion and the wounded were at the west of the airport, what does the eastern part have to do with it? Why close it down? There is no-one attending the tape, so I step under it and furtively run inside the airport. There's nothing strange in here, apart from a few abandoned suitcases on the ground and a bag of rubbish among papers, magazines and plastic cups.

The arrivals area, which is burning, is really run down and a bit outdated. I know because that's where I landed in February. But here, the departures area, that's another story altogether. It's very modern and colorful, there are shops selling clothing and gadgets, lots of cafés and restaurants, there are even wellness areas, from hairdressers to beauty centers.

Man! I can't wait to take the flight back home!

I hear voices coming from the left corner of the building and immediately run toward the opposite side, along the corridor, and I end up right in the airport café.

Cool!

On the opposite side there is also a tobacconist shop which is open, and taking advantage of everyone's absence, I randomly grab a newspaper and rush towards the empty café.

I can't wait to make myself a proper coffee!

Cappuccinos in America are literally *dis-gus-ting*, the only thing that recalls an Italian cappuccino is the cup with *Italian cappuccino* written on it. I go behind the counter and I see that the pods of my future cappuccino are closed inside a glass display case. I try to open the cash register and it opens without any difficulty, with all the money inside. Why on earth would they put the coffee safely away but leave the money unattended? This country is really strange. I take a full bottle of Vodka and I'm about to smash the display case when I hear my cell ring with the tune of *Deep Red*. I know who's calling me. All happy I take the phone from the pocket of the ridiculous gray uniform and scream: "Grandma!"

"What's this deafening noise in the background?"

"Ah nothing, the airport exploded."

"No, I was talking about the sound of glass."

Perhaps she's talking about the glass cabinet I've just smashed with the bottle, "Someone has broken the display case in the airport café."

"Why?"

"I don't know, grandma, there are a lot of crazy people around. What's news with you?"

"Nothing, and you?'"

"Nothing."

"Okay, goodbye then."

What the hell? She hung up on me? I can't believe it, she hung up on me?

As I said before, there are a lot of crazy people around.

I put the phone back in my pocket and start making my cappuccino like they do in Italy, more or less. Once again I think about my earlier letdown: I was sure I was well-prepared when it comes to medicine and healing wounds, but instead I've shown to be a total disappointment here as well. There's not one thing that I can do well. Everything by halves, unfinished, incomplete, I feel like a real failure.

But I don't want to think about this any longer, I'll think about it another day, I'll think about it the day before the day after!

I pour my cappuccino into a very nice cup with *Miami International Airport Café* written on it. What an original name.

I open the newspaper and on the first page I see an article written in big bold letters *Hurricane Alert.* It seems that torrential rains and typhoons will increase this year. Bah, they've been talking about it for weeks but I haven't even seen a hurricane yet. I hear my cell ring again, it's my grandmother again. I answer: "Still nothing new here, grandma."

"How are you? How's Miami? Are you coming to Serbia in August? What does your future husband say? What do you want for your birthday?"

"Well, rain and perhaps hurricanes on the way, of course I'm coming, he's always working, nothing."

"You're not well my dear grand-daughter, I know it and you know it, what I don't know is why don't you want to talk to me about it? You've always told me everything!"

"There's nothing to tell, grandma," I say annoyed, "Stop worrying."

"Your mother said the same thing too, eighteen years ago, when I asked her what she wasn't she telling me! She would reply *nothing mum, stop worrying.* I didn't know at the time that *nothing* was a deceitful code that meant *I am pregnant, I am going to get married and move eight hundred kilometers away,* and now you're saying that..." While my grandmother rebukes me for a problem I really don't want to deal with right now, I take my cappuccino, with the intention of going to sit at one of the empty tables in the café. I'm about to put my foot down the first step when, as I slip on something, I risk going head over heels with the hot cappuccino in my hand. I don't know how, but I manage to keep my balance and I immediately look on the ground trying to understand what almost killed me.

There is a thin red trail on the red floor near the counter. I get closer to it, I look at the almost imperceptible mark, and it's only when I get down on my knees that I realize it's a blood stain. I would recognize that sickening smell anywhere. I look around, but I don't see broken glass or signs of a brawl where someone could have got hurt. There are only tables and chairs moved by people who fled from here after the explosion, which is normal.

Grandmother continues to complain on the phone, but I'm not listening to her. I exit the café, look carefully at the red floor and notice something strange: even thought you can hardly see the drops of blood, it is perfectly clear that the injured person ran toward the café and not the other way. I go back inside and proceed towards the end of the counter, with the cappuccino still in one hand and the phone in the other, and I stop in front of the door to the bathroom.

I put the phone in my pocket - with grandma who, unaware, continuing in her monologue - and I slowly open the door. The first thing I see is the enormous mirror on the wall and on the ground, under the sink, the motionless body of an old man with white hair, face down in his own blood. I walk in without touching anything and put my cell to my ear.

"I liked you better last year when you were telling me you had two personalities in one body..."

"Grandma", I try to interrupt her.

"Now you've only got..."

"There's, a body..." I stammer.

"Yes, yes, this is exactly what I meant. Now you've left with only one, empty and depressed body! You must find yourself again grand-daughter dear..."

"Grandmother! There's a body, on the floor, an old man, in a pool of blood!" I finally manage to say, albeit with difficulty.

"What? Is he dead?"

"I don't... I don't know."

"Do you only want to inform me of this strange thing that's just happened to you or do you also want to check if he's breathing or not?"

"He's face down!"

"I am not interested in his position, but his pulse. If you don't see anything broken, turn him on his back and do what you know has to be done."

"Hang on..." I place both the cell and the cappuccino on the ground and move closer to the old man. He doesn't seem to have anything broken, but I don't know how to turn him because of all this blood, I don't want to get my ugly uniform dirty. I have no other choice, though. I take him with both hands and turn him on his back. His eyes are closed, his face full of blood, and I notice three bullet holes on his chest. It's no use checking for a pulse, I clean my hand on my uniform trousers and take the phone from the floor. "He's dead." I inform her.

"From what? Because he's in a pool of blood?"

"I'd say that it has to do with the bullets lodged in his chest."

"This doesn't mean anything, are there exit wounds? Have you checked his pulse or not?"

"No, I haven't, I'm barely checking mine!" I flare up, "Wait on the line!" I put the cell phone back on the floor and I look at him for a few seconds.

I feel... I don't know what I feel, I feel my heart pounding, but I don't feel any strong emotions, no terror, no disgust at all the blood.

I move closer to the old man. I put my hand near his mouth but there is no sign of breathing, then I check his pulse and again there's nothing. I sit on the ground next to him and pick up the phone again, "he doesn't have a pulse, he's dead."

"What a shame", she says really calmly. She's used to seeing her patients die. Then she begins to speak of... I don't know what; I only know that she's talking. Instead, I'm silent looking at the corpse on the ground and I don't know what I'm thinking about, nothing really. I'm not thinking anything, I'm just here, sitting on the floor looking at the old man with three holes in his chest, the blood on the ground, and I' on the ground as well.

I drink my cappuccino while it's still hot, I don't like drinking it cold. The aroma is no longer the same as before, perhaps the blood on my hands is ruining my coffee. What a pity, I haven't had a good cappuccino in months.

I think slowly. The white tiles, the large mirror, the old man next to me, there is something wrong in all this. I feel strange. All this blood on the ground, the corpse next to me, and I don't feel a thing, no horror, no emotions... a medical explanation would determine that I am a psychopath.

Flashbacks of that terrible evening four months ago come back to mind and... I hear my grandmother scream: "Jas? Jas get up and go away from there! Can you hear me? Jas?"

"Stop yelling", I speak softly and I drink my cappuccino with the smell of blood, and I am... calm.

Is it normal for me to be calm in spite of everything?

"I'm fine."

"No you're not! You've been saying that to me for months! Get out of there immediately and go and look for..."

Suddenly the old man next to me takes a deep breath, opens his eyes wide and seizing my hand he screams: "Me too!"

I scream as well in fright, dropping both my cell and the cup on the ground.

He's not dead anymore!

He fixes me with his small, blue eyes, he's scared too, and then he starts looking around searching for something and, worried, he shouts once again: "Me, too!"

4.

The black BMW X6 arrives from the west side of the airport and parks in front of the south side. The first to get out of the car is Benjamin; with a tough-guy attitude he adjusts his sunglasses and cleans his jacket from the ash that's flying in the air and falling everywhere. Nickolas gets out immediately after; he looks around saddened by the many people dead or injured by the explosion, admiring the firemen, the rescue workers, the people who rushed in, the police, and the many others who came to help.

But when he sees the journalists, instead, he shakes his head. He disapproves of this kind of attitude and information, especially when there are victims involved. Patrick closes the door of the SUV and looks around carefully. "Nick, there's no longer anyone here, they evacuated the area an hour ago."

"I still want to check, we don't know what the terrorist did before the explosion on the other side of the airport. Maybe we'll find something."

They're about to head towards the entrance when they hear an ambulance approaching. It parks next to their SUV, and shortly after they see two interns and Arizona come out of the departures hall. They're quickly pushing the stretcher with an old man on it, while she is keeping her hand pressed on the wounds to stop the bleeding. As soon as the woman sees Nickolas, she turns to one of the two paramedics: "Brendon, he must be taken to hospital immediately and tell them to get the operating room ready!"

The boy continues to stop the elderly man's bleeding, while the other pushes the stretcher towards the ambulance that's waiting for them with the door already open and the sirens on. Arizona cleans her hands with a handkerchief and approaches Nickolas and Patrick, who are trying to understand what's happening and why a victim of the attack is coming out of this area.

"Good morning, you're from the investigation agency, aren't you?"

"Yes, I'm Nickolas Ortega Torres, my colleagues: Patrick Sword and Benjamin Roosevelt of *Watchtower Investigation*."

"I've heard a lot about you", she greets them, with just a nod of her head because her hands are still stained with blood. "I saw you earlier over the other side when you were interviewing witnesses, I don't know if it can be of any help to you, but inside the café, a girl in our..." she thinks for a moment before continuing, "team, found the man a few minutes ago and he is being taken away. He has three gunshot wounds in the chest."

"Thank you very much, and you are?"

"Arizona Jackson, Head of the Jackson Memorial Hospital."

"Excuse me, but can you tell me the name of the girl who found the wounded man?" asks Patrick looking at her in the eyes.

"Why do you need this information?"

Patrick, good observer that he is, immediately notices her hesitation and understands that it is arises from her unease. "You've replied with a question, you're trying to buy time, why is that?"

Arizona blushes. "No, no, it's just..." she pauses again, but she soon continues speaking, intent on telling the truth, "The gentleman was found by..."

At the very moment she's about to say Jas's name, there is a huge roar, a deafening noise that disconcerts all of them.

The other side of the airport explodes as well, throwing both the hospital chief and the three investigators meters away. The fright creates total chaos once again, rescuers rush towards them. Arizona is on the ground, but with no serious injury, while Nickolas, Ben and Patrick are trying to slowly get up, in pain.

All they can hear is the ringing in their ears. They look around disoriented, the rescuers keep asking them something, they see their lips move, but no one can hear any sound.

With their clothes torn and burned, again, and with superficial wounds on their bodies they look incredulous at what has just happened, happy to be miraculously alive.

Meanwhile, the injured man that Jas found is being loaded into the ambulance, where a gray parrot with red tail and black beak looks on inquisitively.

5.

The more I look at our bedroom, the more I wonder how Jas can live in such a mess.

A month ago I got tired of the fact that I'd tidy up and she'd mess everything up all over again, so I decided to stick some red tape on the floor and divide the room in half. This way I clean my half, and she cleans hers. Or I should say she *doesn't* clean.

I'm lying on my bed looking at her open closet with the suitcase on the floor that's been there since February, t-shirts which have already been worn and then just tossed somewhere, shoes under the bed, a computer, a dirty fish-tank, cosmetics and brushes on the desk, lots of books, notebooks, papers and pencils scattered over the bed.

Dear God, I can't even pretend not to see this mess!

What's more, everything is black: black sheets, black wardrobes, black desk next to the black floor mat, even her fish, Highlander, has turned black again. The only touch of color in her half of the room comes from the mysterious detective Jx: the various items and gadgets, or I really should say comes only from her eyes, because no one has ever seen the rest of her face.

I see the door of the bathroom, which is in my half of the room, open and after two hours Jas comes out wearing just the small towel with her blond hair still half-wet.

"An hour and forty minutes", I give her a round of applause, "A new record, Jas. What the hell have you been doing all this time in there?"

She leans with her hand on the door making the bracelet on her wrist swing back and forth and with the face of a great thinker she says: "I was thinking."

"You were thinking? What about?"

"I was thinking that the corpse I saved today was dead..."

"You saved a dead corpse? That doesn't make sense."

"Yes, but wait till I finish. I saved a dead corpse which, however, is alive now."

54

"Ah well, now that you have finished it, your sentence really makes sense", I start laughing, "Perhaps you wanted to say that you saved a man who was alive, but who unfortunately died later."

"Will you stop talking bullshit?"

"Me? You're the one who said you'd resurrected a dead man!"

"Yes, that's right! And so, in short, this makes him a zombie. Do you understand, my love? I have a zombie as a friend now, a little zombie all mine now!" she says like a happy little girl.

"Yes, a little zombie."

Sometimes her imagination is really creepy.

"Jas, if I hadn't taken you away from the airport before Nick got there, right now you'd have two little zombies all for yourself!"

She grins at me fleetingly without saying a word and starts to dry her hair in front of the huge mirror on the wall where the desk is. I sit on the edge of my bed, moving the colored stuffed toys, and I start talking to her an annoyed expression, reflected in the mirror, "I'm happy that you're taking this whole story so lightly, but I had a heart attack when I didn't find you at the hospital, then I had another heart attack when I discovered that you were at the airport where a bomb had just exploded, and then another one when I remembered that Nick was heading over there! Not to mention the heart attack I had before all these heart attacks this afternoon, because of a stupid joke that Franklin pulled! If this keeps up..."

"Let me guess, you'll have a heart attack?" she answers me calmly and unconcerned while I talk to her seriously. I look at her angrily. "I hate it when you do that."

"Do what?"

"When you look at me and respond with that couldn't-care-less attitude! There are a lot of things we have to talk about, things to clarify and resolve, but you don't cooperate and I feel frustrated, thwarted and", I pause, overwhelmed by agitation, "frustrated!"

I become repetitive when I'm upset. She's not paying any attention to me at all. She looks at her hair in the mirror. Pensive. "The hairdressers here don't understand when I speak. I asked him to give me just some natural blond highlights, and I've turned platinum blond."

"Jas!"

"What? What's your problem, tell me."

"I've been telling you for months, I keep telling you, but apparently it goes in one ear and out the other!"

"Tell me again, then."

As if it that's easy!

Looking at me innocently she asks: "What is the problem?"

"Stop asking what the problem is or I swear I'll throw one of these toys at you!"

Okay, I'm not good with threats.

"Talk to me and I'll listen to you, ask me and I'll answer you. While I quickly get dressed," she says, and runs toward the wardrobe looking, in all that mess, for a bra and a pair of knickers.

I give up. "Okay, to begin with it bothers me to be your babysitter and even get paid by Nick."

"Why?"

"Because I'm getting paid for doing something that I do even when I don't get paid. I feel guilty, it's as if I'm cheating him, stealing from him", I point out to her.

"This is not a problem, but a good thing. You're getting paid to do something you like."

"And who says that I like it?"

"I do. Besides, I've never heard Madonna complain when she gets paid after being on stage."

"You're talking nonsense. What kind of rationale is that?" I complain.

"Mine. Get to the next issue." She's getting dressed, running around the room since she has clothes scattered everywhere.

I cross my arms. "We have to talk about our trip to Europe, Jas."

"After Benjamin and Katherine's wedding, we'll leave. We've got everything arranged already, what is there to talk about?"

"For example, about the fact that if you don't recover your memory, neither Nick nor your parents will allow you to leave, and today Patrick asked me bluntly when you're going to decide to find the right time to get your memory back! He knows that I know that he knows, and this makes me feel uncomfortable, and the thing that makes me uncomfortable the most is that he knows this too! Therefore he knows I'm covering for you and that I'm a liar, which

I am not, actually, but I find myself alone in your twisted world where you keep on involving me! And he knows this too!" I let it all out hugging one of my stuffed animals.

"You don't need to worry about Patrick. He's the only one who minds his own business in this building. He won't talk."

"No, he won't, but he's using his psychological tricks to make me talk! He wants me to give in and confess! Each time I see him it scares the life out of me! I love it here in Miami. I swear! But this is the only time I become upset and stressed! When I have to lie, hide things, omit others and have the feeling that they are about to catch me out! There you have it!" I stick my head under the pillow, I feel safe here. I hate secrets. I hate having my own, let alone Jas's, which are always very complicated, big and absurd. And with Patrick around everything becomes more difficult. I don't hear any remark from Jas. I lift my head up and I see her sitting nice and quiet in front of the mirror wearing a short blue dress. She hasn't paid any attention to me whatsoever. "Do you listen to me when I speak or what?"

"Yes, my love, but I'd already given you an answer; everything will be fine, and as for my memory, I'll get it back a couple of days before leaving, okay? Is there anything else?"

"Yes."

I want to know why you told everyone that you lost your memory.

I'd like to ask her, but instead I find myself saying: "What do I do while you're out smooching with Nick?"

I don't want to rub salt into the wound, I know it hurts her. I don't know why she has chosen to play the part of the amnesiac, perhaps because she had really grown fond of that awkward disabled guy, or maybe it's because Jack was the first person in the world who succeeded in pulling the wool over her eyes, and to admit this in front of everyone is not like her. It feels like so much time has passed since that terrible day.

"Earth calling Mina, Earth calling Mina", she mocks me seeing me lost in thought. She puts her heels on and goes to the mirror to do her makeup.

"It's pointless for Earth to call Mina, if Mina is still waiting for an answer from Jas", I point out to her.

"Well, when I don't know what to do, I go and see Will and try to paraphrase what he says. I must say it gives me a sense of personal satisfaction when I succeed. Then of course you have to take into account that there are various levels of difficulty, like in a videogame. When he's calm, it's the first level, the easiest. When he gets upset if someone is quarrelling, the second level begins. But the most difficult is the third one when he sees something dirty: wine spilled on the carpet, dirty dishes or someone sitting on his red chair. I have to admit that the third level, even I haven't been able to finish that yet."

I start screaming with laughter, lying down on the bed and moving my leg upwards. She's too funny when she imitates or describes someone's habits. She turns towards me, and she's beautiful. Her hair has grown a lot in recent months, she's left it hanging loose today, still a little wet, and I must say that the platinum blond really suits her. She has put on light make up and the only piece of jewelry that she is wearing is the bracelet that Nick gave her for Valentine's Day. And the color blue becomes her now that she's so sun-tanned. She stops in front of my bed and with a smile on her lips, she asks me: "So? How do I look?"

"I don't think that..." but I don't finish the sentence, "Ah nothing, I was about to say something silly."

"Like what?"

"I was going to say that I don't think Nick will let you go out dressed like that, but then I remembered that he now approves of everything you do."

"That's not true."

It is though.

The wall clock starts to chime. It's eight on the dot.

"It's eight o' clock, my love, I have to go."

"Ugh, I hate it when you leave me alone to go out with him."

"Stop it", she smiles, throwing a small black bottle on my bed, "Here, I got it this morning, it will help with your sunburn."

"Thanks Jas, but I don't like it when you steal medicines from the hospital for me."

"I said that I got it, and not that I stole it."

"Yes, yes."

She bends down and takes a jar of Nutella from under the bed. I look at her amazed as she eats it greedily with a spoon.

"And I don't like it either when you steal other people's Nutella from the kitchen. If Will sees you you're finished."

"I haven't stolen it, I've borrowed it, I'll put it back later", she closes the jar and throws it under the bed with the spoon.

"Yes, yes, you'll put it back, half empty though. And then at the Sunday meetings you take off with some trivial excuse and I have to sit there listening to the others complain about you."

She pretends she doesn't hear me - as she always does, anyway, when the topic doesn't interest her - she opens the bedroom door and at the same time I see Nick's, opposite ours, open as well. He's doing up the last buttons of his black shirt, the compass that Jas gave him shines around his neck, just like his face as soon as he sees her walk into the hallway.

I haven't seen him crack even half a smile throughout the entire day, if not forced or out of politeness. And then he just needs to see her to turn into the most cheerful of men. He looks at her from head to toe and says: "You slept until two in the afternoon again, you took a test pretending to be a grad student, your former psychologist pressed charges against you, your fish called the WWF and... you're platinum blond! What have you got to say for yourself?"

"Three times three makes nine."

"I thought so." He puts an arm around her neck, kisses her on the head and, laughing, they start along the corridor. "This blond suits you, you're very beautiful, Jas."

So many things have changed. If the same thing had happened only four months ago, he would have been furious and given her a two-hour lecture, explaining to her how what she has done is wrong. Now, on the other hand, he hugs her. How strange some people are; with me Jas seems to be the same as before, even if she's actually not, while Nick is the same as before, even if it seems that he's not. Here everything seems to be but nothing is.

6.

The door to the Hereafter opened, and out came Isobel with a worried expression. In her hands she was clutching *Macbeth* and with a slow step she went to the phone resting on the table near the window. She looked at the clock on the wall, it was noon on the dot, she wasn't expecting any phone call, and yet she had a feeling that the phone was about to ring.

And it did. After only one ring, Isobel picked up the handset. "Hello?" her voice was shaking; her heart began to beat fast.

She heard a male voice on the other end of the phone. "Isobel."

"F!"

"Is the line secure?"

"It's me you're talking to, F", she answered, pretending to be annoyed by the question.

"How are you, Isobel?"

"I'm well now", she said, her voice broken by emotion, "Thanks for calling, I needed you, F! I've missed you so much."

"I've missed you too, you too. Tell me how you are. Please tell me the truth."

Isobel got up from the chair and looked out the window. She saw Nickolas outside, wearing shorts and a t-shirt; he was sitting on the ground and was staring at the fence that separated Italy from Slovenia.

"I feel heartbroken, I feel powerless. All of a sudden I find myself being a grandmother to a thirteen year old who hasn't spoken since the day of the accident. Three months of absolute silence; it's frustrating. I don't know how to communicate with him, nor if one day I'll be able to gain his trust."

"It's of no help to you or him to become disheartened at this time. If he doesn't speak it's because of the shock, his parents died before his eyes, give him time to process his pain."

"The truth is that I was not a good mother and I'm not a good grandmother". She looked at the photo on the desk portraying her daughter Maria with a newborn Nick in her arms.

"That is not true."

"Yes, it is, I have disappointed her, I have disappointed you, and now it will happen with Nick..."

"Stop feeling sorry for yourself and react!" he said with an authoritarian voice. Isobel remained silent.

"You'll be a loved and respected grandmother, Isobel. You just have to wait patiently, earn his trust and all the rest will come on its own."

"Trust is a gift, and not everyone is lucky enough to receive it."

"Luck has no bearing here. Nickolas needs you. You're the only family that he has left."

"And he is the only family that I've got left, thanks to you." She looked out the window again. Nickolas was kicking the ball against the fence with his head down.

It was a summer full of sunshine and very warm, yet in that huge villa all that could be felt was an icy silence, and Isobel wasn't sure if she would ever be able to get closer to her grandson and warm his heart.

"Isobel."

"Yes?"

"I'm sorry, for everything."

"I'm sorry too."

7.

From Jas's diary – A Walk with Nick

Even though I've been here for four months, taking a stroll through the streets of Miami is a new experience every time, because here they're all completely mad and I blend in extremely well among them.

You look around and see women dressed in a strange way who show themselves off as if they were stars, the stars who try to disguise themselves under glasses and hats pretending to be simple tourists, gays dressed extravagantly with glittering fabrics and glistening accessories. In other words, here, whatever you wear is fine and no one is horrified by it. In Gorizia it was enough for me to wear my school tie around my wrist to get dirty looks.

I've had a very adrenaline-filled day today and only now that I'm walking with Nick hand in hand I'm starting to relax a little, even though he's not completely comfortable. I see him constantly looking around, afraid that journalists might pop out and start snapping pictures of us, assaulting him with all sorts of questions, except those that concern his work. He hates them precisely for this reason: they don't publish a story, they create scandals. Journalism here is misleading and unscrupulous.

When I was in Slovenia, Nick would often tell me that he's quite well known in Italy, but not in America; well, since I've been here, I've realized that Nick ignores the meaning of the word *known.* His team is famous throughout Florida, and I don't understand why no one ever spoke to me about it, nor even mentioned it, but it's a known fact that I'm always the last one to know things. The only thing I knew about was the fame of the detective Jx. Over here she's some kind of icon of the law, she's very much talked about because of her secret identity, she's admired for the work she does, and the posters with her dark eyes can be seen at almost every corner of Miami, not to mention various gadgets, like t-shirts, fanny packs and balloons.

"Hi, can I have an autograph, on my breast?" I hear a girl address Nick in a scandalous manner. I turn and I see her: she's wearing extra short shorts and the top part of a bikini. She touches her breast as she looks at him from the bench she's sitting on with a girlfriend.

How infuriating!

Obviously Nick gives her no autograph. He always proves to be the lovely guy that he is: to every scream or over the top behavior of some girl he humbly says hello or, like now, he pretends not to have seen or heard, he holds my hand tight and keeps going. I adore him when he does this. Any other boy would posture if he were in his position and would take advantage of his notoriety. But not him, he gets embarrassed and looks the other way.

He has noticed that I'm staring at him and he says, smiling: "What's wrong?"

"Nothing."

He looks at me suspiciously and then moves his gaze while I keep staring at him. Suntanned with wavy hair falling on his face. It's not my fault if he is so perfect. He studies me again and this time he feels embarrassed. "Stop it, please," he says.

"Stop what?" I ask him. I try to be serious, but can't, I like seeing him uncomfortable about nothing at all.

"Looking at me like that, you're making me uncomfortable."

"Why?" I ask.

"What sort of question is that?"

"Mine."

He smiles and shakes his head. I notice a small smile he's trying desperately to hide. "Sometimes I wish I could read your mind to see what goes through that little head of yours."

"Don't try to get in my head Nick. It's a mess, why do you think I'm seeing a shrink?"

"You pretend to go to a psychologist. It's different."

I shrug. I don't want to contradict him, seeing that last time as well he left ranting down the corridor.

"By the way", he starts.

Ouch.

"How did it go with the psychologist today?"

Just the question I was afraid of. "Let's just say that..."

Tell him the truth without going into details, Jas.

"It went."

63

Yes, good, keep him calm now.

"If it makes you feel any better, I'll have you know that I say almost everything I think, and I think almost everything I say."

"I know. In fact, it's that *almost* that worries me, Jas."

We laugh, even though his laughter is different from mine, as if I'd laughed at a joke and he at the truth.

He hugs me tight and we continue our walk among excited girls and groups of mulatto boys dancing in the street. We see a bald man walking his snake, and a poodle walking its drunken owner.

As I said, this city is full of strange people and I feel perfectly at home among them. Every now and then, however, I can't help looking around, I don't know why, I don't know what I'm looking for, but occasionally I feel someone is following and watching me, perhaps this thing with the journalists is making me paranoid.

After our walk, we go to Espanola Way on his motorbike, passing the magnificent buildings in typical Spanish style. We stop at our favorite restaurant and sit outside. Live music is playing and there are many people dancing between the tables and out onto to the road. A fabulous atmosphere.

The entertainer this evening is doing Tonino Carotone's songs and the more I look at him, the more I'm convinced that it's Tonino himself walking among the diners with the guitar in his hand.

Next to our table there's a Cuban girl celebrating her birthday. During the evening, the waiters bring her a giant cake with twenty-one candles and the whole restaurant sings the happy birthday song for her.

After having drained an unspecified number of glasses of spirits, she starts to dance and gets on stage to sing a Spanish song at the top of her lungs. As well as being off-key she's also rocking on her feet, while Tonino looks at her and smiles happily. She must be very drunk indeed. We all laugh. Nick turns to me shaking his head. "Tell me that in a week's time I won't witness embarrassing moments like this, I beg you." He smiles, even though all of a sudden I don't feel like laughing any longer.

"No, don't worry. The only embarrassing scene you will see will be *Buffy and Spike* on DVD which I'll put on at midnight while we toast."

He looks at me in silence for a little, tales a sip of beer and with a forlorn air he says: "Then you haven't changed your mind?"

"I'm sorry, but why would I change my mind?"

"You're in Miami, America's greatest party town, and you want to spend your eighteenth birthday in your room? No party, nightclub, a midnight swim, drinking alcohol on the sly."

I look at him shocked. He shakes his head and smiles surprised. "I can't believe I said that."

"Neither can I! And to think that only a few months ago I would have given a kidney to hear you say these words. We're really out of sync the two of us, eh?"

"No." He tightens his lips, he doesn't seem at all happy.

"Nick, I just want to spend a quiet evening with you, Mina and Patrick, what's so bad about that?"

"Nothing, it's just that I wanted to organize a nice party for you or take you somewhere, I want the best for you."

"The three of you are the best."

He's got a strange expression, and I realize immediately that, unconsciously, I have disrupted his stupid plans. I can't believe it!

"If by any chance you were thinking of organizing a pathetic surprise party with fifty people I couldn't care less about, you'd better call it off because the guest of honor will not show, have I made myself clear?"

He stares and tightens his lips, a clear sign of surprise, but especially because I was right. He leans back on the chair and, sighing, he says to me, "Oh, alright, it's a party that was meant to be a surprise, but it is not a surprise party."

I look at him with a raised eyebrow. What on earth is he saying?

He smiles amused. "I didn't express myself correctly. What I meant to say, is that I thought I'd give you a surprise you for your birthday..."

"A surprise?" I exclaim, without even letting him finish the sentence. "I don't like surprises!"

"If you'll let me finish..."

"Sorry."

"I know you don't like surprises. That's why I thought I'd speak to you about it tonight", and then, silence.

I was expecting an entire speech on his ridiculous plans for the party-not-party, and instead he sits there in silence watching the passers-by and moving his head to the rhythm of the music. What is he, an idiot?

"And so? Aren't you going to finish what you were saying?"

"Why would I? You've already said what you want to do for your eighteenth and it didn't look like you were leaving room for other options, therefore, it seems useless to keep going."

"I only said that I don't want a surprise party. Come on, tell me!"

He keeps looking around on purpose, without talking.

"I'm leaving room for new options, okay? Lots of room, a universe of options. Tell me!"

His face lights up, he sits up and explains enthusiastically: "Charity night at Villa Vizcaya for the children suffering from cancer and leukemia, the most important people of the investigative and medical world will be there, it will be the most important media event this year and I want you beside me. It will be your first official outing where you'll introduce yourself as a future member of our team and at midnight we'll celebrate your birthday together. What do you think?"

He looks at me with his dark eyes, very excited. I don't know for what obscure reason he is so sure I'd be jumping for joy, but I'm not happy, at all.

I don't know what to say, people around us are having a good time and singing and I can't even fake a smile.

Nick notices. He becomes serious in the face of my silence which is far too long and he leans back on the chair again, crossing his arms and looking at me as if I had just shot him in the heart. I absolutely must say something. "I... don't know what to say."

What a great thing to say! Well done, Jas!

Sighing deeply, he keeps fixing me serious and disappointed. "A *yes* would have been welcome. What's wrong?"

It's quicker if I tell him what's not wrong. "It's just that... I don't understand."

"You don't understand what?"

"The meaning of this invitation."

"This is one of those moments when I would like to get inside your head."

For me, on the other hand, it's one of those moments when I would like to get up and go so I don't know what he's thinking.

"What's wrong, Jas?"

"I don't know."

I see his worried, disappointed face, and the more he asks me what is the matter with me, the more I can't speak; how can I explain to him something that I can't even explain to myself?

He takes my hands and caresses them softly, still with this sad look in his eyes, while I just want to get out of here.

"Jas", he says as he plays with the bracelet he gave me on Valentine's Day. Even if I hate the situation, I love the contact that it creates between us; his hands are warm and pleasing. "Little one, I know you so well now that I understand when there's something you don't want to tell me. Your silence is heart-breaking, but I want you to know that I feel you all the same. It's just that I can't understand what you're trying to tell me, while you do all you can to not tell me anything."

"Nick, please", I wish he would stop talking, his every word hurts me, but I can't shut him up because he's only concerned about me and wants to help me. But no one can help me.

He takes my hand and reminds me: "There must be trust between us, without trust what are we doing here? You know that you can tell me everything, don't you?"

He looks at me with that sincere gaze, hopeful of receiving a logical explanation to a reaction that, to him, is illogical.

"Yes, I know", I whisper. I know that I can tell him everything. The problem is that he doesn't understand everything.

"This is not you, the Jas that I knew would never have reacted like this, the Jas I knew was full of energy, hyperactive, with the desire to live life and not miss out on any opportunity. Where is that Jas? Where are you?"

"I am here, I have always been here."

"Yes, but only physically. When I look in your eyes, you're not there. It's been months now."

I scrutinize him in silence while the psychological torture continues. Why doesn't he see that I'm ill and I don't want to talk?

"Why don't you want to come with me to the charity auction?" he asks.

"Why do you want me to go?" I ask him, "I'm not a detective or a doctor, I'm nobody. And besides, I still don't feel ready to be presented as a future member of your team, because I am still not sure I want to be, and you know it."

"Why are you doing this? Why do you say this?"

"You know why. We are too different, Nick, we think too differently. You respect the law to the letter, but I'm not able to do that. Furthermore, it was you who told me that, if one day I work with you, I'll have to believe in the law and not just pretend to. Do you remember?"

"Yes."

"Well, I'm still pretending, to this day."

Silence again. I knew that as soon as I spoke against his sacred law he would have lowered his gaze and would have immediately gone silent. "I'm sorry", he whispers, thoughtful.

"For what? Why is it that every time I have a doubt or a problem you think you're the cause? You're not the problem, here, I am. I feel out of place, there, you have it. I look around and I see that you all know what to do and how to do it, while whatever I do, I do it by halves. I'm not complete in anything, there isn't *one* thing that I know how to do properly, and at the moment I feel like... nobody."

"Since when have you become so self-critical and harsh toward yourself?

"Since I've stopped trusting in myself, in my feelings and my judgment, that's when."

He cannot understand, he wasn't there, he doesn't know how I feel." And me, do you trust me?""

I look at him straight in the eye. It's the only question I know how to answer: "Of course I trust you. Since the first day I met you."

"Don't trust yourself and consider yourself *nobody* if you want, but know that for me you're *everything* and I know that you're able to do everything."

"Nick, please, that's enough."

"I just would like to understand why..."

"I don't feel like talking about this!" It's only when I raise my voice that I see the doubt cross his face that maybe - just *maybe* - I am not well and don't want to talk anymore.

"Alright. I'm sorry." He fixes his black hair sighing. "You asked me why I'd like you to come to the charity gala with me... Because going with would make it so much more special. That's all. I would simply like to have you by my side", he says in such a sweet and sincere way that... How can I say no to him, now? I stroke his hand, and I do the worst thing I could do to him. "If this is the reason, then I'll gladly go with you, Nick."

Lying shamelessly to him! As I've been doing for months now. He is happy. I see the joy in his eyes at seeing me cheerful again. It doesn't take much to show him what he wants to see. I get up and go to the other side of the table and hug him really tight, so tight that I feel his heartbeat accelerate more and more. "You know I adore you, don't you?"

"Of course I know", he kisses my forehead gently, "Do you really want to come with me or are you doing it just to make me happy?"

"I really want to go", I lie again. I really don't want to go, I want to have a quiet night at home, but seeing the lies that come out of my mouth lately, this is maybe the worst punishment for me, doing what I don't want to do.

He smiles pushing my hair behind my ear. "Jas, if one day you feel the need to talk, about anything, I am here, Mina is not the only one, I'm here too. I want you to know this."

"I know that already." I need to move away from him and put an end to these heavy conversations and the continuous acts. "Good!" I exclaim and go back to my place taking on a much more cheerful and carefree tone, "Now we can start talking about serious things."

"Such as?"

"Such as: why for the whole evening you've been trying to hide the wounds you have on your chest and on your right hand, and what has happened to your hearing?"

He looks at me surprised, touching his chest, and then smiles shaking his head. "I didn't want you to worry unnecessarily. How did you notice?"

"Easy, you kept touching your chest, you were drinking, eating and touching my hand with your left hand, which is odd, for someone who's not left-handed, and then I noticed that you were looking closely at my lips while I was speaking."

He smiles again and puts his bandaged up hand on the table. I stroke it, I can see his lightly burned skin under the bandage and my heart begins to pound in my chest. "What happened, Nick?"

"It all started with a madman who shot at us."

"And you tell me like that?"

"What other ways are there to say it?"

"Just as well you didn't want me to worry! They shot you?"

"Don't be alarmed, I had a bulletproof vest on."

"Luckily!"

"It is not a matter of luck, none of us can go out of the *Watchtower* without the jacket. It's one of the first rules of the team. And the day ended with an explosion at the airport."

I pretend not to know anything about the explosion, while he, completely unaware, continues to relate: "We got out of it with some scrapes and light burns, and the ringing in the ears will go in a few days, it's called acoustic trauma, nothing serious."

We're interrupted by the sudden loud music, and the Cuban girl who earlier looked like she was about to pass out drunk, is back in action. She runs to the tables and pulls people to their feet to dance with her. She comes to our table as well and grabs me and Nick by hand, drags us to the middle of the road shouting and singing Tonino Carotone's song *Me cago en el amor.* Nick and I put our arms around each other and start dancing amused. It's a nice atmosphere of general cheerfulness and also the people strolling in the street stop to look at us. As we dance the music changes to a slow. Nick strokes my back, his fragrance relaxes me. I don't want to move away from him ever again. I look at the compass. I'm pleased that he always wears it, I touch it and ask him: "Do you also have a rule that says: never leave the *Watchtower* without my compass around your neck?"

"Yes, that's your rule."

"And do you follow it?"

He smiles, touching the compass with the wounded hand. "Of course I do, I follow all the rules."

"Good, because it's your lucky charm, and besides, it is the only way to find each other again in case one of us gets lost."

"I don't need the compass to find you, Jas."

We look into each other's eyes and in such sweet moments like this, I don't know why, but my heart always starts beating fast. I like some of what he says very much, I feel loved and safe. He says it without thinking, it's all very spontaneous. I adore him.

"You never know", I reply smiling. I am well again. Being here with him, dancing with him, feeling him close, looking at him. In such moments everything else becomes simply... *everything else.*

***

I was in a deep sleep. I was having a beautiful dream: I was drinking a *good* cappuccino, one of those that only in Italy they know how to make, I could smell the aroma of the beverage just made, I was feeling the warm cup between my hands and I heard... growling?

I open my eyes and I find Katherine's mongrel in front of me, grumbling and breathing in my face, and her butler, Ambrose, behind her looking at me with a swivel chair in his hands. The only thing I can do is to shout: "Nick!"

I sit on the bed furious as hell and Mina instead literally falls out of bed from the fright. The mongrel scrutinizes my every move and keeps growling at me. Katherine comes in from the small balcony to my right. She rushes toward me all concerned. "Oh no, no, no, no, you don't be frightened, sweet pea, it's ok, you're safe here."

She sits on the bed taking my hand.

"What's going on?" asks Mina, as she tries awkwardly to get back on the bed.

"I was wondering the same thing! What are you doing in my room?"

"I am Kath-er-ine, Ben-ja-min's future bride, as well being as young and famous international model", she says to me spelling out the words as if I was an idiot, "You know, the one with the grey hair, well-built and very handsome, who always puts your lawsuits to bed?" She turns to Ambrose and says to him

71

whispering: "Poor thing, she has lost her memory, we must be patient."

"Nick!" I scream again.

"Nickolas is not here, my little salted popcorn."

The dog keeps growling, while Katherine, being anorexic, keeps giving me food-based nicknames.

"Get out of my room!"

"Oh no, no, no, don't scream, don't get upset. Naomi, come here", she picks up her ridiculous dog with a ridiculous pink hat on its head. "Say hi to Jas, come on, say hi to Jas, come on, come on."

"I repeat! What the hell are you doing in my room?"

"But of course, you have been very lucky, girls; Nickolas has asked me to help you buy your dresses for Saturday evening. Isn't that wonderful? It will be your first appearance in public, my dear, and my last appearance as an unmarried woman, and from now on the cameras from *VIP Wedding* will be following me and I'll be in world vision! Isn't all this wonderful?"

8.

At the same time – from Mina's diary

My Jas is still sleepy because since she's been in Miami she's accustomed to sleeping until late. She hugs the pillow and stares at Katherine with wild eyes, no doubt trying to come up with a way to get rid of her.

I, on the other hand, am delighted! Katherine will take us shopping and I can't wait. She knows all the most fashionable shops in Miami. Wherever she goes, they all fall over themselves to please her and they'll do the same with us, how nice! I like to be waited on hand and foot. In nineteen years, this has never happened to me.

The Katherine-Ambrose-Naomi trio is fun. I can see that Katherine has had her beautiful curly blond hair cut shorter to her ears, and she's lost even more weight since last I saw her. I think she's too thin, her butler too, considering how tall he is. But he's fun; despite his age, he still likes clowning around and doing silly things. In this case, while Katherine is talking with Jas who's not paying the minimum attention to her, he's pretending to kick the dog in the butt. Sometimes I get the impression that he'd like to do it for real, given that the poodle often bites him and scratches everywhere. It's a very twitchy and angry dog.

Suddenly, America appears at the door and knocks, even though the door is open, and as soon as she sees Katherine she makes a face, as she usually does. "Excuse me", she starts in the tone that sounds like she's making fun of someone, "Here's the list the boss has asked me to give you", she says disinterestedly as she approaches Katherine. Naomi starts growling again and from America's look I'm scared she's going to punch it, and not for show like Ambrose does. Katherine becomes strange, turns toward the window and pretends not to see or hear her. America puts the sheet in front of her face and Katherine, disgusted, takes it with the tip of her fingernails and puts it on Jas' bed.

Is this the way to behave?

The black woman looks at her like you'd look at someone you don't have much respect for. She turns to go to the door, when Katherine starts screaming: "Wait a minute! No low neckline or thigh high splits, nothing see-through, no high stilettos? Who wrote this list, the Pope? How can I make her look sexy without the basic things that show off a woman's body?"

The list, of course, is about Jas's dress.

"I don't know and I don't care!" replies America in a hard tone and leaves slamming the door.

"What a sour woman, no wonder she's still a spinster. She dresses all colorful with those unsightly braids on her head, she's always angry and to top it off she's black", she whispers the last word, as if it were something shameful, and keeps wiping her hand with a paper towel, "Try as she might, she'll never be able to hide it!"

I am shocked, I didn't know there were still racists around, and before today I hadn't realized that she was.

Jas doesn't seem at all upset. She's still hugging her pillow and travelling far from here in her mind. Katherine gets up from the bed and suddenly falls to the ground like a sack of potatoes.

Jas continues to ignore her, while I, Ambrose and the dog rush to help her.

Anxious, I ask her: "Oh my God, are you ok?"

"Yes, don't worry my little chocolate cake," she says, as if she sees a cake instead of my face.

"Why are you sitting on the floor?" asks Jas, waking up suddenly. Obviously she's not coming to help Katherine, as if. She looks down at her from her untidy bed with raised eyebrows and doesn't move a finger. Ambrose helps her to sit on the chair. I can hear loud rumbling noises coming from Katherine's stomach.

"Would you like me to bring you a glass of water or... make you a sandwich?" I ask concerned.

"Oh no, no, no, thanks, I'm not hungry. I just licked a stamp."

What? What did she say?

"I can't give up right now, I'm getting married in less than a week and I have to be thinner than everyone!" she says, as Ambrose drags her towards the door, chair and all. "I don't want to turn into a colored fatso like Choco, Ben's ex-wife!"

I don't understand this remark either. Fatso yes, but it would be a little difficult to become black by eating.

"Alright, honey buns. I'll wait for you in the living room. Do you know if there's some area there which America can't enter? Or is she free to go anywhere?"

"America is free to do whatever she wants since the fourth of July 1976", says Jas with an acidic tone.

"Bummer." meows Katherine.

Ambrose drags her and the chair outside, Naomi follows them as well, snarling and biting the butler's shoe. The scene is too funny, but I still don't understand the remark about licking the stamp. I turn toward Jas, shocked. "I wonder what criteria Ben has for choosing his wives."

Jas merely shrugs without saying anything. I get to my bed which is opposite hers and lie down. "I can't wait to go shopping with Katherine! I want to feel like *pretty woman!*"

"Like a... prostitute?"

"No, not like a prostitute. Like someone who goes shopping, Jas!"

She hasn't got a clue.

"I like the idea of trying on clothes and trying them on again like in the movie! Katherine knows all the most famous shops! Really Jas, a little enthusiasm...come on!"

"I don't know."

She puts a hand under her bed and pulls out a packet of chocolate cookies. These too have been stolen from the kitchen pantry obviously. She begins to eat and complains: "Right from the start I wasn't enthusiastic about going to this charity gala evening and now that I'm about to go, I'm afraid."

"Why?"

"Because every time I do something that I don't want to do, it ends in tragedy."

I would like to tell her that it's not true, but then flashbacks of last year come back to my mind: she was in her room looking at Jelena and saying *I don't want these stupid fish!* But she kept them just the same and in fact nine of them died, only one survived, which is an overstatement seeing that it has changed color and shape several times in less than a year. Then I remember her

75

saying to me *I don't want to go to a stupid Halloween party*, she went anyway and the same evening she ended up in hospital with a serious head trauma. Not to mention her walking around the school shouting angrily *I don't want to be Jack's tutor!* And then it actually did finis... to tell the truth I don't know if it's over yet.

And these are just the most recent memories. I could make a list of many more.

Scratching my messy hair I look for a way to reassure her: "Okay, maybe it did happen in the past, but now everything will be different. We'll go to a charity dinner, what on earth could happen at a charity auction? That an old man loses his denture?"

Okay, maybe I could have avoided the denture thing. She looks at me again with that anxious face, unconvinced.

"Jas, the lack of confidence and the distrust you've been feeling these past few months makes me shiver, you keep waiting for something awful to happen somewhere and that's not you, it's me!"

"You haven't been paranoid for months now," she says while she drowns in the cookies, "And also, when will you all stop telling me I am not myself anymore?" she puts her head on the pillow again and at this point it's best I leave her alone, otherwise she'll get edgy and I don't want to argue.

I'm about to get back to sleep, when I hear Katherine shouting loudly from the living room: "Aaaagh! Please help me, Ben's little black boy is dead on the floor! Call a, call someone anyway, immediately!"

Both Jas and I continue to sit on the bed amused. It's yet another of Franklin's jokes. For once I'm not the victim and I'm happy about that.

Then we hear America's harsh and authoritarian voice: "Franklin! Get your butt off the ground and quit making these stupid childish jokes!"

"Was I good?" asks Franklin.

Katherine shouts: "A joke? At my expense, when I'm already physically fragile? Naomi, go get him!"

We hear some yelling, barking and further chaos in the living room and start screaming with laughter. I throw myself on her bed, crossing the red line on the floor, and cover myself with the sheet making a few markers and papers fall to the ground. I take advantage of this moment to comfort her a little more and eat a chocolate cookie. "Jas, Saturday we'll go to the gala, drink champagne wearing a beautiful designer dress, we'll help the sick children and everything will be fine. You'll have a wonderful birthday, you'll see."

She looks at me smiling and hugs me tight. I feel that everything will be fine and, after her birthday, we'll think about our next move. First her memory, and then we finally leave for Europe!

"I love you, Jas."

***

Saturday has arrived in the blink of an eye. My heart is racing. We get off a modern black speedboat in Biscayne Bay where, set among gardens and lakes, the property extends for a good eighty hectares. The entrance is lit up in blue, orange, and green, the red carpet leads straight to the wonderful villa which reminds you of Venice, with the poles painted in white and blue stripes.

Nick holds Jas by the hand while they parade as required past the photographers. They look like Hollywood stars, they smile and exchange knowing glances at each other the whole time, while the journalists go crazy. Nickolas is wearing a white shirt and black tuxedo, and Jas is in a wonderful long white dress, which shows off her tan even more.

Ben and Katherine disembark immediately after. They're quite at ease in front of the flashes, answer questions from journalists about their marriage, posing like VIPs. Everyone is particularly focused on Katherine's dress, with a seductive now-you-see-it-now-you-don't effect.

I get off the boat last, totally excited. My dress is beautiful, very tight and red in color. Fortunately Will helps me to disembark and get to the first step.

Even though they don't know me, the journalists and photographers snap pictures of me for the mere fact that I arrived with Nick and the others. I feel important!

We're almost more famous than the Mayor and this makes me walk five feet above the ground. I try to look serious, but the smile does not want to disappear from my face. Will, very shy, walks with his head lowered and avoids making eye contact with anyone, with the usual mumbling sound he makes when he's nervous, while Veronica walks ahead like a horse toward the front door without paying attention to anyone. She was prickly even before we left the *Watchtower*, because of Nick I think, who at the last moment told her Jas would be his date for the evening.

Finally I walk into the villa and when I'm inside I discover the wonder of wonders. The floor is in colored marble, with different circular designs; everything is baroque style, the entry hall has a lot of columns around it, and large and bright rooms. In every corner there is valuable furniture, European artifacts, beautiful statues and huge crystal chandeliers hanging from the ceiling.

I feel as if I'm in a fairy tale, a real princess.

The room is full of important people from the police world: law enforcement agencies, the FBI, the Mayor of Miami, and other political faces of Florida, with their wives or partners all very made up, showing off designer clothes and jewelry. I thought detective Jx would be here too, but then Jas explained to me that she doesn't attend galas, and even if she did, we wouldn't know it's her, since nobody has ever seen her face. What a shame.

As at every gala there are the usual waiters: they wear elegant uniforms, they go around the room holding trays, offering us champagne in crystal flutes, and caviar on decorated plates of fine porcelain. I can't believe it. I have only seen these things in the movies. I am so happy!

9.

Charity gala – From Jas's diary

I'm really depressed. As soon as I arrived at this sort of charity party I found myself exactly where I thought I would: *in plastic-fantastic world.*

The women do nothing but look at each other to see who wins the contest for the biggest boobs or the most beautiful nose or who is wearing the most expensive dress or jewel. A few of them can't even laugh because their lips are so puffy, full of who knows what crap, that they risk exploding in front of everyone, and others are so full of Botox that it's impossible to guess how they're feeling; they seem made of wax, without a wrinkle or a facial movement, they're scary!

Not to mention the esteemed gentlemen. Some are wearing heels, others a wig and still others have foundation on their face, and, like their wives, there are some with the same immobile face. The only good thing about the Botox is that you won't see the pained expression when they have to write a check at the end of the evening.

I turn and see Mina next to me. She looks like Alice in Wonderland, except I don't understand where the wonders are. With wide-open eyes under the red bow she has on her head, she observes every small detail of the room and she even marvels at the most trivial things, such as the waiter asking her if she'd like a drink or the compliment from some old man wearing a wig. At least her dream to be noticed has come true: what with the dress, the bow and the sun burns, she resembles a giant crab.

But our rule is always the same: until she asks me for my opinion, I keep my mouth shut, even if it's difficult.

I, on the other hand, am wearing a dress that is squashing my boobs, I can hardly breathe, my shoes are giving me blisters, my hair stays up thanks to the many evil hairpins which hurt like hell, and I can't wait to go home again.

10.

The charity gala – From Mina's diary

I don't want to ever go home! Everything here is fabulous! After various cocktails and appetizers we move to the large room nearby where they have set up a stage for the occasion, and where each of the selected guests must play a game to entertain the other guests and say something in favor of this donation in order to have the best check signed.

Right now, Patrick is on stage. He came out of nowhere. He didn't come with us, and when he appeared, it was like seeing Prince Charming. At thirty-two, he really is a handsome man, that's for sure.

He walks from one side of the stage to the other, while in the middle, sitting in the chair, there is a chubby gentleman picked randomly from the public. Patrick maintains that he'll need just one look at him to tell everyone private things about him, even if he's never seen him before. Patrick takes the microphone. "This man is about forty-five years old."

The audience begins to murmur and smile because it's actually not so difficult to guess something like that.

Jas, standing beside me, takes a sip of water and then she whispers: "Now comes the *Pat-trick*", she smiles amused, while Nick whispers in her ear.

Patrick pretends to be indignant: "What are you insinuating? That it's something easy? That I'm not a serious fortune-teller?"

The public continues to laugh saying *yes* while Patrick continues to pretend he's surprised. I didn't know this playful side of him.

"Let me see if I can get you to reconsider. This man is five foot six tall."

They all smile again, Patrick starts to walk slowly up and down the stage and then, to everyone's surprise, he begins to list: "He still lives with his mother, has just bought a black and white cat, he plays an instrument", he pauses and looks at him again, "A guitar. He was married but now he's single and..." he looks around. "He would like to have a *liaison* with the lady with red hair there at the back." He turns to the gentleman on the stage and says: "But she is not interested, I'm sorry."

All remain silent. The man on the chair becomes red in the face and asks him embarrassed: "How the devil do you know?"

There's a huge round of applause, the bald man goes off the stage feeling totally embarrassed when he walks past the redhead. He was incredible, but how did he do it? He's not showing any sign of happiness or satisfaction for having had such success; he only smiles with his lips closed, and then immediately addresses the public again: "No, I'm not a fortune-teller. I'm just a great observer. I use my five senses to create the illusion of having a sixth. Put your hands up those of you who have never been fooled at least once in your life?

Some raise their hand, but many others do not.

"Good, and raise your hand now those people who thought *he's delusional* about your friend."

Many start to laugh at this and raise their hand.

"There are a lot of raised hands. And now, raise your hand those of you who think that children with cancer and leukemia will be healed thanks to the illusion that tonight you have donated money for research."

Silence descends. Everyone present is dumb-founded, and even if someone had at first raised their hand, they immediately realized something was wrong and put it down. They are really taken aback. I took a few seconds myself to understand what he said.

"There are illusions that can heal, others that can kill, the choice is yours. Thanks."

I have never seen anything like it. They all put their hands in their pocket taking out their check books, while the women, fascinated by Patrick, applauded madly. Jas smiles and follows him with her eyes as he comes down the stairs with his hands in his pockets. I notice a touch of pride in her eyes, and Patrick notices too, and after smiling briefly at her he leaves, without stopping beside her and Nick. Patrick makes you feel uneasy. When he looks at you it's as if he knows what you don't want him to know, just like he did with the bald gentleman earlier on. Sometimes I wonder how Jas can be so relaxed when she's in his company.

81

11.

An hour later – From Jas's diary

How boring. Nick has done nothing but introduce me to old people all evening. I can no longer keep smiling and pretend that I'm interested in what they have to say.

I look around trying to find Mina and I see her in Katherine's clutches - she is holding her by her arm telling her who knows what, while the butler is nearby putting up with the mongrel biting his shoes. Perhaps my position is not that bad.

I look at Nick, he seems so grown up, so much a man, wearing a tie and his hair pulled back. Finally he bids goodbye to an old couple and looks at me displeased. "This was the only tiring part, from here on things will be better and the fun begins."

"There's no need for you to justify yourself", I smile.

"I'm not justifying myself."

"Nick."

He tightens his lips in the sweetest way. He knows that this type of evening is not exactly fun for me, and that *perhaps* he made a mistake by inviting me. I take his hands and, with a very fake smile, I add: "It's a wonderful night, I've learned to be patient and polite, I've met important people in the investigative world, I've received many compliments... it's true that I would have preferred watching Buffy and Spike kissing but it's not that bad here". I smile.

Nick takes a deep breath and stands in front of me. "And speaking of", he says, tense. He caresses my shoulders with very anxious movements.

"Speaking of what?" I encourage him.

"Speaking of... the kiss", he says embarrassed.

I know what kiss he is talking about, but what I don't know is how to stop my heart which is about to burst out of my chest. He looks at me and waits for me to say something, and all I can do is hesitate. "Nick, I..." I'd like to speak, but the words just can't get out of my mouth. He pushes my hair behind my ear looking at me with strange serious eyes. Instinctively I would like to run away from here. He's about to say something, when a male voice interrupts us: "Nickolas!"

A second later we're a few feet apart, both embarrassed and with our heads down. As always, everything happens in an instant between us, and I find myself standing there red in the face and my heart in my throat.

In front of us is a black gentleman of about seventy, lean and tall, with a moustache and gray hair. I've never seen him before. He comes up to Nick and shakes his hand, hugging him hard. It looks like they've known each other for years, he's very happy to see him.

"Felix!" Nick exclaims. As soon as I hear his name I realize who he is, and I smile.

"I can't believe it!" continues Nick.

"I was hoping to see you before the auction, how are you?"

"Very well, thank you, and you?"

"My retirement is bringing me a lot of fulfillment. Had I known that earlier I would have left the FBI twenty years ago."

"Retirement, sure, and do you think anyone believes you?"

They laugh amused while Felix keeps patting him affectionately on the shoulder.

Nick takes my hand, bringing me closer to Felix. "I want you to meet Jas, my..." he pauses, "Family. And this is Felix Walker, the man who made the concept of *Watchtower* possible", he says with pride. He has told me about him just a few times, but I am happy to meet him at last.

"He's the one I have to thank if I'm here right now" concludes Nick.

"Oh that's very kind of you, but you mustn't exaggerate, now."

He extends his hand towards me and shakes it firmly, looking straight into my eyes. Fortunately, I'm smart enough to be able to say that, instinctively, he didn't like me even a bit.

"I'm pleased to meet you, finally. So, you're the famous and much loved Jas?" he says one thing but means another, clearly. He keeps scrutinizing me with a disapproving look, as if he were trying to understand what I'm doing here and what's so special about me. I decide I should play nice. "It depends, famous for what?" I ask politely.

"I'll wait for you to ask me the right question."

Something he hasn't done with me!

"I have already asked the right question and don't intend to change it", I clarify annoyed, but with a smile on my lips.

Okay, it's not just dislike here, but a hatred that comes from the bottom of his heart. The more he challenges me with his gaze, the more I feel like slapping him, what does he want from me? I have known him for a minute and already I can't stand him.

I think Nick has sensed a slight tension between us, and tries to calm us both down saying, "For forty years he's been the main operative arm of the United States justice system, you know?"

"Yes, I know", I say this with an unpleasant tone, looking at Felix as you do an idiot.

"He talks so much about retirement, but in reality my team and I still collaborate with him," he smiles. Felix and I, on the other hand, don't. In fact he asks me: "Do you know what our motto is?"

"Fidelity, bravery, integrity."

He is surprised by my short reply. "These are the three fundamental adjectives for every type of relationship, not only a working one, don't you think so too?" he asks. He continues to study me and pretend in front of Nick that everything's alright.

"Yes", I answer through my teeth, acting as if I didn't understand his pretense.

"And you? Are you faithful to our Nick, as it apparently seems that you are?"

"I'll wait for you to ask me the right question."

Describing this moment is impossible. There are no right words when embarrassment, challenge and hatred converge at the same time. Unfortunately, the conversation is interrupted by Katherine's scream: "Jas, come with me, right now!" she grabs my hand and pulls me behind the stage with Mina. I only think of Nick and the fact that I'm sorry that meeting that asshole Felix went so badly. Who does he think he is?

In the meantime, Mina screams behind my back: "Jas, I have to tell you something very important!"

"Not now!" I'm too angry! The one time that I make an effort to be polite and kind with someone, I find myself in front of a jerk who draws the worst out of me. And then this story of Nick, me and the kiss... there are too many emotions all together, I can't handle it! I hate feelings! I would like to go back to being my old self, except the only problem is that I don't know how to find me again, I think I'm lost.

12.

Shortly after – From Mina's diary

I found myself in a situation that was embarrassing at the beginning, but in the end it gave me such a great personal satisfaction that I'll carry it in my heart for a lifetime.

I didn't know that we would also be involved in the charity auction.

In a nutshell, we get divided into two groups of women and girls, then we get called onstage in pairs, and five males from among the guests make up a jury sitting behind a table. Each one of them votes for the one he prefers, and the girl who wins may choose which one of the guys that voted for her she'll dance with.

Nick and Patrick are also in the jury, and of course they voted for me.

I won against a woman in a pistachio green dress, orange shoes, and fire red hair. She looked like a traffic light. I received a round of applause, and I danced with the Mayor. We didn't talk much, he's is a very reserved fellow, but I enjoyed myself all the same.

It's five minutes to midnight, Jas is to be called on stage, and from the expression on her face she doesn't look very happy. I stand behind the jury while the presenter, meaning Katherine, takes the microphone to introduce the two new competitors.

The funniest thing of the whole evening is the pair of midget cameramen, who follow Katherine and Ben everywhere. Apparently they'll keep doing this until the wedding, because it's a reality show where they show the life of famous people and the goings on before the wedding. Katherine is really funny. Between one thing and the other she promotes the products of the sponsors, but unfortunately she does it at the most inappropriate moments and she's not all spontaneous: "I would like to remind you again that all proceeds from this auction will be donated to charity for cancer and leukemia research, to save small sick children", she says looking toward the camera, "And now I call on stage the next girl, "Come here, come on little cookie, don't be shy." From her handbag she pulls out a blue bag with biscuits drawn on it and she turns toward the audience smiling with her mouth wide open. "And, speaking of cookies, have you ever tried *Star cookies*, small glazed stars that recall the ancient taste of cookies your grandma used to make. *Star biscuits!*"

Her advertising is absolutely absurd, I feel like laughing, while Jas comes onto the stage looking very annoyed, even if she tries to be polite, smiling in that fake way that only she knows how to do. I see Patrick and Nick look at each other amused, they know perfectly well what she's like, and that she really has no desire to be put up for auction in front of everyone.

"What's your name?" asks Katherine.

Jas is about to speak into the microphone, but Katherine bursts out laughing, "Ah, but I already know, she'll be one of my bridesmaids on Saturday, at the most exclusive and chic wedding Miami has ever seen! Everything will take place on a beautiful beach, Naomi and I will be wearing the same hats created by..." She looks straight into the two cameras that follow her around and she speaks with enthusiasm and excitement.

From the audience Ben motions her to stop, waving his hands and making strange gestures, he's terribly embarrassed, while the others don't properly understand what is happening. Jas looks at her as if she's crazy and she mouths our secret number to me, *twenty two*, which means *go away*. I start laughing.

"Fine, fine, heaven's what did I say!" meows Katherine towards Ben, then turns to Jas and says: "Anyway, this is Jas. She lost her memory, poor thing, we must be patient", she looks straight into the camera hugging her tight and with a suffering look on her face she adds: "I am her only point of reference. I'm like a mother to her."

I look at Jas and I laugh, it's a hilarious scene.

She lets Katherine hug her, even though, with a closer look, it seems like Katherine is leaning on her so as not to faint from hunger, rather than hugging her in a gesture of affection. After a while she pulls herself together and continues to look toward the other side of the stage. "Let the other girl come through."

The curtain opens, and it's only now that I recall what I wanted to tell Jas that was so urgent before we were separated.

Dark, long wavy hair, a sweet look in her big blue eyes. She hasn't changed at all in this year that I've not seen her. She's wearing a black long dress and approaches the center of the stage with much grace and elegance. Jas stares at her with eyes wide open.

"What is your name? I really don't know hers this time," Katherine laughs amused while she approaches the microphone and with a soft and polite voice she introduces herself: "I'm Ginevra, good evening to you all."

I look first at Nick and then Jas; they are both staring at her as if they've just seen a ghost, while Ginevra greets them with a shy and embarrassed smile.

Unaware of everything, Katherine trills: "We can begin now. Patrick, which girl are you going to vote for? The blonde or the brunette?"

My heart races, I don't like this vote anymore, I don't like this war between Nick's ex-girlfriend and his best friend. Jas is clearly embarrassed, moves her gaze to Katherine so she doesn't have to cross Ginevra's. Patrick takes the marker pen, writes a name on the board, and before showing it he looks at Jas giving her a closed smile and shaking his head, as if to say *you're really in a bad situation huh?* Then he turns the board; *Jas* is written on it.

Ginevra smiles, one of those sweet smiles, not offended by his vote.

"Let's keep going," says Katherine condescendingly. From the nametag I see that it's now the turn of a Mr. Felix Walker, a black gentleman. That explains Katherine's tone. Felix, without a second thought, lifts up the board with the name Ginevra written on it, staring Jas up and down the whole time. This attitude seems a bit much to me.

Good God, it's only a game.

The third one to vote is another black gentleman with curly hair, who Katherine pretends not to see at all. The man waits a few moments then, seeing that Katherine is not taking any notice of him, lifts the board; he has chosen Ginevra as well. The more Nick's turn approaches, the more I see him fidgeting in his chair. He is clearly having trouble, while Jas's face stays the same: serious, pale and terribly angry with Ginevra.

"Now it's your turn, Mr Mayor. For those who don't know, among the famous people invited to my wedding, he'll be there too", she starts laughing and seeing Ben motioning her to stop talking about the wedding, she continues all serious: "Who is your favorite?"

The Mayor doesn't think much about it, lifts the board up with a vote for Jas on it, so game over, because it's logical who Nick will vote for.

"Nick, I've chosen a nice dress for Jas tonight, haven't I? She looks like an angel." Katherine looks at Jas, very happy about her choice of dress, forgetting the auction for a moment. Once again we hear Ben coughing from the back of the room. Katherine snorts. "The question seems almost superfluous, but I must ask you, who do you give your vote to, Nickolas?"

To my great surprise, he has stopped fidgeting and now he is simply motionless. He looks at the table for a while and then toward the stage, where Ginevra stands rumpling her black dress in her hands. Jas gazes at them both, she looks jealous. Nick raises the board, and fortunately there is a big *Jas* written on it. Ginevra lowers her eyes with a bitter smile and you can see a touch of sadness in Nick's expression.

Katherine exclaims: "My maid of honor won!" smiling first toward the audience, then toward the cameras. "Now tell me, my dear, who do you want to dance with among the guests that voted for you?

"No one!" she says in an abrupt and unpleasant tone; she turns around and leaves the stage, with everyone looking at her astonished. I'm running after her, when I see Nick quickly get up from the chair and do the same thing.

Damn! After months of peace they've chosen this moment to argue? One minute before her birthday!

13.

I walk quickly through the crowd. The dress prevents me from running. It's long and uncomfortable. I can't wait to get to the exit. I feel strange, sad, I don't even know why.

"Jas! Wait!" Nick calls after me from behind, but I pretend I can't hear him, I don't feel like talking to him, I have nothing to say to him, he can go and throw himself in Ginevra's arms.

He grabs my hand turning me toward him, looking at me with those innocent eyes. "Stop! I had no idea she would be there, I didn't even know she was in Miami."

"You don't have to justify yourself, it's none of my business." I take my hand from his.

"Yes it is, though."

I hate him when he speaks like this. He makes me feel strange and confused. He keeps staring straight into my eyes. I feel uncomfortable. I am not in control of the situation. He comes close, pushing a lock of hair behind my ear, while he lightly touches my shoulder with the other. His face is relaxed, he kisses me on my forehead and with a calm voice he asks me: "What bothered you, Jas?"

It looks like he already knows the answer, as if he could read my mind, but wants me to say it aloud anyway. I lower my eyes, I don't want to talk, why should I bare myself like this? He lifts my head with both hands. "Tell me. Please."

"You wanted to choose her, didn't you? Earlier, when I was on the stage, you hesitated for a moment."

There, I've said it.

My heart is in my throat, but I said it. He smiles shaking his head. "I have never doubted you, ever. How can you not see it?"

I don't know. I must be habit. I feel like an idiot, I don't know why I said that to him.

He takes my hand. "Come here."

We move next to a large column at the end of the room, away from prying eyes. He is still holding my hand, he knows that if he lets go of me I'll run off. He strokes my face and he says gently: "Now listen to me."

I lift my eyes to the sky, he's about to say one of his sweet and heartbreaking things convinced it'll make me feel better, while I feel increasingly worse after revealing myself like that. "Maybe you're too young to understand, but I want to tell you something. As you grow up, you'll often find yourself having to make a choice. At times, you'll be confused because your head will tell you one thing, and your heart another, but in the end, when it comes to people you love, regardless of how much you can think it over and agonize about it, the heart will always win."

"So you were agonizing, before, below the stage?"

He smiles again, shaking his head. "That's not the point, but I chose with my heart. Beforehand, below the stage. And if you choose with this", he puts my hand on his chest, "You're never wrong, or almost never; there are also some rare exceptions."

I feel uncomfortable again, I move my gaze away from him playing it cool. "Are you finished?"

"No", he smiles caressing my shoulders, "Happy birthday, baby."

I look at the huge clock on the wall above the stage. I have completely forgotten my birthday. I hide my head in his embrace hugging him so tight I can feel the warmth: "I had completely forgotten about it."

"Yes, I noticed." He kisses my head while I don't want to ever move away from him again.

I can't believe it, I have just turned eighteen. "It's my birthday."

"Yes."

"It is my eighteenth birthday", the more I say it the more my heart is doing all it can to jump out of my chest.

I look at Nick, and then immediately move my gaze away from him. Isobel had told me what to do, but I don't know if I will be able to do it. He caresses my face and repeats: "Yes, it's your eighteenth birthday, Jas." As soon as he stops we look at each other and in a moment we both turn serious. No more smiles, no more words, only he and I looking at each other in silence, embarrassed. We know what is going to happen, and the fact we don't talk about it but remain standing one in front of the other scares me. He comes closer to me, I feel strange, I look at his full mouth and I feel a strange heat, I'm going red in the face, I can feel it. Meantime he, embarrassed, barely whispers: "I don't know how..."

"Nick, don't say anything..."

The need to flee becomes stronger and stronger, but it isn't as strong as the desire to stay. I gently put a lock of hair behind his ear, watching his uncertain eyes. I see his embarrassment and feel his emotion as he touches me with trembling hands. He slowly moves closer, he wants to be sure that I really want him to, I could stop him, I could say no, move, but I don't.

He comes closer still, holding my face in such a way as to feel my breathing, closes his eyes and the next moment I feel his warm lips touch mine.

Suddenly I hear Mina scream.

14.

I've found them at last. Nick is already wishing her a happy birthday, dammit! Taking small but quick steps I run toward Jas shouting: "Best Wishes my loooooove!"

Nick seems upset, and when I stand between them, I notice Jas is too. Admittedly my entrance was a little reckless, but what can I do if I'm happy? I move her away from Nick and hug her tight. In a week we're going on our long-awaited trip through Europe.

"Thank you", Jas replies in strange tone, she and Nick are both red in the face. I don't understand.

"We must make a toast, love!" I exclaim, jumping up and down like a little girl, "It's your eighteenth birthday! You're an adult, darling! Let's go and get the champagne!"

I grab her by the arm and I'm about to drag her away, when I see Nick take her other arm stopping us both. "Jas, are you alright?" he asks timidly.

"And you?" she asks him.

"Listen up!" I interrupt this unjustified embarrassment between them and separate them, "You've been glued to each other the whole evening, it's my turn now, so you wait here, will you Nickolas, we're going to get something to drink!"

I drag Jas with me down the room. I'm too curious to know how the *Jaskolas saga* is progressing now that Ginevra is back. "I want to know everything! When I saw Veronica speak with Ginevra, I couldn't believe it was really her at first! I was stunned, I swear, but what is she doing here? She doesn't want to get back with Nick, surely?"

"I don't..."

"Jas, maybe it was just my impression, but you looked somewhat angry, anguished, but mostly jealous of Nick, back there."

"What? No, that's not true." Her tone is actually saying quite the opposite. We stop near the buffet table.

"Waiter, could you give us three glasses of champagne?" I politely ask a dark-haired boy with his back turned to us. I am about to continue my conversation with Jas when I hear a very familiar voice answer: "Yes, of course, no problem."

The waiter turns and... I can't believe it, it's Ross. Shocked he screams: "Oh good heavens, it is you?" Immaculately dressed, with his forelock dyed black, he looks at Jas terrified and adds: "And Satan's here too! I didn't know that even the devil was into charity."

"Who is he?" Jas asks me intrigued, while I take a glass of champagne from his tray shaking my head.

"Ah ha, mock me all you want and pretend to not know me, but contrary to you, you crazy psychopath, who only thinks of hurting all the innocent souls on this planet, I want to become someone in this life. Now I serve drinks, tomorrow I will serve food, and the day after tomorrow perhaps I will serve as a living ashtray, but in the end it will be the others serving me, and when I say *serve*, I mean in every sense, if you know what I mean?" As always, he said all this in his shrill voice, in one breath, and assuming a pose like he was a higher being.

Jas goes to him to take two glasses of champagne from his tray, and even though she is smiling calmly, Ross steps back with a serious face.

"Yes, yes, it is better if you go away, Ross, or Jas will have you arrested", I joke.

"What? She can't have me arrested if I haven't done anything!" he exclaims, but he's not entirely sure of what he just said. "Okay, I'm going! But not because I am afraid of you! Let that be clear!" He literally flees behind the buffet table, wiggling his hips like a hysterical girl.

I toast with one of the two glasses that Jas holds in her hand, waiting impatiently for her to tell me what's new in the invisible triangle Jas, Nick and Ginevra, but she says nothing.

"So"?

"So what?" she looks around and I know very well who she's looking for among the crowd. It's so annoying, there's always him in the mix.

"Jas", I pause raising my eyebrows, "I already asked you this a while ago, but now I feel the need to ask you again: what's going on between you and Nick?"

She smiles at me shyly and is about to say something, when behind us we hear someone with a foreign accent ask: "Excuse me, miss?"

We turn around and see a tall man, dark haired, very well-built and full of scars on the face looking at us in a nasty little way with half open eyes. He is pushing a boy with dark hair on a wheelchair, his head turned down. They can't get close to the table because of us.

"Oh, excuse me, I'm the one who should asking your pardon", I stumble over my words, "Please, go ahead, I hadn't seen you."

I move quickly, but the gentleman keeps standing there, staring at Jas annoyed. She raises her eyebrows, she doesn't understand, until the boy in the wheelchair lifts his head and says: "Happy birthday, Jas."

Everything stops in a moment, everything has become dark. I recognize him, it's really him, with the black wig and his eyes hidden by the glasses, it's him: Jack!

My mouth opens by itself from the shock. I can't take my eyes off him, I can't believe it.

He looks at Jas with a tender expression and eyes full of hope, waiting for a reaction, but what is Jas's reaction? I look at her, and if she was pale when she saw Ginevra, now she's white, as white as a sheet. She's stock-still, with eyes wide open. She loses her grip on the glasses which fall to the ground breaking into a thousand pieces.

I don't know how, but I find the strength to squeeze her hand and whisper her name with a trembling voice: "Jas?" I feel her hand also squeeze mine tight, something snaps in her. She closes her eyes for a moment and when she reopens them, I shiver. My old Jas is back. Nasty eyes, challenging gaze and a smile that cries out for revenge. She looks at Jack straight in the eye and the only thing she says is: "What was the first rule, John?" and immediately after that she punches him so hard straight in the face that he falls off the wheelchair.

And then chaos breaks out around us. Everything happens so fast, even if in my head I see people moving in slow motion. The gentleman with the scarred face first of all looks around him and seeing people turn toward us, he bends over Jack trying to help him. The boy's lower lip is bleeding.

Jas is out of control. She throws herself on top of him again, still on the ground. In her path she finds Ross who wants to help the boy; she pushes him so hard that he ends up on Jack and his wheelchair.

"*Jas! No!*" I cry grabbing her arm and trying to pull her away from him, "Stop! That's enough, Jas!"

She looks like she's possessed. That's where all her rage has been in all these months.

I don't know what is happening exactly. The chaos is such that I can't follow everything.

At a certain point policemen arrive. One of them, really nasty, holds Jas who keeps trying to beat Jack. Ross screams like a little girl that he has done nothing, that Jas is the guilty one. The music is turned off. The guests are shocked. The journalists rush happily to Jas to take pictures of her and Nick, incredulous, who is protecting her in spite of everything. He is evidently distressed, but still ready to defend her in front of everyone and everything, hiding her from the photographers' flashes. The first person who runs to his aid is Patrick, looking at Jack and the dark-haired gentleman beside him.

I've often thought of Jack coming back. From the day that he came looking for her at school I was afraid that it might happen, and now that it has, what next? Things have just become complicated and I fear that this is only the beginning.

***

The prison is cold, dirty, on the ground there is an inch of dust, the tiles are icy. To see dawn from the small window on the wall is another story altogether. I would have thought anything, except that one day I would end up in here because of Jas, because she landed a real punch on a fake disabled person.

The policeman who arrested us was thin, with a white beard and white hair; from a distance you could take him for a good friendly granddad like the ones you see on the ads for Christmas pudding, but up close you are afraid that you're the Christmas pudding and that he's going to eat you in just one mouthful.

I don't know why, but I had the distinct feeling that he doesn't like Nick and his group and, as a result, Jas as well.

And speaking of her, she doesn't speak, she hasn't said anything for hours, she doesn't justify or blame herself, there is an annoying silence in this cell, and I don't feel like asking her anything. I'll wait, as I have done for months now, she'll talk to me when she's ready, I'm sure.

Nick will be here in a while. Angry, disappointed, he'll ask questions and he'll want answers. I wonder how she'll explain it to him and where she'll begin. Just thinking back to the faces yesterday and how everyone looked at her shocked, makes me feel ill.

What an awful birthday.

Jack's back and obviously he's back for her. For months and months I just could not accept it, I could not come to terms with the fact that it really had happened and that John and Jack were the same person. Right to the end I kept hoping that it was just a bad joke, like little Franklin's, but now I know that it's all true. John was only an act, a performance worthy of an Oscar, and Jack is the reality.

I hope that Nick is not too hard on her and that among all the punishments we're won't be stopped from going on our trip around Europe.

Ross is sitting on the bench facing us, under arrest as well, even though his only crime - like mine after all - was being in the wrong place at the wrong time. He is very angry with Jas, does nothing but jiggle his leg and glare at her. I think he's about to explode. "When you said that she'd have me arrested, I should have imagined that you were serious, you witch!" he says, addressing me with an annoying tone. Then he looks at Jas. "You've beaten up a disabled person! A poor boy in a wheelchair!" He stands up crossing his hands, while she keeps looking at the floor, I'm not even sure that she's even listening to him. "I guess you'll get a

97

promotion when you return to the underworld again! Will they give you a medal? A little skull to hang on the wall? And what will the next mission be? Setting an orphanage on fire?"

She raises her head, glaring at him. It's enough to shut Ross up and make him sit down on the bench again.

I move towards her cautiously. "Jas? *Twenty three*?" So that Ross won't understand, I ask her in our code if she feels like talking about it. Without moving her gaze from the floor she answers: "*Sixteen.*"

If I'm not mistaken, that was the number for Mr. Rossi our schoolteacher. It has nothing much to do with what we're talking about.

"What *three* to *nine* when *two*?" *what will you tell Nick when he comes?* I can already see him, with that disapproving expression of his and a list of punishments in hand. "Jas, *three*!" *Jas, speak!*

"Oh my God, they're possessed!" exclaims Ross, continuing to say stupid and irrelevant things as he hears us speak with numbers. "I'll write to Jx! She needs to know of your existence, oh demon", he murmurs and gestures looking at Jas.

She remains silent for a while, then with a resolute tone she answers: "I'll say that I need another psychologist."

I look at her incredulous, while Ross nods in agreement with his statement.

"You'd rather make out you're crazy, than finally tell Nick the truth?" I whisper shocked, "If Ja..." I stop. I can't say Jack's name, I correct myself in saying: "If the disabled person hadn't surprised you, coming up from behind like a *thief*", I say, and this is not a code or an analogy, "You'd have never hit him, therefore it's his fault."

"Please God, let me get out of here unharmed." prays Ross with a shrill voice looking upwards. He's getting on my nerves, but not as much as Jas's reasoning to pass herself off as crazy. I just don't get it anymore, and all this not knowing and not understanding is doing my head in, seriously.

I take her hand, and for the first time in hours she looks me in the eyes. She's not well, it's a difficult night for all of us, and I can imagine how her brain must be working overtime, but she must think about it carefully and make the right choice.

"You should tell Nick."

"Tell me what?"

We look toward the bars, Nick is right there.

I didn't know he'd already arrived here. I don't answer his question. His face looks seemingly peaceful. He, like all of us, is still wearing his party clothes. Ross rushes to Nick and clinging to the bars he begins yelling scared: "Oh dear God, Niki help me, get me out of here! She wanted to beat me. She's possessed by the entire Adams family! She lives in an up-side down world where she passes as the victim and disabled people as killers!"

Jas stands up from bench with her head down to go to him.

"Oh God, she's coming, help me!" Then he notices that nobody's taking any notice of him and shuts up. Annoyed, he goes back to sit in his place.

Jas puts her hands on the bars and stands there silent, visibly upset. How is she going to explain it to him now? Telling him she's gone crazy? That she needs a psychologist? I don't think that's the right solution and I doubt he'll believe her. I'm about to have a heart attack. Nick's eyes fall on Jas's fingers, they are stained with ink. She notices and tries to hide them, visibly uncomfortable.

"I have paid the bond. Ben has asked the disabled person's father to drop the charges against you as long as you apologize to his son. It seems to me like a more than reasonable request. Unfortunately we have not succeeded in stopping the journalists. Both the photos and the news have already been printed and you're on all the American newspapers and television networks." Nick lowers his head for a moment, we remain in silence. "Later, we'll think about how to protect you from the media assault. Ben is signing the last forms for your release, and then Will is going to come and get you and take you home". He speaks in a subdued tone; his eyes are worried, but not angry. In the face of Jas's silence, he adds: "That's it. I'll see you later at the *Watchtower*."

He's about to leave when Jas calls him. He stops and only after a few seconds turns and looks at her, but doesn't move closer. He stays a few meters away. "What is it?"

Jas grips the bars nervously, drops her head and almost whispering she says: "Love me, hate me but spare me your indifference."

He looks at her amazed, while she, upset, stays there with her head down. He comes closer to the bars and gently rests his hands on hers, saying: "Is it indifference that you see in my eyes, Jas?"

She lifts her head and looks at him. "No."

"And what do you see?"

They continue to look at each other and stroke each other's hands. I feel strange for them myself. Jas doesn't reply.

"There are many things we have to talk about, clarify and understand," he says.

"Yes, I know, I..."

"But not now."

"What?"

Yes, *what*? I can't believe my ears! I'm as shocked as she is.

"Everything happened too quickly and you'll certainly be confused and", he pauses, "I don't want you tell me anything right now. I'll wait, and when you're ready, I'll be there."

They look at each other like two lovers, and at this point I give up, I really can't understand anything anymore.

He asks her: "You know that you can tell me everything?"

"Yes, I know."

Through the bars he kisses her on the forehead, gently, and smiles at her with closed lips.

"I punched a disabled person," says Jas, as if to remind him what she did.

"Even if you made a very intemperate and unwarranted gesture, it doesn't mean that you don't have a rational explanation for what happened. When you feel like it, I will listen to you, but until then I will respect your silence." He caresses her hand and as he leaves he says: "What's important is that you don't end up like your hamster."

We are all left open-mouthed with eyes staring. Nick leaves with a touch of a smile on his lips, and Jas looks at him speechless.

I figured she'd say something like, *but how is it possible that he didn't yell at me? What's going on with him? Has a miracle happened?* Instead the only thing she says is: "My hamster?"

Ross continues to shake his head with his hands joined. "This man must be made a saint immediately! Even Gandhi would have slapped you in the face a couple of times after what you've done, and instead what does he do? He buys you a hamster! You haven't even apologized to him for making us all look like pieces of shit in front of the entire world! I hate you!"

Sometimes I get the impression that Ross doesn't listen when someone is talking and interprets things the way he wants, but in this case he's got a point.

Jas looks at the corridor smiling happily. I can imagine that, in spite of everything, she's asking herself a thousand questions about the how and the why, just as I am. Perhaps she also has the answers which I haven't. "Jas, I'm a little confused. I mean, I'm happy for you, let that be clear. But I wasn't expecting this reaction from Nick. He didn't scold you, didn't want explanations... Anyone else would have, and then what's this thing about the hamster?"

"I have no idea."

15.

From the window Isobel watched the workers that - on her orders - were building a solid and impenetrable stone wall around Villa Torres. On the other side of the perimeter, she noticed suspicious movement. A Slovenian family had bought the adjacent land and was about to build a house right opposite her villa. This meant busybodies and the end of her privacy.

Her grandson Nickolas was outside, sitting on the grass below the wall of the Italian-Slovenian border, holding his ball and observing the brick-layers at work. She saw he was pensive and in no way inclined to interact with any of them and this hurt her. His silence had gone on for months now, and Isobel's fear that she would not be able to win his confidence and help him in his pain became greater with each passing day.

The three bricklayers worked under the scorching sun all day long. A sip of beer, a laugh among themselves and the wall around the villa grew higher and higher.

One of them came to the boundary and emptied a bucket of water on the lawn where a puddle had formed, little Nick watching on in silence with his ball in his hands.

"Hey boy, want to give us a hand?" asked the man in a nice way seeing him there all alone but, just like every other time, all he received in return was silence.

The other brick-layer sipped his beer and said laughing: "Leave him alone, it seems he has inherited his grandmother's charm." He was alluding to Isobel who, with her severity and authoritarian ways, did not elicit much liking among the workers. The first brick-layer smiled at Nickolas tenderly, not agreeing with his colleague, but the child turned his head the other way, pretending he hadn't heard anything.

He looked at the puddle full of water. Each time one of the masons dumped some more, Nick would see the stormy and violent sea of the night his parents had died. He saw the same water rise inside the jeep, the dark open eyes of his father already dead and the scared eyes of his mother who, despite everything, had tried desperately to save him. Despondency grew inside him. He hadn't been able to help them!

His eyes filled with tears, angry, and without realizing it he kicked his ball towards the puddle. But it hit one of the masons straight in the face, breaking his nose. Blood began to flow and the other masons ran to their friend's aid, as Nick remained motionless, scared and incredulous at the idea of having done such a thing. The brick-layers looked at him indignantly; they didn't understand what had gotten into him. Nick looked up to the window of the villa and saw Isobel staring at him with the same astonished expression. He took his ball stained with blood and ran away in tears, toward the large grounds of Villa Torres.

16.

We are still in prison waiting for Will to arrive, but the atmosphere is decidedly more relaxed and pleasant than half an hour ago.

Ross is still doing his stupid game of walking two fingers on the wall, Jas is lying quietly on the bench smiling and thinking about Nick's unexpected reaction, and I am looking at the two of them in silence.

There are many things I'm not clear on, but as long as I see her happy it's fine with me. I'd like to lie down too, but I don't want to crease my wonderful and very expensive red dress, so I've been sleeping in a sitting position for ten hours already.

All of a sudden we hear the echo of high heels arriving from the end of the corridor. I turn and see a woman around thirty: black hair tied in a ponytail, spectacles, wearing a formal black skirt and a tight white shirt matching her handbag. She looks like a model, with that long-limbed physique, the sensual walk and a confident gaze with which she studies us from afar. She's very alluring, although she's not doing anything particular. She stops on the other side of the bars and looks us up and down with a big sigh. Ross gets up from the bench all agitated. "Oh my God, who is the goddess my eyes have had the honor to set upon? Apparently Olympus still exists and no one told me!"

It is the first time that I hear him pay a compliment to a woman. She fixes him intrigued and visibly pleased about the compliments. "You're a nice little chocolate. I like you."

What a sexy voice she has. She looks at Ross as a cat would, her eyes half-closed.

"And I like you, my Athena! I am inebriated by your presence and your fragrance is..." he can't find the right words, he approaches her sniffing at her from behind the bars, "I am not entirely sure, but it smells like..."

"This is the scent of desire."

What a deep voice. I feel embarrassed to be so attracted to her.

"Oh, I would have sworn it was vodka", adds Ross thoughtful.

"What is your name?"

"My name is Ross. Rossella to my friends."

The woman leans on the bars in a provocative way showing her low neckline and goes on mischievously: "Do you like me?"

"Yes, yes, yes. I'm already wagging my tail, God! Shall we rub noses?"

"And what do you like about me?"

"You're very Gucci, poochi, oochi! Is it the real thing?" he points to the white bag with his finger, excited.

"The bag is, yes. The boobs, no," she says, and begins to laugh with her mouth wide open uttering irritating sounds along with Ross, ruining the whole sexy appearance. "I used to date a surgeon some time back, you understand, yeah?"

They're like partners in crime, as if they've known each other for years, same laugh, same mannerisms. Jas and I look at them astonished and in silence.

"Have you seen Louis Vuitton's latest creation?" asks Ross as he gets closer to the bars whispering: "It's a unique piece. Ab-so-lut-ly u-nique! I'd sell my soul to the devil to have that bag", then he turns toward Jas, "Oh, I got lucky, he's sitting right here behind me", and the complicit laughter explodes once again, their mouths wide open.

"I know," the woman laughs amused, "I am her lawyer."

"You're the devil's advocate?"

"Sexy, right?"

"Oh yes, my God, can I dress up like you for Halloween?"

Their conversations are strange, without meaning, I don't understand them. I have the feeling that they're making fun of us, because no one speaks and behaves this way. Jas looks at them from the bench and with a great couldn't-give-a-damn attitude says to her: "I already have a lawyer, I don't need another."

The woman looks at her bringing her hand to her hip and smiles: "Who? Ben? *One thousand*! He's so busy looking after his ex-wives, his children and his wrinkles that he doesn't have time to deal with your juvenile skirmishes. Go on, come out."

"Take me too, me too!" screams Ross jumping around behind the bars like a dog.

"I can't today, maybe next time, if you're good."

"But I am always good, Rossella very good."

"I am not going anywhere with you, I'm waiting for Will."

"I had almost forgotten how much you are... *you*", she sighs, making a strange grimace, as if she'd known her for years. "However, orders are orders and I don't think you should be throwing a tantrum after what happened at the gala, my dear."

"Love, don't worry, go with her", I reassure her, "If this is Nick's decision, I'm sure there's a reason."

"Okay", she looks at the lawyer and then whispers to me: "But, *Homer*?"

In our secret code it means *alcohol*, but I can't make the connection and understand what she means.

"*Zero*?"

If I see it? But see what? Today, numbers and I aren't on the same page. I smile looking at the lawyer, pretending to understand. Jas approaches the bars, the lawyer looks at her puzzled from head to toe stroking her white bag.

"And how do I get out? The door is locked", Jas points out to her, but we hear a noise, and the door opens suddenly.

"It's not now."

Jas goes out, the lawyer says good-bye to us waving only the fingers of her hand, and they leave.

"Promise me that I'll see you again, my goddess, I beg you..." Ross screams desperately with his hand outstretched towards the lawyer as she goes away with Jas. Then he sits on the bench all sad talking to himself: "That devil called Jas has all the luck in the world."

17.

From Jas's diary – Miami prison

I walk behind my new lawyer and the more I look at her, the more I realize that she's blind drunk. She stops several times to regain her balance and avoid slamming against the wall or fall to the ground. This is absurd, how could Nick employ a person like that to be my lawyer?

We are about to walk out of the station, when I hear a policeman calling her: "Miss White?"

We both turn. Well, she took a little longer, given her alcohol level, and she it did holding steady to the door. At least now I know her surname: White.

She approaches the policeman with a slow and seductive walk. He looks at her from under his glasses, embarrassed. He's the typical goofy boy, shy and who doesn't know how behave with the female sex. Only when Ms. White reaches the counter she asks him: "Yes?"

Holy Mother of God, a simple yes *turns into porno stuff.*

"You must give me, just sign here and you two can g-go."

Poor thing, he's so excited, he stutters, "If I give you, I sign."

She reads his name on his badge. "Scott", she says panting. "What will you give me, do in exchange?" she ends the sentence grabbing his tie with one hand whilst with the other she signs the sheet without taking her eyes off him: he's about to faint. "Think about it until the next time, alright, Scotty?"

The policeman dries his sweaty forehead with a handkerchief, nodding, while he takes his tie back from Ms. White's hands.

We leave the police station. It's cloudy, everything around is gray, the wind is shaking the palm trees lining the road, it's about to rain.

After taking only two steps Ms. White looks at me from the corner of her eyes, saying: "At midnight you became an adult, right?"

"Yes", I reply, as she grabs my arm because she's about to collapse. Incredible.

"And at two minutes past midnight you were arrested for assault and you even resisted arrest, didn't you?"

I don't bother answering her, but where is she going with this?

"I feel that you will make me real proud, my dear."

She's totally insane, this one. I can't wait to get rid of her, and I see the opportunity to do it when I notice Will climbing the stairs. He looks at us surprised, scratching his dark hair and adjusting his glasses with the other hand. "Jas? I was, Nick told me to, because, yes, is it her?"

Too bad that I forgot the decoder at home. I can understand the words one by one, but it's the whole lot that gives me problems.

Ms. White looks at me with a bored expression. "Can we go or do I have to reply to this man?"

"The agreement was that I'd co-come, pk pk damage of with you now?" whatever he's saying to her, he's pretty angry.

"Ms. White. I'm her lawyer", she gets closer to him with the look of huntress. "Tell me, do you like me?"

Does this one here always ask the same questions?

Will doesn't seem to appreciate her behavior, he steps back, stuttering: "No. Withdraw, of the fact, prison and all three pk pk, hjguyhjknssssssss."

"I am not interested! *One Thousand*! No one has ever dared treat me this way! And besides, I got here first!"

"I don't believe that, in the sense, it's frrrf."

I watch them argue and I'm totally shocked.

I don't understand if it's a sick joke or if I'm hallucinating. From the start, the whole situation is too strange and surreal to be true. Ms. White grabs me by the arm, annoyed, and pulls me down the stairs complaining about Will and what he said to her, while he looks at us upset saying something like *kljuihgf DAS* .

"How do you know what he's saying?" I ask intrigued.

"Simple, I used to date a guy who spoke with the same English accent as his."

"English accent? His accent is the only thing you can understand when he speaks!"

She's couldn't care less about me anymore. We walk down the stairs; the taxi is parked in front of us. I was ready to grab the handle when I hear her scream in terror: "Oh no, no, no what are you doing? *One Thousand!*"

I take my hand off the handle in a split second, wondering what the hell I did wrong, and also what the hell this *one thousand* she keeps inserting into each sentence means: "I thought the taxi was ours. How do we get home, on foot?"

"Taxi? On foot? What is this, some sort of code?" she rebukes me.

It must be because I'm really tired because I haven't slept all night, but I continue to see something strange in her, and the way she talks, as if she was a porn star, makes me feel uncomfortable.

She grabs my hand whispering: "Move away from there before someone sees us!"

She pulls me away from the taxi and shortly after a long black limousine with tinted windows stops beside us. She immediately grabs the door handle, opens the door, puts her white bag inside bending so she can show her backside to the passers-by, and only then she gets inside walking on four legs on the seat of the limousine.

"This is not like Nick, and besides, why would he send a limousine to pick me up?"

"Why he would, I'm not sure, but I know why I would. Get in."

I get in, even if my instinct tells me not to. Nick is not a strategist, he's not someone who says one thing and does another, at least not consciously. All of this is really on the nose, and I'm not talking about the stench of alcohol from the drunken lawyer, but all the rest.

Perhaps Nick wants to confuse me, but to what end?

The limousine is an indescribable luxury. I am sitting opposite Ms. White, to my right there is a long bar with dozens of bottles. I briefly read the labels and I notice that each of them indicates an alcoholic drink or a spirit. This explains even more the type of person I have in front of me.

I can't see the driver because the dark glass screen has been raised between us and the driver's seat.

"Give me your leg."

"What?" for a moment I thought she was asking me to give her my leg.

"Your leg."

She takes my right leg and lifts it up onto the seat, between hers. She looks at me as if to seduce me, slowly raises the evening dress up to my knees, she seems totally at ease as she caresses it. Slowly, she pulls something from her bra. It's a business card in a bright red color encrusted with sparkling Swarovski crystals.

Looking at me straight in the eyes, she slots it between the straps of my stilettos. "This is my business card, in case you need a little legal help again one day."

She puts my skirt back in place fondling my leg again. "You're the first girl I know who doesn't have a bag. Why don't you have a bag? You should get one, my dear."

I don't want to give her cause for a conversation. I simply smile and stay silent. She takes a glass looking at the spirits in the showcase. I raise my eyebrows. I can't believe she still wants to drink.

Ms. White presses a button under her seat and the screen in the center of the cabinet comes on. The news is on. It is showing the arrest of a man of Turkish origin, apparently the one responsible for the explosion at the airport a week ago. It seems there is a super witness.

Immediately after, it quickly moves on to Jx's heroic feats during the hurricane alert and then stops on another news item: last night's charity gala. It goes without saying that it wasn't the proceeds for the sick children that drew attention, but me being unjustly arrested.

Frowning, I follow the entire broadcast. They've spoken more about me and the *Watchtower* than the capture of the Turkish man who makes bombs.

I turn off the TV just by moving my leg and pressing the button with my heel.

Ms. White offers me a glass. "Drink this and relax, *sweetie*, you'll need it."

I don't even have time to refuse the cocktail before I feel a very pleasant massage on my back. These seats are cool, I really needed it.

I take the glass, even though I have no intention of starting to drink at ten in the morning. I lean my head on the seat closing my eyes. What a pleasant feeling, I feel my body relax at last. The evening dress I'm wearing all of a sudden seems so comfortable, and everything is becoming so... peaceful.

But unfortunately this feeling doesn't last long. Nothing here is peaceful.

As soon as I relax and I have nothing to do, here come my concerns floating back into my mind.

John is back. He was there in front of me with a ridiculous wig on his head, looking at me.

Happy birthday, Jas.

Was that all that he had to say to me, after everything he's done to me?

To come back here and ridicule me again like that... he knew I'd react badly, he knew it and he did it on purpose to make me look like a fool in front of everyone in Miami. I hate him!

But I mustn't think of him, that's exactly what he wants. I will not allow him to put me in a bad mood or to humiliate me again in any way.

I open my eyes and I see my reflection on the window, and it is not a great sight. I notice that my pulled up hair from last night is now loose and disheveled. The white dress got a little soiled in prison, a shoulder strap is missing. I can't recall if I had earrings on, because if I did, I don't have them anymore, I've lost them.

Perhaps it is better to look out the window. The wind is blowing hard, the sky is even darker and everything reflects my mood perfectly.

"Where we are going?" I ask, not recognizing the landscape, "This isn't the way home."

"And who said we were taking you home, my dear? It will be a surprise, you'll see."

"I don't like surprises."

"Everybody likes surprises."

"Not me."

"To tell the truth, I had a vague suspicion of that, but I pretended I didn't know". She starts to laugh. When she speaks she has this low and sensual voice, but when she starts to laugh she becomes someone else. The tone of voice becomes irritating, too high. And then she has this habit of opening her mouth wide as if

111

she's about to bite something. I just look at her. There are no words for this situation.

The limo stops, finally. I look out the window.

"Here we are!" she says very enthusiastically, taking a sip of her drink and, still holding the glass, gets out of the luxurious car.

"What is this place? What are we doing here?"

"This is a big parking garage and your boyfriend is coming to get you."

"Nick is not my boyfriend", I point out. I put the still full glass on the bar and I'm about to get out as well, when the glass between us and the driver begins to lower. I stand at the open door of the limousine, waiting for Nick to arrive and explain to me the reason for this absurd show.

Ms. White can't stand on her feet, she clings to the door so as not to fall, but she seems happy all the same, lost in her alcoholic world. She downs her drink, throws the glass inside the car and takes a bar of chocolate from her bag. "Would you like a little bit of white chocolate?"

White chocolate? As soon as I hear this, something inside of me snaps. It reminds me of something important, but I don't know what. She's taken a piece and puts it in her mouth like it was... I am ashamed to even describe it.

Chewing, she explains to me: "A doctor I used to date a few years ago... To tell the truth, I was seeing him so I could date his brother who hung out with a renowned mafia boss... anyway, he told me that chocolate increases serotonin which puts you in a good mood. That's why I'm always so cheerful. I love white chocolate."

While she speaks nonsense, suddenly everything becomes terribly clear in my head. My memory starts to bring back old memories to me, I blanch.

Lexi is a lawyer, she's nice, she likes white chocolate...

I stop breathing.

I look inside the limo. A huge man is at the wheel and in the mirror I can see two icy eyes and the many scars on his face. I recognize him. He's the man who was pushing John's wheelchair at the gala.

I look at the woman who claims to be Ms. White. She stares at me dazed, and continues eating the chocolate. "What's the matter, my dear? All of a sudden your face matches your dress."

I take a few steps back. I look first at her and then at the man at the wheel.

I have to get out of here! It's not Nick who's coming!

I start running toward the road as fast as my legs can carry me. I feel like I'm in one of those nightmares where you run and you run but get nowhere.

All of a sudden, I see a black car with a fire red number plate coming down the road. It takes the bend at full speed and blasts into the parking garage. I stop, certain that it's about to run over me, but it turns on its side stopping a few inches from me.

The windows are blacked out, loud AC/DC music is coming from inside. The lawyer or I should say Lexi smiles and beside her the blond driver looks at me in a nasty way.

I don't know what to do. I back up some more, but then I stop. The first time I was taken by surprise, but not now. I am not running away!

The car door opens, the music goes off and it's him, John, getting out!

He places his sunglasses on his blond hair, throws the cigarette to the ground and smiles at me with arrogance. His upper lip is wounded from the punch I swung at him.

Hanging around his neck is a shiny blue stone. My stone, the one I won on Valentine's day.

He leans on the door touching his lip. "As usual, your self-control is enviable, darling," he says in a sarcastic tone.

"I am not your darling! And besides, wasn't the punch on your face enough for you? Do you want me to aim lower?"

Hearing this he smiles smugly. "Sorry to disappoint you, but the only reason you were able to hit me was because I let you."

"Oh really?" I don't know what gets into me, but my hand goes up by itself and slaps his face so hard that his glasses fly off his head. I'm not afraid of him. "Did you let me do this as well, *darling*?"

Touching his cheek, he looks at me with his eyes half-closed and then says with great calm: "You know, I've thought a lot about this moment and about what I'd say to you when I had you in front of me, and the only thing that comes to mind is to tell you that you're a bitch!"

There's no trace of the disabled John in him. I don't know who this person in front of me is. Shocked and becoming even more furious I ask him: "I am *what*?!"

He comes to within a few inches from me and, spelling out the words, he looks me straight in the eye and repeats: "You're a damn bitch."

His effrontery makes my blood boil. I deliver an angry kick at his car and I leave infuriated. He screams desperately looking at the dent on the car. "No! My baby!"

He soon catches up to me, grabs my arm and vigorously turns me towards him. "Where do you think you're going?"

"Let me go!" I push him away from me. "Don't touch me!"

"I came here to clarify things with you, and all you do is hit me!"

"I don't have anything to clarify with you! It is all too clear, go away!"

"No!"

"I'll go then!"

"No!" He grabs my arm again.

"I told you not to touch me!"

Instinctively I knee him between the legs making him bend over in pain. I'm about to run towards Lexi and the stocky man, who are looking at me bored, then I stop, I can't go that way, they'll stop me for sure.

I don't know what takes me. I turn around and seek shelter in John's car, locking myself in. My heart is about to jump out of my chest. What am I doing? He comes closer, really mad. "Get out of there right now!"

"No! Go away!"

With his face stuck to the window he tries to open the door. "Jas! You don't realize how much you're pissing me off right now! Get out of my car immediately!"

"Or what? You'll plant a bullet in my head?"

"Don't tempt me!" he says between his teeth.

I have to get out of here.

I start the car. It makes a really loud noise. It sounds like an animal, a roaring tiger. I stare in surprise, while John puts himself in front of the car completely changing his tone of voice and expression. "Okay, okay, okay. Calm down, calm down, breathe deeply, nothing's happened, nothing's happened." He speaks to me slowly, articulating the words as if I were a moron and motions with his hands for me to stay calm.

"Stop talking to me like I'm crazy!"

"Okay, okay, okay. We got off on the wrong foot, okay? What say we start over, eh?"

He is repeating exactly what I said to him months ago! Apparently he is continuing to take the piss!

"How about turning off the engine, getting out of there, and we can talk about it calmly, far, far away from my little jewel?"

"I don't want to talk to you. You must disappear from my life, get away from me!" I push the accelerator, going a few meters forward and almost hit him.

His expression and tone of voice change again. "Stop! Get out of this car! Jas! I'm ordering you!"

"You're *what*?"

"No, no, I'm not ordering you... I was joking..."

I put it in gear and take off at full speed, and he jumps on the hood of the car. What with several spasmodic burst of the car and sudden braking, I end up on the main road. It's my first time ever at the wheel, I don't even know which gear I'm in and I have a guy on the hood!

I am angry, scared and excited all at the same time. "Have you got any more orders to give me, you stupid son of a bi... aaah!" I scream. I end up in the opposite lane. A van is coming towards me.

"Be careful!" shouts John.

I turn the steering wheel sharply, avoiding it by a hair. My heart is about to jump out of my chest, I'm shaking all over. John instead continues to scream from on top of the hood: "You'll wreck my car! Put it in second gear at least, you'll kill her!"

"No!

"Be careful!"

"No!"

"You'll make me fall off like this! Open the window and let me in!"

"No!"

He's in front of me on the other side of the windscreen. His bright blue eyes are staring at me, distracting me again.

"Nooooo, be careful!" he shouts, holding onto the wipers. I get back into my lane, with other cars honking impatiently.

John manages to reach the window on the passenger side, and almost crying he says to the car: "Oh, please forgive me little one. And you watch the road...!" he orders me and with his left hand punches at the window and breaks it into a thousand pieces making them fly as far as my seat.

I don't know whether to look at him or the road. He jumps inside very angry, moves the glass from the seat, tossing it onto the floor, and shouts: "You're completely out of your mind!" He points at me with his finger, which is bleeding. "Slow down!" He puts his hand on the manual gearbox and repeats: "Brake!"

I step on the brake immediately, and he scales down the gears. The motor stops screaming, but I don't. "If you try to put a single finger on me, I swear I'll destroy it!"

He looks at me breathing deeply. With the healthy hand he pulls back his long blond hair, while he hits the dashboard with the other, leaving us a little bit of blood on it. "Dammit!"

He takes a handkerchief from his pocket and wraps it around the bloodied hand. "Why do you behave like that? Why?"

"Why do I behave like that? Hmm, let me think for a moment. Perhaps the fact that you lied, cheated, stole the headmistress's crucifix and killed three men in cold blood before my very eyes could be a clue? John!"

"My name is Jack."

"I don't give a damn what your name is! What do you want from me?"

"Hmm, let me think for a moment. The fact that I supported you, listened to you, defended you and saved your life *twice* could be a clue!"

"You're a liar! A murderer!"

"I cannot believe that out of the four months we lived together, this all you remember of us."

"Us? There has never been any *us and* there never will be!"

"Ah no, eh?" he looks at me and smiles in a provocative way. I know that he's about to make me get even more angry. "Well, as far as I can tell, our clues have one thing in common."

"You and I have nothing in common!"

"How strange, and yet I thought you were the excited girl that I was kissing in the school courtyard."

I open my eyes wide, shocked. *This is too much!*

I swerve the car suddenly, ending up in the other lane again, with the risk of causing another accident.

"No, no, no, no! I was joking..."John whines, worried about the safety of his car.

"Excited girl?"

"No, no, don't do it! No!"

I crash through the fence that runs alongside the road, ending up right in the middle of the beach, and go straight for the lifeguards' lookout. The car grinds through the sand, but I continue to press the accelerator.

John grabs the steering wheel trying to stop me. "Let go of the steering wheel! Get your hands off it!"

"It's all yours!"

I open the car door and jump out with the car still moving, roll in the sand for yard after yard and really hurt myself. I see the car destroy part of the lifeguards' lookout and head toward the sea.

My heart is going crazy now. I don't know how, but I find the strength to get up and I go away hobbling, in the rain, without looking back.

18.

In the rain, on the edge of the road, a black limousine pulls up. From the open window, Vladimir watches Jack's car plunge into the sea while the latter, enormously angry, blasphemes and kicks the sand.

The Russian shakes his head. "How embarrassing! He's at war with a girl and she is winning!" he says with his very pronounced Russian accent. He continues to look at Jack, who is emitting a sound similar to the snarl of an animal. "I hate her!"

Lexi, sitting in the back seat, also opens the window and adjusts her black wig. She looks at her brother despairing for the loss of his beloved car and smiles: "You're just jealous because she's crazier than you are."

Vladimir looks at her in the rear-view mirror growling again, as the black Kawasaki Ninja ZX-10R appears unexpectedly next to the limousine. Koki, in the saddle, sees a group of onlookers taking photos of Jack's car as it sinks, and bursts out laughing under the black helmet, followed in turn by Lexi.

"What do you have to laugh at, you two?" asks Vladimir annoyed.

Laughing, Lexi responds "I don't know, I'm laughing because he's laughing", and continues to giggle between one sip and another of her cocktail.

"I warned him that it wasn't going to be easy," the Japanese adds amused, and all three continue to watch Jack on the beach, who continues to despair in the rain, not just for his car, but also for how things went with Jas.

19.

From Mina's diary – Watchtower, evening

I feel ill. I have something that feels like a huge stone on my chest that stops me from breathing and any moment now I'm going to start crying. I should control myself and stay calm, but I don't know how to.

My leg swings by itself because of the agitation I feel, making the bench I'm sitting on creak. All I do is stare at the clock on the wall opposite America's counter. The television news is talking about us and the agency and the bad end to the charity gala with the pictures of Jas being arrested and Nick protecting her from the assault of journalists, and the faces of all those present shocked from what has just happened.

The same pictures are in the newspapers scattered all over the counter, which I avoid looking at. The agency switchboards are clogged by the endless calls that have been arriving since this morning and the only thing that America continues to repeat is *no comment*, but this is not enough to make this thing stop. The deafening sound of phones that never stop ringing is giving me a headache.

And speaking of phone calls, Jas's cell phone has started to vibrate as well. I pick it up off the bench and I see the photo of her grandmother on the screen. She's wearing her doctor's gown and a mask covers her face. She has been trying all day to contact her and so too have her parents, but no-one has received a response.

I'm here though, I'm here and I'm waiting, but my phone doesn't ring, why doesn't she call me?

Where have you disappeared to Jas? Who is this lawyer, because Nick knew nothing about it?

I raise my head and I see America staring at me from under her black braids, with raised eyebrows and mouth curled. She can see that I'm upset, and even if she doesn't say anything it's clear that the continuous rocking of my leg is annoying her. I stop. I even stop breathing for a moment and get up to go to the elevator, when it opens and Ben, Veronica, Nick and Will get out in a big hurry, shoving each other as they compete to be the first to the counter.

Will is dragging his red chair with difficulty, pushed around by the others as the dispute continues. Despite the funny scene, I cringe.

I sit down again on the bench, stiff and even more nervous than before, while others are talking over each other asking America a lot of questions.

"Silence!" she yells shutting them up in an instant, and lowers the volume of the TV. Only now I see that Patrick is also there with them. He goes to his usual place, watching us all from a distance, with his back resting against the wall. I feel trapped, I can't get out, I can't go to my room, whatever I do I'd be noticed and this is the last thing I want at this moment. I decide to sit here in silence. Perhaps they'll go without asking me anything after America has given them the usual news and information. Will and Ben start shoving each other around again.

"Get in Indian file!" says America in a loud voice.

"What do we have to do?" asks Ben, incredulous.

"You heard me! In Indian file, at once!"

They can't even agree on which order to get in a line. The only unruffled person is Nick.

America raises her eyes to the ceiling. "In alphabetical order."

"Ha haaa, B is before V and W", Ben teases them, pointing at both Veronica and Will, as the latter adjusts his spectacles angrily.

"And who said we're going in name order?" Veronica asks him, "Usually you say the surname first, and Banderas comes before Roosevelt and Smith." She too boldly points at Ben and Will as she goes in front of them.

I, on the other hand, am deliberately avoiding Nick's gaze like the plague. I feel that he is staring at me. He definitely wants to ask me where Jas is and I really don't know what to answer him, seeing that I don't know where she is.

I feel ill. My leg starts to swing under the bench. Perhaps Jas is coming and I'm fussing about nothing.

America in the meantime takes the files from the counter and seeing the others fighting in silence takes a sigh before saying: "Ben, come here."

"Ha haaa." Ben exclaims, passing in front of Veronica and dancing about happily.

"This isn't fair!" protests Veronica.

"I have a family."

"I have one too! I have a father, three brothers and a bull!" complains Veronica, trying to prevent him from reaching the counter by putting herself in front of him, but Ben answers her as he continues to dance: "Yes, in Spain, a long way from you. Try to beat two former wives, a girlfriend, three children and a dog, here in Miami."

Resigned, she gets in line behind him joining her hands.

I thought I would find them in another state of mind after last night, and instead, apart from Nick who is visibly worried and lost in thought, the others seem quite calm, as if nothing had happened. I don't understand.

America leans on the counter looking inside the files. "Benjamina said to tell you that she will not talk with you anymore and that you know the reason already, insensitive father prohibitionist ogre."

Ben stares, surprised.

"They're her words, I'm just reporting. Then afterwards she ran away weeping."

"Where is she now?

"At her ballet class. One of them though who actually went to class this morning, but came back home after only an hour is..."

The sound of a cup or something fragile breaking into pieces comes from the kitchen and soon after that Ben's thirteen-year-old son arrives.

"Is Pavarotti", America finishes the sentence. He's wearing super low jeans and his hair is more disheveled than his younger brother Franklin's. He's playing with the portable Play Station as he walks.

"Why did you come out of school?"

"I've been suspended," responds Pavarotti in all tranquility, as he goes toward the central hallway that leads to his bedroom. Ben takes the toy from his hand.

"Benjamin! Give it back!"

"Don't call me Benjamin! I'm your father!"

"Whatever. Give it to me!"

"No. Have you been suspended from summer school? What happened?"

"I don't know and I don't care."

"Pavarotti! Why were you suspended?"

"Because one of my classmates broke the school's aquarium with his head," he replies irritated and tries to take the console from Ben's hands.

"And what has that got to do with you?"

"In your opinion, who pushed him against the aquarium?" The boy takes the Play Station back and goes towards his room.

"Now I'm going to call your mother and tell her everything!" Ben threatens, trying to be the tough man with these threats.

"Do as you like, Benjamin."

"Dad!" he corrects him.

But Pavarotti, disinterested and fed up, disappears into his room.

"Don't say anything to his mother or she'll kill me", Ben wails in America's direction placing his head on the counter.

"That's if you don't kill yourself. On Friday, the day before your wedding, you have a dinner with your ex wives and my answer is no. "

Ben lifts his head looking at her like an abandoned puppy. I feel sorry for him. "Please, I beg you."

"I'd rather be the dinner of two hungry hyenas, than accompany you to dinner with those two monsters!"

"What's this? A joke?" exclaims Veronica.

"I never joke, Veronica." America points out.

"I'm talking about this!" She points to the TV hanging on the wall. Nick appears on the screen, it seems to be an interview. Veronica takes the remote control and turns up the volume, while below the images a large written text slides by: *Jas, Nickolas's girlfriend, has had a nervous breakdown!*

"Since when has Jas been your girlfriend?" she asks annoyed.

I, however, cannot believe that Nick has said in front of everyone that Jas has mental problems. *How does he dare to say that?*

I jump up from the bench, my eyes wide. Patrick sees me. He knew that this news would have bothered me.

Nick responds very calmly to Veronica's question: "This was not the news that I wanted to clarify in the press release."

But of course, you wanted to say that she's mad!

Ben sits on the bench next to me looking at the floor, while Veronica continues to complain: "Nobody told me you'd issued a press release!"

Meanwhile Olivia Fox, the nastiest journalist in Miami, is on TV saying: "The most famous detective in the peninsula reveals the ultimate gesture of his girlfriend."

The video of the press conference starts where Nick explains: "Jas had a very traumatic experience four months ago, a trauma that she has not yet got over, unfortunately. Her gesture is not justifiable, I'm the first to say so, but we need to be able to understand a girl who is going through a very difficult period of her life, and forgive. After all, we're human beings and we all make mistakes. The important thing is not to be in the position to repeat them." As he talks, he transmits a sense of self-confidence and sincerity, but that does not justify the fact that he has blabbed all Jas's personal problems to the world. I don't dare to even imagine how she'll take it when she comes to know about it.

Patrick leaves his position and begins to walk around the room, making me become even more nervous, and Veronica continues to criticize my Jas: "How can you justify her after what she did? We're the ones who should be enforcing the law, the ones that protect people in difficulty, the weak and defenseless from dangerous and sick people! And now everybody knows that one of them lives with us! She has made us look really bad in front of the entire Miami that counts! She is ruining our reputation!"

"Between our reputation and Jas it's not difficult to guess where my choice lies. I live life with the certainty that what I do is right, and I've done the right thing. Jas has not been well since February, she needs help and the charity gala has only added confusion to her confusion."

"I can understand everything, and I know that it hasn't been easy for her in recent months, but if you can see that she has a problem she can't resolve even with your help and your understanding, maybe it's time to think of a more drastic solution."

"What? Close her in some psychiatric center?"

They more they talk, the more I feel I'm getting close to bursting. I am so angry that even the presence of Patrick no longer has any effect on me right now.

Veronica, meanwhile, continues: "Well the fact that the psychologists disappear after only one session with her and describe her as *unstable, aggressive and self-destructive*, should be an alarm bell. And you shouldn't speak of these organizations in that derogatory manner; these centers have been the salvation for many people who have had much more serious problems than hers."

"I can't believe you're saying this."

"I'm saying it for you and for us. You've spent years getting where you are now and we all know how many sacrifices you have made and what you had to go through. Then in an instant there is the risk of all that being destroyed because of the problems of a little girl that you can't manage! This is not only about you. If you go under, there will be a chain reaction that will take all of us down, people who have sweat blood for the *Watchtower*!"

Silence descends. Will is visibly uncomfortable. He sits on his red chair as if he wants to hide. I also sit down again, distraught, next to Ben. He doesn't seem to have followed the conversation very much and I have confirmation of this when he turns his head toward me and asks: "Will you accompany me to dinner with my ex-wives?"

I become hostile. "Thanks for the invitation, but no!"

"And if I give you a stamp? I have a stamp collection to die for."

I don't answer. America coughs and gets our attention. "I'm really sorry to interrupt this pleasant embarrassing silence among you, but I think I should inform you that no one will go under, because the polls show us on the rise since yesterday evening."

"What?" Veronica goes to the computer behind the counter, skeptical.

"There has been some controversy, yes, but not everyone has the same negative opinion. After the press release a few hours ago the situation has been completely reversed. Nick could have prevented Jas's arrest, given his position, but to the surprise of many, he didn't. He left her in prison the whole night, spoke with an open heart of her unresolved problems and asked for people's understanding and forgiveness. All this has made him a kind of hero, a standard to follow. That means more work for us, guys."

"So now we also have to thank her." Veronica bursts out, "I mean, she punches a person with a disability and becomes a saint!"

"Not her, the boss", says America.

"From my experience, it's never bad to tell the truth," comments Nick.

Veronica fixes him scathingly. "Can you say the same of Jas?"

"Up to now she hasn't given me any reason to state the contrary."

I stay silent. It's better if I don't list all the lies that she has told him in these months and show that the Spanish viper is right.

"I can't believe it!" The girl is upset.

Will stands up from his chair and goes to her behind the counter. "Yes, I know, I know, prf pk pk, a-a-let's go to our ro-rooms." With one hand he pushes her down the hallway trying to mollify her and with the other he pulls the red chair.

"She always wins! And the good, polite and nice girls take it in the..." she continues to complain in Spanish all the way along the corridor.

"Don't sa-say that paaf jhkunyb frff."

They go, but the moaning in Spanish can still be heard from her room.

It would seem that here, the more trouble you make and end up all over the tabloids, the more things go well for you. Thank goodness we're in America. If we were in Italy they would have already closed down the agency.

"Nick?" starts Ben, but can't even finish the sentence before Nick replies: "Not now."

Turning toward me, Nick asks me: "Is Jas in her room?"

"No, she's out", I respond bleakly.

"Out where? Without you? Alone?"

"No, her imaginary friends are with her too", I whisper. Now at least he clearly understands that I'm not blaming him. In fact he approaches me and sits down between me and Ben. "Mina, at this moment perhaps you don't understand what I did, but..."

"It is not what you did that I don't understand, but your words. You're passing her off as crazy."

"It's not true. I'm passing her off for what she is: a young girl who needs all our support and understanding. I'm passing her off as a human being who has feelings and problems like all of us, even if she does her best to hide it."

I don't know what to say; on one hand he is right, but on the other hand he knows how she protects her private life, and it was not nice to blurt everything out to everyone.

"Did she tell you by any chance why she asked for another lawyer and where she found her? I told her that Ben had resolved everything, I don't understand why she made this decision."

"I've already told you, if you want to know something which concerns her, ask her. I'm not saying anything." Because what's more I don't know anything.

"You're right, forgive me if I continue to ask you questions, but I was anxious to have some answers."

And he says this to me? I've been waiting all day for Jas to give me some answers!

I hear the doors of the elevator open and my face lights up. Perhaps my Jas is back!

But when I look toward the doors I see Patrick stepping into the elevator with his hands in his pockets. Surprised, Nick asks him: "Where are you going?"

"I'm going to look for a permanent center of gravity."

We all look at him astonished. What does that mean? The only one who doesn't miss a beat is America, who gives him some advice as she writes on the computer: "In that case, it's best if you go out via the back door."

The doors of the elevator close, Ben gets up from the bench and seeing little Franklin go past asks him desperately: "Do you want to accompany me to a family dinner?"

"Family dinner," reflects Franklin aloud, "I gladly accept, I'll finally see my mom live."

Ben embraces him moved. "Thank you son."

"Not at all daddy."

They go down the corridor with their arms around each other.

Nick and America look at the email and talk about work. I remain sitting on this bench not knowing how to move, not knowing what to do. *Where are you Jas? Why don't you call me?*

I'm about to pick up the cell phones and go to my room when I see that Jas's phone has disappeared.

I stand up, checking under the bench and nearby, but the cell has literally disappeared. I sit on the ground, unbelieving. I don't understand what's going on.

What has happened to Jas? And where is her cell phone?

20.

From Jx's diary – Streets of Miami, the same evening

He holds Jas's cell phone tightly in his hands, as it continues to vibrate with the insistent calls from her parents, and above all from her grandmother, Danica. He puts it in his pocket without responding, stops in the middle of the road and looks around slowly, in no hurry, observing all and everything that his eyes can see. Of the passersby, in his mind he disregards all colored people, all the girls with dark or red hair, short hair, all those dressed in a provocative or eccentric way, but there is no trace of Jas in the crowd.

He walks past colorful restaurants with signs big and small, loud live music, and others which are more peaceful with a romantic atmosphere and couples affectionately embraced.

There are hundreds of buildings with bars, pubs and restaurants for every taste: Latin-American music, Spanish style, Cuban evening, Italian... but he doesn't stop in any of these places to look for her. No-one comes near him, but girls recognize him from a distance and murmur, smiling, *that's Patrick Sword! He's so mysterious and solitary; they say that he knows how to read your mind. I've heard that he hasn't had a girlfriend since his girlfriend was killed.*

Patrick doesn't listen to the comments from the people he passes and continues on his way, but after almost an hour of walking, his hands in his pockets, a particular bar attracts his attention. He smiles.

It's not one of those places full of colored lights and glittering posters like Miami offers tourists. It's a small place immersed in lush foliage and surrounded by palms and multi-colored flowers. There are two huge spotlights that turn slowly lighting the sky. The bar is called *Black Cat*.

He passes under a large arch with two wood carved black cats at the door, and enters. The entire bar is made of wood and is frequented mostly by young local people: some are playing darts, other billiards; a tattooed boy with long brown dreadlocks is tuning his guitar on the mini-stage near the bar. And right behind the same counter, sitting on a swivel chair, there she is, Jas. She has her back turned and is still wearing the white evening dress, her hair loose and a lot of empty cocktail glasses in front of her.

As always, she has found a way to obtain alcohol, even here in America where it is prohibited to people under twenty-one years of age.

She is talking with a Latin American girl and two boys who are standing in front of her. Patrick approaches without being noticed.

"First the money," says Jas in a slow slurred voice.

"But you haven't told me anything yet," complains the girl, looking at Jas who is waiting for her money as she swings on the bar stool.

"And I'll continue to not tell you until I see five bank notes with the face of George Washington in the palm of my hand."

The girl opens her wallet, unsure of what to do, while the two boys behind her smile and shake their heads.

"Even one banknote with the face of Abraham Lincoln on it will be fine, eh."

Although she thinks that it's a scam, the girl gives Jas the five dollar bank note. Jas grabs it quickly and puts it on the counter under one of the many empty glasses, and then turns to her closing her eyes. "Now I'll tell you what I see."

"But you have your eyes closed!" the girl protests.

"I see the ghosts closing their eyes, so don't interfere, woman!" Her breath smells of vodka and other spirits.

The girl crosses her arms and raises her eyebrows. She is getting upset.

"I feel a presence near you. It's on your right."

The girl moves and looks to her right, incredulous.

"It's your mother speaking to me, now I can hear her. She's telling me that you're suspicious because you've been tricked many times in your life."

The girl becomes serious, looks at the two guys who are with her. Jas opens her eyes and, looking closely at the girl and the boys from top to toe, she continues: "She says that after her death, and because of the continuous beatings from your father, you ran away from home taking your brothers with you. Since then you've done

129

nothing but work and you've brought them up practically one-handed, being mother, father and sister to them. You've made sure they had everything and their happiness was enough for you to go on..."

The girl holds her brothers' hands with tears in her eyes, while they look to the ground, saying nothing.

"She says she is proud of you, because she knows that if you could go back you would do exactly the same things again without thinking twice, and she says that she regrets that she wasn't able to live longer so that she could help you", she addresses all three of them, "And give you all the love that she still has for you."

The girl holds back her tears and sobs: "I still feel your love, mom."

"She says that she's there, that she is always watching over you. Now that your brothers are grown, it's time to think of yourself a little. So don't be a pain in the ass and get married!"

The three boys look at her testily despite the emotion.

"Okay," mumbles Jas, thinking she should correct herself, "I added the last bit."

All three of them embrace, moved, as Jas looks at them bored, anxious for this torment to end.

"Mom knows what is the right thing for you too, she will be near you," says one of the brothers in a broken voice, "They're not all like our father. Look at the two of us."

The girl smiles, caressing her brothers, and says to them: "I love you, I love you." Then she looks at Jas and thanks her sobbing: "Thank you, Buffy, may God bless you! You're an angel! An angel from heaven!"

"Yes, yes", answers Jas, fed up with these tear-jerking speeches. Then she turns toward the counter on her stool and ignores them.

Patrick watches everything from behind her and smiles; he's proud of her and what she has done, but he is especially amused by the way in which she has decided to earn money to pay for a drink. She is not a seer, and she doesn't speak with ghosts, obviously; but the skill with which she has been able to read the small seemingly insignificant details of the Latin American girl and her brothers has surprised him. Small clues that gave her a lot of information about the person that she had before her, but you must be able to look, observe and connect things in the shortest possible time, and she knows how to do this.

With a feeling of pride he goes closer; with her head resting on the counter she waves the banknote she has just earned without saying anything. The barman, a huge colored boy, raises his eyes to the ceiling and asks her annoyed: "Have you finished with your little games?"

"Yes," Jas replies waving the money near his face.

"What do you want?" It's clear that he doesn't like Jas very much.

"Vendetta", hisses Jas.

"I've finished, do you want something else?" he takes a couple of glasses from the counter waiting for her to answer.

"Then make me a *JasTwentyfive.*"

"I don't know what that is. I can make you a *B52,* if you like."

"I don't want a *B52,* I want a *JasTwentyfive!* How come you don't know it? In Italy it's very famous, and one of the most popular."

"Listen, little girl, I don't have time to waste. We're not in Italy here, this is America."

"Nice shit!"

The barman glares at her. He cleans the counter and listens to her as she goes on talking in a garbled way: "You come here chasing the American dream and you find yourself being chased by a nightmare!"

The man goes off, tired of her, while from the small stage near the bar the guy with the dreadlocks starts to rap. Jas looks at him with one eyebrow raised. The boy is awfully thin and on his t-shirt is written *skeleton.*

There are words that I said: I lied
There are things that I took: I stole
There is a place where I've been: I got high
There are people I've hurt: I am sorry
I don't know if I'll ever be forgiven: I understand
I don't know if I'll ever be able to forgive: I forget
I don't know what I have to do: it hurts

Everyone applauds, except Jas, who with raised eyebrows complains: "This isn't rap! What about the rhymes?"

She turns her head the other way and sees Nick on TV, outside the *Watchtower* speaking with a journalist. She grabs the remote control from on top of the bar and turns the volume up.

She listens carefully to Nick's press release and doesn't like it at all. She shakes her head, disappointed. "The truth before all else", she smiles bitterly, takes a glass from the counter and after drinking it down in one gulp throws it on the ground breaking it into smithereens.

"Hey!" the barman protests angrily.

"In Serbia we do this when we're happy."

"We're not in Serbia, this is America."

"Nice shit!"

The bartender goes to her, perhaps to throw her out, when Patrick stops him, raising his hand as if to say *forget it, I'll take care of this*. The colored man freezes instantly, tightens his lips and shaking his head turns to Jas: "These five dollars are for the glass you've broken!" He takes the money and leaves annoyed.

Jas rests her head on the bar, disconsolate. Patrick slowly approaches her chair and, not wanting to frighten her, he says almost under his breath: "Happy birthday, Jas."

He gets the opposite reaction. Jas snaps from the stool without even looking at him, grabs an empty glass from the bar and is about to throw it at him when at the last minute she realizes it's Patrick. "Patrick! Are you crazy to come up on me from behind? You could have got a glass in your face!"

"Why? Who did you think it was?" he asks. He sees the shiny business card inserted in the straps of her high heels and then the bruise on her arm, but acts like he hasn't noticed.

She doesn't reply to his question, but turns to the bar and puts down the glass. "How did you find me? I don't think I left bread crumbs behind me", she says curtly.

"Don't put on an act with me. If I found you it's because you wanted me to find you."

Their eyes meet and for a few seconds they look at each other without speaking. She says nothing, he asks nothing, and yet they say more than they could ever do with words. But this game of glances is interrupted by a boy who calls out in a loud voice: "Jack!"

Jas jumps around again. Startled, she looks at the entrance where the call came from, but it's a false alarm. She sighs deeply, and sits up straight on the chair, while Patrick continues to look at her without commenting.

She justifies herself: "Alcohol is playing bad jokes on me."

But he knows that it is not because of the alcohol and that she's edgy for very different reasons. He looks at the TV for a moment where images of the catastrophic charity evening are still being transmitted and in a calm voice says to her: "You can fool everyone for some of the time, and some people all the time, but you can't fool everyone all the time, Jas."

"Why not? You've been doing it for years."

"Yes, but if things go wrong, I can cope with them, you can't."

She takes one of the newspapers from the bar and throws it in front of him. On the cover there's a photo of her being arrested at the gala. "Is there something you want to tell me, Jas?"

"No. Is there something you'd like to ask me?"

"No."

Silence falls again between them. Patrick does not want to insist. After looking closely at him, she smiles. "You were a very quiet child from the time you were small, weren't you?"

Patrick looks at her with interest. It rarely happened that someone would ask him questions about his private life or his personality. He smiles and decides to respond: "I listened a lot and I thought even more, so as a result I had little time for talking. Everyone likes to talk, I like to listen. This is sometimes a drawback in life, but it helps in my work."

"Lately I don't like to talk and I have never liked to listen. As far as thinking is concerned though, I don't know, I'll have to think about that," she says swinging herself around. More than once, as she speaks, she comes close to falling from the chair. Patrick smiles at her. "You've had a little too much to drink today, eh?"

"A little?" the barman interrupts, "She's been drinking for two hours now! Apparently it isn't anything new," he says angrily, getting more empty glasses from the table and taking them away.

"The situation is getting out of hand, Jas. You can't continue to lie like this. You'll make things worse and deeply disappoint Nick."

"That's rich coming from you!" she comments, giving him a nasty smile, "Who's been lying to Nick for eight years? Who's looking for his girlfriend's killer and planning a terrible revenge even though he knows that his best friend is against revenge, summary justice and murder? Who?" She challenges him with her gaze. Rarely does anyone dare to do this with him. "Do you think you won't disappoint him when he comes to know about it? Of course you will. He'll probably never speak to you again. At least I don't intend to kill anyone. For now. And anyway I don't lie. I just keep my mouth shut."

Patrick does not let his emotions show, but he is not accustomed to people speaking so directly to him, confronting him in such an outspoken way. People usually avoid him for fear that he can read them inside and that he could reveal some hidden secret of their life. But not Jas, she doesn't avoid him; unlike others she has always looked for him. Just as on the other hand he always seeks her.

"What is the reason for your silence?"

"Does there have to be a reason?"

"I do it for her, for me and for an *us* that will never exist again. I'm not saying that it's a valid reason, but it's my reason. And what about you? What is your reason? What is the purpose of your silence?"

"I listen a lot and I think very much, therefore I have little time for talking", she smiles.

Silence falls between them again and Jas starts to look at him puzzled. "Why are you still here?"

"To tell you that Mina has been covering your back since this morning and that this telling lies to Nick is giving her a rash all over her body", he answers looking at the bar. From his tone of voice Jas notices that there is something wrong. Much as he wants to hide his emotions, he doesn't succeed with her; perhaps, deep down, he doesn't want to. Jas knows that she could have avoided the discussion about Emily and the lies he tells Nick. She takes one of her empty glasses, pours half of the cocktail the barman has just served into it and moves it toward Patrick, who looks at her surprised.

"Do you feel like making a toast with me? I haven't been able to do that yet, today. If the truth be known, I haven't even been able to celebrate my birthday."

Patrick smiles, he knows that she wants to cheer him up. The empathy between them is very strong now and he takes the glass. "Gladly, what's the toast?"

She thinks about it for a moment. "I don't know, to the two of us."

"To us, who don't speak for fear of being listened to."

"To us."

After the toast, Patrick takes Jas's cell phone from his pocket and puts it on the table. She looks at him in surprise.

"Call Mina, tell her that you are well and that you're on your way. Your birthday is not yet over and you should spend it with the people who love you."

Jas looks at him without saying anything, happy and surprised by his gesture, then gets up from the chair and, wobbling, goes to him and hugs him.

Patrick is embarrassed; he keeps his hands away from her. He doesn't know what to do.

Jas's embrace is warm and sincere and he feels pleasure in spite of his discomfort when he has physical contact with girls. His heart begins to beat very fast, he closes his eyes and slowly his hands return the embrace.

"Take me home, I beg you", she whispers without breaking away from him.

"Here you are, *Buffy*", the barman interrupts them in an annoyed tone, and places a cocktail on the counter. "The girl down the end there is offering it to you."

Patrick and Jas look in the direction indicated by the bartender and see the Latin American girl of before and her brothers who are smiling at her and raising their glasses. Jas reciprocates the greeting, Patrick instead smiles at hearing the bartender call her Buffy.

"This is not the *JasTwentyfive*!" she protests.

"I've already said that I don't know how to make it! I don't even know what it is!"

"You know what they say in Slovenia, that the easiest thing to say is *I don't know how to do it* if you want to avoid doing something."

"We're not in Slovenia here and I don't even know where Slovenia is! This is America!"

"Nice shit! And don't touch my straws! They're mine! You brought them with my drinks, I paid for them, so hands off!"

The barman turns to Patrick annoyed. "What is she, a relative of yours by any chance? Because even if she is, I'm telling you that I won't put up with her behavior much longer! And anyway I'm not even sure that the identity card she showed me is genuine. Tell me the truth, Patrick, is she really twenty-one years old?"

"Do you know this hillbilly?" asks Jas, surprised.

"The hillbilly has a name," says the bartender.

"And what would it be? Big Jim?"

"I'm Big Bob!"

Jas bursts out laughing. "Big Bob? Lovely name. And why do you think I'm related to him?"

"Because you both break people's balls the same way! And furthermore, it's forbidden to use cell phones in here! Can't you see the sign on the wall?" he points toward a sign on the wall faded by the time, and goes away.

"We break balls in the same way?" repeats Jas looking at Patrick puzzled, "What's he talking about?"

"Ah, I have no idea."

***

Seven years earlier

For some time, Big Bob had been looking at the blond boy sitting at the bar; long disheveled hair, beard stubble, torn clothes. He was visibly drunk; you'd take him for a tramp, and yet he was somehow different from the others. For four hours he had done nothing but sit in silence and drink alcoholic beverages, then, when he had finished his money, he had looked around and had started to tell people's fortunes, thus arousing the curiosity and amazement of customers who paid him for his performance.

It was evening now and the boy had his head resting on the counter. He was out for the count. Big Bob went to him. "Have you finished with the tricks?" he asked him, not happy.

"Yes," he replied him in the same tone.

"Do you want to order something else?"

"Yes, revenge."

"I've run out of it, do you want something else?"

"Then give me a double revenge. You know, it's very famous here in America."

"Listen, boy, I don't have time to waste."

"I'll buy him a beer, Bob."

The man turned and saw Nick arrive. He sat down near the blond boy and put the money on the counter, giving him a big smile.

"Do you know this boy?" Bob asked him surprised.

"My name is Nickolas", said Nick, extending his hand to the young tramp, who looked at him for a few seconds as if he was examining him, and then he shook his hand, "I'm Patrick."

"I know him now," said Nick turning to the bartender, "Bring him a beer, and for me a soda, please."

Big Bob made a strange frown and then went to get the drinks.

Patrick continued to fix Nick attentively. "Not many people offer a drink to a tramp", he remarked.

"We've all been homeless at least once in our life."

Patrick looked him up and down and smiled, finding himself opposite an elegantly-dressed guy with well-kept hands and a polite manner; he obviously came from a well-to-do family.

"And you were homeless, *when*?" he asked, "When there was no water in your swimming pool?" Patrick's tone was hard and disdainful, but Nick did not react to the provocation. He took the beer that Big Bob had just brought together with an orange-colored drink; he handed it to him and responded politely and kindly, saying: "No, when my parents were killed when I was thirteen and I became an orphan."

Patrick's expression changed suddenly; he bowed his head, regretting what he had just said.

"I'm sorry, I was..."

"It doesn't matter, you couldn't know."

"How did it happen?"

"Corruption, manipulation, injustice and another fifty adjectives like these."

"Were the murderers arrested?"

"No, killed."

"Killed?" asked Patrick surprised.

"Yes, I've never found out what happened exactly. But I'm not happy about the way it ended. I would have preferred to see them in prison for life." Nick remained in silence, looking pensively at his soda, while Patrick looked at him.

"You seem to be an honest guy, Nickolas."

"I am."

"Then why do you pretend you don't know who I am?"

Nick stared at him, surprised. "I wasn't sure it was you. I've been looking for you for weeks now, but I didn't expect to find you right here, in this bar."

"Who sent you?" he asked in a hard tone, "Who do you work for?"

"Felix told me about you, but he didn't send me, no one sends me, and now I work only for myself", he tried to reassure him.

Patrick squinted at him. "What do you want from me?"

"I know what happened to you and I know that you no longer have a job."

"You don't know a damn thing!" He rose from the chair, annoyed. "If I no longer have a job it's because I don't believe in my work anymore!"

"I want you to believe again."

"*You* want to do *what*?" Patrick could not believe his ears. How could that boy even think of making him believe again in something that was much bigger than him? He didn't even know him.

Nick decided not to give up and, looking him in the eyes, went on: "After the murder of my parents, I got back on my feet thanks to an unknown person who spoke to me from the other side of the bars. Now I am the unknown person who is speaking to another unknown person. Not all the world is dirty, Patrick, there are also honest, hard-working people, good people, and I want to find them and get them together. Listen to what I have to say, please, and then decide."

Patrick looked at him with tears in his eyes. "Look at me!" he yelled, "Look at me! I don't exist anymore, I'm a ghost now, a dead man walking, don't you see that?"

"Hey!" intervened Big Bob annoyed, "No yelling in my bar! Can't you see the sign?"

He pointed to the sign hanging on the wall where it said *No shouting*

"Let's play pool, Patrick. Only one game, and if you don't like my ideas, my projects, I won't bother you anymore."

Patrick was motionless, he wanted to leave, but for some strange reason he was interested in what Nick had to say. Nick took advantage of his hesitation, stood up, took a cue and threw it to him. Patrick grabbed it in full flight.

21.

From Jas's diary – My eighteenth birthday

"Mom, please don't listen to grandma. She's doing it on purpose to make you paranoid, don't you see? I'll be home straight after the wedding... no, not mine. Ben's! I'm not marrying anyone, I'm not pregnant and I'm not relocating to Miami. So, please stop worrying... Okay, say hi to dad and thanks for the good wishes, mom."

I hang up and I'm exhausted, as well as terribly drunk. Grandma has to stop this. I understand that she hopes to see me transferred somewhere at least eight hundred kilometers from Slovenia, so as to get her revenge at last on what my mother did nineteen years ago, but she goes too far. It will give her a heart attack.

And speaking of people who are plotting revenge, Patrick is here beside me. After listening to the hilarious phone calls with my grandmother and mother he does nothing but smile and shake his head. I still feel very drunk. I put my head back on the seat of the taxi for a moment's rest, but I see that we've already arrived at the *Watchtower*.

"We're here. Mina is coming down to get you."

"Aren't you coming up?"

"I'll come later, it's best to avoid being seen together."

He is always so nice to me, he's always there when I need him, and has been for years now.

"Nick is your best friend, and yet this isn't the first time that you've supported me, you help me and protect me when I need it and hide it from him. Why?"

"Why do you want to know?"

"Why don't you want to tell me?"

"I haven't said that I don't want to tell you."

"Wow, Patrick, we've got to the double negative."

He smiles, enjoying our debate.

"Well, I'm saying that you can't not answer my question. As long as you keep lying to Nick for Emily I can understand it, but when you lie to Nick for me, no. I don't understand it." My head is spinning, very much, and I don't know which Patrick to look at, so I speak a little bit with one, a little bit with the other so as not to offend either of the two.

I smell of alcohol. And, now that I think about it, I've been wearing the same dress for twenty-four hours now, so I smell of other things as well.

I look at the two Patricks: one is a serious one and the other is lost in thought. Although I feel like throwing up, I hold back pretending nothing is wrong, just to hear what his answer to my question will be.

Wait a minute... What was my question?

"Oh my God, Jas!" screams the voice of my Mina. She has come to get me.

She smells clean, and even her comfy jogging suit has a lovely perfume. She's so lucky. She looks at Patrick all angry and asks: "What happened? Where was she, but above all *who was she with*?"

"She just needed to let off steam by herself."

"And why were you there too in her solitude? And why didn't you call me?"

"Why won't you talk with Jas? Jas wants to talk with Mina", I whine looking sulky.

"She didn't have a cell phone, but as soon as I gave it to her you were the first person she called." The two Patricks continue to defend me, they're so nice.

"And how did you find her?"

She goes on with the questions and continues to ignore me, I can't believe it!

"It was just luck." He is protecting me again, or perhaps he's just protecting himself from Mina's jealousy, I don't know.

"Jas?" says Mina.

She has finally decided to address me!

"My love! You know that I love you, don't you?" I'm slurring my words.

"Yes, yes, get out of the taxi."

"I forget how to do it."

141

"Jas, please, come on..." she seizes me and pulls me out of the car, "Nick is losing it, for God's sake. If he sees you in this state he'll go out of his mind!"

"He can fuck off! Not only did he let them arrest me, but he also said I was mad in front of the whole United States! *She has some unresolved problems,* fuck off! I'll never forgive him for that! He's done with me! In every respect! I don't want to celebrate my birthday with him!"

"Yes yes, okay, we'll celebrate just me and you, come on."

"And Spike, you me and Spike."

22.

At the same time – From Mina's diary

Jas is filthy drunk. She can barely stay on her feet. I help her reach the front door as she says bad things about Nick. Before going inside the *Watchtower* I turn and Patrick is still there, sitting in the taxi looking at us and smiling at Jas's cussing. I don't like the idea that he was the one who found her, I don't even like the idea that he went to look for her, that he stole her cell phone from me, and that he spoke to her before I did! I'm her best friend!

I already have to battle with Nick, now there's him too. And in all this, as well as wondering what exactly he knows about this whole matter, I also wonder why he didn't come upstairs with us.

23.

From Jas's diary
A few days later, dinner with Ben's former wives

Choco chews slowly, very slowly, extremely slowly. Her every move, every gesture is so... s*low*.

It's like watching a movie in slow motion and, sitting opposite her, I'm often instinctively looking for the remote on the table to press *play* and see her finally swallow that cursed piece of fish. I play footsie with Nick, seated on my right, without taking my eyes from the woman, who in real life is an opera singer, and ask her: "Hey what's up, Choco? Did they sedate you?"

He smiles, sipping his wine, and comes closer, whispering in my ear. "Quit making quips, there are cameras".

What quips?

Nick is still smiling but I still don't understand. Can I be the only one who sees that there is something wrong with the movements of the huge colored woman sitting opposite me?

The two dwarf cameramen are going around the table and they put the camera on us. I don't know what they're looking at... feet perhaps, while I continue to watch Choco.

She's dressed as if she were still on the stage of a theater, wearing a *Gone with the wind* red dress. Perhaps she had a show before coming here and hasn't had time to change clothes?

She turns her head towards Ben and still in slow-mo says to him: "Benji, Benji, Benji", pauses shaking her head, or at least I think she does, maybe she's just stretching her neck, I don't know, this is all too slow to understand. "What must I..." she pauses again to drink a little wine, "do with you?"

She takes so much time to formulate a sentence that you forget the question, for Christ's sake!

Ben, instead, is... oh what a pitiful scene: he looks like a boxer at the fourteenth round going to the corner. He can barely breathe, he's sweating, and waits agitated for his ex-wife to finish the scolding.

"Getting married for the third time", she takes a breath, still slowly, "With a model twenty years younger than you", she wipes her mouth, as everyone looks on in silence. "I am saddened by your choice which is so... sad."

I notice that even when she closes and opens her eyelids she does it in slow motion, incredible!

"And to think, I was gone only three months." She puts a piece of fish in her mouth and starts to chew so slowly that all of us present at the table are chewing in time with her, thinking that it can help her hurry up, for once. "And Franklin is becoming a great prankster. His teacher has had to seek medical help."

I look at the first wife, a terrible Asian lady, who is shaking her head, annoyed.

"And Pavarotti continues to get into fights and hit people and take it out on the weak."

Once again the two wives look at each other and then both of them turn to Ben who is wiping the sweat from his forehead.

"They're children. Who hasn't misbehaved a little when they were young?" Ben tries to justify them, but the two former Mrs Roosevelt do not seem to agree.

"But I'm solving the problem. Work has kept me busy lately, but we will solve everything."

"Benji, children are much more important in life than work or than a marriage with that one there", continues Choco, putting her hand on her heart. She doesn't seem very credible. "Seeing them grow and", she pauses for a sip of wine. "And grow, and there is nothing in the world which is more rewarding."

I try hard not to laugh. Coming from someone who sees her two sons, Franklin and Pavarotti, once every two months on video calls, seems more like a joke than anything else.

The two ex-wives nod, backing each other. So now Ben, the only one who really does look after the boys, must also justify himself? I don't understand these adults.

The other wife wipes her mouth. I'm thinking she'll be the one giving him shit next.

Ling is always so serious, with those elongated eyes that look at you in such a... Chinese way... It's her gaze that is nasty. I'm sure she must be a huge ballbreaker.

145

There's an urban legend going around about her: it seems that the only time that she has been seen with a half-smile on her face, was when a competitor of hers died. She raises her hand to call the waitress, who immediately runs over to our table, all eager.

"Do you know who I am?" asks Ling in a patronizing tone and with the attitude of someone who knows perfectly well what the girl's response will be.

"It's obvious that I know, Madam Ling, you are the greatest organizer of parties and events in the United States! The seventieth birthday party for the Mayor of New York was memorable! Blocking the Brooklyn Bridge for the toast? Spectacular!" She's very excited, she praises her, speaking with a very strong French accent, then adjusts her spectacles and the very short blond hair, hoping to be beautiful enough for this chat with the cameras of the two dwarves trained on her. Ling looks her up and down, even though she is sitting, and in a disapproving voice says to her: "Perfect, and now that I know that you are aware of my identity, I would like to bring to your attention, at this time, to the imperfections on this table at which I am sitting."

She looks at the centerpiece disgusted, as Ben sighs deeply resting his head on one hand; he looks desperate.

"The tablecloth clashes with the gold colored decorations of the plates and glasses. And, with regard to the latter, there is a distinct difference between pouring the wine into the glass and outside the glass, so see that the fat waiter who served us is fired. The bread in the baskets is scattered haphazardly, the flowers aren't fresh and you should change the name of the restaurant. *Maria* is too, how can I say, old-fashioned. Here you have the list of names that I have chosen for you; take them to the manager."

"At once, Mrs Ling."

"Miss Ling", she corrects her in an unpleasant manner.

"Excuse me, Miss Ling, we will immediately see to the replacement of everything." She stands still, looking at her with admiration and fixing her hair.

The Chinese wife just makes a gesture with her hand, and the waitress disappears in an instant.

Pity Mina isn't here to see these scenes. We would have laughed like crazy.

"Benji, Benji, Benji!" Ling's tone, unlike Choco's, is hard, authoritative, and huffy. "Your marriage with the undernourished, racist and materialistic blond? There is only one word to describe it: shameful. But I don't want to speak badly of her; I don't do things like that."

I look at Nick who is smiling inside, though with his eyes he is telling me to be a good girl.

"Our daughter Benjamina is still with that long-haired tattooed guy who dresses in smelly rags, and is devoid of any education and behavioral code. She has missed many of her classical dance lessons and tonight her lipstick clashes with her dress! Why is all this happening, Benji? "

She is talking to Ben as if they were alone at the table, or rather, as if Benjamina were not present. But she is, and how! She looks at her mother with tears in her eyes, holds the fork in her hand and trembles. I expect her to start crying at any moment.

Ling makes a disappointed sigh. "Why do I always have to do everything?"

Choco gets involved, "Being a mother is so... difficult."

"You're right Choco, men cannot understand. The sacrifices that we mothers make are unbelievable."

"Amazing, incredible," agrees Choco.

"Benji, why does our daughter go out with a bear?"

Ben stammers random justifications. "No, it's just that, we cannot choose who to fall in love with and..."

"Benjamina is half American and half Chinese, so they're the races she should focus on!"

Then she turns to Choco, given that she is colored, "No offense, it's just that the other races would not look good beside Benjamina, she's a classical dancer, sweet and refined, and can't be with a nonentity of that kind."

"Skeleton is not a nonentity!" screams Benjamina, her eyes filled with tears.

The name of her boyfriend sounds familiar.

"Skeleton is a fantastic rapper, even the President of the United States adores him!" she continues to sob, "He is romantic and sensitive! He loves me and I love him! You can't judge him just by his appearance. It's not fair, mother!"

There, I knew it; she has started whining as usual.

She hides her face under her long black hair and dries the tears with a white handkerchief. That too will certainly clash with the lipstick, according to her mother's strict rules.

Ben sits there in silence listening to the two argue, while the two cameramen are filming everything.

"Skeleton?" Choco starts to laugh, and to my great surprise I find that even when she laughs she is annoyingly slow; first she opens her mouth and then emits the sound, but how is this possible?

"Of course it's fair, daughter! These days, the image prevails on what you are inside as a person. I organize dream parties and weddings, so I'd know something about image, or not? Why do you think I'm the best in my field? I want you to leave the monkey man immediately!"

"No! You're bad!"

"Me, bad? I brought you up and loved you like a daughter!"

"But I *am* your daughter!"

"It was just an example."

Ben tries to calm the situation: "There is no need to argue, please."

Disconsolate, he turns to the two dwarf cameramen saying in a low voice: "You'll cut this."

"Perhaps we should put Pavarotti in college", reflects Choco.

"What? In your dreams, old girl!" protests Pavarotti.

I'm about to die laughing, I'd forgotten Pavarotti was there too, since he hasn't opened his mouth all night because he was too busy with his portable Play Station.

And anyway who of the two called him Pavarotti? Can anyone be so idiotic as to give a last name as a name to a son?

"Benji! Did you hear what he called me?" Choco complains.

"I am angry about your rudeness, but it was only to be expected. Only children are always like that!" concludes the colored woman.

"I am not an only child!"

"Ah, it was just an example", the Chinese wife intervenes.

Suddenly I hear an anguished scream. I turn and see Ben's youngest son with the fork stuck into his left hand.

I'm about to get up and run to help him, but Ben is already on him, worried. "Franklin! What have you done? Let me see!"

Choco screams, a scream that sounds like a song: "Oh *heeavvens, I'm aaabout to faint!*"

It's only when Ben takes Franklin's hand that we realize it's a fake hand and that it's a prank.

Fantastic!

To everyone's amazement, he starts to laugh at the top of his lungs. The only other one who thinks this is funny is me.

"There, you fell for it, you fell for it! Was I good, mamma?"

"That's enough of these pranks, Franklin! I almost..." Choco complains as she waves her napkin to recover, "passed out from the shock!"

"It wasn't a prank! I was acting. I'm an actor, mom."

"A *what*?"

"An actor, that's someone who characterizes or interprets a part or a role in a movie, television, radio or theater, like you mom."

She looks hard at Ben, indignant. "I have invested time and money for his education and I won't allow it to be wasted in this way."

Meanwhile, Pavarotti is explaining: "You won't be able to put me in college, let that be clear!"

"You won't be put in college", Ben reassures him.

"Of course he'll go," reiterates Choco.

Ling, in the meantime, orders her daughter: "And you'll leave the shaved horse you're with and you'll dedicate yourself once again to classical dance one hundred percent."

"*No! I hate you...*" Benjamina screams getting up from her chair.

"Where do you think you're going? Benjamina!"

"To get a tattoo, mother!" and she runs off weeping hysterically.

Ben turns to the cameramen once again. "You'll cut this."

They're all fighting. They're shouting at each other and their cries overlap. The cameramen run up and down and record every detail of the fight. The other people sitting in the restaurant look at us indignantly.

Suddenly, I start to feel strange. The situation is almost identical to the charity gala, only this time I'm not the protagonist, just a spectator.

Only Nick and I are silent. We are so out of place in this situation that I feel I want to throw myself into the fray and argue too. Now I know how you feel when you have a clear conscience.

I feel Nick's eyes on me, I look at him. In spite of the yelling and all the noise around us, he appears calm, and this reaction is not like him. He's not helping Ben to calm the situation, he's not embarrassed about others who are assisting at this scene in the restaurant, nor for me; usually he tries to protect me and not let me see disputes or ugly things. He plays with the bracelet on my wrist and looks at me. He is very handsome.

All of a sudden Pavarotti tears the camera from the hands of one of the dwarfs and begins to run around the table. So it ends up with Ben chasing the dwarves that are chasing Franklin.

"And I thought I had problems", I remark.

Nick says nothing, smiles as he looks at Ben who has now reached his son, and is trying to take the camera from his hands. This is a family of mad people.

I hear Pavarotti say in a loud voice: "Hey, parents, you want to see a trick I know how to do?"

He grabs the tablecloth and pulls with all his might, causing a great disaster. Bottles, plates and glasses shatter on the floor.

In one moment we are all wet with water, wine, juice and soiled with ten different kinds of fish.

Choco, who is the most sensitive, begins to complain when she sees her dress all dirty. Ling is probably going to start criticizing the imperfect order of the plates and cups which are overturned and cracked on the floor, while Pavarotti laughs with the tablecloth in his hand saying that on YouTube the plates had remained on the table. Ben, meanwhile, continues to repeat despondently to the two cameramen. "Cut this."

The cameramen will have already recorded everything except the faces in view of their small stature. With the cuts that Ben wants, I really want to see what will remain of this premarital video. If somebody had related to me the scenes that I've witnessed this evening, I would never have believed it. America is really a continent of crazies.

"Are you alright?

"Of course I'm okay, Nick, he only threw a bit of fish and wine on me, not the table."

He smiles and helps me to dry my clothes with a napkin. He cleans me up in silence. I don't know why we are silent, and I don't know why this is creating some discomfort in me. Our eyes meet, he caresses my face. What an odd situation. I'd have so many things to say to him, and I think he also wants to talk to me after all this, even if I am not entirely sure I'm ready to deal with the matter. As soon as we get closer to each other, one of the dwarfs appears between our feet to film us. We jump back, embarrassed, as if we'd been caught red-handed doing who knows what.

"Okay, I'm going to clean myself up in the bathroom," I say nervously.

"Yes, alright."

Nick is embarrassed. He goes to Ben, sitting with a sad face as he listens to the complaints and screams of his ex-wives and two children, and even the French waitress who curses as she mops up after the disaster.

I go to the end of the restaurant, toward the stairs that lead to the bathroom.

This place is strange, it's like a museum, with many paintings of angels, Virgin Marys, crucifixes and other biblical things. The atmosphere is somehow disturbing.

A very robust guy with a blue cap is on a ladder in front of the bathroom door to adjust something on the ceiling with a lot of wires hanging from it. I step under the ladder to be able to get to the bathroom.

Once inside, however, I am flabbergasted: there is a fountain in the middle of the bathroom. A real fountain with carved angels, flowing water and coins on the bottom.

I'm starting to clean my blouse when in the mirror I see someone spying on me from behind one of the four doors inside the bathroom. I see short gray hair and I realize that it's a male.

I pretend I don't see him. I look at the fountain and walk around it until I reach the door, then unleash a vigorous kick. The only thing I hear is a man's loud cry of pain.

"Get out of here, you pervert!" I'm in combat position, unafraid.

For a few seconds silence reigns, and then the door opens, and to my amazement out comes Ambrose in jeans and a t-shirt, followed by Katherine who is wearing an enormous pair of glasses and a hat just as huge. Her mongrel Naomi is wearing the same hat, but smaller. As soon as it sees me it begins growling, while Katherine seems very embarrassed.

"And what the hell are you two doing here?"

"Why? Do you remember me?" asks Katherine, incredulous.

"Yes?" I look at her with raised eyebrows.

"Naomi had to do a little pooh and..."

I continue to look at her with raised eyebrows.

"I wanted to make a wish throwing a coin in this antique fountain and..."

Noticing that I do not believe a single word of what she says, she sits on the bench that runs all around the fountain and, desperate, says to me: "Oh. Okay, okay you've sprung me. I couldn't stand the idea of Ben seeing his former wives again, with all the children, his best man and my bridesmaid! This perfect family, everyone happy and having a good time, with the video-camera recording everything, overwhelmed me! I came here to spy on you all, but in the end I got stuck in this bathroom and couldn't get out!"

"Why couldn't you get out?"

"There's a ladder outside! You can't pass under a ladder because it brings bad luck! And tomorrow I'm getting married! I would never want to bring bad luck to my own wedding, little fish, you know?"

I reach the door and open it, saying to the maintenance man: "Listen, you, can you move the ladder?"

The guy gets down without saying anything, moves the ladder a few feet, climbs back up and gets back to work. I look at the trio showing them the road to freedom with my hand.

"How did you do that?" asks Katherine, surprised, "Thank you, my pizza capricciosa, you're my salvation!"

She approaches the door and opens it, hoping to be able to see Ben and the others from here.

I look at her and say: "You didn't really camouflage yourself all that well, so if I were you I'd leave from the back."

"But there's no back here."

"There's not one blind person there, though, so how did you think you'd pass without being noticed?"

"Ah no, we're not understanding each other. I have no intention of hiding, but I want Ben's ex-wives to see me in all my splendor and advertise this perfume before I faint from hunger." She takes the perfume from her bag, holding it in her hand as if she was in front of the television cameras.

I sigh. "Good luck."

The whole situation seems crazy to me. I'm about to go to the washbasin again when she stops me saying, "Wait a second", and comes close, looking hard at my shirt. "What is this? A piece of fish?" Her eyes light up.

There's a piece of food on my shoulder, she takes it and goes to put it in her mouth and eat it, but Ambrose strikes her and takes it from her hands. "No! This is wrong! You can't do that! Naughty!"

"I know, I know, thanks. You saved me from the temptation. I'm desperate! I'm hungry!" Then she looks at me, distraught. "Tell me, Jas, what's it like to eat? Nice?" she asks, her eyes bright with tears.

"You're not normal."

She doesn't take me very seriously. She grabs my hand and says to me: "Anyway, now that we're alone I'd like to take this opportunity to tell you that I am totally on your side!"

"Concerning what?"

"About that young disabled man that you hit at the gala. Know that I understand you." She gives me a wink of understanding and leaves with Ambrose and the dog. I can't believe it. She thinks I hit that idiot John for the fun of it. That is, yes, in the end she's right, but I certainly didn't hit him because he was a person with a disability! Instead, I did it precisely because he's not.

I approach the washbasin shaking my head. This whole evening is absurd and I'm really enjoying it. I think my grandmother is right to torment my mother: I really will relocate to Miami.

The red wine stain does not want to leave my white pants. The more I rub, the more enormous it becomes.

Suddenly I hear a strange noise coming from outside, as if someone bumped against the door. I go to open the door, smiling, sure that I'll see Katherine with another unsolvable problem, and instead the smile dies on my lips when I find myself facing the big guy from before. I'd recognize those icy irises and the scars on the face anywhere.

I open my eyes very wide, quickly closing the door with my heart going crazy. I try to stay calm, to breathe and concentrate on not let myself panic. I grab the chair resting against the wall next to the washbasin and shove it under the door handle. I see the handle move. He is trying to get in.

The handle continues to go nervously up and down. I look around me, agitated, searching for any object so I can attack him and escape, but don't find anything.

I rush to the other wooden chair beside the second washbasin, slam it against the wall, breaking it, and I take off one of the four wooden legs. I'm ready to defend myself, but at a certain point there is silence.

I look at the door and nothing happens. Silence inside and out, and when there is a silence like that I begin to get scared.

The door opens with a crack, sending the wooden chair flying. At the door stands him: John.

He looks at me angrily, and comes toward me at a fast pace snarling: "You destroyed my car! You drowned it!"

I hide the piece of wood behind my back and step back. "Really my intention was drown who was in it, but apparently I failed." On the outside I'm a bully, but inside my heart is going mad.

He stops in the middle of the room staring at me in anger, with only the fountain between us, while his friend full of scars locks us inside.

John looks at me. "You know, the time has come to make a few rules between us, to better address our troubled relationship."

"There is no relationship between us, and there never will be!"

He keeps staring at me with that challenging air and begins to come closer. "First rule, you must never more, and I repeat *never more* smash my car! Fuck! It took me more than a month to steal it!"

"Ooooh, poor John!" I exclaim sarcastically.

"My name is Jack! Jack!"

"What? I finally learn your name, and you change it just like that? You disappoint me."

He takes me unawares making a quick jump and stops a few inches from me. Scared, I begin to strike him on the head with the piece of wood.

"Stop it!" He tries to stop me. I give him a hard whack in the stomach that makes him bend over in pain. I take this opportunity to escape, but he grabs my foot and I fall to the ground screaming: "Let go of me!"

"Stay still a moment with this leg! Stop kicking me!"

"No!"

Thanks to a strange contest of hands and legs, I don't know how, but I find myself sitting on top of him, and he is blocking my hands on his chest.

"Don't touch me! You have to stay away from me!"

"Why are you behaving like this? You continue to offend me, push me away and hit me, why?"

"I've already told you why! You're a murderer, a thief, a liar!"

"I'm not only this! I saved your life!"

"I didn't ask you to save my life, but to tell me the truth!"

I manage to throw him off me hurling him against the door, but he is so agile that, after a somersault, he lands perfectly on his legs without getting hurt.

I dart to the other side of the fountain; he looks at me furious. "All I ask of you is a damn chance to be able to explain, that's all!"

"Forget it. I'll never give it to you!"

Silence falls. We are both breathing fast. My heart is pounding in my chest because of the tension and the adrenaline though I do everything I can to hide it. We begin to walk around the fountain.

"You've had four months to report me, to tell your *boy-scout* friend everything, but you haven't."

"And what do you know?" I reply bitterly.

"I know everything! You haven't told him anything, Jas, have you ever wondered why?" He looks at me as if he already knows

155

the answer. "Answer me! Why haven't you have said anything to your dear and inseparable, perfect friend Nickolas?"

"You're not to even pronounce Nick's name!" I become angry, without replying to his question.

"Oh excuse me!" he says ironic, "I didn't want to talk about *Nickolas* and your disgusting friendship. I have never understood what you had to argue about so much! What kind of relationship is that?"

"I don't intend to psychoanalyze my relationship with Nick with you!"

"Then what about psychoanalyzing our relationship?"

"You and I don't have a relationship!"

"Then why not psychoanalyze the relationship that we don't have?"

"You're crazy!"

"Coming from you, that's a compliment!"

I make a move toward the door and start to scream, but he prevents me and stands in my way again. "Where do you think you're going? Why do you want to run away from me? "

"I'm not running away."

"Yes, you are! There is something between us, there was when I was John and there still is. I feel it. You have feelings for me. You already had these feelings last year, but you were too afraid to admit it because I was a disabled person and now you don't want to admit it because you think that in reality they don't exist!"

As I listen to his absurd theory I take some steps backwards until I get to the fountain again.

"In Gorizia you told me that you'd get together with me if I wasn't a disabled person!"

"I said that to John, so he didn't suffer!" I point out, as we start to go around the fountain again.

"Oh shut up. You said all sorts of things to me! You've treated me like a piece of shit!" He stops walking around the fountain, and I stop too. The whole situation is surreal. I still can't believe it is really happening. The only thing I know is that the more I look at him, the more I want to slap that presumptuous and arrogant face of his.

"You're afraid of what you feel for me and what your friend, the champion of the law, would say if he found out. You look for refuge in his arms so you're not tempted by me," he says, with such assurance and conviction that I burst out laughing. I can't stop myself and he looks at me as if to say *you laugh but you know that it's true.*

"Apparently, John was not a recitation", I continue to laugh heartily, "You're really stupid. The only thing that I feel for you is contempt! How could you even think that I liked you? And what is even funnier is how you could even think you could compete with Nick? Have you taken a good look at him?" I laugh with amusement while the smug look has disappeared from his face. "Nick is wonderful, he's the boyfriend that every girl would like to have; he's sincere, faithful, has values and above all earns his living in an honest way. He's loved and respected by all. Someone like you doesn't even come up to his ankles. You're an inferior being."

I don't know when or how, but I suddenly find myself squashed against the bathroom door. His hand is squeezing my neck and his blue eyes are looking at me like a man possessed. "You, on the other hand, you're living proof that saving someone's life brings more consequences than taking it!"

"I'm not afraid of you", I gasp. He clenches me but not too tight, because he doesn't want to hurt me. He comes close to my face; I can feel his breath on me. "You should be", he whispers with a menacing air.

I know the situation is tense, that maybe I'm wrong and he actually wants to hurt me. Maybe I won't get out of this alive, but I can't help it and burst out laughing again.

He is clearly confused, perhaps he expected me to beg him not to kill me, that I would tremble in front of him and instead I'm laughing. I think back to Gorizia, to his tearful eyes, and his last words.

"Jas, help me", I begin to imitate him, making fun of him. He looks at me shocked; his hand is still firmly on my neck. "I love you, I expected anything to happen but not you", I continue to ridicule him, "You should have seen your face! You were pathetic!"

My laughter only lasts for a second, because the moment after I find myself with my head pushed under the water in the fountain. I don't even have the time to be afraid of drowning. He pulls me by my hair lifting my head out of the water. "Wash out your mouth before you speak about me and my feelings, damned iceberg that you are", he hisses a few centimeters from my face, "You're a fucking piece of shit! You know nothing about me! Nothing!"

He lets go of my face and I take advantage of it to knee him between the legs making him bend onto the floor again. I run toward the chair that earlier had flown away from the door, and quickly pick up one of the broken legs that has become a sharp stake. "Come near me again and I swear I'll stick this straight into your heart!" I scream. I dry my face without taking my eyes from John who in the meantime has got up from the ground.

"I tried to be understanding and patient, but now you have gone too far!" He glares angrily at me without coming closer. "If it's war you want, war it is! I'll track you down, I'll follow you, and wherever you turn you'll see my face, just so you know. I'll be after you day and night, you'll be my prey. I will torment you until you go crazy, until you give yourself up and give me a fucking chance to tell you what happened!" His voice, his threats, his language makes me shudder.

I try to pretend nothing's wrong, saying arrogantly: "Then get ready because I will never give in!"

"We'll see about that. You don't know who you're dealing with!"

"You're wrong - I know very well! This room has no windows, there are no rear exits, you have no way of escape! The only way to get out of here is going past Nick, who – I'm sure – will be waiting for you with open arms! "

He smiles at me, looking at me straight in the eyes. "Not only will you not say a word to him, but my brothers and I will go out of here through the main door, with head held high and passing in front of your friend Mister Super-mega-hunk!"

I take hold of the handle and hear him say: "Ah, and another thing."

I look at him annoyed.

158

"As well as your mouth you should wash your right hand too, princess!"

My right hand? I look at it and it's all covered in blood. I don't understand. First I clean it with my other hand, and then on my white trousers, beginning to feel myself going white too.

I begin to feel sick, to such a point that I can't breathe properly, my vision is blurred and I feel dizzy. I collapse onto the floor asking terrified: "Is this my blood?"

Everything's blurry, I'm going to faint. The only thing I can see clearly are John's blue eyes looking into mine a few inches from my face. "Do you give up?" he asks me.

"Never! Ugly son of a bi..."

24.

Jas has fainted because of the phobia that she has when she sees her own blood. Jack stoops down beside her, moving the wet hair from her face with a tender and affectionate gesture. He looks at her with a different expression, gentle, now that she's lying there unconscious, now that she can't see him.

He gets up, opens the door and goes out.

In front of the bathroom, disguised as a maintenance man, Vladimir is waiting for him; he greets him with a growl before heading to the exit. Jack is not disguised, he is simply Jack: in jeans, white t-shirt and black leather jacket.

After a few steps Lexi joins them, disguised as a French maid, and all three start walking to the door.

At Nick's table confusion reigns; the two former wives are quarreling with Katherine, the children are complaining, the cameraman is running from one place to another, Nick is comforting his friend Ben. Jack glances at him with an amused smile as he leaves the restaurant, as he goes out the main door with his brothers.

25.

If someone left me on a desert island with Nick for a week, I am sure we'd never exchange a word, unless it was to talk about Jas.

We've been in this hospital room for almost two hours, in total silence. He continues to look out the window all brooding, and I'm sitting by Jas's bed in the hope that she wakes up as soon as possible and saves me from this embarrassment.

Jas's hand is bandaged, but Nick acts as if she's missing an arm.

If you ask me his anxiety is uncalled for. I see Jas's hand move, and then her eyelids open slowly. I jump to my feet, happy. "Love, how are you?"

She looks around disoriented. The speed with which her eyes scoot around the room is amazing; she's like a computer that puts together the pieces of the puzzle to comprehend what's happened. Then they stop on her bandaged hand.

"Jas, are you alright?" Nick rushes to her before she's even had the time to answer my question. "You've made me worry so much!"

"You've made *us* worry!" I stress, looking at him reprovingly but he takes no notice. "How do you feel?" he repeats.

"Am I in hospital? I can't believe it; you brought me to the hospital for a scratch on my hand? You brought me to the hospital, and", she looks at the pajamas; "Oh good God, and you made me put this horrible thing on! How ridiculous!"

"Ridiculous? In your opinion it's ridiculous to bring you to hospital after finding you unconscious on the floor of the bathroom, soaking wet, with a wounded hand and everything around you demolished?"

"What?" I exclaim shocked. "You didn't tell me that!"

Nick looks at me. "I'm sorry. I didn't want to worry you."

I turn to Jas, angry. "And you say that all this is ridiculous?"

"But whose side are you on?" she rebukes me.

"On the side of who's right, Jas", Nick answers for me.

She protests: "That's enough now. You're giving me a headache."

Nick keeps on at her: "Can you tell me what happened in that bathroom, please?"

"Of course I can. There was a mouse, actually no; it was a disgusting and annoying rat. I tried to kill it with whatever I had available, but then I tripped and fell into the fountain, I hurt myself and as soon as I saw the blood, it was good night Jas."

We're silent, looking at her, both astounded by her hardly credible tale. Nick closes his eyes for a moment, sighing, says: "I'm going to speak with the doctor, to sign a couple of papers and bring your clothes." He seems sad and disappointed. "You don't move from here." Before leaving the room, he asks her, "Did you hear me?"

"Yes, daddy", she responds annoyed looking at her bandaged hand.

I cross my arms, now it's my turn to ask questions, and I want the truth. "Jas?"

"Do you think he believed me?"

"Do you think Nick is stupid?"

"Okay, you think he didn't believe me."

"Not even a deaf person would have believed you! What happened in that restaurant, Jas?"

Instead of answering me, she rolls up the sleeves of the pajamas and, with wide-open eyes, stares at her arm. "They've taken my blood!"

"Was that a question or..."

"Damn it... they took blood!"

Okay, it wasn't a question.

She sounds frightened and she instantly jumps out of the bed and heads to the door. "All this for a cut on the hand!"

"What are you doing? Nick said not... but what I'm doing here wasting my breath." I follow her and notice that, as well as being barefoot, her backside is showing. I have never understood why hospital pajamas are so open on the back. "Where are we going?"

"To save my ass."

"You could start by covering it, Jas."

162

She covers herself her hand and hurtles along the corridor. I don't ask anything else, I'm sure that she'll give me the explanations I want by herself; the problem is that instead she continues to take no notice of me. She starts to open every door she encounters along the corridor and looks inside.

"Can you tell me what it is we're looking for or not?" I ask running out of patience.

"My friend Zombie!"

"Your *what*?"

I follow her into a room. Like all the other rooms it's bare and white, except that it's much smaller. It has only one window. An elderly gentleman is sleeping in the single bed.

"He's the old man that was dead at first and then resurrected, don't you remember? I told you about him."

"I thought you were kidding." I had no way of knowing that the story she'd told me was true, I thought it was one of her usual ridiculous tales to divert some issue that made her uncomfortable. She takes the man's medical record hanging at the foot of the bed and sits next to him as if he was her grandfather, as if he were a relative, a normal thing in short.

"Jas! Get off there," I whisper scared, "You'll wake him up like this!"

She still takes no notice of me and reads his medical record. "He still hasn't been identified. Firearm wound to the chest, but he is now stable, in a semi-comatose state, dialysis twice a week..."

I don't understand a thing of what she is muttering. "Which, translated, means?" I say in a low voice; if the man wakes up he could have a heart attack.

"That he's... a parrot!"

"Okay, medical terms are not my forte."

A strange sound draws my attention. I look toward the window and to my great surprise I see a parrot, a real little parrot. It's very beautiful, gray, with a long red tail, and he continues to open his black beak repeating *kooooo*.

"A parrot", I say under my breath, "Jas, did you see it, a parrot." I go to the window, talking to it like a child. "Little one, what are you doing here all alone?" I try to pet him, but he flies off. "Oh nooo... why? I wanted to pet him, did you see how pretty he was, Jas?"

"Yes," says without having even heard my question.

"You couldn't care less, right?"

I go to her not talking about the *parrot* any more, even though it's not normal to see one in a hospital. "What happened in that bathroom?"

"Oh, the parrot's back!" she cries. I look toward the window and he is there again. *How cool is that!*

The parrot begins its call once more.

"You've come back, little one?"

"Me too. Me toooo" the parrot squawks, flying around the room.

"Did you hear that, Jas? It knows how to speak", I whisper, despite the cries of our feathered friend.

"Me too". That's what my Zombie kept saying before he went into a coma."

"Is he in a coma? Why didn't you tell me that at the start? I've been speaking softly for hours so as not to wake him!"

"Me tooooo, me toooo", the parrot keeps repeating, while Jas looks at him as she remains sitting on the bed, and this time she's intrigued as well.

"You're his parrot, aren't you?" she asks, pointing to the man in a coma. The parrot, to my great surprise, flies straight toward Jas landing on her shoulder and repeating "Me tooooo, kooooo!"

"That's not fair!" I complain.

"Get it off me right away!" says Jas petrified, without moving her mouth too much.

"Why does it come to you and instead flies away from me? I'm the one who loves animals, you hate them." I look at her upset. "She hates you, you know? Come here to me, come on!"

"Me toooo", it screams and takes off again, flying out the window.

"This is not fair."

"Hello, Jas."

I turn and see a little girl, in the dark near the door, with a giant stuffed toy in her hand. She takes a step forward, and I stare. She has a bald head under a yellow bandanna and is very pale with dark circles under her eyes. She looks at Jas and smiles. I can't say anything, I'm stunned. Of course, the same thing doesn't apply to Jas who looks at her from under her eyebrows and snorting says: "Oh God, it's you again."

"How come you're here, Jas?" the sick girl asks curiously.

"And how come you've still got the same hairstyle?"

"Are you really sick or did you steal the pajamas from someone?" she speaks with a strong English accent and seems happy in spite of everything. "The other time she stole Arizona's gown and pretended to be her", she informs me quietly, as Jas gets up from the bed irritated.

"I didn't steal it, I borrowed it, okay? By the way, where is the chief?"

"Why is your hand bandaged? Did you steal the bandage or did you really hurt yourself?"

"Didn't you have to go away with Nightmare?" she asks and goes out of the room holding the pajama with one hand to hide her bare backside.

"It wasn't Nightmare, it was the black man!"

"Where are you going, Jas?" I ask, yelling at her from behind.

"I'll be right back, wait for me here."

I fail to understand her lately; she's even more mysterious than usual. She avoids conversations, twists words, disappears, faints and then doesn't give you any explanation.

As soon as she gets back I'll take hold of her and put her with her back to the wall!

I feel a tug on the sleeve of my shirt; it's the little girl who looks at me with her big brown eyes and smiles. "My name is Diana, what's yours?"

"I'm Mina, nice to meet you."

"And he's Yellow Cat!" She proudly shows me her toy. Her arms are skinny and she looks so... weak. I try to pretend it's nothing even though it tugs at my heartstrings. "What a nice toy. Do you know that I have lots in my room? They're all spread on the bed and are all in pretty colors."

"Yellow Cat is my favorite, he's my best friend. Did you know that if a cat is bitten by a snake he'll then be afraid of a rope? And that a cat doesn't let anyone own him? Daddy has promised me that when I'm better, he'll buy me a real cat."

She is very sweet and innocent. I have tears in my eyes. I take a deep breath so I don't start to weep in front of her. Why am I so sensitive?

"You know, it will be my birthday soon and the black man will come to get me and will sing me a beautiful song and I'll have a party."

"Wow, that's great, and will you invite lots of friends?"

"Yes, I'll invite nurse Pamela, she's nice, and also Arizona and two new friends that I met yesterday. They're in my section."

"Wow, how nice", I repeat stupidly. I don't know what else to say and I feel ridiculous always saying the same thing.

"Yes, I am lucky", she smiles caressing her cat.

I have seen hundreds of healthy kids that do nothing but complain, cry and throw tantrums for stupid things, and she who is ill, with no hair and closed in a hospital to go through painful chemotherapies, is full of life and optimism. I kneel down and hug her hard. "You're a very courageous little girl."

"I wanted to invite Jas to my birthday party, but I don't know if she'll come, I'm not really sure she likes me."

She wants to invite Jas? But if she treats her like a little piece of shit?

"I like her very much though."

"Really?" I ask surprised, "Why?"

"Because she doesn't look at me like you do", she floors me. I feel really bad. I wasn't expecting a response like that. I didn't want to do anything wrong, I don't even know how I have looked at her. Or maybe I do know, like a poor sick little girl. She says goodbye to me and runs out leaving me there in the room feeling like a cretin with a shocked look on my face.

I look around me. The old man is still sleeping, or better, is still in a coma, and there's no trace of the gray parrot any longer. I pick up the medical record; I put it back in its place and go out to look for Jas. It's the umpteenth time that she has mysteriously disappeared with no explanation. She doesn't talk about Jack, doesn't speak of our trip to Europe; she doesn't talk about Ginevra's return and certainly not about what happened in the

166

bathroom of the restaurant. I wonder how she manages to keep everything inside, how she doesn't explode.

I look toward the end of the corridor and I see her speaking to a colored lady. The lady first rebukes a Chinese boy and then sends him away, mentions a laboratory and then turns back to Jas very worried. The closer I get the more I see the lady despair. It seems she is trying to explain something important to her, she shows her the sheet she has in her hand and waves it.

In all this, Jas is completely disinterested, with one hand clutching the pajama so as not to show her bottom seats to anyone going by and with the other is trying to take the sheet from the lady's hands. As soon as he sees me she changes expression, says something to the colored woman, in less than two seconds, the lady give her the sheet of paper and goes off with a depressed look on her face. It doesn't take much for me to realize that Jas has just scared her with some last-minute threat and being in such a hurry to join me makes it clear that she wants to avoid me meeting the woman.

This time she's not going to get away with it! This time she won't be able to divert the conversation and butter me up as she usually does!

I go to meet her with a determined step and only one thing in my mind: to make her talk. "Jas."

"Hey."

"What were you talking about? What's written on the sheet in your hand? What happened in the bathroom of the restaurant? And see that you answer me."

"You know, I was thinking about our trip to Europe."

"Our... really? You don't know how overjoyed I am to hear that, Jas. After everything that has happened in the last week I was sure that you weren't thinking about it anymore."

"Are you kidding? I think about it constantly."

"Do you know what I want to do when we arrive in Spain...?"

***

"Wake up! Get your lazy butt out of bed and don't let me have to repeat it twice! It's Ben's wedding today, so we must keep to the schedule and the timeline I've prepared that I put under your door! I give you five minutes then I will come to get you one by one and kick you out of bed!"

I wake up with a start to the screams of America amplified by the megaphone. She is walking along the corridor and knocking on all the doors so hard that she makes them bounce from the wall.

Despite the bad awakening, I'm in a good mood and full of energy. Today it's Ben and Katherine's wedding and I can't wait to go.

Since I arrived in Miami, I feel as if I've been living in a wonderful fairy tale. I have seen and experienced many more things in the past two months that in my nineteen years of life, and if I think that I'll have to go back to Gorizia in September I feel sick.

I look over to Jas's bed and between blankets, pillows and a few books, her blond hair sticks out all disheveled. I get up and go over to her bed and with a smile on my face I start singing softly: "Looove, ge-e-et up...!"

"Khmngag."

I can't understand her, she speaks like Will.

"We don't want America to come in and throw us out of bed, right?"

"What time is it?" she asks with a slurred voice, she can't even speak she's so sleepy, I can barely hear her.

"It's six in the morning, come on, get up, we have a beautiful day ahead of us."

"Six o'clock in the... it's still hours till the wedding", she complains, and puts her head under the blanket.

"I know, but there are so many things to do and places to go... come on, up, up." I try to lift her up or at least put her sitting on the bed. "Jas, get up!"

"Why do I have to get up ten thousand hours early? Give me a valid reason."

"I'm telling you now!" I jump off the bed and go to the door. Everything is in darkness both inside our room and in the hallway. I pick up the white sheet that America has left outside the door and jump onto her bed quickly, thus preventing her from getting into a horizontal position again. I turn on the bedside lamp and open the note. Jas is sitting up only thanks to the support of the pillows. She rubs her eyes with the bandaged hand and yawns all unhappy.

"So, we need", I begin to read the note, "to have a shower, have breakfast, get dressed and then a taxi will take us into town where we will try on our bridesmaid dresses, and I can't wait to see my dress!" I say excited, "Then we have the body and face massage at the beauty center, manicure, pedicure... I can't believe it!" I scream again all happy but Jas doesn't seem enthusiastic like I am. I continue to read: "Then the taxi will bring us back to the *Watchtower*, where the helicopter will be waiting for us on the roof to take us to Fisher Island, and finally, after make-up and wig, there'll be the ceremony on the beach. And I am dreeeeaaming!" I jump up and down on the bed with joy. I yell like someone crazy, I can't believe that all this is actually going to happen to me!

"Can you lower your chirpiness a billion tones, please?"

"No! I want everyone to hear that I love Miami! I love America! I mean, did you listen carefully to what I just read?"

Instead of giving me an answer, Jas asks me: "What's the time?"

"It is time to geeet uuupp..." I jump on top of her and start to tickle her. "Get up! Then tomorrow you can sleep until noon like you usually do, come onnnn..."

"Stop it! That's enough!"

I know that, if she wanted to, she'd push me off the bed with a single movement and the fact that she continues to suffer my tickling torture makes me very happy. When she wants to play it means that she is well and has no bad thoughts in her head.

"Well? Are you getting up or should keep on with this?"

"I'm getting up, I'm getting up. But I need a cappuccino, a big, huge one like the one Massimo at the Forum makes for me."

"Yes, yes, okay, I'll go and make it for you, but you have to get up though."

"Okay, will you also open the drapes, love? I need some light, the sun, to be able to see the terrible day I have ahead in a more positive light."

I immediately run to the window which opens onto a balcony. "Instead we're going to have a wonderful day, I'm so excited! I've never had a massage or a manicure before and I'll ride in a

169

helicopter as well. Do you realize that! It feels like a dream!" I open the black drapes with one motion, the sun comes into the room and lights it all up, and outside there is... I hastily close the drape.

Today will be a bad, bad, ugly day!

I have my back to Jas, holding the drapes tight in my hands. She must be wondering what the hell is wrong with me.

"What's the matter?"

I knew it!

She will certainly be expecting some explanations, but I can't speak. I keep holding the drapes closed and with a terrified face I stammer: "Jas, don't... don't move, stay where you are, okay?"

I should have known that as soon as I said not to move, she would have got out of bed and would be coming toward me. She always does the opposite of what I say, but I insist: "Jas, please, listen to me, don't open this drape because you won't like what you're going to see and maybe it's better that I clean up and..."

She pushes me away with the force of only one hand, as if I was a part of the drape. In an instant the sun enters the room lighting up her face: an angry face, a very angry face as she looks at the balcony in front of her full of garden gnomes.

Lots of gnomes, of various heights, widths and colors, all turned toward our room and smiling happily, all with some object in their hand, all thoroughly hated by Jas. On the skyscraper opposite the *Watchtower* there is a huge white billboard where written in black is: *DO YOU GIVE UP?*

The only thing I can manage to do is swallow my saliva.

"This is war," she says between her teeth with a demonic voice and immediately afterwards she rushes toward the desk drawer. She opens it, takes out a glittering red business card and begins to look around enraged.

"Jas, no! Please, calm down, think a moment!" I try to make her reflect, but she takes no notice of me. She picks up the cell phone from the table and from among all her clothes scattered on the floor grabs the first two things to put on and rushes toward the door.

"Please, Jas don't do this!"

"Do what?"

"Think! From thinking about it to doing something idiotic, it will take you less than a second!" My attempts are useless. She's already out in the corridor. "Jas! He's doing it on purpose! Jack is provoking you and you're falling for it! You're not dealing with shy and nerdy John any longer, do you understand or not?"

"Damned bastard!"

I see little Franklin come out of his bedroom, still sleepy and still in his pajamas. He is rubbing his eyes with one hand and in the other is holding his glasses. He doesn't even have time to say a word before Jas the grabs him by the neck saying, "You! Come with me!"

"I haven't done anything, I just woke up. I don't do pranks anymore because my mom forbade me. I didn't do it", he justifies himself without even understanding what he did, poor little thing, as Jas drags him away with her. I keep hoping to see America behind her orange counter, at least she could stop her, but she's not there, all you can hear is her voice coming from the living room.

Damn!

Whatever it is that Jas wants to do at this moment is certainly foolish and terribly stupid!

The situation worsens when I see her getting into the elevator with Franklin. "Jas, what are you doing? Where are you going? What do I tell Nick?"

"I'll be back before him!"

"I'll be back? Singular? And Franklin?" I'm worried.

The door closes and Jas in knickers and vest disappears with little Franklin who is all scared; but not as much as I am. What do I say to the others now? It's the day of the wedding and they'll all be tense and nervous, there are so many things to do and organize... I feel sick and hear America coming toward the hall. I literally flee to my room.

Damned Jack! He's the one to blame! Since he has reappeared in our lives only awful things have happened! He does nothing but get her into trouble and make her angry and he's doing it on purpose! What do I do now, but more importantly, what does Jas intend to do?

26.

Three hours later – From Jx's diary

A 1966 black Pontiac GTO speeds along the streets of Miami. At the wheel is Jack. Dark glasses, wearing a simple white t-shirt, one hand out of the window and his blond hair blowing in the wind. He is listening to songs by AC/DC at full volume, singing, and is hand is beating the rhythm on the door of the car. He's relaxed and satisfied with how the day is going, when he realizes that a police car is following him with lights flashing.

He raises his eyes to heaven, lowers the music and pulls over to the side of the road. He takes off his glasses and puts them on the passenger seat, takes the gun from the back of his belt and, pushing a simple button on the CD player, it opens revealing a secret space inside. He hides the weapon, closes everything, and quickly looks into the rear-view mirror. A thin policeman of average height, with a greying unkempt beard, gets out of the car. He closes the door and with an intimidating posture and gaze approaches Jack who grunts again, understanding immediately the kind of difficult and severe person he's about to deal with. The policeman reaches him.

"Good morning, mister officer", Jack greets him with a big smile, "Please don't tell me that I've broken the law again, I couldn't take it," he exclaims clearly ironic.

"Hello, I'm agent Christoph Waltz, license and registration, please", he asks in a serious and authoritarian voice.

"It's good to have an attitude, agent. That way you can intimidate potential criminals."

"Seriously?"

"Your work must be very difficult, especially because you are fighting two terrible enemies every day: crime and the lack of means to combat it."

"Our means are very efficacious", replies the agent, annoyed, "License and registration, please!"

"By means, I don't mean avant-garde technology, I was talking about brains", he starts to laugh amused while Christoph looks at him with a serious expression.

"Which you, of course, have", adds Jack, still in an ironic tone.

"Driving license and registration!"

"Just kidding", he lifts his hands in sign of surrender and takes his wallet from his pocket of jeans. He opens it, and the only thing inside it is a small white piece of paper with the words: *WHAT IS THE FOURTH RULE, JOHN?!*

Jack stares in surprise. He immediately realizes that Jas has something to do with this phrase, but doesn't understand how she did it. She couldn't possibly have been able to get near his car without him knowing it, let alone the wallet in his trousers. He rests both the sheet and wallet on the seat and opens the dashboard where he finds another small white piece of paper. He opens it.

DON'T MAKE ME ANGRY OR I WILL MAKE YOU PAY DEARLY FOR IT!

He can't comprehend how something like this could happen and is visibly confused.

"Is there some problem?" the policeman asks warily.

"No, it's just that, by a strange coincidence, I changed wallets and I don't have the license here with me, but..."

"Get out of the car!"

"There's no need for this mistrustful and unfriendly treatment, I've just forgotten my license, I haven't killed anyone," and then adds murmuring as he turns the other way, "today." He gets out of the car still astounded by what has taken place.

"Open the trunk!"

"The trunk? Are you kidding?"

"Christoph Waltz never jokes!"

He speaks of himself in the third person!

"Christoph said to open the boot!"

Jack looks at him incredulously and smiles. Everything seems inexplicable, he doesn't understand how the note ended up in his wallet and even less the agent's suspicious attitude or because he speaks of himself in the third person.

"Well, if Christoph Waltz said it, then..." he continues to make fun of him. He goes to the boot and opens it, looking condescendingly at the agent, wondering what on earth he thinks he will find in there. Suddenly the agent grabs his gun and points it at him. "Stop. Put your hands up!"

Jack doesn't understand his sudden reaction, turns his head toward the boot and stares.

Inside is little Franklin gagged and bound kicking his legs scared and crying out in fear! On his pajamas are the words: *GIVE UP? NEVER!*

The only thing that Jack manages to say before being handcuffed is: "What the fuck?!"

27.

A few hours later – From Mina's diary

I swear that this time, when I get hold of her, I'll strangle her with my own hands!

Because of her I'm so agitated that I'm getting an ulcer.

This morning, when they asked me where she and Franklin were, I said I didn't know, because it was also true, and the good thing about this whole story is that nobody worried that much. The only thing America did, after rewinding the security video and seeing the two of them leave the *Watchtower*, was shake her head and turn off the video. What sort of country is this? Jas went out barefooted in her underpants with a child in pajamas by her side and nobody asks where they are, what they're doing, or if maybe they should look for them, seeing that they're not answering the phone.

When Nick finds out about it I'll be fired. I'm supposed to be the mature and responsible one, the one who takes care of Jas and always knows where she is and what she is doing when he's not there, and instead I know nothing about nothing. This thing is starting to annoy me. I'm about to go crazy. She went looking for Jack, I can feel it. She went to look for a thief, someone who has already killed. He could be a madman.

Oh my God, I feel sick!

This whole situation seems crazy. I can't believe that I am the only witness.

"Ben! Telephone!" yells America as she runs from one corridor to another trying to avoid the many young boys who have come to pick up the various boxes to take to Fisher Island, piled on the floor in front of the elevator. Only the three of us are still here on this floor, while all the others are having massages, manicures and pedicures, and I'm here, dammit, sitting on the bench in the hall watching the elevator and waiting for Jas, as usual.

Ben burst out: "I told you not pass me any phone calls, today! No-one ever listens to me!"

"It's something serious, Ben!" says America with a worried look.

I don't know why, but I stand up as soon as she pronounces the word *serious*. Perhaps it's nothing to do with Jas, but every time I think that, it duly turns out that it is, and how. Ben goes past America saying: "Call me when it's something very serious!"

"Your son has been up to another one of his pranks, having an innocent boy arrested for kidnapping! It that serious enough for you, sir?"

Ben stops in amazement and the next moment he rushes to the telephone. I sit on the bench with my head in my hands. I can't believe it.

The elevator opens and out comes Jas, still barefoot, visibly worried and nervous. I shoot to my feet with my heart pounding.

America is about to ask her something, certainly about Franklin, since she's the last person to have seen him, but Jas goes straight ahead ignoring her.

I follow her. "Jas, you're back at last! What's happening?" I ask in a low voice, "Ben is talking to the police, about Franklin", I continue to whisper as I follow her at a fast pace along the corridor.

"Yes, I know."

"Where were you till now?"

She goes into our room and begins to get dressed, put on some shoes and do her hair, all nervous and agitated. The confidence and anger of this morning have disappeared from her face.

"Jas, there is no need for me to tell you this, but things are becoming slightly complicated here and I don't know what I should do!"

"Yes, I know", she says bluntly and leaves the room.

"Dammit, Jas!" I grab her by the arm stopping her in the middle of the corridor. I can't stand it anymore, living in this not knowing, I haven't known anything for months now. "What is happening?"

"It's all because of that idiot!"

"This is the only thing I know already! Tell me what I don't know!"

"I intend to tell Nick the whole truth."

"Are you serious?"

176

Suddenly something inside me changes. I feel lighter, I feel relieved. "Oh my God, thank you!"

She turns and continues on her way toward the hall. I follow her, but am assailed by a doubt: "Wait a second, the truth as you intend it? Or the truth as it is intended by the rest of the world?"

"Truth, truth!" She responds and then adds, "More or less."

I shudder. I know her half-truths and they're scarier than a whole lie. "What does *more or less* mean, Jas?"

She doesn't reply, but goes straight to America's counter – who by a very bad coincidence is singing *Hit the road Jack* - and asks her like one possessed: "You! Do you work here?"

America looks her up and down adjusting her black braids, leans on the counter and says annoyed: "I won't fall for your provocations like the others do. No, I will not. And now open your ears good and wide! I was working here well before you arrived with your white ass and..."

"A yes or no was sufficient", Jas interrupts her abruptly, "Where is Nick?"

I dare not even look at America's expression; nobody dares to talk to her in this way.

They are both silent looking at each other like two tigers. Not having received a response, Jas turns around and goes toward the third corridor leading to the living area and kitchen. I follow her, again, and I'm about to ask her the umpteenth question when we hear Nick's voice from the other side saying astonished: "Ben? What are you doing still here?"

"Franklin has got himself into trouble, I'm going to police headquarters to find out what happened," Ben replies putting on his jacket.

"To police headquarters? Is he okay?"

"He's trying to boycott my wedding. That's a clear sign that he's not okay!"

"Do you want me to come with you?"

"Yes, please, if you can accompany me you'd do me a favor. I don't have my car here, and my head's not right to drive."

Jas races into the hall. "Nick!"

"Jas? You shouldn't be here," he says to her as well, astonished, and looks at me immediately with rebuke, seeing that I'm the one responsible for taking her where he tells me to.

"It seems that no one is where he should be, today," murmurs Ben waiting in front of the elevator.

America looks at the security cameras and shakes her head. "Boss, we have visitors. And they're not exactly pleasant ones."

Jas quickly takes Nick by the hand leading him away from the elevator. "Nick! I have to talk to you about a very important thing!"

"Calm down, you're trembling, what's wrong?"

"I'm in a real mess, I don't know what came over me, I lost control of the situation, but I have an explanation for everything, you must believe me!"

"Tell me, tell me what happened. Whatever you've done, we'll work it out together, you know you can rely on me."

"Yes, I know, but unfortunately I don't have time to explain now."

"Why not?"

The elevator door opens and Scott gets out, the very shy policeman that I saw at police headquarters when I was released. He is uncomfortable, he seems scared, and I also understand why when behind him I see the bad cop that arrested me and Jas at the gala party. I shudder again.

He walks toward Jas with a satisfied air and handcuffs in his hand. "Jas Herzog, you are under arrest. Again."

"Here we go", she murmurs displeased, and I blanch.

"What? What is happening?" asks Nick shocked, but despite the situation he stands between her and the bad cop without thinking twice. "Wait a minute!"

"What is she accused of?" Ben asks quickly in an authoritarian tone. He is different from usual, very serious, with the attitude of someone you don't mess around with. The agent starts to list: "Car theft, driving without a license, kidnapping, attempted murder and defamation with the involvement of a minor."

"What! No! It's not true, Nick!"

"There must be a mistake!"

"Agent Christoph Waltz never makes mistakes!"

178

He uses the third person with himself, raising his chin. He seems even nastier when he caresses his grizzled beard.

"It's not true! I just played a joke on an asshole!"

"Agent Waltz confirms the truth only on his last statement, but on the rest, no", he continues to use the third person about himself. He tries to handcuff Jas, but Nick doesn't let him get near and I, instead, watch everything motionless, incapable of saying or doing anything.

"Wait a minute, I said!" Nick raises his voice, terribly serious.

Jas looks at him desperate. "Nick! You must believe me! It's not true! I haven't done all those things!"

"I believe you!" he reassures her patting her shoulders, "Don't worry, we'll resolve this misunderstanding! I believe you!"

"I have to tell you, I have to talk to you..."

"You can talk after Christoph Waltz has read you your rights!"

"Why? I've also got some rights, now?"

"Yes, you have the right to remain silent, for example."

"Jas, say nothing!" Ben intervenes, turning nasty, "I am her lawyer!"

"I want to see the evidence! She is innocent until proven otherwise!" growls Nick.

"Everything you say may be used against you", continues the policeman, ignoring Nick and putting the handcuffs on her aggressively.

"Do you really need to put handcuffs on her?" protests Nick.

Jas makes a moan of pain, and then hisses: "You damn asshole."

The policeman sneers. "Offending a public official."

"Jas! I've just said not to talk." Ben remind her, angry. The policeman cuffs the other wrist in a violent manner and Jas, without thinking twice, kicks him hard on the leg.

"And aggression to a public officer." adds the agent.

"Jas!" Nick berates her.

"I haven't spoken! I have not spoken!" Jas points out.

"This was not aggression, but unconditional reflex", Ben tries to justify her. The elevator door is closing. The bad cop massages his aching leg, while the other one that hasn't said a thing the whole time, remains in a corner all scared. Nick, very worried, continues to reassure Jas until the end: "Everything will be fine, don't be afraid, we will resolve everything."

I have the impression he's trying to reassure himself more than her.

As soon as the door closes, the first thing Nick does is look at me.

"I don't know anything! I don't know anything and don't ask me anything", I burst out frightened and still in shock from everything that has just happened. I hear America cough behind us. She doesn't believe a single word of what I have said, and perhaps not even Nick does, staring very serious at me. We are silent watching the numbers of the elevator as it descends slowly toward the ground floor, each of us immersed in our own thoughts.

I don't understand the meaning of half the things the policeman listed, but if Jas really has decided to tell Nick the truth, then eventually all this complicated, tangled and unbelievable situation will be resolved.

She's very lucky to have a friend like him.

Despite the policeman's thousand accusations, he hasn't batted an eyelid; he has had no doubts about what to do and who to believe. Has total trust in her.

If I were Jas I would feel terribly guilty toward him. I look at him out of the corner of my eye. He is silent, with his hands in his pocket, very thoughtful.

"So Franklin did not want to boycott my marriage", rejoices Ben.

We turn toward him, incredulous. How does he manage to stay so calm after everything that has happened? He, continuing to gloat, explains to Nick: "Well, in any case you would have had to accompany me to the police station, wouldn't you? At least, you're not doing it for nothing now."

Nick doesn't deign to reply while Ben, in the face of his silence, shrugs and adds: "They're children."

***

I'm agitated. I am in one of the many corridors of the central police station in Miami, sitting on the wooden chair between the

180

interrogation room, where Jas is being held, and the policemen's room. I don't know how you call the room where they can see Jas on the other side of the dark glass, but she can't see them. In front of me, in another room with normal windows, are Nick, Veronica, Will and Patrick. They've been behind a computer examining the video for a good hour now.

Will is the only one sitting, and I couldn't believe it when I saw that here too, in a different building, in a different street, he has brought along his inseparable red chair. Perhaps it is a kind of lucky charm for him? I find no other logical explanation. He is concentrating on his work at the computer, he presses the keys on the keyboard at an absurd speed, sometimes also on two keyboards simultaneously, incredible.

The most nervous is, logically, Nick; he walks up and down the room, fidgets with his hair continuously, takes deep long sighs, and Veronica's behavior is certainly not helping him. She does nothing but look at him with a satisfied air as she points to the computer, trying in every way she can to make him understand something, and I also know what that is: that my Jas is mad and it's time to close her in a psychiatric facility.

Damn her!

The only calm one in this whole situation is Patrick, leaning against the wall behind the others, with his hands in his pockets, watching the whole scene in silence. He will always be a mystery to me.

At the end of the hallway is Ben. Earlier he was talking with the bad cop, a certain Christoph Waltz, and they even quarreled, so for the second time I am witness to the fact that Ben, when he's on the job, becomes a true warrior. I, on the other hand, can't do anything. Except sit on this bench. I wonder why Nick brought me here.

"Thank you for your privacy and the trust that you are giving us, and we'll see that this misunderstanding is resolved as soon as possible ", Ben says to timid Scott.

Scott retorts: "You don't have to thank me, it's the least I can do, after all we're colleagues."

Little Franklin appears on my right and, full of enthusiasm, runs to Ben and throws himself into his strong arms exclaiming: "Daddy!"

"Son!"

"Jas put me to the test and I passed it! I passed it!" he explains all happy.

"Which test?"

"She asked me to play a joke on her friend and said that if I managed to have him arrested it meant that I am a really good actor, and I did it! I passed the test! When the policeman saw me in the trunk, he arrested him immediately!"

"Son", begins Ben, his face is more shocked than mine, "Do you know the meaning of the word *arrest*?"

"Of course I do, daddy. Stop, prevent the continuation of a movement. Hold a person to bring him to justice. Now tell me, daddy, was I good? Are you happy? Are you proud of me?"

Ben looks at him bewildered. Of course Franklin, even though he is a small genius, is always a six year old child and is unable to understand certain things, such as revenge and manipulation. He smiles at him, caressing his head. "Yes, son, you've been", he pauses and adds sighing: "very good."

I watch them hug each other. They are so tender and moving. Ben becomes someone else when he is with his children, a real daddy bear. My father has never hugged me like that. I feel like weeping.

Franklin wriggles out of the embrace, looks Ben in the eyes all happy and asks him: "Can I tell mom?"

"*No!*"

***

The video is clear and unequivocal: Jas jumps out of a black car as it runs toward the sea and immediately after a blond boy also jumps out. The car plunges into the water and the video stops. Nick walks nervously around the room, waiting for a response from Will, which comes shortly after: "T-t-the-video is o-original," he stammers with difficulty. "I-I'm sorry."

We're all silent for a moment. Why have they made me come into the room with them? I felt better in the hallway watching them through the glass. Now I'm overwhelmed by anxiety. I hope they don't ask me anything.

"Are you sure? Are you absolutely sure that it has not been modified or altered in any way'" insists Nick.

"Yes, Nick."

"I can't understand this!" he raises his voice, incredulous, addressing Patrick, "There must be a logical explanation to all this! What was she doing at the wheel of the car, and why did she involve Franklin in the fake kidnapping today?"

"I don't know why. You're asking the right question to the wrong people, Nick."

"She's there on the other side of the corridor, what's stopping you from going to ask her?" Ben asks him in a polite way, even though it was his son that Jas got mixed up in the prank, but it's Veronica who answers in a hard voice in Ben's place. "Fear, that's what is stopping him, the fear that he will have to arrest her himself. But if you like I'll simplify things and I'll do it!"

"Stop it! How is it that I'm the only one to see that in this entire story there is something wrong?"

"You've heard the witnesses, you've seen the video, you have the evidence before your eyes and you continue to justify her! All this is crazy. As long as she gets into trouble by herself stalking that boy is one thing, but this time she has involved Franklin as well! Her behavior is inexcusable. Jas needs help!"

Ben says nothing and fortunately Nick continues to justify Jas's actions. "She isn't a stalker! In the video she was wearing the dress she had on at the charity gala, so it must have something to do with the punch she gave the disabled guy, it has to be connected with him or his family. Will, what do we know about that family? Try to find out where..."

"You're incredible!" Veronica interrupts him sharply, "Now it's the fault of the disabled person? Nick, do you hear what you're saying? She will be your ruin, and now she's becoming ours too! You can't go on protecting her even when we have the evidence! Why do you behave this way? It's about the Borak story isn't it?

183

Why not admit it, for once? Do you think it's still your fault that she was attacked that night and now...?"

Nick intervenes, slamming his hand on the table and I tremble in the corner where I'm sitting, "That's enough! Say another word and you're fired!"

"What?" she asks looking at him in disbelief. We all look at each other amazed.

Ben tries to calm him down: "Nick, please."

"I've had enough of her! I've had enough! This does not help me!"

"I just wanted to say..." Veronica begins again, but Nick interrupts her another time. "I'm not interested! The next time you're about to say something about Jas, don't say it!" He bangs his hand on the table again.

"Hey, hey, hey, guys, what's this? Calm down", Ben intervenes again. "What Veronica was trying to say before she expressed herself badly is that we do not yet know if all the accusations made against Jas are true or not, and defending her a priori without first speaking to her to verify if..."

"I believe her!" Nick interrupts him. They're all speechless, all except me. "Despite what I see and what I feel, despite the testimony of this James Dean, I believe her!"

He looks at the guys one by one. "I am not asking you to trust her, I am begging you all to trust me", he leans on the table with a sad face and my eyes fill with tears.

"I know that to you I look as if I'm out of my mind right now, and perhaps I am, but... she listened to me when nobody was able to hear me. She took me by the hand, held it tight and never let it go, stopping me from falling and losing myself again. I gave her the most precious gift, trust, thus feeling once again that I was part of something, part of a family. This does not concern Borak - even if it did, I feel responsible for what happened - and it is not feelings that bind me to her. This is about truth. And there is no truth here; there is no light in this story, only shadows. Jas may have a thousand defects, but she is neither a thief nor a presumed stalker or a murderer! I know it, I believe her and I will show you that. Patrick."

"Yes?"

"Make sure that Waltz is not listening to us."

Patrick goes from the room immediately and enters the other, the one with the dark glass. Nick leaves the room too: Veronica watches him with a sad and at the same time annoyed look. I am still sitting on the chair in this corner, drying my tears and sobbing like a child.

Ben goes to Veronica sighing. "Come on, this is not the worst thing today, there is still my marriage to celebrate."

I don't know where he finds the strength to joke in spite of everything. Will also goes over to her and stammers something.

Veronica pouts. "When it's about her he is not objective, he can't see clearly."

"I would do the same for my children."

"Jas is not his daughter. I wonder how she managed to make him turn into her servant for life!"

All of a sudden, Christoph Waltz comes out from the room next door, and after giving us a nasty look goes away. Veronica, Will and Ben rush to Patrick, and I do too. I go into the room and I see Jas through the tinted glass.

She is sitting on the chair alone and with her head resting on her arm. She is moving her hand nervously and the only thing that you hear is the noise of the bracelet that hits against the table.

The other members of the team are nervous too.

The door behind Jas opens and Nick enters looking sad and worried. Too many sensations run through me in a single moment. I look at Patrick; we both know that the moment of truth has arrived and that when we leave this room nothing will be the same as before.

"I don't want to end up like my hamster", whispers Jas with broken voice.

Nick stares for a moment, his face serious; he sits down in front of her and remains silent. While I ask myself why she keeps talking about this hamster, Ben joins me and signals to me to leave. I go out upset and displeased at not being able to stay there with them, but before closing the door behind me, I hear Jas start to tell the story from the beginning. "He arrived at my school last year and introduced himself as John..."

28.

From Jx's diary – Twelve years ago, Villa Torres

The wall was very high and it covered almost half of Villa Torres. All you could see were the windows of the third floor, protected with heavy drapes which prevented anyone seeing inside.

Nickolas was sitting outside, on the unpaved road, leaning against the fence that divided Italy from Slovenia. He was scrutinizing the open door on the balcony of the villa. The drapes, moved by the wind, looked like the waves of the sea; his eyes filled with tears.

"Hello, little boy."

She heard the soft voice of a girl behind him. He turned sharply and met two enormous brown eyes. Standing on the other side of the fence, he saw a young girl with long brown hair and a huge smile on her face. Nickolas wiped away the tears and looked at her surprised without saying anything. The eyes of the little girl reminded him very much of his mother's.

Behind her, twenty yards away, was a white Kalimero parked on the dirt and a big man who was taking a shovel from the trunk as he spoke with his wife in a language that Nickolas didn't understand.

"I'm Jas", the little girl introduced herself, placing her hands on the fence, "Did you hurt yourself?" she asked seeing his scraped knee, "My grandmother says that we must immediately difse, difinsect, disinfent..."

She didn't know how to say the word *disinfect* and Nick realized that. He continued to look at her enquiringly.

"After you defect the hurt, you have to put a plaster on it, if not it becomes even more hurt." Jas seemed very proud of herself for knowing how to give him some advice on a thing that she had evidently just learned from her grandmother. She smiled satisfied.

Nick continued to say nothing, but he did not want to leave, and she, with her smile and large eyes, transmitted a sense of tranquility to him. "You're the child who doesn't speak, right? My

186

mummy was saying to daddy yesterday that you and your grand-mother are strange."

Nick bowed his head hurt.

"But she says the same thing even about me and my grand-mother, you know?"

She looked around and continued with her questions: "There are no houses here except yours so who do you play with? Have you got some friends to play with? My mom and my dad are going to build a big house and I will have a bedroom all to myself. If there are no other houses with other children we might become the best friends in the world and you can come and see me, what do you think?" She stopped asking him questions. She looked him straight in the face. It seemed that she liked his dark eyes and, despite being so small, she guessed what his problem was.

"There is no need to speak, you know, you can just nod your head. In Slovenia if you do that," she said, nodding. "It means *yes*, and if you do that it's *no,* understand?"

Nickolas smiled a little at this final pearl of wisdom and nodded yes with his head.

She smiled happily and began to applaud. "Bravo! You learn quickly! This is a *yes*."

The hours passed and the two children spent the entire afternoon together. Jas spoke non-stop and asked questions continuously with Nick replying simply with a nod of the head or giving her a smile.

For the first time after more than three months of absolute silence and sad faces, Isobel, hiding behind the front door of the villa Torres, saw her nephew smile and more than anything communicate with somebody.

The girl was only five, but for some inexplicable reason with her way of doing things and talking she was quickly able to find the right key to his wounded heart.

On one hand it surprised her and on the other hand it made her happy. She sensed that that little girl would not be just a passing thing in the life of her nephew, but that she would become a very important part of it.

***

Night had fallen now and Jas's parents were putting away the lasts tools scattered on the ground where they were building their house. Jas and the little boy were still sitting on the grass talking, divided by the Italian-Slovenian border.

"Jas! In five minutes we're going," called Jelena. She was helping Senad put the tools in the car.

"Yes, mummy", she yelled and turned to him again. For a moment they looked at each other in silence, both of them sad because they had to separate.

"I don't want to go home," she said pouting her lips. They remained silent for a little and then suddenly Jas took his hand through the grating. He was surprised, but did not pull away.

"My dad bought me a hamster at New Year. He didn't speak either. And then one day he died," she said in sad tone. "Daddy said that I am ier... iersponsible because I hadn't given him anything to eat or drink every day. How could I know what the problem was if he didn't tell me?"

She looked at him, his scraped knee, and the football that he didn't leave for a second, then at his tender gaze that reassured her so much, and squeezing his hand through the grating added worried: "It doesn't matter to me if you don't want to talk to me, I am not in a hurry, I'll wait. Just promise me that you won't end up like my hamster. You're the only best friend in the whole world that I have."

"Jas! Let's go!" her mother could be heard calling. She let go of his hand and got to her feet, shouting, "Yes, I'm coming, mommy." Then she turned again with a smile on her lips "Now I have to go, see you next Saturday, okay? Ciao..." she wanted to say his name, but she realized she didn't know it.

"I don't know what your name is yet", she smiled, "Sooner or later you'll tell me, I know you'll tell me, I'm your best friend."

And she went running away toward the white Kalimero. Nick saw her take Jelena's hand and before she got into the car he instinctively called out: "Jas!"

She turned around abruptly, surprised.

"My name is Nickolas", he said timidly.

"You have the same name as my grand-father! Mommy, did you hear? He's called like grand-father!" she screamed all happy as Jelena was trying to make her climb into the car.

"Yes, I heard, I'm happy that you have a new friend, but now get in."

"He is not a new friend, he is my best friend in the whole world, mommy."

"Okay, Jas, but now get in the car, please, before dad gets angry."

Nick stood behind the fence with the ball in his hands watching Jas climb into the Kalimero with her parents. He felt happy, and a smile appeared on his face as Jas continued to wave to him from the window.

29.

From Mina's diary – Central Police Station

Nickolas has been closed in the interrogation with Jas for over an hour, while on the other side of the glass the other components of the team are listening to everything that's being said. I, on the other hand, am still sitting on the bench in the corridor and there is no-one except me on the entire floor of the building. The fact of not being able to talk to anyone makes me even more anxious. What will happen now? Will Jack be arrested? If so, I have to admit that it would displease me a little. He became dear to me both as John and as Jack, because in both cases he saved my Jas's life. However, he is still a criminal, and it is right that justice take its course.

Suddenly, the door to my right opens violently and I see Nickolas come out, furious, with his eyes half closed, a dark expression on his face and visibly upset. Without saying anything, he goes past me and proceeds along the corridor at a fast pace. Immediately after, the door to my left opens too and Ben comes out. "Nickolas! Wait!" he cries running after him.

Veronica and Will also come out and rush into the room opposite looking shaken and worried, and in all this commotion I don't know who to look at or where to go. I turn to my right and I see Jas with bright eyes and a sad face. She stops on the threshold without being able to say anything, she just looks toward Nick. I jump to my feet and go over to her worried.

"Jas? How are you? What..." I don't even know what to ask exactly and I don't even have time to think of a question, when I see her pass in front of me and go quickly along the corridor.

She wants to join Nick, of course, but Patrick comes out of the other room and blocks her, grabbing her hand. I am shocked at the physical contact that Patrick manages to have with her, but not only that. They look straight into each other's eyes; there is a strong understanding between them. Even if all this takes place very quickly, as usual I see the scene in slow motion: their hands held tight, their looks that meet and quickly understand the other's and then again total indifference, as if nothing had happened, as their hands slowly part, gently brushing each other's.

Patrick goes to Nick and Ben who are at the end of the corridor, and Jas sits down on the bench with her hands in her hair without saying anything. Since when does she do what he says? I don't understand.

I sit next to her in silence, I caress her back to calm her and as I watch Patrick go away, I think back to the scene I've just witnessed. I am well aware that the situation is tense. At this moment Nick knows everything about Jack, Jas is desperate, and yet I can't think of anything else but their understanding, their hands gently holding each other's, their complicit looks, which apparently they are doing their best to hide from the others, even me. Why? And since when are they are so intimate?

30.

A minute before – from Jx's diary

Mina is sitting on the bench alone, feeling anxious. There is no one except her in the corridor or in the entire floor of the building. Suddenly the door to her right opens violently bouncing back against the wall so hard that it makes it close again. Nick is furious, he is looking resolutely in front of him, and his sole objective in this moment is Jack, how to find him and arrest him, so he can put him away for life.

Benjamin follows him worried. "Nickolas! Wait!"

Nick feels only anger inside, nothing else exists. He walks at a fast pace toward the table at the end of the hallway as Ben continues to call him, but his shouts serve no purpose at all.

Nick reaches the table where his jacket and the Beretta are lying; he picks them up and is heading toward the elevator when Benjamin flings himself on him. "I told you to stop!" He grabs him with force and slams him against the wall. "You have to calm down, my boy! Can you hear me? Are you listening to me?" he asks in a sharp and threatening voice as he holds him still. Nick is breathing fast and looks at Ben annoyed; he does not seem entirely himself. "What were you planning on doing? Eh?" He continues to hold him immobile, impeding any movement with his arm.

"Find him!" he responds angrily.

"And then what? Have you thought about it? Knowing does not mean proving, Nick!"

"Let me go!"

Benjamin does not loosen his grip. "No! I will not allow you to make a reckless gesture that you might regret!"

"I won't do anything, let me go!"

"No!"

"Leave him", a voice interrupts. Benjamin turns around and sees Patrick behind him, with his hands in his pockets and his face relaxed. He looks at him surprised, unconvinced by his words, but Patrick insists, "Let him go, he won't go back on his ideals in order to arrest him."

Ben lets him go, slowly, while Nick throws the Beretta and his jacket on the table to his left and places his hands on it, breathing heavily without saying anything. A few seconds pass and then he starts to pound his fists to the table top, one after the other as hard as he can. The two friends regret seeing him in this state, but know that they are unable to help him, not until he has time to vent.

Veronica and Will arrive from the end of the hallway, looking very serious, holding sheets of paper. Patrick approaches his friend as he continues to throw punches at the table with tears in his eyes, until he splits it in two. The others look at each other taken aback.

"Have you finished?" asks Patrick in a courteous tone.

"He has been doing what he wanted for months and I didn't notice a thing!" he says in a broken voice and breathing quickly. He stares at the broken table and clenches his fists in uneasiness.

"None of us noticed."

"I told you that Jas was innocent! I told you!" Nick insists irate, looking at Veronica. She bows her head without commenting.

"Guys, at the moment it's a tense situation for all of us, but we must calm down and solve one problem at a time," says Ben, trying to quell the spirits. "I don't know who Jack is, but it is obvious that he knows what he wants and how to get it without undergoing any consequences. And characters of this type are not apprehended in one day, with reckless actions and no precise plan."

"I can't sit on my hands and wait! He's dangerous and has been obsessed by Jas from the outset! We have to begin looking for him, find him and stop him! He has to keep away from her!"

"And you have to keep away from him", Felix orders, having just walked out of the elevator. They turn astonished and, dark in the face, he approaches them.

Nick was not expecting to see him here.

"What are you doing here?" asks Veronica, surprised, while the others say nothing. Felix looks first at the broken table on the ground and then at the woman, saying: "Give me the file."

She looks at Nick, he's her boss after all, and only after he agrees with a nod of his head, she hands the sheets of papers to him.

Nick asks the same question: "What are you doing here? How did you know that...?"

"Who's the blondie?" interrupts Felix addressing Veronica. She again seeks Nick's approval before starting to fill Felix in with the information. "His name is Jack. He's a boy who, for four months recited the part of a disabled person named John Dillinger at Jas's school. He stole an ancient crucifix, smashed up the school, framed two innocent people and lastly he has killed three people."

"As far as we know," Nick points out.

"Yes, it's true, and seeing the latest discoveries, we think he is much more dangerous than his angel face would lead us to believe. But I'd mentioned him, don't you remember?"

"I do remember now, yes", reflects Felix and then asks Nick: "Didn't you go to his villa in Gorizia, the same night of the attack on Jas?"

"Yes, a colored man opened the door and presented himself as his father, saying that his son had just gone to sleep. Since he was a disabled person, we supposed that if he had seen something he wouldn't have been sleeping so quietly in his bed. Then, when we compared the evidence and the time we arrived at the conclusion that he wasn't there when Jas was attacked and we didn't investigate further."

"We didn't know that the father was his accomplice", Veronica defends herself. Nick knows that if Felix is here, there is a more than valid reason and he is afraid to find out.

"This photo is not genuine", says the man looking at it carefully.

"No, all the video and photographic material concerning Jack inexplicably disappeared without leaving a trace, or has been manipulated", continues Veronica, "As he appears, so he disappears. His true identity is unknown. Today, for example, he presented himself to agent Waltz as James Dean. We had an old photo of when he played the part of a disabled. With the help of the computer, Will has modified it by removing the glasses, changing the colors of the blue eyes and the hair according to the descriptions that Jas gave us."

"And you didn't notice anything?" asks Felix turning to Patrick, "I thought you were the best in your field."

"And I still am", answers Patrick without turning a hair, in spite of the clear provocation. Ben and Will remain in silence, distinctly uncomfortable.

"Yet you didn't notice anything," he insists.

"No, he's a great quick-change artist", Patrick continues to inform him, still imperturbable, "He is able to adapt his body language to the character that he is interpreting with precision and extreme ease and manages to avert any suspicion, even mine. People who are able to do this are rare, and I've had the good luck to stumble on one of them."

"Luck?" asks Felix surprised.

"Yes, luck. I have had the opportunity to see his extraordinary interpretation with my own eyes and today I can say I know strengths and weaknesses of the subject, something that will help me for future investigations."

"Unfortunately, you won't have the opportunity to study him further because it will not be your team investigating him."

"What?" ask Nick and Veronica in unison. The others open their eyes wide, but continue to make no comment. Nick frowns. "What are you talking about, Felix?"

"I'm saying that I don't want you on this case, Nick."

"But why?" blurts out Veronica.

Nick protests: "You can't do that!"

"Of course I can, there are certain rules, Nick. You're too involved. You're bound to her by a relationship of friendship and this can sway you in the investigations."

Nick refuses to accept this decision. "We've been dealing with him since last year. We have material and contacts which will help us frame him and arrest him! My team has to finish what it started!"

"I said no and I don't intend to continue with this discussion. The FBI will take over the case and my team will deal with it."

Nick insists: "Felix! Sooner or later Jas will be part of my team, I already have to face up to my fears, but I can't do it if I am away from her! I can do it! And besides you don't know as much as I do about the case!"

"I know you well, and you're not ready yet to work alongside her. You're too involved and this could harm the investigations", he says, explaining his reasons clearly as he starts toward the elevator. "Tomorrow please send me all the documentation that you have on him."

"Wait", Nick stops him, with the hope of being able to persuade him, "I agree, I accept to move away from this investigation, however, my team is perfectly capable of..."

"No, Nick, no!" he interrupts him.

"They could deal with it without any problem! You have always worked with them in the past, even when I wasn't there! My judgment could perhaps be clouded by Jas's presence, but theirs? Is theirs blurred too?'"

"This is not what you need to deal with, it's Jas!"

"What?" Nick asks surprised.

"You have to stop spending your time fixing her problems and begin to do your job seriously!" Felix orders, raising his voice. Veronica changes expression, this time she is perfectly in agreement with the man.

Nick remonstrates: "What are you talking about? She has no blame in all of this! She has been arrested twice because of that criminal, she's the victim!"

"Is she? Are you sure?" Felix asks doubtful, "Then why are you discovering all this just today?"

"She suffered a serious shock in February, she lost her memory. I told you about it!"

"When did she recover her memory?" Felix wants to know.

"At the charity gala."

"At the gala? How do you know that? Who guarantees that it's true?"

"She does! What are you insinuating, Felix?"

"Well why has she has confessed everything only now?"

"Confessed? This is not about confessing, but talking, Felix!" protests Nick.

"Talking, confessing, there's no difference, it's still information, information that she kept to herself until today, why?"

"All this is ridiculous!" he exclaims running his hands through his hair. "She didn't tell me immediately because I was holding her back, I wanted her to take her time and tell me about it when she felt up to it! I can't believe that you doubt her!"

"Very well, let's say that's how it went."

"It did go like that!" he insists annoyed.

"Okay. Let's say that her latest misfortunes are all due to this Jack. But what about all the other times, though? Whose fault was it?" insinuates Felix.

"What are we talking about? What other times?"

"You trust this young girl far too much, she will be your ruin, both sentimental and workwise and I'm not going to stand here and watch while this happens!"

"It's not like that", he continues to defend her. He turns toward the end of the corridor and sees Jas and Mina listening to their spat. He knows she has heard everything, and he regrets it. Veronica has nodded her head the entire time, visibly in agreement with Felix, while the others listened in silence.

"Since she arrived in Miami, there has been nothing but defamations, offences and arrests! She has often put the reputation and the good name of the agency in jeopardy, which means tarnishing my name, and I will have no more of it!"

For a few seconds silence reigns, Felix takes a deep breath and with a calmer voice he continues: "Nickolas, you have always been like a son to me, and you know it, but I can no longer tolerate the lack of respect that Jas shows toward you, toward your colleagues and those you represent! You have to send her home. This is no place for her."

"Home? She is the only witness we have."

"With the evidence I'll collect, there will be no need for any witnesses, least of all her", Felix states.

"I can't, not right now, not after what I learned today", he answers, speaking in a low voice so Jas cannot hear him.

"I'll take care of Jack. You take care of putting her on the first flight to Italy."

"You're judging her without knowing her and this is not like you, why this relentlessness?"

Veronica shakes her head, thinking to herself that Nick, even after the words of a respected and experienced person like Felix, is unable to accept the truth about Jas.

"You're a responsible guy, with healthy principles, you believe in the value of friendship and in the honesty of the people who are close to you and who admire you for this, really. Your parents would be proud of you, just as I am". Felix lowers his gaze for a moment. "But I don't trust her, because she is exactly your opposite, Nickolas, and I wonder if she is as sincere with you as you are with her! I don't think so, and I will think this way until there is evidence to the contrary."

"Me too", murmurs Veronica looking at Felix with a complicit gaze.

Nick shakes his head, it is evident that Felix has already formed an opinion about Jas and he certainly won't change his mind by talking.

"Mr Walker", calls the authoritarian voice of Waltz who bursts into the corridor, "the car is downstairs waiting for you, sir."

"Thank you very much."

"It is an honor for me to assist you, sir", he says, smiling in admiration for his mentor.

Felix does the presentations. "I don't know if you have already introduced yourselves, this is Christoph Waltz, the Mayor's cousin, and in a few months he'll be an integral part of my team."

Christoph looks at them self-importantly, with a forced, insincere smile. The boys do the same.

"And they are..."

"Christoph already knows who they are," he interrupts him smiling, speaking of himself in the third person again. "They are the dummies, um, I meant to say the detectives from *Watchtower*", he says, smiling at the word *detective,* "That you yourself founded, sir."

The tone of his voice, his gaze, sounds very much like he's making fun of them; even a blind man could see that he hasn't the least respect for them.

"That's not exactly right, I just lent a hand," says Felix.

"But of course, sir. In any case, we have already met."

The guys don't know what to say faced with an individual of this kind; they look at each other, saying nothing.

"Send all the information you have on Jack to my agency before closing time, and when I say everything I mean *everything*, including the evidence you collected in Gorizia. My team will be on his tracks starting right now."

He approaches Nick, giving him a pat on the back, something that visibly bothers Christoph. "I give you my word that we will be able to keep him away from Jas. I'm sure that in the meantime, you will adopt adequate protection for her, but understand that my men will also be around," he says, and then addresses everyone, "If Jack is able, in any way, to contact her or approach her again, regardless of which continent she is in, you are not to do a thing. I don't want you interfering in our investigations in any way. Is that clear?"

Nick remains silent.

"Nick, did you hear me? You are to stay away from the *Jack case!*"

"Yes, I heard you."

"I will keep you informed of all developments, see you at the wedding." He leaves with Christoph Waltz who is doing everything he can to attract his attention. As soon as the elevator door closes, Nick rushes to the other end of the hallway visibly worried.

"Where are you going?" asks Ben.

"To Jas! She heard everything!"

Veronica raises her eyes to heaven with Ben calling out behind her "Nick! The case is not ours any more. Nick! In less than two hours I'm getting married... and you're my witness!"

Nick just lifts his hand and keeps going, leaving his friends alone in the hallway looking at Ben as he nervously puts his hands in his hair and stares at his watch.

31.

Two minutes before – From Mina's diary

I look at myself in the huge mirror in front of me and it makes me feel strange to think that behind it, usually, there are people listening to the various interviews that take place here. Who knows how many thieves and murderers have sat on this very chair where I'm sitting now. Just thinking about it makes me shiver. I don't feel very comfortable here and of all of the rooms that I could choose, I don't understand why I have chosen this one to escape from Nick and Felix's shouts.

That awful person. Why has he got it in for my Jas like that?

I haven't understood much of what they were saying, because they were also speaking in Spanish, but from the look on Jas's face, who knows the language, it's obvious that they were not nice words. And that horrible Veronica, you could see that she agreed with everything Felix said. I'd already seen them huddled up at the gala, those two.

But it doesn't matter, even if at this moment Jas is lying on the table in front of me and feeling as if the whole world has fallen on top of her. I know that talking to Nick was the right thing to do and that things can only improve from now on. I'm proud of her.

I hear knocking; Nick appears slowly from behind the door. "Can I come in?" he asks softly. He advances cautiously, not knowing what kind of mood she's in.

Jas raises her head, "Have you calmed down?" She looks at him with sad eyes even if she tries to pretend it's nothing.

Nick sits down close to her. "Yes. Excuse me for before, I was beside myself." He begins to caress her, as she looks at a fixed point on the table without saying anything. "They've taken the case from me."

"Yes, I heard," Jas whispers, "How come you let them do that?"

"It's a long story. But it doesn't matter. His days are numbered now, that crook!"

"Do I have to stay? Do they need my testimony?"

"No, not for now."

200

"That's good, because I want to go home."

"What? Why?" Nick asks surprised.

"I want to leave here because at this point I no longer have any reason to be here. My memory has come back, the secrets have been revealed, John will be arrested and Mina and I still have a trip to Europe to do."

"I'm sorry but I can't let you go, Jas. If Jack has followed you as far as Miami, he'll also follow you in Europe and I couldn't protect you from here. I don't want you away from me, not now."

"I want to leave."

"Give me just two weeks, two more weeks to see how things are proceeding and then you can leave."

I try to mind my own business while this goes on and not put myself in the middle of it, but I can't swallow this thing of staying here longer. As much as I like being here in Miami, I am too interested in our trip to Europe. We've been planning it for two years, and in two weeks I'm afraid something will happen that prevents us from leaving. Again.

He continues to beg her, pushing her hair behind her ear. "Please Jas."

"I don't know, Nick..."

Oh God! From *no* we've passed to *don't know*! It's finished!

"Jas, after what happened," says Nick, then after a pause he says, "I can't go on without you by my side. Stay with me."

"What are you talking about, exactly?"

They have both become serious. I don't understand this strange reaction of theirs. They look embarrassed or something.

"What do you think I'm talking about?" he asks, biting his lips. She moves away from him, saying: "Two weeks, Nick, only two."

"Thanks litt... Jas."

While the two of them bill and coo and exchange languid glances, I lie down on the table snorting.

Another two weeks. In the life of Jas two weeks correspond to two months. That's a whole lot of days! I already know that the two of us won't be doing this trip this year either, dammit! I understand their feelings in this moment; however someone needs to understand mine as well.

"Do you feel like coming to the wedding?" Nick asks her.

"Of course she does!!" I scream without even realizing it.

They both look at me surprised.

What the heck, I haven't gone for my massage, manicure and pedicure and now not even to the wedding? It's not fair!

I snort again, put my head on the table without another word. Goodbye marriage! Goodbye my shattered dream!

"If you don't want to don't worry, Ben will understand", Nick reassures her.

He's still insisting! Why doesn't anyone ask me if I'll understand?

"And will Felix understand?" asks Jas decidedly ironic, but I still wonder, *and what about me?*

"I told you, don't listen to Felix, he's a cynic. He has had many disappointments and low blows in his life, so it's normal to be distrustful, but he's a good guy."

"How did he know that we were here and what we talked about?" asks Jas.

"I think Christoph Waltz played a fundamental role in all this. What do you want to do Jas? Are you coming to the wedding?"

Of course she's not going to the wedding. I'm too much of a loser to go by helicopter to an island where there is a private mega-party with VIPs, dressed in a beautiful dress that recalls Rossella O'Hara and have a heap of fun.

"Yes."

"Yes? Yes!" I can't contain my joy. For the second time they turn to me amazed at my behavior. I don't want to seem insensitive to what just happened between Jas, Jack, Felix, Veronica and others, so I recompose myself and trying to hide my smile, I add: "No but, if you don't feel like it, no problem, I'll stay with you."

I'm not at all credible. Jas smiles and shakes her head while I start laughing covering my face with my hands. What else can I do if I'm so anxious to go to this wedding? After Miami and the trip to Europe, if we get there, who knows when I'll have a chance again to go somewhere, what with study, work and looking after my mother! Oh God! I don't want to even think about my mother, it makes me feel so ill. From one day to the next I expect a phone call to tell me that she died playing with the electricity outlet, or that she has set fire to the house playing with matches or she's been kidnapped because she talked with a stranger.

In short, I don't miss her at all.

I look at the two lovebirds. The usual annoying scene: him caressing her, her looking at him, smiling, me being ignored.

"You're safe now, Jas. Jack's days are numbered, it's over. It's over for him", he reassures her kissing her on the forehead, and I think about one thing only: we'll be here for two more weeks... and the word *over* is not the most appropriate...

***

God in Heaven, if this is a dream don't let me wake up ever again! And if it's reality, then I'm happy to be awake! In the space of a few months, I have traveled for the first time on an airplane, in a taxi, in a very fast elevator and today I've been on a helicopter too! It came to pick us up on the roof of the *Watchtower* and took us to Fisher Island, an artificial island south of Miami Beach. Wonderful! No bridge connects it to the mainland and it's accessible only by ferry, boat or helicopter. Katherine and Ben have chosen it for this reason, so their wedding is not invaded by fans and photographers, because they've already given exclusivity to a very well-known TV program in the United States.

Among the residents of this island I've discovered that there's Ricky Martin, Julia Roberts and Oprah Winfrey! What a feeling! Everything is so perfect! The only slight problem that I've had was getting out of the helicopter; the wind lifted my skirt and my posterior could be seen, with my Bridget Jones slimming knickers on show, damn! Embarrassment apart, everything else is beautiful and I still can't believe I'm a part of it. After the hairdresser and make-up in a luxurious villa, we got dressed and went down to the beach where I was about to faint from the excitement: white beach, red carpet up to the altar, white chairs with red bows on them and lots of balloons everywhere. Three Chinese girls sitting near the altar were playing the violin as the guests arrived on the island with boats and helicopters.

One day I'll find my prince charming, we'll fall in love, he'll ask for my hand and we'll come and get married on this wonderful romantic island. Yes, one day I'll come back.

32.

From Jas's diary – Ben's wedding

I will never come back here ever again!

That anorexic doll has squeezed me once again into one of those dresses she chose; only this time it's worse than the others. The dress is repulsive, all colored, and full of stripes and strange little squares. They've inserted Hello Kitty pins in my hair that have nothing to do with the overall look. They've put the false eyelashes on me and the make-up is obscene.

She has really done her very best to make us bridesmaids look terrible.

I can't stand it anymore! I'm about to explode!

Here all those people who were with me at the police station are trying to pretend nothing's wrong and focus on the marriage, with forced smiles, but you can see a mile off that they're tense and worried, and Felix's presence certainly does not help their state of mind. *That man strikes terror!*

Today that part of me that I don't know and that I can't manage has appeared. I don't know what came over me, but as soon as I saw all those dwarfs on my balcony, that sign in large letters on the building opposite: *Do you give up?*, something snapped inside me and I became blind with anger. I have to learn to control myself. I have to learn not to do things instinctively. I must try not to create more damage. I can't wait to get out of here and forget about everything, forget John.

33.

The ceremony begins in five minutes, at last, and I can't wait. Looking around the room, I've realized that I've had America only a few meters away from me for all this time, but I didn't recognize her, with that stylish dress, her hair up and adorned with many lots of little white flowers. I am certain that, dressed like that, she even looks feminine.

My Jas, on the other hand, hasn't said a word for an hour and I don't know what to do with her. She's not impressed with anything, and if all this manna from heaven doesn't make her happy and help her to forget her problems, then what could?

"Jas?" Here's Nick. I imagined that he would turn up immediately after I'd been thinking all that.

"Hey," Jas replies cordially.

"You are... beautiful."

"Have you taken a good look at me? They didn't dress like this even at a Maya party."

Nick smiles.

"I'm ridiculous! I should have taken those American films and stories about maids of honor clothes more seriously, dammit!" Jas goes on complaining.

"Stop it!" he smiles amused, while I still don't understand what's wrong with our dresses; they are gorgeous. We move towards the altar, where Ben is already waiting all nervous for his bride. Pavarotti certainly isn't helping him, seeing he continues to run around among the crowd, and move the cutlery and decorations on the buffet while America and Will try to stop him. A laugh escapes us.

"Good day, Nick", I hear an unmistakable voice behind us, I turn and see Ginevra.

She looks at Nick with her beautiful blue eyes, they're so sweet, and she plays with her black hair, distinctly ill at ease. I dare not even look at Jas, so as not to meet her gaze and be pulverized by mistake.

I had completely forgotten Ginevra. Poor Nick, between a rock and a hard place.

I haven't been able to retain the grimace of fake pain on my face while he is obviously embarrassed.

"Gin. How, how are you?" stammers Nick. I can't believe this, he really stammered.

"Well, thank you," she replies in a calm and friendly way. She is really very polished. "Hi Jas", she also greets her very politely, and of course Jas, very rudely, turns her head the other way. The most she is able to do is raise her hand in a sign of greeting.

Ginevra smiles and continues to speak with Nick as if nothing had happened. "The last time we met we didn't have much time to talk."

Jas pulls a face knowing that the last time was precisely at the auction where disaster struck, while Nick cannot utter a single word. She looks straight into his eyes and continues her monologue. "You look good in a tuxedo."

What with me scrutinizing her every gesture and Jas who is ignoring her, she can't feel very at ease.

"Thank you, you too... you look beautiful."

"Yes, you're as beautiful as when you left him," Jas bursts out.

I feel myself sinking beneath the earth.

Ginevra looks down for a moment and then continues talking, once again as if nothing has happened, despite her discomfort. "In the end you succeeded in realizing your dream, I am very happy for you, you deserve it."

"Thank you", he whispers, speechless for a few seconds before asking her: "What about you? I thought you were in Rome."

"I was, but I'm here now."

Jas, seeing these huge embarrassing pauses between them, raises her eyes to heaven. I swear I can't yet figure out if this reaction is from jealousy or resentment toward Ginevra, seeing that she left him and went away from one day to the next.

"Ben and Veronica didn't tell me you would be coming to wedding."

"I know. I begged them not to say anything, unless you asked about me", she pauses tightening her lips, "And apparently you didn't."

She seems displeased. She is looking at him all the time with such a sweet look, I think she still feels something for him.

"How long are you thinking of staying in Miami?"

"It depends."

"On what?"

Ginevra closes her eyes for a moment as she touches her black hair and then gently responds: "On the reasons that will compel me to remain."

Nick is clearly baffled by her response. Once again there is an embarrassing silence, but Jas is happy to break it and taking Nick by the arm, saying, "You stay if you like, we have to go!"

"Yes, we do," agrees Nick, giving Ginevra a tense smile, "It was nice seeing you again, Gin."

"For me too."

As we go, I peek over my shoulder to see her expression, when she calls him again: "Nick! One of these days, we could have a cup of tea together."

"Nick!" Jas interrupts annoyed. Okay, she is officially jealous. As we go, I look at Ginevra again, and to my great surprise I see Veronica approach her and hug her.

I can't believe my eyes. She's consoling Nick's ex pretending to be her friend, while all know that she too is in love with him. I'm right to detest her, she's nasty and a hypocrite.

34.

Shortly after – From Jas's diary

In the end, to my great surprise, I wasn't bored at this kind of Maya wedding. The ceremony was an absurd situation comedy. I could hardly stop myself from laughing. Katherine is too funny.

Apparently, the latest product she had to promote was teeth whitening strips, with the result that we saw her for the entire time with her mouth wide open to show her sparkling white, far from natural, smile. As she approached the altar and stared at the cameras, she looked like Jim Carrey in *The Mask*. Everyone there seemed stunned, Ben included.

I, on the other hand, had two admirers that eyed me the entire time; the first was Franklin who, having passed his acting test, greeted me waving his little hand and sending me loving little kisses, and the second was Felix. Only he didn't wave to me, no. And rather than send me little kisses, I think he would have gladly told me to get fucked.

35.

From Mina's diary – Ben's wedding

It is all so romantic, so perfect in every detail and Ben is so excited as he looks at Katherine and Naomi - with the same little white hats on their heads - walk down the aisle and come closer to the altar. I can't stop crying.

And then the marriage vows that they exchange are so tender, we are all moved. The atmosphere would be even more perfect if Jas wasn't sniggering the whole time behind the bouquet she is holding. Apparently their marriage vows are a kind of joke that amuses her. Everyone is glaring at her: the other two bridesmaids, the guests, even me, but not Nick and Patrick, who seeing her laughing are trying hard not to laugh as well.

Anyway, I am excited, I'm not sure why, given that I've known Ben and Katherine for a little over two months. And yet my heart is beating fast, I feel very taken by it all and I'm truly happy for them.

After the ceremony all the guests throw themselves on the buffet, while the bride and groom, the witnesses and we bridesmaids remain near the altar to have our pictures taken. Another experience that I'll keep in my heart.

Behind us now there's a beautiful sunset, the whole island is lit by shades of red and orange, and the photographer is really trying hard to take the best shots. In short, everyone is happy except Jas who has been huffing and puffing for half an hour now, while Nick smiles at her trying to mollify her with his gaze.

We're ready to take a last photo, when we see a black helicopter flying toward the island. Ben is trying to figure out who is arriving, but above all why this helicopter is landing a few meters from where the ceremony is taking place thus creating a disaster all around us; the sand is blowing up, the wind is making the decorations fly from the tables, the women are holding onto their skirts and the large hats on their heads, while the men are desperately trying to keep their toupees in place.

Everyone is surprised by this landing. Katherine is smiling, but in her eyes you can see the disappointment for that disaster. I don't get it.

I go to Jas and Nick holding my skirt, while people are moving to make way for the helicopter to land at the beginning of the aisle leading to the altar. The violinists stop playing, and everyone begins to stare silently at the tinted windows and the door of the helicopter with curiosity.

The door opens and after a few seconds we see a beautiful leg get out and then its owner: a knockout of a woman with red curly hair. She looks around with a kind of cunning air, smiles and adjusts her red dress. She is holding a bouquet of flowers and a picture.

The pilot gets out immediately after, a great big muscular man. One entire arm is tattooed black and he looks at us with eyes narrowed, a very serious face and his arms crossed. They stand in front of the helicopter, not saying and not doing a thing. I turn toward Jas; she is very pale, staring wide-eyed. She grips Nick's hand and whispers: "It's them."

Nick's face turns nasty in a heartbeat, and at the same time Ben looks around and tries to catch the gaze of the other members of the team.

My heart begins to beat hard, I know who is arriving, and in fact it's him who now comes out of the helicopter. White pants and white shirt, blond hair ruffled by the wind and a confident gaze pointed at us. He comes towards us, while the red-haired woman follows him winking at the children present.

It's Jack! Jack is here! He really is here!

Jas is strange. It seems she wants to hide behind Nick. Jack is just as I remembered him the last time I saw him at school without a mask: of striking beauty, poised, eyes of ice, not in the least afraid of the unpleasant gaze of Nickolas and his team that is slowly approaching the altar. I wonder why he has come here. Does he want to give himself up?

Nick tightens his lips making a gesture to Jas, as if to encourage her to stay calm.

Jack reaches us, stops a few meters from us, and smiles as he sizes Jas up from head to toe. She avoids his gaze, angry.

"Good sunset to all!" Jack greets politely, pointing to the guests around us. "First I would like to apologize for the sand and the disorder which my helicopter caused as it landed", he smiles, seeing other people smile, and then calmly turns to Nick with a low voice, so as to not be heard by the others: "Do you know who I am?"

"It's not hard to imagine", he answers in a hard tone, but without losing his composure, so people won't see the tension that in reality reigns between them.

Jack smiles again and continues aloud: "Let me introduce myself. My name is Jack Black and they are my brothers and sister: Lexi."

The redhead slowly turns in a circle with a cougar gaze.

"Over there is Vladimir", continues Jack, and indicates the beefy fellow next to the helicopter, who is staring at everyone with contempt and makes no greeting.

"And he's Koki."

I haven't a clue where this Koki has appeared from. He wasn't there before and now he's standing next to Lexi and Jack, and greeting us, raising the black hat from his head and smiling at the girls around him.

"It so happens that I saved the life of one of Katherine's beautiful bridesmaids", the guests begin to murmur while Jack continues, "and I have saved her life twice." He behaves as if he's on stage and has to entertain the audience; he has such charisma and such an engaging way of speaking that everyone is listening to him, marveling at his heroic undertaking.

"And do you know something else? She didn't even thank me."

I hear murmurs of dissent from the people around, while Nick's face darkens more and more. Jack approaches him again asking him in a low voice: "So? Did you imagine well?"

Nick clenches his fists without responding. Jack smiles and asks Jas: "Do you give in?"

"Stay away from her", the detective says between his teeth putting himself a breath away from his face.

"What's this, a threat? Aren't there laws against these things?" he asks sarcastically. I look at him and I can't make head or tail of him. There is no longer any trace of John in him; before us now is another man, arrogant, provocative. I really can't believe that John and Jack are the same person.

I'm expecting Nick to arrest him at any moment, and instead nothing happens. They challenge each other in silence with icy looks, each of them expecting the other to make a move. I don't understand why Nick doesn't react until I see Felix in the midst of the guests, and his eyes say it all. Nobody in the team does anything because they can't do anything.

"What do you want?" Nick asks him again through clenched teeth. Jack suddenly turns and continues his monologue in a loud voice: "And then I said to myself, but I don't want her thanks, you don't save a human life to be praised. After all, I did it for love", and murmurs softly to Nick, "And because you were not there and nobody else could help her, except me."

"That's enough!" Jas bursts out suddenly, "Stop it!"

It's the first time she has spoken since Jack arrived. She is angry, very angry. If it weren't for Nick, she would have already thrown herself upon him, I'm sure.

He smiles insolently continues aloud: "And with the same love, all I ask you today is: Jas Herzog, will you come to dinner with me?"

"Never!" Her *never* is categorical and clear. The audience begins to murmur and go *booo*. I see Nick's team in difficulty. They look at each other and try to communicate with glances about what they should do.

"No, don't do that", says Jack addressing the guests who are now hanging on his words, "I know why she is holding back, because I have not asked the permission of the fearless Nickolas Ortega Torres to see his", he makes a pause and looks at him, "Girlfriend? Am I right?"

"You realize that this place is full of detectives and other law and order forces, right?"

"Obviously, that's why I am so cool!"

I cannot believe his reply which is so... domineering and bold. As shocked as I am, his behavior attracts me more and more, and I'm not proud of it.

"Well then, Nickolas Ortega Torres, do you give me permission to go out to dinner with Jas?"

"Never!"

"I'm afraid I didn't hear that", he continues to provoke him, when from the crowd a hard and authoritarian voice is heard saying: "Of course he grants you permission, you saved the life of that young girl. Nobody could deny you." It is Felix. He approaches, though remains in the midst of the other guests, and looks at Nick severely while the audience applauds and roots for Jack. The situation is so compelling that I'm about to applaud too.

"Like I always say, the public is always right. Well then, Nickolas? Can I take your *girlfriend* to dinner?" After his question, silence falls. Only the sound of the waves can be heard.

The sun has set now and everything has become darker.

The guests are waiting impatiently for Nick's reply. Jas seems to becoming more and more confused, while Felix observes everything from afar with arms crossed and eyes squinting. This suspense is taking my breath away, and then finally Nick responds: "At most, you can take her to breakfast!"

"What? No!" Jas blurts out unbelieving.

"Breakfast it is, then!" says Jack in a loud voice gaining all the applause from the people around him, as Jas looks at Nick enraged. "Before I go, I have a gift for the bride and groom."

Lexi goes to Katherine with sinuous movements and gives her the bouquet of flowers.

"And of course, for Nickolas." He takes the picture from Lexi's hands and the only thing I can see are the faces of Nick, Ben and Veronica which are even angrier than before. I don't understand this reaction of theirs, while with a smile on his lips he continues to needle in a whisper: "Medusa was the only one able to paralyze with just one look, but from your faces, I see that I have been successful too." He shows everyone the painting of Medusa. "A little something for a great team, good luck guys", his tone of voice is again sarcastic. He gives the painting to Nick, turns to the guests and bows thanking them: "Thank you for your cooperation." Then, with a large satisfied smile at Jas, he says to her: "And we'll see each other tomorrow. I'll pick you up at eight", he pauses and adds: "in the evening."

"We said breakfast!" Nick insists.

"I'll make some brioche" replies Jack, turns around and goes toward the helicopter. I cannot help but admire his rear end and I feel myself going red in the face, embarrassed by my impure thoughts.

The Japanese boy follows him immediately after smiling at Veronica who looks at him frostily. On the other hand, there's something familiar about Lexi. The way she moves, her way of pandering to people around her reminds me something. And then I get it! She's the lawyer who came to get Jas in jail! She looks at Will blowing him a sensual kiss and off she goes, as he murmurs something all embarrassed and scratches his head.

Nick is ready to burst as he watches them boarding the helicopter. He is breathing deeply, clenching his fists.

I see the rest of the team becoming agitated, two gorillas dressed in black, accompanied by Felix. They take the painting, and then the flowers from Katherine's hands, while Jack meanwhile takes flight with his helicopter without being stopped or questioned. He goes as if he had never done anything bad in his life and this leaves me stunned.

After all, he is a thief! A murderer! I look to my left, but Jas is no longer there.

36.

A minute later – from Jas's diary

They've let them go! They've let them go! He looked at me with that shit of a face, with that all-powerful expression. He did what he wanted, and they have let him go!

Felix, Nick, their team, they are all ridiculous and so small that I am ashamed for them.

I can't believe it! They watched the situation from a distance; they could hear every offensive and provocative word from that imbecile and didn't do anything about it! I can't believe it! Ridiculous, all of them!

"Jas, stop!" screams Nick. I pretend not to hear him. I enter the villa on the beach and nervously begin to take the little pins from my head.

I don't want anyone to see me talking to him after making me look like shit the way he did! I don't know him!

"Jas, please!" He is following me. Perhaps I'm going to pretend I know him for two more minutes, just long enough to tell him to his face what I think of him and his shit team. I turn around pointing my finger at him. "For every tiny mistake that I have done in the past you have criticized me, punished me and sometimes even humiliated me! For every little vulgar word, for every impulsive gesture that I have done, even if for a good reason, you have mortified me like nobody has ever done in my life, and now? He arrives! The one who cheats, manipulates, steals and kills arrives, he stalks me, he has me arrested, and you let him leave like that? You listened to him and put up with his provocations! He was laughing at you, Nickolas, and what did you do? Nothing! Nothing!"

"I couldn't! With which charges Jas? There are procedures to follow, permits to..."

"On what charges?" I interrupt him screaming, "Procedures? Permits? Are you taking the piss?"

"No! It's just that it is not that easy. Knowing does not mean proving, Jas!"

"What? What are you...? You're saying that we know who, how and when, but it's not enough because there is no evidence linking the crimes to the bastard?"

"For the law, without evidence, it could have been anyone who committed those crimes."

"This is absurd! And then you wonder why I don't believe in justice! Because it is more complicated and unjust than injustice itself, that's why!"

"Jas, I beg you, listen to me..."

"No! You listen to me! I told you everything precisely to avoid meeting up with him again, I wanted you to arrest him, and instead what happens? That not only do I see him again, but I even have to go to breakfast with him!" I'm furious.. "You just stood there looking at him while he put on his little show in front of everyone! I'm not going out with him! He can get stuffed! He roams the world and does whatever the fuck he wants, does this seem right to you? It's not fair!"

"No, it's not fair, it's not fair! And that is precisely why we need you! Don't you understand? You're our bait!"

"What? No!"

"While we're all looking for him he's looking for you! You're the only one that can get close enough to gather the evidence to be able to arrest him. It's your chance. You have always wanted to work in my team, and now you have the chance. The chance to make everyone see what you're worth, Jas."

"Do you listen to me when I speak?"

Now I've had enough!

"I've been telling you since February that I don't know if I want to work with you! And after today I don't think I need to explain the reasons to you."

"Jas, please, it's your duty to help in the investigations!"

"No, that's not true! I have already done my duty! You're the detective here, so go and investigate! That's if you're capable of it!"

"That's enough! What kind of behavior is this?" Felix reproaches me, interrupting our furious quarrel.

37.

A moment before – From Mina's diary

I go into the villa and see Felix opposite Jas and Nick shooting daggers at them and his face so tense that a throbbing vein is sticking out on his neck. You can cut the air with a knife, while Felix continues his speech in a hard and severe way addressing Jas: "No one regrets more than I do that it's you who is involved in this case, but unfortunately I have no other choice and now we will have to find a way to collaborate, whether you like it or not."

"I don't have to do a damn thing! You should have arrested him when you had the chance instead of letting him leave." Jas does not seem to be afraid of him; indeed she challenges him and I have the feeling that she can't wait to attack him as only she knows how.

"The reason we have not detained him is because without evidence we're going nowhere, and for now he is only a suspect, because we don't have the evidence." Felix reminds her.

"Evidence! Evidence! Everything revolves around this! And what am I?" she asks infuriated.

"A witness or perhaps someone with an attention-seeking obsession who has invented everything just to draw attention to herself."

"What did you say?" she asks like one possessed. She's about ready to beat him black, and it may seem like a bad play on words since Felix is black, but fortunately Nick grabs her quickly around her waist which keeps her from hitting him. "You damn..."

Nick covers her mouth with the other hand, holding it before she says something silly which she may regret, while she angrily flings herself about.

I see Veronica and Will come in; they are shocked by the scene and at first don't know what to do.

"Jas, please, calm down." implores Nick, but she manages to break free from his hand and begins to hurl curses at Felix, as he looks at her icily.

Nick continues to hold her still. "Will take her away please!"

He, poor thing, opens his eyes wide in fright, adjusts his glasses stammering something, then approaches Jas, takes her by the shoulders and lifts her from the ground, taking her away. She continues to scream: "I haven't made up a damn thing!"

Will tries to comfort her. "I know, I know DAAS."

"Fuck off!"

"Khyghnk yes, frrrf , I know..."

While the three of us go out trying to mollify her, Ben and Patrick are closing the door behind us. In all this chaos, however, I certainly don't miss Patrick's watchful eyes turned on Jas, as she is carried away.

* * *

Time passes, it's about an hour now that I've been sitting outside on the stairs with Jas. It's dark around us, the wind is blowing and the humidity is suffocating me. This day never ends; it seems to have lasted an eternity.

Too many things have happened in too little time, one after the other. So many emotions all together that I'm not even sure what I'm feeling at this moment. Jack's back, everyone hates him, but I can't get him out of my head. His looks have completely bewitched me from the first moment that I saw him.

We hear voices and yelling come from inside the villa where we left the others, and although I am aware that Jack is a criminal, I can't understand all this agitation. He didn't kill anybody, I mean he did, but he saved Jas's life. Good God, we mustn't forget that.

"I want to leave here", I hear her say something at last, after an hour of silence. She's sitting on the steps with her bridesmaid dress that is half torn and is looking at the people who are cleaning and putting away the chairs and tables of the ceremony. The guests are in the villa celebrating and instead we're here, sitting on the ground.

Jas murmurs annoyed: "Of all the places where they could have got married, they choose this island which I can't escape from. Damn them."

I don't have the time to say anything to her, before I hear the door open behind us and I see all the team come out, plus Felix.

They've all got serious faces, except Patrick who is the last to come outside and he looks at Jas as she gets up from the steps. Felix comes up to her; he seems more relaxed than before. "There are some procedures to follow and everything has to be legal. This means that the evidence must be collected in a lawful manner, with proper mandates for both search and arrest, and so on. We will draw up a detailed plan tonight and tomorrow, when you have calmed down, I will let you know my decision about your involvement in this case."

"I don't give a damn about your decision!" explodes Jas.

Nick implores her: "Jas, please." Nick's voice is sad, his face disconsolate.

"I don't want to be involved in this story!"

"You are already involved, unfortunately. Of course, by law we cannot force you to do anything you don't want to do."

"You, because of the law you can't even do what someone wants, let alone if he doesn't want to, so nothing doing!"

Felix shakes his head looking at Nick, while the others remain silent, not daring to say anything. I don't understand why this Felix has all this power over Nick. The man looks at her condescendingly and leaves. Jas also is about to leave toward the helicopter, I believe, but Nick grabs her arm. "Jas, wait a minute."

"Get off me! I want to be alone!" she protests wriggling free, and she leaves Nick with a sad face to watch her go away. I, of course, follow her but before disappearing into the darkness that leads toward the helicopter I hear Patrick ask the others: "It is not strange that they came to us? Why risk being arrested?"

***

The hot air that enters the room wakes me. Jas is not in her bed. I look at the clock on the wall; it's five in the morning.

I get out of bed and go toward the balcony; I see her leaning on the railing wearing only underpants and vest looking at the advertising hoarding on the skyscraper opposite, with the sign *Do you give in?!*

Is it really so hot out here and there is a frightening silence. The only thing you can hear is the wind blowing through the skyscrapers. It is really a nice show.

I approach slowly so as not to scare her and whisper: "Jas?"

She looks at me, by no means surprised, with a half-smile. "Hey."

"Why are you still awake?"

"I can't sleep." She turns once again to the skyscraper with a deep breath without adding anything else. I feel I'm in the way, perhaps it is better to leave her with her thoughts. "Do you want me to leave you alone?"

"No."

I feel that she's sincere and she really doesn't want to be alone out here. I lean on the railing too. "Why can't you sleep, Jas?"

I wait for her reply, even a monosyllable, but nothing. This time she doesn't even look at me, she stares into space and the only thing she does is shrug her shoulders. Silence is over-rated; I always say that, even if in this moment my Jas has told me more than she would have wanted to. I look at the writing opposite and say: "Wait for me here a moment."

I don't know what to do. I run into the room, straight to my closet, almost tripping over once or twice, I take the red packet from the drawer and return to the balcony. Jas looks at me with raised eyebrows.

"This is my birthday present for you", I say. I take her hands and give it to her, as she continues to look at me with raised eyebrows.

"I was waiting for the right time to give it to you and something tells me that this is the right time."

She smiles and starts to shake the gift near her ear trying to understand what's inside. "What is it?"

"Open it."

She tears the red paper and throws it from the fiftieth floor of the building. She looks at the gift. Her face finally lights up, and then she asks me: "What is it?"

"A diary, Jas." It seems obvious to me.

"Our new stupidiary!"

"No, it's just a diary", I take it from her hands and open it. "I've seen that you only had a few pages left in yours so I got you a new one. That way everything you aren't able to say out loud, you can write it in words, here inside, inside your diary."

"I don't want to write diaries anymore", she whispers.

I hit her on the head with the diary. "Yes you will, instead", I insist and I give it to her again. She begins to flick through it with a sulky face. I hug her hard. I would have preferred that she talk with me, but I understand what she is going through and I am more and more convinced that this diary will help her to understand. I know my Jas and I know that she doesn't talk to me because she doesn't know what to say and not because she doesn't want to.

***

The day after

Highlander has transformed into a piranha. Now I'm afraid to go anywhere near the aquarium. Every step I take to go from there onto the balcony it stares at me with its narrow eyes, follows me and shows its teeth. Who would have ever said that the little black fish of last year would first change its color to red and immediately after change back to a black fish again, big and bad. What is most disturbing in all of this is that it seems happy; it splashes around inside the dirty aquarium watching us, and every so often takes a bite at the plastic container, but it's happy.

"Where are you?" I hear my Jas call. She's out of the bathroom at last. She looks around trying to figure out where I am.

"Here", I answer popping out from under the bed. She looks at me raising her eyebrows. "What are you doing sitting on the floor?"

"I was taking the measurements; I'll soon have to put it in a bathtub, Jas."

"What are you talking about?"

I indicate the aquarium with my thumb. "Highlander! He's getting bigger by the day! In a few months we'll have a shark for a pet!"

She comes to the table smiling at my bad quip; as soon as the fish sees her it begins to swim all happy from one part of the aquarium to another. For a moment it seems to be smiling at her with its pointed little teeth.

Jas sighs. "You know, I'm beginning to have a certain respect for him. I've been trying to get rid of him for almost a year but he's still here, happy and stronger than before, my big little mutant." She starts to talk to it as she feeds it, as if it's a little child: "You're my little mutant, aren't you? But of course you are. My darling little mutant."

What a strange scene. As she panders to Highlander, it looks at her and wags its tail like a dog. Incredible.

I lie down on my bed and exclaim: "Something normal in your own life no, eh? You have a mutant fish, a zombie friend in a coma, you've got a crush on a vampire and you", I take a good look at her and note with astonishment, "You have dry hair?"

"I don't understand the connection, but..."

"You've been in the bathroom for an hour and a half and you come out with dry hair? What the hell have you done in there all this time? I don't understand."

"There is nothing to understand", she cuts short going to get dressed behind a door of the closet. There is an incredible mess on the floor, what with clothes, suitcases and stiletto shoes. Maybe I shouldn't complain about her extended stay in the bathroom, after all, it's the only place she always keeps clean.

"Well, anyway, while you were in the bathroom Patrick came by looking for you", I tell her.

"Patrick?" Her head comes out of the closet immediately. "And what did he say?"

This interest she has in him annoys me. "Nothing, he just asked where you were."

"And what did you say?"

I cross my arms. "And what should I have said, excuse me? That you'd been in the bathroom for an hour."

She doesn't ask anything else.

I'm tired of all these mysteries.

While she finishes getting dressed I move my leg nervously on the bed. Why doesn't she talk to me about him? Why doesn't she tell me what's going on? I can't stand it any longer. I recompose myself and begin: "Jas, can I ask you a question?"

"Of course", she says absently, continuing to poke around into the disorder and ending by throwing the clothes right and left.

"What is there between you and Patrick?"

Clothes instantly stop flying and silence falls. She doesn't come out from behind the open door for quite a while. Then I see her blond hair poke out and her face tells me everything. She is clearly surprised by my question, looks at me in silence and is about to say something when I hear someone knocking at the door.

"Jas, can I come in?" Damn. It's Nick. He enters and I raise my eyes to heaven. His extraordinary timing is annoying. Very annoying.

"I don't understand why you ask when you're already inside?" she replies irritated, obviously still angry about what happened yesterday at the wedding, while I am for what has happened now.

"Can we talk?"

"If you mean in the literal sense of the phrase, yes. You and me, on the other hand, no!" She sits on the bed, annoyed by Nick's presence while he turns to me and I know that it's time for me to clear off.

I stand up from the bed huffing, again. "Okay, okay, I get it! I'm going... to clean the handle, as usual."

"You're not going anywhere to clean anything!" Jas instructs me.

I don't know what to do, or where to go. I feel myself surrounded, just like has been happening to me often, lately. They all stare at me and their eyes do the talking.

Nick tells me *to go out immediately*, Jas *don't even try it*, and Highlander *come here and I'll bite you.*

I sit on the tape on the floor that divides our room, crossing my arms angrily. I don't think it right to be put in the midst of their bickering, I have nothing to do with it.

Nick sits down on my bed pushing away the colored soft toys with one hand, while holding a magazine with the other, or perhaps just some rolled up paper, I can't tell from where I'm sitting. With a serious face he turns to Jas, sitting on the bed opposite him. "I don't know where to start what I have to say. I'm really in difficulty right now and I'd ask you to please not interrupt me, if possible". He makes a big sigh and Jas continues to look at him incensed, "On your birthday..."

"I don't want to talk about it now", she interrupts him and looks at me. I don't understand this thing.

"I spoke to you about choices", Nick finishes anyway and looks at her in a strange way. I can see her biting her lips, "About how sometimes it is difficult to know the right thing to do, which road to take, decide, cut off. Whatever you do, it always ends the same way: you must make a choice. Today I will give you the chance to do this, and your future will depend on this choice."

I don't understand where he's going and from the way Jas looks at him I don't think she understands either.

"Since February you've kept telling me that you don't believe in justice."

Jas raises her eyes to heaven.

"And at this point, I don't blame you", Nick pauses briefly and she and I both look at him in surprise, "I look at the facts and the facts have shown that, every time I've reassured you about something, I've been proven wrong. Yesterday was one of those times too. I'm so very sorry. I don't want to push you to do anything you don't want to do, but unfortunately, given the recent events I can no longer wait, Jas. It's time to make a choice, now. You're either in or you're out, you can no longer choose a middle ground."

"Middle ground? But what are you saying?" she raises her voice annoyed.

"You must let me explain..."

"Explain *what*? I hate the middle ground! You don't know what you're saying!"

"I know perfectly well what I'm saying, but I never manage to speak and finish a concept because you don't let me", he reproaches her, "I can never express myself as I want to because you continue to interrupt me, or stop me or run away."

"I don't run away!" she interrupts him again. They're silent for a moment and then she adds with a calm voice, "Talk. Why are you here? What do you want from me?"

"A choice. That's what I want. But to make a choice you need to know between what you're choosing. That's why I'm here."

He gets up from my bed, goes to the door and sticks a poster on it. "Do you want to be this?" He moves and I see that the image on the poster depicts Jas dressed in school uniform. "A light-hearted high school student, live a normal life with normal problems, study so that one day you find a good job and create a family? Or do you want to become like her?" He attaches another poster to the door and he moves away I recognize the image straight away; the dark eyes of the mysterious detective Jx. "Or like Jx?" he continues, "Follow and force people to follow the rules, live a dangerous life, yes, but with many personal satisfactions and achievements. Make the world you live in a better place?" He kneels in front of her, taking her hands and speaking to her gently: "You can choose to be what you want, Jas, because you have the possibility to do so, and I'll give you my support in any case; however, you also need to see my world up close. You already know how to be the student, but what it's like to work under cover, what it's like working with me, is something you don't know. I want to make you believe again in law and justice, but to teach you how to change your idea, you need to touch my world with your hands, see it with your eyes, and feel it, as I do."

I see Jas in great difficulty. I know that gaze, it's the look in her eyes that says *I don't feel like it, don't ask me this, I don't feel well*, it's the gaze that Nick can never see or perhaps does not want to see. Jas pulls back her hands, separating them from his, takes the diary that I gave her tonight from the bed, and begins to crumple it nervously. "What are you proposing? That I work with you? But you've even been taken off the case because of me"

"I haven't been taken off the case because of you. I'm not asking you to work, you're too young, and you still have a long way to go before becoming a detective, I'm asking you to cooperate with the law, and find out for yourself what I've been trying to tell you for years. Then you can decide what to do with your life. I need you to tell me, I need to know how to conduct myself with you, not only in this difficult situation, but in the future as well."

Jas looks at the two posters stuck on the door next to each other, her eyes bright with tears. My instinct is to get up and go and hug her. Can't Nick see that she is ill and this is perhaps not the right time to be talking about this kind of thing?

"Jas, say something, please", I urge her.

"I am not able to... I don't... I don't know." She can't even speak and I feel bad for her. Sitting on the floor between my half of the room and hers is as if I had a different perspective - somehow in a clearer way - of both of them. Nick has unclouded and well-defined ideas, like my half of the room where he's kneeling, which is clean and has bright colors; and Jas is confused, disoriented and sad, like the disorder and the black that prevails in her half.

Nick moves the diary out of her hands and starts to stroke them gently. "I want to talk Nick to Jas? Is that okay?"

She nods her head.

"The idea that you can go out with that delinquent terrifies me, believe me, but if you think about it perhaps it's the best thing that has happened to us."

She looks at him with an expression of someone wondering what is good about it.

"It isn't possible to predict everything and this is as true for us representatives of the law as it is for criminals. If you choose to get to know my world, her world," he says pointing to the poster of Jx, "and if you agree to help us, we'll frame Jack because he won't be expecting your full involvement. With this arrest not only will it show you how the system works, if you just follow the rules, but also demonstrate to Felix and others that I am able to work with you without losing control. I want you believe again." He puts a lock of hair behind her ear.

"I'm afraid", admits Jas in a small voice.

"Of what?" he asks kindly.

"Of doing something stupid, to go too far, to... I don't know how to follow the rules Nick."

"I trust in you, and I know that you can do it."

"It's me who doesn't trust me anymore. I am afraid I'll be manipulated once again, tricked. I have already lost my way once, Nick, I am afraid of losing myself again."

227

"Nothing will happen, this time I'll be there with you, you won't lose your way, and I'm going to show you the right road, Jas. I'm sure that if you accept to get to know my world, you will follow the rules to the letter. I know it. You won't lose your way, I promise."

Jas has tears in her eyes. She lets go of Nick's hands and covers her face. He sits on her bed, and hugs her tightly. "Do you think that I'm not afraid? I'm more afraid than you. Except that I do everything I can to hide it in front of the others."

"Afraid of what?"

"The usual, the thing that made me say last year that you weren't fit to work with me, the fear that something will happen to you, the fear of not being able to control myself when I think you're in danger and shoot him if he even tries to touch you!" he says to her with an angry tone, holding her face tight in his hands looking straight into her eyes. I wait for him to continue with the speech, or get up and do something, but nothing happens. They look at each other in silence as Nick's thumbs gently stroke her face.

I feel uncomfortable, or perhaps it is not only discomfort, but also a feeling of being in the way.

As I look at them open-mouthed and move closer to finally see what everyone has been expecting for years, Jas notices me and moves away from Nick, breaking the spell.

I'm there like an idiot in the middle of the room, on all fours with wide-open eyes and I say to justify myself: "I was looking for the... little ball, no, the Highlander's... bone." As usual I never know how to say the right thing at the right moment. Nick looks at me like I'm a ballbreaker and with my head down and tail between my legs I return to my original position, still on all fours.

How embarrassing!

Nick turns back to Jas. No titillating scenes this time; he sits down at an appropriate distance, clearly embarrassed, and continues his speech: "What I wanted to make you understand is that it will be difficult to look at Jack, withstand his provocations and not be able to do anything, but I'll face up to him. Together we can do it."

"Okay."

"Wait, wait," he quickly interrupts her, "Before you decide definitively, I want to talk to you also from detective to victim."

"Meaning how?"

"There are moments where you have to choose with your head, and others where you have to choose with your heart. When it comes to work, your choice must be dictated always, always with your head. Do you understand what I mean? "

"No."

"Do you know what the difference is between revenge and justice, Jas?"

"Yes. You take revenge because you're angry, because you need it. It's a personal thing, it makes you feel better. And justice is what you do because the system imposes it on you. If you can do that, okay; and if you can't, amen, let's look at another case."

"It's not really like that. Justice is balanced by a human being's other qualities. It is driven by the noble sentiments. It is directed against someone who has done something illegal, or anyone who has done a wrong, to prevent that person from continuing to hurt others, whereas revenge is dictated solely by a negative feeling, bitterness and hatred. It is a settling of accounts that always ends with bloodshed, one bad action that generates more bad acts. If you choose to accept it, you must give me the guarantee that is not revenge that you're looking for, Jas, but justice. Bringing Jack to justice for the crimes he has committed, so you have to choose with rationality, with your head. If you think you can't do it then please, I beg of you, don't accept. This is my only condition. As much as I want to have you rethink my job and have others believe in you again, I could not tolerate taking part in your personal revenge."

"I'm in" Jas pledges.

She gets off the bed looking at the two posters attached to the door.

Nick remains seated, visibly concerned. "Jas, I need to be reassured."

"He saved my life. I think that should be enough to reassure you."

In a flash Nick stands up, embraces her hard and kisses her on the forehead. "Welcome to the team."

I am not sure I've really understood what has just happened in here, but the more I look at the two posters stuck on the door, the more I realize that they have absolutely nothing to do with my Jas.

38.

From Jas's diary – Breakfast at dinner time, preparations

I still don't know if I let myself be convinced by Nick to collaborate, or if I only pretended to let myself be convinced. The fact remains that in the end everyone was convinced of something, except me.

When Felix arrived this morning with his four men dressed like the looser version of *men in black* and said *follow me* with that serious and authoritarian tone of voice, the first thing I thought was a huge *twenty two*, meaning *go away!*

It was only the first in a series of numbers that shortly afterwards multiplied and changed into a series of swear words.

39.

My Jas has been closed with Felix and his gorillas the entire afternoon, in the offices of the *Watchtower*, while Nick and the rest of his team can only look on from afar.

It's not easy for anyone.

We walk up and down the corridors, agitated, making even America get so jumpy that she eventually shuts herself in the living room with Ben's kids.

Who knows what Jas is doing? Who knows if she is able to put up with Felix, but above all who knows how she is feeling in this moment, because it's only ten minutes until her appointment with Jack.

I feel my heart in my throat. I look at the others and notice that they're worse off than me: they're staring at the wall clock in silence, swinging their legs and drumming their fingers on the table.

What tension! I don't know how long I can resist. Meanwhile my nails have become non-existent I've bitten them so much.

"I don't care!" we hear Jas shouting angrily. Her voice resounds from the other side of the wall. We look at each other without saying anything and the next moment we're already in the hallway that leads from the living room toward the hall. Jas is near America's counter, she is adjusting something on her trousers, while Felix and one of his henchmen, both very annoyed, are trying to make her stop.

"Do you understand that it hurts me, or not?" she is protesting.

"Just stop complaining for once!" says Felix at this point fed up and very, very tired. While we others stop at the end of the counter, Nick immediately approaches them and asks: "What's going on here?"

"She doesn't want to collaborate! She is wearing us all out!"

"What? I am collaborating! I've been doing that for twelve hours! It's not my fault if you can't keep up with me!"

Felix sighs, exasperated: "Nick, please, say something to her! She even told me to go to hell earlier!"

"Go to hell?" she smiles amused, "To tell the truth, I was more precise!"

"Nickolas! Tell her to stop this!"

While they bicker, I notice that I am the only one watching and listening to them in a normal way, because the others around me are using tactics which are, to put it mildly, comic as they do the same thing and I don't understand why. Veronica pretends to talk on the phone, Will is sitting in his usual chair reading a magazine, but he's holding it upside down, and Ben is pretending to watch TV, trying to change the channel with the remote control of the microwave that has inadvertently been brought from the kitchen.

America, on the other hand, is really doing her work and, from the way she is looking at them, it is clear that she doesn't like this farce in the lease. Nick in the meantime is trying to understand why Jas and Felix are squabbling. "What's the problem, Jas?"

"Have you had a good look at me? I look like Robocop!"

I can barely hold back the laughter; in fact she is full of strange gadgets all over her with wires popping out from her t-shirt which one of the gorillas is trying desperately to disguise. I have never seen such a thing.

"And what's more the bracelet is too tight, take it off me!"

Nick signs and explains to her: "Jas, there is a localization system in it, and this wire transmits audio and video to a remote receiver, which is our computer. It will allow Felix to follow and protect you in every moment. It is for your safety."

"And to gather evidence", adds Felix.

"Yes, and to gather evidence", he repeats just to make him happy. Then he turns to look at Jas, who continues to look at Felix scowling. "Come here", he says to her, and they move toward the display in front of the desk, thinking they'll be away from prying eyes, but in reality Ben and the others have ears like Dumbo. Nick whispers: "Did they tell you that you need take note of every detail when you're at dinner? You must not neglect any detail, everything is important."

"Nick, what are all these things for?"

"You are about to go out with a criminal! For your safety it's..."

"No, you don't understand. Do you really think he is so stupid not to expect me to get out of that elevator fully fitted?"

I think that with *he* she is referring to Jack, and her question is actually sensible; it's just a pity that Nick doesn't have time to answer it, seeing that Felix goes between them putting something in Jas's ear. "Through this earpiece I can communicate with you."

Jas yells in pain, which Felix completely ignores and tells her: "And you have to say and do everything I tell you."

"But of course!" exclaims Jas.

"Let's do a test," says Felix, and puts a tiny microphone near his mouth and shouts into it, "Test!"

Jas screams and protests: "Are you doing this on purpose?"

I see Nick in difficulty again. He takes her arm and leads her away from Felix.

"Don't go on like this, please", he kisses her on the forehead, trying to calm her.

"Guys, all go to your positions, it's eight on the dot! Is the van ready?" Felix speaks to no-one holding his hand over his ear, as he goes toward the offices. Jas continues to look him up and down saying a low voice: "I can't stand him! How do you manage to get along with that Kunta Kinte?"

"Jas, stop it, it's not polite to speak in this way", he whispers to her, hoping that Felix hasn't heard her, "Remember that there is no success without the team, and he is part of the team."

"I don't give a damn, I don't want him around."

"Be quiet, you made a choice, you said that you want to know my world, so stop complaining", he rebukes her, "From today onwards you have to work together, follow all the rules, but especially the law. You can no longer afford to be arrested, denounced by someone, or throw punches at people. You know this, don't you?"

"Yes, yes, I know," she says short and not happy at all.

"Remember that you're doing it for a good cause."

She doesn't seem at all convinced by his words.

"Jas?"

"Yes, yes, I heard, it's for a good cause, okay."

While they continue to do their usual sappy scenes, I turn toward all the others who are following Felix and his gorillas with

234

their gaze and watching their every move, but still pretending to do other things. They make me laugh.

"Chief, a box is coming up," says America turned to Nick while the elevator door opens. Everyone leaps in front of it: Felix, his men, Nick, while the others in his team are still pretending they're not interested in what is happening. The door opens and much to our surprise there really is just a box inside, all black with a white bow.

We look at each other, surprised, and immediately after we look at America who, with great composure, answers us as she continues to write on her computer. "I told you a box was coming up."

Felix's men slowly approach with some strange equipment that emits lights and sounds which are even stranger. Only after they have checked it out do they pick it up and put it on the counter. They all look at it intrigued, except Jas, who is sitting on the bench under the pegboard where I usually sit. Felix takes the card which is sitting on the box and reads: "For Jas."

"What? For me?"

She literally jumps off the bench, running toward the counter, as Felix has just pulled out of the box the most beautiful dress I've ever seen in my life. It's gorgeous, all black, interlaced front and back, with glittering stones sewn on the shoulder straps and from inside the box shines a beautiful pair of high heels. Both the dress and the heels light up the room leaving us all agape.

"Wow..." I whisper, dazzled by such beauty.

Felix puts the dress inside the box screaming nervously: "Damn him! Plan B, hurry up boys, quick! Plan B!" He runs toward the offices to do who knows what.

Nick is dark in the face. He takes the dress in his hands and in an angry tone exclaims: "No, no, no! She is not going to wear this!"

Nobody dares to say anything. Ben, Veronica and Will pretend not to see or hear, one is still reading the magazine upside down, the other is speaking in Spanish on the phone with mister *nobody* and Ben gets angry with the remote control of the microwave because it doesn't change channels on the TV.

Felix returns to the hall and Nick reiterates: "She is not going to wear this!"

"You're not the one who'll decide!" Felix points out and takes the box from the counter. "Jas, you have to change clothes, hurry up!"

"I'm coming, I'm coming!" she exclaims, but before she leaves she pats Nick on the back and with a smile on her lips says to him: "Nick, don't be like that, from now on you can't be protective and jealous anymore, so stop complaining. You have to follow the law, you have to collaborate, there is no success without the team, remember that you do it for a good cause", she smiles looking at him with her cheeky eyes and follows Felix all satisfied to the offices of the *Watchtower,* leaving Nick standing there in the hall and not happy at all.

Only after they have gone, Ben and the others stop acting like clowns and approach Nick with serious expressions. They don't say a thing, they just stand close to him and it seems strange to me that Patrick isn't there too; he's usually the one who knows how to calm Nick in these situations.

America breaks the silence: "Boss, a black limousine has just parked in front of the *Watchtower*", and continues to write on her computer as she speaks. Ben, Will and Veronica dash quickly behind the counter to look at this limousine in the security cameras. I go over too, curious, when I hear the elevator door open. I turn and see Nick enter the elevator with a black bag in his hand.

"Nick!" Ben calls immediately, worried, "Where do you think you're going? You can't interfere, remember?"

"It's my building and I'm free to move around inside as I like", he states without turning a hair, and disappears behind the closed door of the elevator.

40.

Two minutes later – From Jx's diary

The elevator stops in the basement of the *Watchtower*. The door opens, and out walks Nick, very serious and tense. His eyes are fixed on the exit where Jack is waiting for him, leaning on the black limousine with a smile on his face.

He goes toward the panoramic glass door and down the steps of the skyscraper without acknowledging him. He puts the black bag on the ground, slowly, looking closely at Jack's Beretta which pokes out from under the stylish jacket.

"What's the matter? Does the gun clash with my evening suit?" asks Jack with a bold air, still leaning on the limousine. "It's registered, if that's what you are interested in."

"Don't dare use that weapon in front of her, I'm warning you!" says Nick harshly, but Jack's reaction is not that of someone who is afraid of him and his warnings. On the contrary, he begins to laugh amused, bending over as if the laugh is about to stifle him. "You are warning *me*?" he ridicules him, "I lose sight of you for a few months and here you are again with a sense of humor." He pretends to brush the tears of laughter from his eyes and then approaches Nick becoming suddenly serious. "Let me explain something to you, Big Boy. You don't represent a risk for me, just a nuisance, a nuisance that I'll get rid of very soon."

They look straight in each other's eyes.

"What do you want from her?"

"An opportunity to tell her why I did what I did," says Jack.

"What you did?" repeats Nick and shakes his head outraged. "What you did has a name, it is called mass murder!"

"It's called whatever you decide to call it," replies Jack with great simplicity.

"Of course, who knows better than you? And you, what have you decided to call yourself today? John Dillinger? James Dean? Jack Black? Or have you chosen to use some other false identity for the occasion?"

"It is not the name that counts, but the personality," he scoffs, smiling in his face.

"Always pretending to be someone else, you end up being no-one."

"No-one", repeats Jack pretending to be surprised. "You say that with contempt, as if it were an empty word, without depth or importance."

"Because it is, and you're the living proof."

Jack smiles again. "And yet, in the history of mankind, it has often been the *no-ones* that have made the difference. You should know something about that."

"What are you talking about?"

"What? Now you're pretending that nothing happened? You've already forgotten? I'm talking about the Valentine's Day evening. I can still see Jas's terrified eyes, while you reassured me telling me that you'd come to save us from the Albanians. But you didn't arrive, not in time, at least. And do you know who saved her from Borak and his lovely little friends? The one you are looking at with contempt, describing him as nobody!" he says his voice becoming louder, "I made the difference that night, *I* did! I'm great!" He goes toward Nick until he is a few inches away from his face. "And what did you do? Nothing! And doing nothing, Nickolas, is worse than being nobody. So get that expression of superiority off your face when you speak to me."

Nick remains in silence, clenches his fists while the memories of that cursed evening run through his mind. Jack smiles again, knowing that he has cut him to the quick. He moves away from him and leans on the limousine once again. "You know, I like it when you're nervous, and I like it when I am the cause of your nervousness", he continues to provoke him, "And do you know what it is that I like most about you?" he asks looking toward the entry over Nick's shoulders. His blue eyes light up.

Nick responds with clenched teeth "No. "

"Jas."

Nick turns around, and is gob smacked.

41.

A minute before – From Mina's diary

I can't take my eyes off her. If last year I thought she was wearing a sexy dress at Halloween, now I don't know which word to use to describe her. Being blond, the black dress suits her to a tee, the dizzying split and the plunging neckline make her look like a real woman.

She doesn't look at herself in the mirror of the elevator, she crumples the very elegant evening bag in her hands while I just try to avoid looking at the size of her breast that seems to shout *look at me, look at me.* Time tends to lengthen when you try not to do something that you desperately want to do.

The elevator door opens and the first thing I see are Jack's deep blue eyes looking in our direction. He's at a distance, yet his eyes speak, and it is not difficult to understand what he's thinking after seeing Jas. He says something to Nick and when he also turns toward us he is turned to stone. First he is amazed at the beauty of Jas and then gets angry because of the provocative dress.

The closer we get to them, the more agitated I feel. Jack has a strange effect on me. He' leaning on the limousine, elegantly dressed and his blond hair blowing in the wind. *Damn!*

He smiles, a perfect smile of course, and gives Jas a compliment: "Darling, you're beautiful."

Jas does not even look at him, she goes straight to Nick with a concerned air and the first thing she does is ask him: "Nick, is everything okay?"

"Yes", he answers, more or less convinced.

She hides in his arms for a moment and then looks at him gently putting his hair behind his ear. "It's not true, what happened? What did he say to you?" she asks, looking daggers at Jack.

"Nothing, don't worry", he replies in a calm voice caressing her back, carefully avoiding to look at her from the neck down.

Jack is becoming green in the face. He squints at them as they continue to whisper together, locked in their impenetrable world.

He lowers his gaze, annoyed, saying in an angry tone: "We must go."

"We?" asks Jas, turning angrily toward him, "You have to quit putting you and me in the same sentence!"

"Do you know some other way to say that we're late and that we have to go without putting us in the same sentence, by any chance?" he needles her.

"Jas", whispers his Nick, and the pulls her close, "Self-control, self-control", he repeats and meanwhile lifts her wrist touching the bracelet.

The more the seconds pass, the more I see Jack become edgy.

Jas takes a deep breath. She nods her head and, whispering, she asks him: "And if I cross the line? And if I get lost?" She seems worried, insecure of herself, and to see her in this state is a total shock for me. I would never have expected it from her. Nick, though, is unphased; he smiles and puts Jas's hand on the gold compass hanging around his neck. "If you get lost, I'll find you."

These words are enough to tranquilize her. Jas smiles, while Jack behind her says: "Have to go!"

I can barely hold back my laughter. I can't let it be seen on the outside, but inside me little Mina is laughing out loud, lying on the ground and with one leg raised in the air as I laugh usually. Jas looks at him askance and then says goodbye to Nick: "See you later." She is also about to say goodbye to me when Nick stops her. "Wait, before you go I have to give you something else."

He kneels next to a black bag on the ground and takes a bulletproof vest from it. She quickly holds out her handbag to me smiling, and with Nick's help she puts it on as Jack stares at them speechless, totally incredulous. Nick smiles at her and whispers: "What is the first rule?"

"Never go out without your bulletproof vest."

They exchange this complicit gaze. After which she looks at me and winks, then goes to the limousine where Jack, very elegantly, but still with an annoyed face because of the vest, opens the door for her. Jas says nothing, she gets in without objecting. Jack gives Nick a provocative smile and, when he is about to climb into the car as well, the door closes in front of his nose.

"Hey!" he protests surprised as the window is lowered and Jas with a challenging air goes: "I am forced to dine with you, but not to travel with you to get there, so go and sit in front."

Without looking at us, Jack walks all the way around the limousine and sits next to the driver, not happy at all. Nick smiles with satisfaction, the limousine departs, and as soon as it turns the corner, Felix's men appear, running to a white van which has just pulled up on the sidewalk. Felix is the last to come out; he rests his hand on Nick's shoulder and tries to reassure him, saying: "We won't lose sight of her even for an instant. Don't worry." He gets into the white van as well and they disappear rapidly around the corner.

It's now just me and Nick standing outside the *Watchtower*. Embarrassed by the silence that affects us every time we're alone, I'm about to go up the steps and leave when I hear him say in a low voice: "I'm not worried."

I don't know who he's talking to, perhaps he's just reassuring himself.

I arrive at the elevator, I push the button, the door opens and I see myself reflected in the mirror; still all red in the face from the discomfort that Jack causes me every time I see him, and still all red all over my body from sunburn and... still holding Jas's handbag!

42.

From Jas's diary – Breakfast at dinner time

I am good at manipulating people, at lying, at saying one thing and thinking another. I spend most of the days not revealing the truth about what I really do... so why do I feel so strange and very uncomfortable doing all these things, now? I'm nervous, my heart is about to go crazy and Felix's continuous instructions through the headset certainly don't help me. "Take a good look around inside the limo to see if there's anything, like a used glass or a hair on the seat, or on the ground. Pick it up nonchalantly and put it in your handbag without being noticed."

"Oops."

"Oops? What does *oops* mean?" he asks.

"That I don't have it, my bag," I explain.

"What? What do you mean you don't have your bag?"

"It means exactly what I said," I murmur annoyed, "I gave it to Mina so I could put on the flak jacket and I forgot to take it back."

He doesn't even reply. I guess he's cursing, letting off steam with his looser *Men in Black.* I look around, but apart from Lexi's usual alcoholic drinks I don't find anything that can be of help to the investigation. And even if I did have my purse, I wouldn't be able to stick the bottles inside it. But they are very beautiful and colorful. I've never seen such multicolored hard liquor. I take a bottle, but just to see what the drink is called, when I hear Felix's irritating voice yelling in my ear: "Put that bottle down right this minute! You don't drink alcohol during a mission!"

Who wanted to drink? I'm sick of him!

The limousine stops. I look out the window and I recognize the district. This is the Art Deco District, full of pink, lavender and turquoise buildings. I see John come to the door and open it for me with a great big smile. He holds out his hand to me which of course I don't take, even though actually getting out of the car with the very heavy flak jacket and the vertiginous heels is not easy.

"I'm going home by taxi", I state. I want this thing to be clear. He makes a strange face raising his eyebrows, and still with his hand outstretched he gestures to me to enter the building in front of us.

We go inside. Everything is very sumptuous, without a shadow of doubt, full of mirrors and objects of inestimable value. Everything's nice, yes, if it were not for a tiny detail: there is not a living soul here except us.

While we cross the huge hall to reach the elevator, the only thing you can hear is the echo of my stiletto heels. Terrifying situation.

We go up in the elevator. To avoid his gaze, I look at the numbers that light up as we climb; he does nothing but stare at me. The elevator door opens and I find myself in front of... darkness. All you can see is a table close to the panoramic window, illuminated by some candles on table candelabra, while all the rest seems to be deserted.

I turn toward John who continues to smile, all proud, confident that he has made who knows which grand gesture and I spontaneously ask: "What happened here? Has the restaurant gone out of business?"

The smile disappears from his face. "No, it hasn't gone out of business. I booked. Everything. The restaurant," he says slowly, annoyed and disappointed by my question.

I raise my eyes to heaven as he goes to the only illuminated table in the whole restaurant. I approach the table too, when suddenly someone moves my chair. I turn suddenly with a fright and I see Koki, the Japanese I saw at Ben's wedding. I have no idea where he sprang from. He's dressed as a waiter, with his black hair tied in a ponytail, white gloves and a chef's hat on his head. He smiles. "Good evening, Miss Jas, would you like to take off your bulletproof vest so we can better admire your décolleté?"

"No!" I reply, and I sit down glaring at him. I'm distracted for just a moment and Koki disappears just as he had appeared. I look around but he's no longer there. *How did he do that?*

I'm alone with John in a dark, empty restaurant, and with Felix who is, according to him, reassuring me that his men are outside in a building opposite with their weapons pointed at us.

I look out the window, terrified, taking a deep breath. *I can't do this!*

243

"Do you like what you see?" he asks again with the same confident and bold air.

I retort: "The only thing I like in here is my bulletproof vest."

"You've forced me to do all this; all I wanted was a chance to be able to explain myself."

I want to jump onto the table and take him by the neck. But I will not, Nick has said that I have to know how to manage myself. *Self-control Jas, self-control*, I repeat touching the bracelet on my wrist. Felix also continues to tell me to control myself. I take a deep breath before speaking: "I'm here now, so explain yourself. I do want to hear what you have to say, John!"

"My name is Jack! Jack!"

"Since when?"

The atmosphere is already heating up. He fixes me irately with those blue eyes of his that stand out in the darkness around us, while I pretend I can't give a damn even if in reality this whole situation is making me somewhat nervous.

I hear yelling behind me: "You deceived me!" Lexi arrives at our table, with her *very sober* manners and turns to me with the glass of Martini in her hands. "When you called me, you said you wanted to surprise him!" Obviously she is referring to the idiot in front of me and the *prank* with Franklin.

"In fact he was very surprised."

"But you had him arrested!"

"I know."

"Well, you didn't tell me that was a nasty surprise!" she reproaches me.

"I didn't tell you it was a nice one either."

"You said that you hate surprises!"

"If they play them on me, not if I do them."

"*Thousand*! You don't even deserve the embrace of peace from me! You don't do things like that! And above all to my little brother!" She can barely stand up. She's wearing a waitress's mini-dress up to her armpits, red lipstick and a black wig of very short hair. Her every gesture seems to come from the scene of some sexy Italian film from the eighties.

The typical girl who doesn't like to show herself off, very old-fashioned I'd say. The girl next door, yeah, a girl all peaches and... I don't remember that other word.

Lexi interrupts my sarcastic thoughts when she stoops down to me with the intention of showing me her neckline, and without letting John hear her, she tells me breathing in my face: "If ever you're interested in working for my law firm, this is my number. We need people like you", she almost wheezes as I slip one of her red business cards, covered with rhinestones, into the bulletproof vest.

Another?

She goes off swaying somewhere, disappearing into the darkness of the restaurant, and Koki arrives with a tray with various fruit juices, tea, milk, coffee, and a freshly squeezed orange juice. I can't believe this; it seems John was serious when he said that he was inviting me to breakfast.

My first instinct is to throw myself onto the just made cup of cappuccino. The aroma is the same as the ones they make in Italy, the froth is calling me, but I restrain myself. Felix told me not to drink or eat anything, and I will not do so, even if I'm very tempted to.

"You can take a first sip if you don't trust it."

Apparently he has become aware of my hesitation. "*If* I don't trust it?"

He lowers his gaze for a moment, then takes the straw and puts it into cappuccino and takes a sip of it.

"Didn't your mother tell you that the coffee makes you edgy, John?" I ask provoking him, but he doesn't reply and a frightening silence falls again. I don't want to talk to him, nor do I want to hear his pathetic justifications about what happened in Gorizia. But what I want at this moment is not important, especially because I continue to hear the irritating voice of Felix encouraging me to speak and ask him questions.

I look to the heavens, while John decides to ask me: "Do you have any questions for me or would you like me to start at the beginning."

"Don't be too direct, that's best," Felix suggests to me via the earpiece. I take a deep breath and immediately ask my first *not direct* question: "Are you a killer type?"

"What the f...?" the half vulgarity from Felix is appropriate, actually, but I couldn't help it. John looks at me with a strange smile. "I work for one person, who worked for another person, who wanted to see some people dead."

My question may have even been direct, but his response has nothing direct about it. He does this on purpose. Felix, nervous now though, threatens to do I don't know what if I do I don't know what again.

I continue with the non-direct questions: "Are you a thief?"

Okay, this was more obvious, rather than non-direct.

Felix hisses my first name and surname in the earpiece as a sign of reproach.

John answers me with the same little provocative smile: "I procure very, very rare objects for a select clientele, for information which is even more rare and important than the objects themselves." Once again he has replied in a vague kind of way. He speaks but doesn't say, and this is beginning to irritate me. "Is that why you stole the headmistress's cross?"

"The cross was stolen by the Nazis from a Jew in Switzerland, seventy years ago. All I did was to return it to its rightful owner." Not only does he continue to give me idiotic answers, but he's also beginning to take the piss. A Nazi who steals a cross? From a Jew? Who does he think he's talking to?

I stand up from the chair and I head towards the elevator.

"Where are you going?"

"If you think that I'm going to stay here and let you keep on with this bullshit you're very much mistaken!"

"What? What have I done now? Stop!" he exclaims. He even seems to be surprised by my reaction and follows me to the elevator.

"What have you done? Do you think I don't know history? A *Nazi* goes to Switzerland to steal a *cross* from a *Jew*?"

"But it's true!"

"Fuck off! I don't believe you even if you lie to me again." I nervously push the button for the elevator with the hope that the door opens as soon as possible. John instead tries to stop me. "There has been a misunderstanding! Let me try to explain!"

He calls this crap that he talks misunderstandings, apparently.

I don't even reply, it's not worth wasting voice and words for him. My mission as an infiltrator has ended before it even began. Just like everything else that concerns my life.

The elevator door opens at last, and who do I find in front of me? Vladimir the mountain. He grips his gun snarling in my face like a rabid animal.

"Down boy..." I murmur peeved, sure that he'll move, and instead he gets out of the elevator and takes a step toward me. Instinctively, I step back; from the way he is looking at me he definitely doesn't want to give me a friendly greeting, and I have confirmation of this when I see John intervene. "Everything is okay, Vladi" he reassures him. He puts himself in front of me, trying to take the gun from his hands, "All is well, give it to me." He speaks to him as if he's mentally unbalanced. Vladimir gives him the gun without removing his icy eyes from me.

Felix, in the meantime, despite the questionable situation, orders me to go back to my place.

I clutch my bulletproof vest in my hands and back away again, while John pats Vladimir on the back, trying to calm him down like a master does with his ferocious dog. Lexi arrives now, but with more tranquility, given her precarious drunken equilibrium; she puts her hand to Vladimir's mouth and says to him: "Come on, come on, you have to swallow them, good boy." She tries to stuff some pills into his mouth, but without success.

And I'm here, standing stock-still watching this scene and expecting that at any moment I'll see someone arrive with the cameras following them shouting *it's a joke*. But this is not the case.

Vladimir continues to growl and fix his eyes on me like someone possessed. I return the gaze, astonished, while John holds him with both hands.

"Vladi! Naughty! Swallow them", Lexi spurs him on, fed up. In the end she pulls a stun-gun from the belt of her skirt and uses it against him, making him collapse on the ground. I continue to back away in fright.

Only like this Vladimir swallows those damn pills.

Koki appears out of nowhere and together with Lexi drags him toward the kitchen. Meanwhile, Vladimir, despite the effect of the stun-gun and the tranquilizers, continues to growl like an animal and repeat: "I hate her."

I find myself closed in a dark and empty restaurant with armed people who are also sick in the head. I can't believe that this is really happening.

John dries his sweaty forehead with the sleeve of his shirt, and with the other hand he brushes my bulletproof vest to accompany me to the table.

"Don't touch me!" I snap annoyed.

He lifts his hands as if to say okay. We sit down again. I hope to get out of here unscathed.

"Excuse him. He's very protective about us. You wanted to leave and he lost control, let's say, when he saw me in difficulty. But he's not bad, he just forgot to take his medicine", he tries to defend him, "Vladi is a good guy."

I look at him without commenting. He stares at me for a moment, waiting for me to say something; instead I just cross my arms and look at him condescendingly.

"I see you bothered by what has just happened, but not scared."

"Listen!" I raise my voice, "I have no desire to be part of this farce, okay? Tell me what you want to tell me, truth or bullshit as it may be, because I'm fed up with the lot of you!"

His gaze changes, he becomes enraged. "Whatever I say, you attack me!" he slams his hand on the tablecloth. "It's difficult enough for me to speak, and the way you carry on certainly doesn't help me!"

"I am not here to help you! Damn piece of sh..."

"Stop offending me!"

"If you didn't want to be offended, you had to stay away from me and leave me in peace!"

"No! I will not leave you!" He thumps his hand on the table again. We look at each other in silence.

I will not leave you.

I don't know why, but as soon as he said it I become stuck, I'm unable to continue speaking, I can't do anything and this does not being able makes me deeply uncomfortable. I'm angry with myself. He closes his eyes for a moment, adjusting his hair, and after taking a deep breath he begins to speak, looking at a fixed point on the table. "I had to come to your school, in Gorizia, to do an inspection, make sure that it was really *that* crucifix that we were looking for, and leave immediately after the coup. But unfortunately when we got ourselves organized, we were not able to complete the job." He continues to look the table, but his expression is different. It's serious, and maybe even sad.

The more I look at him, the more he seems like an actor worthy of an Oscar. He knows extremely well how to behave to get someone's attention; it's just that, in this case, that someone is not falling for it any more. "Who did you come to Gorizia with?" I ask, not giving a hoot about his false state of mind.

He looks up surprised. "With Lexi and Cyrus," he answers, his face still strained, "Koki and Vladimir joined us later."

"Why act the part of the disabled? You could have come, taken the cross and left without any problems."

"We always try to work in a clean way; we tend not to do damage, not to make ourselves noticed and not leave traces. A disabled person is an invisible person. He can move freely through the hallways of the school, and even if I'd been caught poking around in the headmistress's office it would not have been difficult to explain my presence there. But thanks to you and your continuous woes I didn't need any excuses for being there" he, smiles.

I'm not smiling though. "You are the people responsible for the threats to the school?"

"No. All the threats, the slander and the persistence of the journalists against the school were not our work."

"Why did you have to blame those workers for being responsible for the theft?"

With great simplicity, as if the reason that pushed him to place the blame on innocent people was perfectly obvious and normal, he replies: "Everyone wanted *a* guilty person and not *the* guilty person, and I made them happy." Perhaps he feels my contempt is climbing, but he immediately adds: "I knew that they would be acquitted, sooner or later." He takes the napkin, lays it on the handle of the cup and begins to drink the cappuccino, still with the straw. What a cunning move. That way he doesn't leave any fingerprints.

"You said that you work in a clean way, but the way you damaged my school the day of the theft, that didn't seem very clean to me!"

"Like I already said, the day we'd planned to do it, we didn't do it."

"Why? What went wrong?"

"You."

"What?" I ask amazed.

"We were supposed to steal the crucifix the evening of Halloween. It was the ideal evening, everyone in the gym, drunk and busy having a good time, while we would have had easy access and no-one would have noticed a thing. And the following day everyone would have been a suspect. Everyone except disabled people. When the accident with the lamppost happened in the gym, Koki was already dropping down from the roof of the school. I immediately ran to warn him that we were not going ahead anymore, because I was wounded and I would have left too many tracks. He was about to take me away, when we heard the sound of stiletto heels coming down our corridor. He life quickly climbing back up the rope and then you appeared... and you know the rest already."

I am speechless, so many things were happening behind my back and I didn't realize it. *How stupid of me.*

"Those Albanians you killed, did you know them? Did you know who they were?"

"No. I didn't know. I was as surprised as you."

"You killed them very simply and coldly. I imagine it was not the first time that you'd killed someone."

I see him take a deep breath, and for a moment his light blue eyes fix mine. "No." he answers me, "It was not."

Now my questions are finding answers which are clear and direct, and above all sincere. His eyes tell me that he is telling me the truth. I don't understand why this sudden change.

"Then you're a liar, a thief and a murderer. Like I said."

He starts to say something, but we are interrupted by Koki and Vladimir, the latter with a bare chest and decidedly calmer than he was a few minutes ago. Evidently the dose of tranquilizers has had an effect. He is pushing a trolley to the table and fixes me with that face full of scars, while Koki is carrying a tray full of food. "Are you hungry?" he asks in an ambiguous way. I am about to answer back when to my surprise he begins to quickly put the dishes on the table. He's very fast and very accurate, takes one thing, moves another, and all very quickly without breaking or spilling anything.

I look at him dumbfounded.

At the end he launches the empty tray in the air, grabs it behind his back with one hand while with the other he takes off his chef's hat and bows to me. "Enjoy your meal, miss."

I can't hold back a smile. I've only seen things like this in Jackie Chan movies.

After Koki's performance, the table is set perfectly and full of everything: bread, breadsticks, toast, jam, Nutella, cookies, but also various meats and cheeses. No doubt about it, this is a real breakfast, it's just a pity that I can't eat or drink anything, otherwise Felix will rip me to pieces. And speaking of Felix... I haven't heard him say anything for quite a while. Why the silence?

I look out the window. I know they're looking at me and I also remember the weapon pointing in the direction of our table in the event John does something foolish.

I feel his eyes on me, and I turn to stare at him.

"Where were we?" he asks.

"We were talking about how you'll give the crucifix back to the headmistress."

Vladimir grunts; maybe in his own language it means that he's laughing, I don't know, but in any case as he prepares the crêpes on a sort of trolley with burners, he makes comments in his own way every so often.

"I cannot return the cross."

"Why not?"

"Because it was part of an agreement; I gave the cross to the client, the client gave me the information. That's the way it works."

"And if someone tells you he wants that particular cross for other information? What do you do?"

John smiles at me shrewdly. "Something like that is very improbable."

"Improbable but not impossible", I retort, serious.

"In that case, I'd evaluate whether the information that the client wants to give me is really important enough to risk stealing the cross again. Although the risks would be so great that I don't think I'd accept. Stealing from the man for whom I stole brings a series of consequences."

"I want that cross back, John."

"What do you care about the cross? You're an atheist anyway."

"That's not important!"

He leans against the backrest of the chair and, looking at me with a wily air, comments: "Admit that you're attracted to me and I'll bring it back to you tomorrow." He looks at me straight in the eyes, with such a bold air that I want to pull him by the hair and drag him around the entire empty restaurant.

"I don't like you!"

"Yes, you do."

He is unbearable. And as if that wasn't enough, I hear Vladimir growling again. I turn toward him and I become totally petrified. I leap in fright as Vladimir looks at me demonic.

It's not his expression that shocks me, but the fact that he has his left hand resting on the flaming burner. You can literally hear his hand cooking, the smell of human flesh fills the restaurant, and soon there'll be the sound of me throwing up.

I bring my hand to my mouth to hold back the vomit and John shouts, "No! Vladi! The hand!"

He flings himself on top of him, quickly pushing his arm aside, puts out the dressing on the little finger that has caught fire and checks what is left of his hand. Vladimir meanwhile looks as though he isn't aware of anything. No expression of pain, no complaint, his only concern at this moment, it's absurd to say but... it's me.

Koki suddenly appears next to them and takes Vladimir away shaking his head as he looks at his deep burn, probably fifth degree. Before entering the kitchen he looks at me again, saying: "I hate her."

I can't believe it! What the hell has this got to do with me now? I'm totally in shock. I've never seen anything like it. It must definitely be a joke!

I don't want to sit down. I'm afraid. John fixes me, and it is clear that he's searching for something sensible to say after what I've just witnessed. I turn and go rapidly to the elevator saying: "I want to get out of here!" And this time I have really decided to leave.

At this point he has confessed and Felix has recorded everything, so my work here is finished. I hear him shout behind me: "No, wait!"

"You are a pack of sick people. I don't feel safe here with a murderer, a drunken woman, a sex maniac and someone who cooks his hand instead of the *crèpes!*"

"Wait, wait!" he says putting himself between me and the elevator. He looks at me with his light blue eyes staring and keeping his hands on the elevator buttons so that I can't press them he says to me: "I have an idea!"

***

I am still in the same restaurant as before, sitting at the same table as before, with the same idiot as before in front of me, but the situation, is decidedly not the same as before.

I've seen an incredible film, but not one you normally watch sitting relaxed on your sofa at home, no. It's a film fast forwarded at double speed, where the images change second by second, and I'm there concentrating and trying to understand what is happening and hoping not to miss even one sequence it's so interesting.

The lights are now lit, there is merry music in the background, and the restaurant is full of rich stuck-up people who are dining, while others are waiting impatiently at the door. The restaurant is really beautiful, luxurious, the predominant color is white, and at the end of the room there is a beautiful piano made of glass or some other transparent material. But that is not what has left me speechless. I'm dumbfounded by the organization of this bunch of weirdoes, by the speed and the harmony with which each of them moves and keeps things under control.

Even before the clients entered the restaurant Koki arrived, and in a moment he set all the tables with a precision and speed never seen before. It seemed he was flying between one table and the other. Shortly after, still with her precarious step, Lexi arrived with the first customers. Her every gesture, glance or word was *very* concupiscent, *very* provocative and created *much* embarrassment to the men who were accompanying their ladies and were trying not to give in to her advances. Vladimir, on the other hand, was nowhere to be seen. They closed him in the kitchen, but after what happened before, I feel like vomiting even imagining him at the stove.

I witness another scene in which Koki gets a mouthful from a girl sitting with a girlfriend at the next table. I smile: he hasn't got a clue how to deal with women.

"Do you feel more comfortable and safe now?" John asks me seeing my astounded expression.

"If no-one among them is a friend of yours, yes." I'm actually so much at ease, now, that the thing makes me uncomfortable.

"Aren't you hot?" John asks again looking at my bulletproof vest as he removes his jacket.

"No" I answer, but in reality I'm lying. I'm feeling uncomfortably hot and from the way he is looking at me he knows that very well. He begins to unbutton his shirt and looks at me straight in the eyes. I don't understand his little smile until I see the blue stone at his neck. *My* blue stone.

"I want my necklace ", I order.

John touches the stone. "You want it?" he asks me with a provocative smile, "then come and get it."

I'm taken by surprise, and I don't know how to respond.

He continues to look at me slyly leaning on the backrest of the chair. "What's the problem Jas? Are you afraid to get close to me?"

"Did it ever cross your mind that maybe I don't like you? I don't know... does it happen?"

"That is impossible."

His ego is frighteningly large. It touches on the ridiculous.

"You stole my stone and you'll give it back to me. It's mine. I won it for Valentine's Day!"

"And what do I win for saving your life?" he inquires. He becomes serious and adds, pretending to rebuke me: "That's not the way to treat a hero."

I smile, not believing what I just heard. "After all the talking you've done about your job, you have the courage to compare yourself to a hero?"

"Oh no", he smiles amused, "to tell the truth I compare myself to God."

"You *what*?"

"We have a lot more things in common that you could imagine, you know?"

"Yes, I know. One of these is that you don't exist. You are an illusion, a lie to better manipulate the minds of human beings to convince them to do what you want."

"What were we saying about superheroes?"

It is obvious that he is trying to change the subject as quickly as possible, whilst I give him a filthy look. "We weren't talking about that at all!"

"I think Superman is coolest of all."

He insists on talking bullshit.

"Superman is the uncoolest of the superheroes."

And I even answer him.

"You don't like him only because I like him."

"If you really want to know, I don't like him because he's false."

"But you do know who Superman is, yes?"

"Of course I know! He's an alien that by day acts the part of a human and at night he's a hero. He is never himself with anyone. He spends his time disguising himself living his life under false pretenses. He is ridiculous, squeezed inside that red and blue suit. But then it's easy to be a hero if you come from another planet and you have extraterrestrial powers. It's not a fair battle, so, as I already said, he is false and wrong in everything he does."

John looks at me baffled for a moment and then asks me: "And which would be the superhero you like?"

255

"Batman", I reply promptly, and John raises his eyebrows surprised.

"Yes," I continue, "First and foremost he's a human being, and his unique powers are his values. He's brave, athletic, intelligent, honest and is also a gorgeous hunk. And then he's rich, has a large villa, a butler, not to mention his big car and the multi-equipped cave and the black Batman costume that looks great on him."

"Even Batman has an identity", John points out in an annoyed voice.

"Yes, but Bruce Wayne is not a mask, he's a real person with real feelings. And he doesn't hide his double identity to the people he loves."

"Jas", says John becoming serious.

I don't know why, but this makes me shoot to my feet. "I have to go now." Yes, I have to get out of here. And then the fact that Felix has been quiet for quite a while makes me nervous.

"Wait", John stands up surprised. "Is that all? Couldn't you ask me something else?"

"No, I already know everything that I wanted to know. Why? Did you want to tell me more?"

"No," he says, and looks at me displeased, "Actually I was also thinking the same thing. I was just afraid that you wanted me to ask me some other question."

"For example?"

"There is no example because there is nothing else to say. Right?" He looks at me as if he is hoping that from one moment to the next I say something. But, as he said, there is nothing else to say. I'm about to respond when some yelling in the room attracts my attention. I turn my head and see people running away from a man in flames near a table at the end of the restaurant. I stare wide-eyed and look at him open-mouthed, while a group of terrified people run toward the elevator.

I hear the voice of Lexi behind me: "Uh, guys we have a small, *huge*, disaster happening."

Next to her there are also Koki and Vladimir, who of course fixes me enraged, ignoring the delirium behind us.

"Which of you did it?"

"It is not our doing, Jack", Koki defends himself.

"Do you mean to say that he transformed into a human torch all by himself?"

"He was quietly eating looking at my boobs and poof, he started to burn. It's not my fault if I have this effect on men! I'm mortified!" Lexi apologizes. She speaks with a German accent and shakes her head regretfully taking on one of her sexy poses, while continuing to drink one of her strange alcoholic concoctions.

I continue to be very shocked.

"Someone put him out, Holy God!" screams John and looks at me not knowing what my reaction will be.

Vladimir pulls his gun from his belt and points it at the man in flames, who continues to run screaming in pain between the tables of the restaurant.

"Not with that!" John rebukes him.

The other lowers the weapon with a kind of disappointed expression.

Koki, instead, approaches our table and grabs the tablecloth with both hands. Before we know what he has in mind, he snatches away the tablecloth without making any of the dishes fall off. I can't believe my eyes. He managed to do what Pavarotti wasn't able to do the other evening. Then he goes to the flaming man trying to cover him and put him out with the tablecloth, while I continue to watch him still dumbfounded.

"If they said it wasn't them, it wasn't them", John tells me believing the words of his brothers, regardless of what I think.

Lexi takes Vladimir by the hand and swinging it back and forth says to me, still with the German accent: "Come on, give each other a peace hug, you two."

"Me and him *what*?" I ask disbelieving.

"The hug of peace. It's the embrace we give to apologize for something *bibi* that we've said or done," explains Lexi, "and he behaved very *bibi* earlier, ruining the romantic breakfast. So go on, hug each other."

Bibi, I understand even less than usual.

Vladimir looks at me with icy eyes, opens his arms clearly unwillingly, but without moving closer to me.

"No! He must stay away from me! Do you understand?"

"But it's a family tradition," insists Lexi.

"Lexi please, forget it", intervenes John.

"But Jack, I only wanted to remedy the *bibi* situation! *One Thousand!*" says Lexi in a disappointed voice then goes off wiggling.

For the umpteenth time tonight I feel the adrenaline running through my veins. Too many emotions all together in one evening.

Koki puts out the flambé man while Vladimir, in his own way, tries to reassure people growling in their faces with the gun in his hand. John and I, in the meantime, look at everything from our table as if we're in the cinema. Could it be possible that all this is really happening?

Perhaps I'm not just watching a movie. Perhaps I've literally ended up in one.

***

The paramedics load the stretcher with the man-lighter - or what's left of him - into the ambulance. The policemen standing in front of the restaurant interrogate people, still frightened and shocked by the horrid show, and even the fire brigade arrives, thinking they had to put out a building and not a man, already extinguished, apart from anything. In short, there is huge chaos here, chaos which I look at with interest from the other side of the road, sitting on the sidewalk with John sipping the water that the hospital chief kindly offered us. Spontaneous combustion: that's what happened to the scorched man. Incredible. *I can't wait to tell grandma about it!*

In forty years of honorable career as a surgeon, she has never had the good fortune to assist at anything like this.

In the end I remove the bulletproof vest and the reasons for doing so are so many.

First: Vladimir and the others took off before the ambulance arrived, so I feel much safer without the crazy chef around.

Secondly: even if John has remained with me, I have nothing to fear given the presence of all these policemen around us.

And thirdly: I feel *hot.*

I turn toward the street and see my taxi arrive. I pick up the vest, stand up and go to meet it.

"Are you leaving without saying goodbye to me?" John calls behind me.

"Oh, excuse me, goodbye John."

"Goodbye?" I hear his footsteps come closer. "Then we won't be seeing each other anymore?"

"Of course we'll see each other. I'll come to see you in jail after Nick arrests you."

"He'll never succeed."

"Yes, he will! And I can't wait!" While I smile looking straight into his eyes, he smiles looking straight at my décolleté. I cover the neckline with my hand, annoyed, and I'm about to take hold of the door handle of the taxi when he blocks the door with one leg. "Come and have dinner with me."

"What? No!" I try to open the door, but his leg blocks it firmly. "Look me in the eye and tell me that it wasn't the most exciting breakfast of your life."

"No!"

He comes even closer, touching my body with his. I let go of the handle, quickly backing away from him, and smiling he says: "No, because you don't want to look me in the eyes; no, because you don't want to say it; or no, because it wasn't?"

"No because will I not go to dinner with you!"

"You like to be begged, huh?"

"You wanted a possibility and I gave it to you! And anyway we have nothing more to say to each other."

"And who wants to talk?" he grabs my chin looking at me mischievously. "There are so many other things that we can do together."

"You're a sleaze!"

"And who isn't?" he says shrugging. I'm about to reply when I hear a voice calling me.

I turn pale and see Nick arriving with a serious face and closed fists. From the jeep behind him Benjamin and Patrick get out too.

"Nick!" I say terrified. He comes near looking at John scornfully. "What happened? Why are the fire brigade, ambulance and the cops out here?" he asks angrily addressing John.

"No, he has nothing to do with it", I intervene.

John smiles. "Nickolas, it's always a displeasure to see you."

Nick doesn't bother to answer him, he looks at me, and his eyes fall on the bulletproof vest that is hanging over one arm. I soon realize that he's angry with me. *I shouldn't have taken it off, dammit!*

"I felt hot and..."

"Wait for me in the car." He stops me abruptly. I bow my head unhappy. I don't like it when he raises his voice with me, I don't like it when he gives me orders, but I made a mistake, I deserve it. I go toward the jeep to Patrick and Ben without saying anything, without greeting anyone, and without anyone greeting me.

43.

Jas is sad because she has disappointed Nick, for having removed the bulletproof vest in spite of his advice. She gets into the jeep, leaving him and Jack near the taxi one in front of the other. Behind them, there are many agitated people; the lights of the police, ambulance and fire brigade continue to blink. Jack smiles, a bitter smile. "You say *jump* and she jumps. I'll feel a subtle pleasure in changing your sickening relationship." His voice is serious and threatening.

"Never try to touch her! Did you hear me?"

"Otherwise?"

"Nick!" Ben interrupts them calling them from a distance. Nick pretends not to hear, he addresses Jack once again, worked up. "Thank God there's a law!"

"Which law?" he smiles. "The one that prevents you from arresting me for lack of evidence?"

"No, the one that thanks to the evidence will see you brought to justice!"

Jack moves to within a few inches from Nick's face whispering threateningly: "I'll show you the true face of the world for which you fight. I'll take away all your certainties, and I will take Jas away with me too, far from this corrupt temple that you call justice!"

"You can try!"

They stand facing each other, not moving, serious. Ben intervenes again raising his voice: "Nickolas!"

Nick moves away from Jack signaling to Ben that he has everything under control, and straight after adds through clenched teeth: "I'm letting you go for now."

"Thank you very much," replies Jack, clearly ironic.

"But be aware that I'll soon apprehend you and throw you into the only place that you deserve to be, in a cell!"

"You can try!"

At that point, Nick turns back and gets into the jeep.

44.

Usual orange bench, under the usual board, America staring at me with the usual expression and me waiting for the usual person: Jas.

The elevator door opens and I see Patrick, Ben, Nick and finally my Jas, with a sad expression on her face. I jump to my feet running to meet her. "Jas!"

She doesn't even have time to look at me before Felix appears from the corridor as angry as a hyena. He goes toward Nick shouting: "How dare you! I could dismiss you for interfering in an investigation!"

"Interfering? You lost all contact with her hours ago! You were not properly prepared and you were not ready to tackle someone like Jack."

"You're putting in doubt my work ability in front of my men, this is unacceptable!"

"I don't think it's the time or the place to tackle this conversation", Ben points out, trying to defuse the tones.

Slowly, they all start toward the red corridor, which is *off limits* to me because I don't wear any badge. I stop, but Jas grasps my hand pulling me along with her.

Veronica fixes me irritated, but without commenting.

We enter one of the offices, Ben's I think. The walls are full of hanging frames, with stamps inside on full view. On the table, lots of pictures of his children. I turn and see Nick's whole team, Felix and his four black gorillas behind him. The atmosphere is very heavy.

"We have the audio recordings up to when she got up from the chair. Once she reached the elevator, something got stuck. But she was never outside our field of view! She was not in danger!" Felix justifies himself, in his abrupt tone as usual.

"We already know what went wrong!" Nick raises his voice, becoming irritated "It's called white noise; it prevents any video and audio interception in any place or building!"

"O-our entire bb-building and all of the te-te-teeelephones are protected from white noise PRAFFT", stresses Will.

"It's the first thing we have to be careful of when..." continues Nick getting fired up.

"That's enough!" Felix interrupts him, "Unexpected things happen, we were not ready for such a powerful device!"

"We were!"

"That's not the point, Nickolas! You shouldn't have interfered in any case! You had promised me!"

The situation is becoming increasingly tense. Felix opens the door, making a sign to Jas and his men to leave; the others don't say a thing. I remain alone with all of them, in silence and tremendously uncomfortable.

45.

In the meantime – From Jas's diary

I leave Benjamin's office. Felix accompanies me into the next room, while his men look at me with seriously, showing me the chair I have to sit on. Felix sits on the other side of the table. "Tell me everything from the beginning," he encourages me.

I put my hands behind my head and rocking on the chair I begin: "There was a Japanese, a Russian, a Fin and an American. And no, it's not the start of a joke", I smile, seeing Felix size me up and take a deep breath.

46.

An hour later – From Mina's diary

"We had very little time to organize ourselves, the next time we will be more prepared." We hear Felix's voice resound in the corridor. Shortly after, the door of Ben's office opens and he and Jas step out.

"I'll get back to you in a few days. If Jack reappears you know what to do. He'll be watched by my men, however", he gives her the final instructions and turns toward Nick, "I will not accept any further interference, I'm warning you. You will read about the developments of the case in the newspaper when we have apprehended him."

He goes away without adding anything more, closing the door behind him. I don't know what to do, whether to go to Jas or wait for her to come to me. I just know that I am tired of sitting on this chair and being ignored by all. Nick's team stares at her insistently. In fact, she realizes that too. "What is it?" she asks demurely.

"Tell us what you know!" Veronica bursts out without wasting words, now that Felix has gone. Jas raises her eyebrows looking at her annoyed.

"Veronica", Nick reminds her and then turns to Jas: "We would just like to know how it went, Jas."

"Bad."

"Why?"

"Because that idiot Felix didn't record anything", she complains.

"But what did you find out?" asks Veronica, unable to shut up.

"He admitted that he stole the cross for a client and that, in exchange, he gave him valuable information."

Ben intervenes: "Information concerning what?"

"I don't know, Ben."

"Why didn't you ask him?" Veronica asks her again in an aggressive way.

"I don't know, I didn't think about it!"

265

Nick rebukes Veronica with just the force of his gaze, then approaches Jas and caresses her back. "It doesn't matter."

"He also admitted that he framed the two workmen, and that it wasn't the first time that he has killed someone."

My skin crawls just hearing that.

"Did you ask who he works for? And did you get some napkin or any small object that one of them used during the dinner?"

"No, Ben, they were very careful not to touch anything, and in any case I'd forgotten my handbag, so..."

"Then this is all you can you tell us after spending hours with them?" snorts Veronica, but Jas this time doesn't take any notice of her and exclaims: "I don't understand. What do you need the information for? You're not able to investigate the case."

"I've fffound it. He put the wh-wh-white noise on her bullet pr-prooof jacket frrf", says Will, with a small round object as big as a button in his hands. Ben takes it from Will looking at it with curiosity.

"This case was to be ours!" complains Veronica meanwhile, crossing her arms and launching a dirty look at Nick, certainly convinced that it is his fault if the case has been taken from him.

"They di-didn't know cmghntr how to protect themselves from wh-wh-whiite noise", Will reflects stunned.

"I don't wish to speak ill of one of my colleagues, however Will is right", comments Ben, "their organization was not very... organized. There were huge gaps."

Nick asks: "Have you found out how far we can move legally with this case?"

"Legally, we can move as we want. You and Felix have a non-binding contract of collaboration, you're the one who doesn't want to oppose him and I don't understand why."

"Ben," Nick admonishes him, giving him a dirty look.

Ben shakes his head in a sign of giving in. "We can take advantage of the theft of the Medusa painting from Michael George. By doing so, you wouldn't go against Felix, also because we'd be investigating Vladimir and Koki, and not Jack."

"Good. Jas", he whispers stroking her head, "you can go and take a nap now, you've been superb, I'm proud of you."

Veronica makes a strange face; it's clear she does not agree with Nick at all and from the look on Jas's face, I think that for once she and Veronica think the same way.

"They've been thumbing their noses at us for months! And while they know everything about us, we know nothing about them. And the little that we had, Felix has taken it from us, who knows why?" explodes Veronica in a sarcastic tone looking at Jas. "This investigation is a complete disaster."

Jas and I ignore her and we're about to leave the office, finally, when Patrick stops us "Wait a second, Jas."

He's been silent the entire time and he decides to speak right now?

"I too would like to ask you a question," he adds.

"Go ahead", Jas invites him, but she seems frightened, perhaps because she is convinced she doesn't know how to respond as they would like.

"Can you describe Jack's friends to me?"

"Describe them?"

"Yes. Forget the investigations for a moment. And tell me simply which part of their personality, gestures or physicality has made the most impression on you, this evening."

"Okay." She remains in silence for a little while. Veronica looks at the clock, sure that she won't say anything interesting.

She is so awful!

"Don't let yourselves be taken in by the accent and unsteady gait that Lexi has", she pauses again looking into space, and then continues, "Despite being a drunk and a rather good quick-change artist and knows how to speak several languages and..." again she pauses scratching her head, "Okay. They are a kind of X-Men, but in the real world!"

Everyone except Patrick turns to Nick and I really don't like the expression on their faces. Jas notices but just pretends not to and then starts again with more confidence: "Lexi exudes an outrageous amount of pheromones and this makes all the men to be sexually attracted to her, as if they went into heat for her, they want to possess her, please her. In a few words, she is able to do anything she wants to many men. Koki, on the other hand, is clumsy with women and does nothing but get rebuffs, but he is not clumsy when it comes to movement. He is very agile, accurate, and everything he does, he does it at such a speed that he's almost invisible. He appears and disappears continuously without you even having time to notice it. Vladimir instead is a raving madman. He adores blood, death, and gets angry very easily, and to calm him down they use sedatives and stun guns. And as if that's not enough he suffers from Type Four Familial Dysautonomia", she concludes.

From the way we look at her she realizes that we have no idea what she's talking about.

"It's a syndrome that doesn't allow him to feel any physical pain. He needs continual treatment because he risks death on a daily basis, even for stupid things, seeing that his body doesn't send him pain signals. However, in compensation, where others might stop, he continues. In my opinion you can't stop him even with a bit of lead. He is a very strong fighting machine."

Silence falls. We all look at her amazed at what she has just been able to list with such simplicity.

Patrick instead, who usually does not show any emotion, smiles. You can see from his face that he is proud of her.

Nick and Ben look at each other satisfied.

Veronica is stunned while Jas obviously is not yet aware of anything because she goes on to say disappointed: "I don't know anything else unfortunately. Can this help you?"

47.

"Jas, no! You can't cross the border like this, it's prohibited!"

Jas throws an innocent look at Nick. "Who said so?" she asks as she tries with difficulty to crawl under the netting and pass into the Italian part where her Nick is waiting for her.

"It's written on that board, in large letters, Jas", he points to it.

"I didn't see anything."

"You don't see and don't hear only when it's convenient", he smiles shaking his head and giving her his hand to help her to her feet.

"I'm sorry but why do I have to go the whole way around if I'm right opposite your house?"

"Because you can't do it, it's illegal, the police will get you", he explains for the umpteenth time as they head toward the *Cat's eyes.*

"If the police come I'll start crying" remarks Jas with conviction.

"Your fake crying won't work, Jas."

"Then you'll come to rescue me."

"I can't be always getting you out of trouble."

"Yes, you will. I don't understand why they had to put this fence in the middle. All it does is annoy me."

Nick sighed. "It's to divide the Italian state from the Slovenian one."

"I don't like boundaries."

"I've noticed," he said, smiling at her again.

"You're the one who wants to be the cop, not me. I don't need to follow the rules to the letter. I can follow them to the non-letter."

"I want to be a detective, not a cop. And the rules are important, Jas, think of a world without laws, there would be chaos."

"You're boring", Jas smiled, knowing perfectly well what was about to happen. Nick looked at her with eyes half-closed and asked: "I am *what*?" These were Nick's usual last words before he started to chase her all along the street leading to the tree house. Jas laughed happily and at the same time shouted for fear that he would catch her; she was still too small to understand that, if Nick wanted to, he would have reached her instantly.

Isobel was sitting on a blanket under the huge tree where the little wooden house was built, in the shade. She saw her two darlings arriving. They were happy and smiling and pulling faces at each other as they ran toward her.

"Be careful, my children, slow down", she warned them, seeing Jas fall over on the grass. Nick took her in his arms and lifted her up.

"Let go of me! Set me down, Nick!"

"Who's boring?" he asked her pretending to be angry.

"You're boring!"

"Take back what you said right now!"

"No! Put me down!" the girl protested.

Nick put her down and they both came to sit near Isobel who continued to look at them with a certain melancholy. "Why do you say that he's boring?" asked Isobel, even though she knew very well what the answer would be.

"I crossed the border again and he yelled at me, saying that you can't do it."

"Every so often we must cross it to see what's on the other side", she agreed.

"You can cross it without breaking the rules, you just have to go around, grandma", Nick pointed out.

Isobel smiled and said: "Sometimes it's precisely the going around that prevents you from seeing the most important things, Nick."

"See, grandmother is on my side", exclaimed Jas crossing her arms.

"I'm neither on your side nor his."

Jas stared in surprise. "And whose side are you on?"

"Always on my own side, Jas," replied Isobel looking pensive. Nick took her by the hand; he knew why she had become silent and it saddened him. "Grandma, I know that you don't approve of my departure for America."

"It's not America that scares me, but what you want to do there in the future," the elderly woman admitted.

"Nothing will happen to me, I promise."

"There are so many other jobs that you could do, dear grandchild."

"I know, but I want to be a detective, I want to help the innocent and make life impossible for criminals."

Isobel squeezed his hand and reminded him: "You'll never save the whole world, Nickolas, your father wanted to do the same thing and have you seen how it ended?" She was tired of repeating this to him.

"It's enough for me to be able to save and protect my world," he says, tightening his hand on hers and taking Jas's hand, "You don't have to worry about me, I'll be fine."

He got up from the blanket and looked at Jas whose eyes were already filled with tears. "I don't want you to go away from me!"

Nick knelt beside her and caressed her dark hair.

"They're not fake tears, they are not.", the girl assured him.

"I know, little one", he whispered wiping away her tears. Nick's eyes became bright with tears too. "I'll be back soon."

"How soon?"

"Before your birthday."

"But I've just had my birthday." the girl said with dread.

Nick opened his arms. "Come here."

He hugged her tightly, with an immense desire to say *Jas, come with me*, but he knew he could not do so. "When I return I'll teach you everything that I learned in America, so one day you can work with me, in my agency."

"I don't want to work with you and I don't want you to go!"

Nick smiled and kissed her on the forehead, looking for a last time into her big dark eyes. "I will call you every day, I promise, little one. I'll miss you a lot." He hugged her to himself again; he just couldn't let her go, and then turned to his grandmother and said: "Please, take care of her."

"I shall", she answered in a sad voice and bowed her head, not wanting to watch him as he went away, along the lawn, so green it looked like a dream.

"He loves his work more than me," said Jas crying a lot as she watched him disappear into the woods.

"That's not true, my dear little one."

"Yes, it is, I hate policemen!" she said sobbing, "I hate the law! His work is taking him away from me!"

"It's not true, it's not true", she tried to console her and hugged her very hard. "I will not let this happen again. I will not allow it."

48.

From Jas's diary – Miami Hospital

Justice? Synonymous with rip off! You do an exam in medicine, you get top marks and as a reward you find yourself cleaning all the corridors of the hospital!

Of course, the *you* I am talking about is myself. And to humiliate me even more, they've also dressed me as a cleaner, putting a ridiculous gray and black uniform on me and horrible shoes on my feet. *Damn them!*

"Hello, Jas."

I turn and see the girl with her hair shaved and the usual yellow toy in her hand appear from behind the cleaning trolley.

I continued to mop the floor, ignoring her.

"Have you stolen the uniform or are you really a cleaning lady in the hospital?"

I continue to do my dirty work hoping that she goes away, but instead she decides to repeat it. "Have you stolen the uniform or are you really a cleaning lady?"

Apparently, washing the floor is not the only sad thing that has happened to me today.

"Did you steal the unifo...?"

"That's enough!" I interrupt. "No, I didn't steal it and no, I'm not a *cleaning lady*, but a temporary housekeeper, okay? Am I wrong, or do girls with the same hair hairdo as you have to stay on the fourth floor?"

"Yes."

"So then what are you doing on the sixth?"

"I've come to invite you to my birthday."

I don't want to listen to her. I haven't celebrated my own birthday as I should, so imagine if I feel like celebrating hers. I leave the cloth on the ground and go into my friend Zombie's room. He is still very pale. I take his medical record and sit on the bed next to him.

"Who's he? And why is he sleeping at this hour?" the little girl asks me. I look at her irritated. I do not know who is worse off, Zombie or her with those dark circles under her eyes.

"He's called Zombie and he's not asleep. He's in a semi-comatose state."

"But can he hear you?"

"No", I cut short while I read his chart.

"Perhaps you're wrong and when he wakes up he'll tell you that he heard you talking to him."

"I don't talk to him."

"If you can write to Jesus on Facebook, you can also speak to him."

"Will you stop it?"

"And do you talk to God?"

"No."

"And why don't you talk with God?" the little girl asks.

"Because he owes me some money."

She looks at me with her mouth open and eyes wide, incredulous. I barely hold back my laughter.

"Meeeetooo, ooooooo", calls the parrot. I turn and see it fly straight onto the bed near the old man. I knew that it would have been able to open the window by pushing from the outside.

"A parrot! A parrot!"

"Shut up, little girl, don't yell!" I look toward the door for fear that someone has heard her, while with a sort of sulk she whispers: "You said that Zombie is in a coma and can't hear."

"He's not the problem, it's the chief", I explain to her, "If she gets to know Metoo, she'll take him away and I don't want that."

In the meantime the parrot rests on Zombie's chest playing happily with his beard. Perhaps he wants to wake him up, or simply have fun with this sadistic game, I don't know, however, it is interesting watching them together. The sudden silence of the little girl starts to make me suspicious. In fact, I turn toward her and I see her staring at me with a sly air and arms crossed.

"What's that face?" I ask diffident.

"And so you don't want them to take the parrot away... What are you willing to do for my silence?"

"Are you blackmailing me again? For someone so young you're already a great little piece of shit, you know?"

She shrugs her shoulders, by no means offended by my offense. I feel offended. "Tell me what you want and keep it brief."

"Will you come to my birthday?" she asks raising the arches where there should be eyebrows and smiling in this sly little way.

"Kooooooo", calls the parrot, noticing that the old man doesn't want to wake up. Diana though is still waiting for my answer.

"But of course I'm coming, how could I ever refuse blackmail like that?"

"That's great! You'll meet the man black too!"

"I'm trembling with excitement already, look", I remark in an infantile way.

"Even the parrot is trembling."

I look at him. Actually Diana is right, Metoo is trembling.

"Is it sick?" she asks worried, hugging her yellow cat.

"No, it's just hungry", I try to reassure her, even though in reality I'm not sure that its problem is being hungry. I get off the bed and make a sign to Diana to be quiet while I go out into the hallway. It's lunchtime and nurses are going from room to room taking food to the patients. I approach the trolley full of trays, and pinch a little salad and a glass of water, and then run back into Zombie's room.

Diana is all happy to see me, as if I'd been gone for hours and not just a few seconds. I go to the parrot slowly to give him the salad, but he flies off and perches above the window.

"He's afraid."

"Metoo is strange. One day he sits on my shoulder and the day after he's scared. I don't get it."

I go to the window and he is already looking at me cross-eyed squawking: "Koooooo!"

I leave both the salad and the water on the ground and move away immediately.

"Why do you call him Metoo? Metoo isn't a name."

"I don't have a clue. The choice was between *Metoo* and *Kooooo*. I chose the more obvious name. Come on, let's go before someone arrives."

"Koooooo, Metooooooo!" the parrot continues to scream his new name, I continue with my new job as Cinderella and Diana continues to pester me with questions: "When I heal from the cancer, my daddy is going to buy me a real cat, you know? Did you know that people don't like cats because they're free and don't follow orders like other animals do? A cat understands you very well but doesn't obey you, you know? Do you have any animals?"

"Listen, do you want to go to your room and do some drawing?" I ask, trying to get rid of her, but she continues to follow me along the corridor.

"What do you want me to draw?"

"Whatever you want, for God's sake. Why are you making it so difficult?"

"An animal? I could draw a yellow cat and Metoo, I could..."

***

I unjustly have had to clean the whole hospital and I had to do it with a ridiculous outfit and I had a little pain-in-the-ass girl at my heels all the time.

Am I annoyed? Of course I am! But not as much as I'm annoyed by the fact that I need to do this and put up with it FOR FREE!

I have washed and changed and now I'm in the elevator to meet Nick who is waiting for me at the hospital entrance for fear that I have some unpleasant encounter. The elevator stops on the fourth floor, the door opens and I find myself right in front of him. The unpleasant encounter. All dressed up as if he's a manager, with even a black suitcase in hand, a tie and blond hair tied back. As soon as he sees me he smiles, pretending to be surprised. "Darling? What are you doing here? When fate gets it into its head..."

I quickly push the buttons to close the doors of the elevator, but John blocks them with the briefcase jumping inside.

"Fate has absolutely nothing to do with it! What are *you* doing here," I ask riled.

He places the briefcase on the ground and begins to look at me from head to foot. "I have to be somewhere."

"Well, avoid being where I am!"

"You know, I understand when I'm not welcome."

"And in spite of this you're still here..."

"You're a terrible actress, Jas."

"I'm not acting! Are you tailing me, by any chance?"

"Usually I do, but this time I'm here for work."

"And what did you have to do? Steal the Bible from an atheist patient?" I ask sarcastically. He smiles in a strange way and begins to come closer. "Do you know what I like about you?"

"No."

"Neither do I."

I don't understand his idiotic answer, but this is not my concern at the moment. With all the backing away from him, I now find myself with my back to the wall of the elevator and him very close to my face.

"Move, you're depriving me of oxygen!" I protest pushing him back.

He smiles amused and as if nothing's wrong he proposes: "Come and have dinner with me."

"No! I've already been once and that's enough for me." I look at the numbers that are lighting up as the elevator descends and can't wait for the door to open to get out of this situation.

"That was a breakfast, not a dinner, Jas."

We get to the basement and the door is about to open when John raises his leg and pushes the STOP button with his foot.

"What the hell are you doing?" I'm about to push the button again but he prevents me, seizing hold of my hand and putting me with my shoulders against the wall. "Let me go!" I find myself stuck at two millimeters from his face.

"Come out with me."

"No!"

I try to push him back and pass under his arms, but I can't, he seems made of stone.

"Come out with me."

"No!"

"Come out with me."

"No! And then I'll also write it on the side of your car, so you understand better," I growl.

"Rule number one says that you can't touch my car, remember?

"Instead my rule number one says that you're not to talk, remember?"

"Apparently it's in our blood to break the rules."

"Stop it!"

But he insists. "Come out with me."

"I see you have a big problem understanding the word *no*!"

"Oh, on the contrary I understand very well. *No,* is that annoying sound that sooner or later will transform itself into a beautiful *yes*."

"Never!"

"What are you afraid of?"

"Not you!"

"Then where's the problem? Tell me what I need to do to transform your *no* into a *yes,* and I'll do it." He gazes at my lips and this bothers me; having him so close to my face makes me nervous.

"Alright then..." I give in.

His blue eyes light up. He moves away from me, waiting anxiously for me to finish my response.

"I will go out with you..." I take advantage of the suspense to push the stop button again, the elevator door begins to open up and I add quickly, "When you pick me up with the Bat-car."

He opens his eyes and stares at me as I quickly get out. I feel like a winner, I'm much more cunning than he is, but this feeling disappears when I find Nick in front of me. His eyes meet John's who is still inside the elevator, and in an instant they both assume an unfriendly attitude.

"No, Nick, everything's fine!" I grasp his hand.

"Oooh the fairy godmother of justice has arrived", says John sarcastically, "Another one or two meetings and you'll make an honest man of me, Nickolas" he smiles; this too is clearly a joke.

"Was he harassing you?" Nick asks me, completely ignoring John.

"No, no", I lie. But only because I don't want them to start a fight. "He only asked me to go out with him again."

"But, apparently, she doesn't go out more than once with beautiful, wealthy and virile men like me", he says with great artlessness and then, looking hard at Nick, adds: "You, though, you might have a chance", he smiles amused, while the elevator door closes. I am alone with Nick. Still visibly upset, he turns toward me, lifts up the strap of my t-shirt and holding me hard to him he whispers: "I don't like the way he looks at you."

"Arrest him, and he won't be able to do it any longer."

49.

From Mina's diary – Watchtower, a few days later

It's evening. While Jas is lying on her bed eating Nutella with a spoon and watching TV, I walk up and down the bedroom talking on the phone: "Hello, mom? Can you hear me? What do mean who is it? Who else calls you mom? Forget it! I just wanted to let you know that I will not be coming home in a week's time, but in about two weeks. Got it? Of course I had to come back! What? My room? Mom? Hello?" I look at my phone, shocked.

"I can't believe it!"

"*I* can't believe it, not you, Jas! She told me that she has rented my room to a German boy until the end of August and she hung up! I can't believe it! I've been so relaxed during these months when I haven't seen her or heard from her and now I only have to talk with her five seconds and I'm already nervous and angry! She is driving me crazy! Where do I go to sleep now, in the kitchen?"

Jas takes the biscuits from under the bed as well and, dipping them into the Nutella, continues to complain: "I grew up with the television series *The Robinsons*! It was the television series of my childhood, of my best years and now what do I discover? That the original surname of the family is Huxtable!"

"That German will never leave my house, I already know it! Just like Luca, her toy boy! Do you know what will happen in the end? That when we return from Europe my house will be full of my mother's concubines! Of course, *if* we're going to make this trip to Europe seeing that every year someone prevents it; Nick last year and this year it seems that the *someone* will be Jack", I continue to complain walking up and down the room, "So do you know what the conclusion of this speech of mine is? That anyway you look at it, my problem in life is still men! Not only the ones that I've had, but other people's as well!"

"I don't know what to say. *Huxtable*?"

"And anyway I want some answers, Jas! I know that giving explanations is an unnecessary complication for you, but I've been silent for months without asking for a thing and now I've had enough!"

"This thing is really ridiculous," she says. She is still referring to the television series, I suppose.

"I don't even know what to ask you, the situation is so complicated!"

"And do you know what *Mom I missed the plane* is really called? Another film from my childhood. *Home alone*! And *Mom I missed the plane again and I'm lost in New York? Home alone 2*! I'm going to write in and complain about the Italian translation!"

"And you know, I understand that what Jack has done is wrong: he passed himself off as a disabled person, he stole the crucifix at the school, he killed three people, okay, it's wrong, I know. But here you're all forgetting that he saved your life, Jas! And he saved it as both John and Jack and this counts for something, I mean, we're not about to make him into a saint now, but I don't understand this hatred they have for him. It seems to me it's overstated."

"Oh God! And what about this! You know how Eddie Murphy laughs? Eddie's beautiful and particular laugh? In reality he has a normal laugh! But can you believe that?! It was the Italian voiceover people who changed it and made it funny, while instead it's really a normal laugh! In a nutshell, all the memories of my childhood are fabricated, I've been cheated! But I'll press charges against the lot of them!"

"And then I wonder: how do you intend to arrest Jack if you refuse to go out with him again?"

The clock on the wall interrupts our discourse marking eight o'clock on the dot. I look at Jas. "Shall we go to dinner?"

"Yes."

We leave the room, curious to discover what good things Will has prepared for us, leaving our monologues incomplete. For now.

***

After three days closed in the house, today I went out at last and I keep repeating in my mind: *Yes, this is the life!*

281

I'm surrounded by painstaking salesgirls who are satisfying my every whim, as I stand in front of the mirror trying to find the most suitable dress which will hide my sunburn and highlight the best parts of my body, though at this moment I don't know what that could be. I love shopping with Katherine, especially today when she's particularly happy because in a few days she'll be leaving with Ben for their honeymoon.

I see her come out of the change room wearing a micro-swimsuit. Her skinniness makes me stare. The pandering salesgirl approaches her immediately, rubbing her hands together.

Katherine reflects making a lot of doubtful muttering as she looks in the mirror. "I can't choose."

"Choose?" asks the salesgirl, "No, no, you don't have to choose, it's too stressful Mrs. Roosevelt, take them all", and as she talks she continues to rub her hands together hoping to make her buy all the swimsuits. I barely restrain my laughter. Katherine turns to face me again with that undecided expression and asks: "Should I lose a few more ounces do you think?"

What on earth is she saying? Even if she wanted to lose them, these ounces, I don't understand how she could because doesn't have a trace of fat.

Of course the salesgirl reassures her about her weight and tells her that she's beautiful. I look at Jas. She is still lying on the loveseat next to us staring at the ceiling and yawning. Naomi instead is busy chewing Ambrose's shoes.

"You know, Mina," says Katherine, "at the beginning I wanted to go to Milan for our honeymoon, to do a little shopping in the capital of Italian fashion. But then I remembered that the sales are on at the moment." She looks at me peeved. I don't understand where the problem lies. "Do you understand? I can't possibly buy discounted handbags and clothes. What would they think of me?" And while she sighs depressed because of the dreadful sales that have hindered her plans, in my mind I go through the memories of last year: me pulling the discounted t-shirt from one side and Susy from the other, both of us like people possessed as Chanel tried to separate us. How shameful.

"When Ben was at dinner with the former wives, I saw Ling. The Chinese viper had a Valentino handbag from last year's collection", she says disgusted, "And the black fatso was even fatter and blacker than she was last year, can you believe that? Would she have been doing tanning lamps?"

"Ooookay!" exclaims Jas, clearly fed up with Katherine's talk. She gets up off the little sofa and goes out of the boutique. "Where are you going, little Big Mac menu?"

"To smoke a cigarette."

"Oh, go on then, no problem, in the meantime I'll have my Naomi try on a swimsuit."

I immediately run after Jas, almost stumbling on the carpet. "Jas, but you don't smoke."

"I'll take it up if you don't take me home right away." She opens the door and finds Will there. As soon as he sees her, he begins to move in a cautious way, saying: "Khjnhitym frrrf"

"Will you stop looking around as if you were my bodyguard?" she rebukes him.

"I am your b-bo-bodyguard, Jas."

"Oh please", she responds with contempt, "How the devil do you think you're going to protect me, can you explain that? Look at you."

"I can havvve it if ghnfht frrrf strong!"

"Strong? Who, you? You risk having a stroke simply trying to open a jar of mayonnaise."

"It's not true kjhijn DAS of mayons brtl Frrrf in with him." He adjusts his glasses, scratches his beard nervously and stammers things even more incomprehensible than usual. I think this must be difficulty level two which Jas was talking about to me the other day. I almost laugh watching them argue outside the boutique. All of a sudden I hear a roar come from the end of the street; everyone turns around, curious to see what kind of muscle car is arriving. At a distance I can see people smiling, but the closer the car gets, the more my jaw drops.

It's not *a* car, but *the car*: The Bat-car!

I am, to say the least, astonished. I turn toward Jas and see her trying desperately to hide the big bright smile that breaks out on her face, but without success.

I don't understand her reaction until the Bat-mobile stops right next to us and the window is lowered. The first thing I see are the marvelous blue eyes that look at Jas saying *I'm the number one,* and immediately after I see Jack's whole face saying practically the same thing.

Jas goes over to the window, visibly surprised and amazed, an expression that I haven't seen on her face for months. It has a strange effect on me.

"Are you're trying to impress me by any chance?" she asks him trying not to smile.

"No" he answers calmly.

"Because just know that I'm not."

"Obviously."

"I'm impressed by the car, not you."

"Of course, of course..."

"How did you do that?" she smiles as she examines the car in all its details, just as all the passersby are doing too.

"Simple", he says to her, "When I want something, I get it."

I like his self-confidence and presumption. There's something too sexy and irresistible about him. I move my gaze, embarrassed at having thought such a thing. *After all he is a criminal, a thief, a gorgeous hunk! Help!*

I turn to Will who, all nervous, is trying to call someone with his cell phone, very probably Nick, but he's so full of anxiety that he can't even open the phone, poor thing. Jack meanwhile continues to look at Jas, all happy because he sees her happy.

"Will you stop trying to look cool?"

"I'm not trying to look cool, I *am* cool. So? What are you waiting for to get it? It's not nice to keep a superhero waiting like this."

"I do not consider you a superhero in the least."

"Yes, I know, you see me as a supererror!"

His answers send me out of my mind.

They look at each other for a few seconds without saying anything, and then Jas suddenly liquidates me with a *twenty two,* which in our code means *I'm going.* She walks all the way around the car and gets in, leaving me alone on the sidewalk.

Jack smiles, happy to have captured his prey, gives me a wink and the next moment they disappear around the corner aboard the Bat-mobile.

I can't just get out of my mind Jas's reaction as soon as he appeared with the big car, and I can't understand if I'm worried that she's gone off with him, or happy that she did.

"Heeelp, heeelp, thiiief!" The scream coming from an elderly lady interrupts my thoughts. I turn and see a little old lady pointing at Will who is trying clumsily to take a small black bag from his back. It seems to be glued to him. The lady screams and hits him on the head with a rolled up newspaper and the passersby, instead of giving a hand, are laughing in amusement. I go over and try to help him, but I find myself being hit on the head as well by the old lady, and when I think that it can't get any worse, I find myself looking at Ross.

"Hello *M,* ciao *W,* ciao her that's beating *M* and *W*", he greets us as if nothing had happened and goes off with his thousands of shopping bags in his hand.

"*Ross!* Where are you going? You're not going to do anything?" I scream desperately. He turns quickly around and almost embarrassed he exclaims: "Oh God, yes, how stupid!" He takes the phone from his pocket and starts to film the old lady as she beats us with the newspaper because she wants her purse back, but it won't come off Will's back.

"I'm going to put this on *RossTube!*" he adds excited.

"Ross! Can you can help me, please?" I beseech him.

"Hmmmm, no! The last time that I threw myself into the fray to help you and that antichrist friend of yours, I ended up in prison!"

"But Jas isn't here, I beg you, Ross! Do it for *W!*"

I can't believe I actually said that!

I'm starting to talk like him, but apparently it works. Ross curls his lips, doubtful about what to do, after which he places the shopping bags on the ground and snorting he approaches Will who is still wriggling around and trying to run away from me and the angry little old lady.

"But that's a Valentino bag!" screams Ross like a little girl, looking at the bag stuck to Will's back, and immediately throws himself on top of him. It's a preposterous situation. Like so many others that I have experienced recently, I might add. I stop and look at the disaster all around; it couldn't be worse. But as soon as

I think that, I see the bad cop from the other time racing towards us: it's Christoph Waltz.

50.

In the meantime – From Jas's diary

I've been looking around curiously inside the Bat-mobile for the last five minutes and, whilst at first I had some doubts, now I'm sure: it is exactly the car that Michael Keaton drove in Batman in 1989. I remember it very well.

Every object in here, even if it's fake, is so very interesting. You can see from my face that I'm excited and this annoys me to death. He is smiling satisfied; he looks at me, expecting my praise, even if of course it will never come.

I cast a glance outside the window and I realize that we are going toward the airport.

"But...?" I look at him astonished, "You know what happened here a few weeks ago?"

"Yes. The usual thing", he responds and shakes his head as if it were a routine thing. "A guy gets out of bed one day and asks himself: *What can I do today? I could do some shopping, prepare a Burek, give the cat something to eat and, why not, blow up the Miami airport*. Right?"

"Nice summary, that's for sure. And you, when you got up this morning, what did you ask yourself? Just so I'm prepared."

"I asked myself..." he pauses and then shouts, all pumped up, "*How come I'm so cool?!*"

Then he bursts out laughing really amused and jumping up and down on the seat like a child.

I look at him speechless. I'm not even sure why, since it has already been clear to me for a long time that he is a hothead with delusions of omnipotence.

I look at the road. We are driving on the airport runway. But how did we get here? I remember that after the explosion it was all sealed off with barriers and yellow police tape stuck everywhere.

The closer we get to the building, the more my jaw drops. The Bat-mobile stops and so does my breathing.

John fixes me in silence, with the usual satisfied little smile, while I try to get over what I am seeing.

I get out of the car.

In front of me there is a boxing ring built right in the middle of the runway. On the ground there are still the remains of the rescue attempts: bandages, some dirty blankets, bottles of water, but above all the many stains of blood which have not gone away despite the rains.

Only a few weeks ago, there was a huge mess here, full of dead and wounded people. Wounded people that I wasn't able to help, apart from Zombie.

I look at John with an astonished expression still on my face.

"Come on", he makes a sign to follow him as he jumps into the ring.

"And what does this mean?"

"It means that the time has come to get rid of this sexual tension that there is between us, my love," he replies, and leans against the ropes of the ring with bravado.

"Will you quit talking bullshit?" I'm so busy staring around that I can't even get angry or answer back as I should. The sky is becoming dark; the wind is beginning to blow hard. Behind us are the remains of the burnt airport. Everything is black, half demolished by the explosion. I turn my back to John. I don't want him to see. I don't want him to understand. I don't want... to be so happy.

I'm angry with him. He shouldn't have given me such a beautiful surprise. I hate surprises.

I hear him arrive behind me and ask me: "Do you like what you see?"

He brushes my hair lightly. I feel a shiver down my back. I turn suddenly and without saying anything I unleash a punch straight at his face with all my strength. "Yes, I do now, yes I do!" I reply, asking myself what the hell has come over me.

He stares at me putting his hand on his face. "May I ask why the devil you did that?" he says surprised and angry at the same time.

"Never try ever again to touch me, understand?"

"You're completely off your head! One moment you're happy and the next moment you get mad! You're not normal! Why are you doing this? I don't understand you!"

"It's easy to understand: Do. Not. Touch. Me!"

288

We begin to circle around inside the ring.

"You say one thing, but you think another. It's not true that you don't want me to touch you."

"The punches, the slaps and the continual refusal are clear indications that I don't want to be touched by you."

"These are not indications, they're red herrings. When I say that I don't understand you I mean that I don't understand why you try to resist me", he comes closer, cheeky, "the physical attraction that we feel for each other is obvious".

Instinctively I try to punch him again, but he moves with agility.

"Stop beating me up!" he protests.

"I'm sorry, it's the physical attraction that's at fault", I retort ironic.

"Is this the way to thank me after all I've done for you?"

"Thank you?" I feel my blood pressure enflaming my face. "What for exactly? For having me arrested twice? For making me look like I'm crazy in front of all Miami?"

"First of all, it was your I-know-it-all friend who passed you off as crazy. Secondly, you had me arrested too, sweet thing, and you made me look like a pedophile kidnapper, closing a child of six years in the trunk of my car!" he comes back at me.

We start going around in circles again.

"I came all the way to Miami so I could clear things up with you, and you, as a thank-you, punch me in the face and *drown my car!*" he continues.

"But you on the other hand nearly drowned *me* in the fountain in the restaurant! I confessed to you that I have a phobia about my own blood and you used that against me to escape! You filled the balcony with evil dwarves despite the fact that I'd told you I hate them! You remember that I told you, don't you?"

"Yes, yes, of course I remember..."

"You're a bastard liar!" I interrupt kicking him in the stomach.

"Stop hitting me, Jas!" he orders, pointing a finger at me. "I saved your life! And you haven't even thanked me. I wasn't asking much. Just a gesture was enough. A. Simple. Gesture", he spells out.

"Here's the gesture." I make a vulgar gesture at him and as he's turning his head to look at it I release the umpteenth punch in his face with the other hand. "You destroyed my school." I take this opportunity to give him another punch. "You stole the headmistress's cross." Then I kick him. "You lied to me from start to finish. All you did was use me, you bastard! And you're continuing to do so!"

The last punch makes him fall to the ground.

I'm breathing rapidly and all I feel is anger, rancor. A great thirst for revenge.

"It's not true!" he snarls. With one hand he cleans his bloody lip and hits the floor of the ring with the other. "It's not true." His voice is changing now. It becomes more serious, sad.

I don't like the atmosphere that is being generated. I don't like his capitulation.

He is sitting on the ground with his head down; then he lifts his eyes looking at me from below. "How is it that you don't understand?" His eyes glisten in all this grayness which surrounds us. His gaze is sad, an expression similar to John's. But he is not John: John is dead.

"How can't you see?" he continues to fasten his eyes on me with such a sincere look, so repentant. "Jas, in your opinion, why am I here?" His voice is shaking.

I don't know what happens inside me, but something clicks. I approach him slowly and kneel in front of him.

He seems so fragile: the arrogance has disappeared from his eyes and blond hair hides his face, as he cleans the wounded lip with the sleeve.

My heart begins to beat very hard. I move the hair from his face, but without touching it. He looks at me in silence, surprised. He is trying to understand what I'm thinking, why I'm looking at him in this way. He seems so harmless and sweet that I impulsively say to him ironically: "Oh, my little one. Is that emotion that I see on your face?"

His expression changes suddenly.

"Are you going to start crying?" I go on.

"Be quiet!"

What's he thinking? That I'll fall for it again?

"Why don't you try cutting your arms, pretending to be a self-harmer? It worked last time," I suggest maliciously.

290

"Jas, that's enough", he says through his teeth. His gaze is changing every second and the real one is finally re-emerging, the bastard one. He gets up from the ground, nervous, like someone who feels he's been made a fool of. Like me.

"Or better", I continue, "Why don't you tell me the pathetic story about feeling guilty for the death of your equally pathetic dear little mother?"

"I said enough!" He slaps me, very hard, and I finish on the ropes of the ring. It takes me a moment to understand what happened.

John, looking as if he's possessed, comes over to me. "You're an evil vampire, you're icy cold and insensitive!" he exclaims. He makes a quick movement with his leg and I find myself on the ground again.

He kneels down and starts to speak in a spiteful way a few inches from my face. "I can't touch you, but hit you? Can I do that, little princess?"

I unleash a header out of rage, hurting both myself and him and get to my feet. Still dazed by the strikes that I've received, I turn toward him. "You're talking too much for my liking", I say, as if everything is fine, and kick him straight in the stomach, so hard that he bends in half. But there is not a shadow of pain on his face, only a great anger.

"You should start sticking to the first rule, John."

"My name is Jack!"

I feel a huge pain in my stomach, and shortly after I literally fly out of the ring ending up on the ground near the Bat-mobile. I can't even get up. Everything is hurting. I am breathless and still feel the blow I received.

John leans against the ropes of the ring and smiles. "Oh sorry, did I hurt you?"

This time he's the one who is speaking sarcastically. I quickly check whether I have a serious wound. The sight of my blood would not benefit my situation at this moment. Then I get up as if nothing had happened. "You didn't hurt me at all", I lie. I throw myself toward the ring again, and he continues to stare at me with anger and resentment.

"Not yet...", he whispers.

51.

In the meantime – From Mina's diary

To be arrested unfairly twice in less than a month is humiliating in itself, but to be arrested both times with Ross is unbearable. *May I and my idea to ask for his help be damned!*

If we also add that it was Christoph Waltz who arrested me both times and that Will was with us too, it turns into a Greek tragedy.

So I find myself in a cell which is two meters by two, with Ross yelling like a little girl hugging the bars and Will curled up on the bench and... I don't know what he's saying, I'd need Jas to translate the FRRF and hgujhki for me, but she is not there, because she has fled with Batman.

All this is incredible. If I related my adventures in Miami, I'm sure that no-one would believe me.

"It's all your fault *M*!" Ross cheeps, looking at me furious.

I raise my eyes to the ceiling.

"Every time I come near you, you small provincial duck, the policeman appears and my freedom disappears! I have always had the suspicion that you and that demon friend of yours were conspiring against me! Is it my femininity that bothers you both so much? Is this what triggered the envy in you? God, why?" he whines falling to his knees. "Why did you make me so beautiful, why?" The more Ross asks for an explanation from God on a beauty that God has not given him, the more Will tries to explain something with his incomprehensible stuttering, something that God has definitely given him.

I rest my head against the wall behind me, desperate, when I hear a noise of stiletto heels coming from the other end of the hallway. I turn, and my desperation increases: Lexi - dressed as a lawyer again like last time - and Christoph Waltz are coming. She looks at him in a mischievous way as she adjusts her black wig, and he is totally charmed by her. Waltz drooling over a woman is even more frightening than usual.

"Oh God Almighty, thank you! You have sent Athena to my rescue!"

"They are the last to arrive," Waltz explains to Lexi, leaning against our bars with a macho attitude. "Of course spotted, seized and locked up safe in here by Christoph in person." He looks at her with the eyes of a hunter, still speaking of himself in the third person. All three of us remain silent and look at him dumbfounded.

Lexi pushes him away with one hand and moves closer to the bars. "Oh, how sweet these little bipeds are."

She speaks as if we were little furry animals in a cage.

Ross begins to bark all happy.

"We also have some others, small, large, hairy and not", he jokes, putting himself in front of her again, trying to attract her attention. "I'll show you the way, if you wish, Miss White."

"Of course I'd like it", she wheezes, caressing his untidy beard, "But I'm in a hurry today, unfortunately." She moves him aside again and looks at us attentively, trying not to lose her balance. Jas is right; Lexi is an alcoholic.

"Let's see who we have here. There's Pink."

"Yes, yes, it's me *I'm trouble...*"Ross begins to sing. It's a song by Pink, the singer.

"Then we have Cinderella." Addressed to me of course.

"And Rain Man," she says, looking at Will amused as he continues to repeat his frrf and pk pk pk in silence.

"Don't be so *bibi*, Willy, and you don't need the phone to call home seeing that I came here precisely to have all of you released."

I don't know how she figured out from Will's stammer that he wanted to make a phone call, but from his reaction I think Lexi was right. "Jas hjknmjih Jack kijuhn DAS together, batman!"

"You were going to call Nickolas. I had to stop you somehow."

"Ghnhigj old of paff lady, false i- i- identity for three, with frrf to straff."

As usual I don't understand what he's saying, but I have the impression that the old lady and Lexi have something to do with this discussion. Want to bet that the old lady was Lexi in disguise?

"You do beat around the bush, one *thousand*", she snorts, "Now I'll get you out, guys, also because I'm in a hurry, there's a yacht waiting for me to take me to the Virgin Islands", she smiles embarrassed turning toward Christoph. "Virgin, I haven't said this word since I was fourteen years old", and continues to laugh in an unbearable tone, "Virgin", she repeats and, together with her, Ross begins to laugh also with his mouth wide open.

"Christoph", asks Lexi, "you'll watch me as I go out won't you?"

"Christoph watches everything and everyone in a very precise and attentive way, Miss White", he answers, he too obediently wagging his tail. Waltz has gone by now, his brain has turned off, and... something else has turned on.

"Well then, I'll shake my booty for you," she whispers. Waltz tries clumsily to take the bunch of keys to open the door of the cell, but he isn't able to do it because he's looking at Lexi as she goes waddling away in an unnatural manner, without even saying goodbye.

"Don't go, wait, my goddess!" screams Ross desperately, "Oh my God, she's beautiful. Isn't she the most perfect human being you have ever seen in your life?"

I prefer not to answer. I'm in too much of a hurry to get out of here. Will instead is watching her from behind the bars and comments: "She's not all that be-beau-beautiful! Spurukaft!"

The sound of heels departing suddenly stops. Lexi stands motionless at the end of the corridor for a moment, then she turns, looks at Will with eyes half-closed and in a voice like someone possessed asks: *"What did you say?"*

52.

Miami Airport – From Jas's diary

We can barely stand on our feet. We are exhausted and sore from all the blows we've given each other, but neither of us has wanted to be the first to give in. We're both leaning on our own part of the rope around the ring. We're sweating, one opposite the other and trying to quickly catch our breath, without taking our eyes off the other.

John barrels at me again and tries to hit me with his leg doing one of his acrobatic leaps: I move just in time, avoiding the blow and I punch him on the back as I run to the opposite side.

He smiles and grasps the rope of the ring. "You know how to dodge blows very well."

Of course I know how to dodge them, Nick did nothing but teach me this for a decade.

"And you know how to take them well."

We are both wheezing and as we carefully watch to see that the other one doesn't do anything funny, we both slowly sit down on the ground at the same time.

"I have already explained to you, Jas, you're only able to hit me because I let you."

"Then this is the lie you tell yourself to feel better."

"Well, coming from someone who does everything possible to convince herself to hate me..." He smiles and rubs his sweaty forehead; then without any warning he takes off his tight long-sleeved shirt and is left in just his t-shirt. Seeing him like this has a strange effect on me, but I can't help but look at him. His arms are so strong, so excessively muscular, with lots of powerful veins, but there's something missing now: the scars. His skin is smooth and intact, with no cuts, no bruising, only one scar which is almost unnoticeable; it's the one he got at Halloween saving me from the lamppost. He realizes that I'm staring at his arm so I look away, but it's too late, he has caught me out.

295

"I like it when you look at me this way," he says. He is fantasizing again about non-existent possibilities; I didn't look at him in any particular way.

"It's a look that lasts two seconds more or less. Two seconds isn't much, but if it's full of meaning it's like they last an eternity."

Sitting on the other side of the ring, he looks at me strangely, untroubled, but the even stranger thing is that he is speaking to me quietly.

"Will you stop talking bullshit?"

"I am not talking bullshit, Jas, and you know it."

"It's amazing how you always know what I know, want and think, before I do."

He smiles and stretches out on the floor of the ring. He looks at the gray clouds that cover the sky and for a little while remains silent. I feel uncomfortable, I don't know what to do; if I look at him, then he thinks that I really like him, and if I look at the sky instead... he still thinks I like him. He pulls back his blond hair and starts talking: "For almost an hour you have been slapped, kicked and punched. You feel tired, sore, and in less than an hour you'll be covered in bruises. And yet, you've never felt better in your life. Am I right?"

"You can't even imagine what I feel or what I think!" I say, but I don't think it. In reality I'm terrified because it's a century since I met anyone who could read so deeply inside me.

He looks at me. "I don't need to imagine it, Jas, I know, I see it", he tightens his lips and adds, "I feel it."

He looks at me quietly, relaxed, like someone who knows what he is saying and doesn't need anyone's approval, let alone mine. I feel unnerved again, I don't know why. He is a lunatic, his mood changes continually, first he laughs and says stupid things; then he gets angry, insults me, beats me and shortly after that he turns into a nice quiet guy again, who speaks to me in a level-headed quiet way.

I don't understand him; I didn't know where to place him when he was John and I don't know where to place him now either.

We are silent, he looks at the leaden sky above us and I look at the ruins of the airport in front of me. I like the whole scene; everything is so dark, mysterious, and unusual.

296

"The day I arrived at school, in Gorizia", he begins to relate, "My state of mind was reflected perfectly in the weather. Everything was like today. The sky full of gray clouds, it was dark all around me and it was about to rain. When I arrived you weren't there, but for the whole week it was as if you were. For five days all I heard was people talking about you. *Jas won the award, Jas didn't come to the awards ceremony, Jas took off from school on the back of a motorbike, Jas threw my camera into the vending machine, where is Jas my amorrrr?*" he smiles after he imitates Rodrigo, "you have no idea how curious I was to meet you. On the following Monday, Mina started talking to me and while she explained to me how the roof of the cube opened and closed, information which by the way I needed for the robbery, you arrived."

A thunder clap suddenly interrupts his discourse and immediately after there is a very bright flash of lightning which illuminates the sky. "You arrived just like a flash of lightning, with no warning. You were different from the other girls, the way you moved, the way you talked, thought... You were telling Mina that you had been to Maribor and you looked at me in a strange way without saying a word to me, and when you finally decided to speak", he pauses and looks at me, "you called me Jack". He smiles and shakes his head. "I was about to die. I'd spent weeks and weeks taking on the part of John, studying every minimum detail, movement, behavior, trying to make this my name and then you arrive and", he begins to scream with laughter, "and you call me Jack, do you understand? Of all the names in the world that you could choose, you chose to call me with my very own name", he continues to laugh and to tell the truth I can hardly stop myself from laughing too. I'd never thought of this particular thing.

"You made my life impossible without even realizing it."

"There were a lot of things I didn't realize, apparently", and I didn't even realize that I'd said this aloud. I stare at the floor of the ring, I do not want to meet his gaze, I don't want to see his expression, whatever it is. I hear only his voice say: "Jas."

I look up; he has sat down and is looking at me unhappy. "How much longer are you going to hold the past against me?"

"What if I do so for an indefinite period of time?"

"That's the same amount of time that I'm willing to take too, as long as I can make amends for my errors. But how do I regain your faith in me if you don't give me even a chance?"

Regain my faith in him. He never had it. He doesn't understand anything. Everything around us is black now, it's raining, and the only spot of color, again, are his eyes and the blue stone around his neck. I stand up. "Even if I gave you another chance, nothing would change. I gave my trust to John, a boy who doesn't exist, not to you. I don't even know you!" I jump down from the ring with a leap, going away.

"Jas!" he calls me, and gets down from the ring too, "Everything I told you as John was the truth! Stop!" I don't listen to him and I continue on my way, "Jas! Where are you going?"

"Home! The first round is finished!"

"Don't be silly, I'll take you!"

"No, thanks, I prefer to walk!"

"Jas!"

I walk in the rain, agitated, angry, disappointed, sad... I leave without turning back and he goes away without following me. It's the proper end for a relationship that has never had a beginning, for a relationship that has never had anything true about it.

Everything that he did in the past, and that he's still doing now is part of a precise plan, all deliberate, calculated down to the last detail. Everything he says as well as what he doesn't say is an attempt to confuse me, to get me to capitulate. The only thing that I don't understand is: why?

But I will no longer let myself be manipulated by him, this time I'm prepared. This time I see and feel, unlike last year. This time I have Nick close to me and he will never allow me to lose myself again.

"Jas!"

I turn my head and I see Nick himself in front of the *Watchtower* waiting for me in the rain.

"What are you doing here in the rain?" I ask Nick surprised. I am so happy to see him.

"I've been waiting for you."

I really need him at this moment. I need a little truth and sincerity that Nick knows how to give me with just one look.

"Come on, Jas, let's go inside."

"No, wait just a moment." I do not want to move away from him.

"But it's raining."

I remain glued to him like a koala; I don't even feel the rain, just the warmth of his embrace.

"Jas, you'll catch a cold, please, let's go inside." I don't like the tone of his voice. I look at him. He seems worried and distressed, but why? He knows that Felix's men are keeping an eye on me all the time. I'm wearing the bracelet with the built-in GPS. We enter the Watchtower and he immediately takes a towel from one of the sofas and begins to dry my wet hair. My Nick is always so solicitous with me. He always knows what to do and how to do it. My life would not be the same without him. He looks at me again with that anguished expression without saying anything.

"Nick?" I ask taking his hands, "What's wrong?"

"I'm sorry, Jas, I'm so sorry", his voice trembles, and so do his hands.

"Sorry for what?" I ask, "Nick, what are you talking about?"

He drops the towel on the ground softly touching my arms. He looks at them with tears in his eyes and continues to shake like a leaf.

I look at him too and I'm shocked.

I can't believe that they're my arms. They are crimson! I had not noticed anything, and it doesn't hurt, even if from the color and size of the bruises it would seem the opposite.

"Patrick reassured me that Jack would never hurt you, instead look what he has done to you that animal!" he says in a broken voice as if it were his fault, as if he'd given me the bruises.

I take his face putting his hair behind his ear. "Nick, I'm fine. It doesn't hurt, it was just combat. And what's more I can guarantee you that he's worse off than me," I assure him trying to look cool.

"You should not have fought with him, Jas, you shouldn't have. Promise me that you'll never do it again."

"Nick, look at me, I am okay", I smile, "I chose to know your world remember? And this is part of your world. Don't try to protect me, I beg you. It would not be the right thing to do and you know why."

He shakes his head caressing my arms all sad. "I knew that it would be difficult, but not like this."

"As you said, we have to face our fears. Together we can do this, Nick."

"Yes," he sighs. He doesn't seem very convinced. It's strange for me to see him in this state.

"How did you know where I was?"

"I always know where to find you, Jas."

I was expecting him to say something about my fight with John, after all I was good, I gave him some fantastic blows, but he says nothing. He picks up the towel from the ground. "Come on, let's go and change."

I'm upset. It is true that I came home with a lot of bruises, but I gave John just as many too. Why doesn't he congratulate me? I was incredible, even though I haven't trained for months. But him, nothing. We move toward the elevator, he's brooding, I'm sulking. The door opens and there's Veronica in front of me.

Great, from bad to worse!

"Veronica? Where are you going?" Nick asks.

Of course, Veronica replies only after squaring me from head to toe. "To look for Will. It's right on eight, dinner is not ready yet and his tracker is turned off."

"Has he spoken to his parents?" he asks with a touch of concern.

"Do you know any other reasons why he'd feel the need to isolate himself?"

"No," Nick admits.

"Let me know if he comes back," says Veronica. She comes out of the elevator, but after a few steps turns to me and tells me: "Ah, Jas, your friend has disappeared too."

"What?"

Nick and I look at each other with wide-open eyes and we hurtle into the elevator in one instant.

My Mina doesn't ever disappear! Something has happened!

53.

In the meantime – From Mina's diary

I'm still in the police station, but the situation has definitely turned into a comic scene which has no end. I'm sitting on a chair with a hamburger in one hand and a can of Coke in the other, and to my right are Lexi and Ross, each with a glass of Martini in one hand and the bottle in the other. It's like being at the movies, looking at the same person in the same direction: .Will still in the cell waiting for Lexi to have pity on him and let him go.

"Well then, Willy", she urges him, takes a sip of her drink and looks straight into his eyes. "I am...?"

Sitting on the bench of the cell, Will continues to sway looking at his watch. He scratches his head nervously and repeats for the umpteenth time: "The most be-beautiful."

Only after two hours of psychological torture, Lexi finally achieves what she wanted: a compliment from Will, even if it is anything but sincere.

"The most beautiful..." repeats Lexi, doubtful. It seems that Will's response was not comprehensive enough. "Woman that a-a-I have ever seen," he ends fed up. "I have the right to a te-telephone call PAAAF! I had to prprr dinner a-a-a-at eight o'clock! I'm late pk pk pk."

Lexi doesn't pay any attention to his complaints, but continues with the questions while sipping her drink, and I snigger. She gets up and starts strutting her stuff from one side of the room to the other, then stops in front of Will. "You have become a good little pet, you know? You deserve a little cookie." She bends over so he has to see her décolleté, but Will doesn't seem at all interested in her goods. Between one bite and another of the hamburger I'm about to choke from laughter.

"Rossella, what do you think? Does he deserve my little cookie?" she asks wickedly. Ross shakes his head amused.

"Willy", she continues to provoke him, sticking her hand inside the cell. "If you give me your paw I'll give it to you, your freedom."

After her phrase with a double meaning we are all waiting in silence waiting impatiently for what Will is going to do.

I reckon a new comic pair has been born today, even if the people concerned haven't realized it yet.

Will gets up from the bench with a sulky expression on his face, and surrendering to his cruel fate approaches Lexi giving her his *paw* muttering: "Ghftn frrf DAS paffff..."

***

I'm definitely hopeless at drawing. I realized just today that I still draw humans like kids do in kindergarten, with geometric shapes: the head is a circle, the body is a square, rectangular hands and feet... It is very humiliating to see that Diana can do it better than me, and it seems that she has realized it too, from the way she looks at me and laughs up her sleeve. This is not right. However, I've realized one thing: that I don't look at Diana any more with teary eyes of compassion like before. Her bald head, the pale skin and the dark circles under her eyes have no effect on me anymore. I see her for what she is: a little girl like so many others who wants to talk, play and learn about the world. I am happy I've been able to go beyond her appearance.

While Diana and I are lying on the ground drawing, Jas is sitting on Zombie's bed. She is writing something on her laptop and with the other every once in a while she throws a little red ball onto the old man. The parrot chases after it, takes it in its beak and brings it back to her. She's turning it into a dog too.

"Got it!"

I jump. "Holy God, Jas, you scared me! What have you got to scream about?"

"We don't know the identity of my friend Zombie, but now", she turns the computer toward me "we know the identity of Metoo!"

I get off the floor and go to the bed, intrigued. Diana instead continues to color in her book with her crayons, totally disinterested in Jas's discovery.

"Look here," she says showing me the screen, "Metoo is a *Psittacus Erithacus*, he comes from the Congo, eats seeds, fruit, vegetables and insects, and is one of the most intelligent birds." She looks at it and in a little girl voice she says to it: "You're smart aren't you? Yes of course you are!"

The parrot moves its head all happy; it seems to understand her, it's too funny.

"They associate human words with their meaning", she continues to read, "they have a vocabulary of a thousand words, they are the best imitators of all parrots and", she pauses and then looks at it surprised, "they growl?"

"That's why it brings the ball back to you, it is imitating a dog", I burst out laughing.

"But listen to this, they grow morbidly fond of their owner, they're like kids of five and tend to get bored very easily." She looks at it again as he continues to play with the ball on the old man in coma.

"You're like me, then? I get bored very easily too, Metoo." She smiles at the play on words. The parrot looks at her curious, as if it knew that she is talking to him, and starts to yell: "Kooooooo..."

Jas blocks her ears and, still looking at her laptop, tells me: "I knew that it was intelligent from the beginning. I left the window ajar on purpose, the other day, and since then he opens it with just a simple push and comes inside. And so you're African, eh?" Then she looks at me and asks me all upbeat, "Why don't we go to the Congo one day?"

"But if we can't even manage to leave for Europe." I say sourly, but even so I have all the reasons for the world to do so! Jas snorts. "What we need here is a nice *twelve*!"

"No, instead, you won't change the subject, Jas! What are we going to do about our trip? You just have to tell me loud and clear *we're not going to leave for Europe* and I'll come to terms with it, again."

She closes the laptop, puts it on the man in a coma and says to me, all serious: "Let's do this, tonight I'll speak with Nick and then I'll let you know, okay?"

"Really?"

"Yes really."

"Kooooo..." intrudes Metoo.

Jas laughs. "What have you got to yell about, you?"

303

"Kooooo", continues the parrot, and moves the ball toward Jas's hand with its beak.

"How sweet, it wants to play with you, Jas."

"Hey, go and grab it" she says as she throws it. The ball flies out the window, and behind it the parrot flies out as well.

"Nooooo!" I scream alarmed, "You've thrown it out the window, you're mad! Noooo, it threw itself down! You've killed it!" I stand still looking at the window trying to get over the shock that took my breath away. Metoo jumped down! She killed it! It's dead! I turn toward Diana and Jas; they're staring at me, both of them with one eyebrow raised.

"Mina? It's a bird", Jas informs me.

As if I didn't know that!

"And birds don't die if they jump out the window, but guess what: they fly."

I start to laugh like a crazy lying down on the floor and shaking my leg. I can't stop myself. What an idiot I am, how did I forget that parrots know how to fly?

Jas shakes her head in amusement; little Diana instead seems to be shocked by my behavior.

"Jas! What are you doing here?" I hear an angry voice shout behind me. I turn and see the hospital chief looking at us stunned, and it's no wonder: Diana and I are lying on the ground in the midst of various drawings, pens and sheets of paper, and Jas instead is sitting near the old man in a coma and has put her laptop on top of him.

"What are *all of you* doing here?"

"We have come to see my granddad," answers Jas very calmly.

"He is not your grandfather!" she protests. She takes the laptop off the man and puts it on the nightstand.

"But I found him, so it's as if he were."

"Don't say it aloud, do you want to get me into trouble?" she whispers all frightened and checks on whether there is someone near the door. "I didn't mention your name to the detectives and you also know why!"

"Chief, chief, don't you know you shouldn't tell lies?" Jas teases her.

"You should talk", she whispers.

Diana is drawing on the floor without taking any notice of us.

"Diana, what are you doing there on the ground?" asks the chief.

The little girl simply shrugs her shoulders and doesn't answer.

"Diana? I asked you a question."

"Arizona, you know that I cannot speak", she whispers, "It's Jas's first rule, if I want to stay here. Otherwise you'll have me thrown out!"

"Out of here", she orders raising her eyes to the ceiling, "go right back to your floor or I'll have your blood drawn by one of my interns!"

"Oh bother", snorts the little girl, taking her yellow toy with her.

"And you, get back to work," she says pointing to Jas, "the break is over."

"Oh bother", Jas snorts too and goes out with the mop in her hand.

The chief closes the window. "And another thing, why is the window open? It's terribly hot outside, it has to remain closed. Understood? You'll drive me crazy! Crazy!" She leaves the room in desperation and after rebuking a Chinese boy telling him to go back to his laboratory she turns to Jas. "And make sure you clean the whole room of this patient!"

"Why? What harm can it do to him? He's in a coma."

Arizona sighs exasperated. "I'll go crazy, I'll go crazy." She goes off fiddling nervously with the stethoscope. Thank heavens she didn't send me away too. I go into the room of the man in a coma, adjust the blanket and begin to tidy the mess on the ground, but a doubt assails me suddenly... I get up and run toward the window, I have to make sure that the parrot is really alright.

54.

In the meantime – From Jas's diary

I get into the elevator with mop in hand, I still have one floor to clean and then I can finally go home!

The door opens and there's Lexi dressed like a nurse. Every time I get into this elevator I run into a member of the Black family. This time she's wearing a wig of blond hair tied in a bun, a miniskirt up to her neck and about six male nurses buzzing around her.

How sad to see the males on heat; they smile for no reason, make pathetic jokes, and when they talk looking at the woman in the eyes, I'm convinced that her face must be between her neck and her navel.

Unfortunately Lexi notices me. "Oh, Jas!" she looks at me surprised and disgusted at the same time. "Nice..." She points at my *cleaning woman* uniform, "dress", and then looks at the mop. "And your...." she pauses, "stick is nice too", and then tilting her head at the garbage bag that I'm holding in the other hand "And what a nice, uhm, bag."

I look at her and shake my head while she adds in a low voice: "Darling one, when I told you that you're the only one that I know who doesn't have a handbag, I didn't know that you'd take the first one you came across..."

"Goodbye Lexi!"

"Wait!" She stands square in front of me hampering me from passing her. "What are you doing here?" she asks, with this usual amazed question which is anything but credible.

I approach her whispering: "Actually, I am not here, it's only your imagination."

I look at her with a serious face and leave slowly. As I go I hear her ask the nurses if they saw me. I'm speechless.

"Hey, wait! *One thousand*!"

I hear the ticking of her heels approaching and without turning around I ask her: "What do you want?"

"Jack is still angry with you. He says that you don't understand anything and that you are... I don't quite remember what... unfortunately my attention span is very short if it's not about me, but any way it was a *bibi* thing."

I feel a strange rustling behind us. I turn and see the nurses and the interns walking behind us, shoving each other.

"Why do you treat him like that? Jack is a rich, beautiful, strong, powerful and combative boy. Why don't you want to go out with him?" she continues to ask me idiotic questions.

"Why? I look at her annoyed. "Well, the fact that he's a thief and a ruthless murderer are only two of the reasons that make him impossible to date!"

"Why?" she asks astonished, "Bad boys are sexy", she smiles, adjusting her blond wig, then winks at the boys behind us.

"He hasn't a chance with me, and explain it to him properly when you see him", I tell her.

"Jack will never give up, that is why you'll end up falling madly in love with him."

I look at her like you look at someone who doesn't understand a thing, while I keep walking along the corridor.

"We women love having men fight for us."

Meanwhile a dispute among the nurses has commenced behind us. Lexi looks at me and smiles. "There is nothing less sexy than a man that respects the restraining order, or a priest that respects the vow of chastity, or a husband who is devoted to his own wi..."

"I understand", I interrupt her, "that's enough now."

For a moment she is silent, she caresses her hair in a sensual way, thinking of who knows what, and then says: "Tell me something...did Willy ask about me?"

"Will?" I feel like laughing. Actually, because of her, Will has done nothing in the last week but to clean the most absurd places in the Watchtower saying things like FRRF SPRAF, PK PK, just to get rid of his agitation.

"More than ask about you, he has cursed you. Why?" I ask wondering.

"That's all, just simple curiosity. Excuse me, now I really have to run," she says as she runs toward the elevator on the other side of the corridor, risking of toppling over, what with her dose of alcohol and the people that are running after her. "I have an important appointment this evening and I need to find a dress that matches the seats of my private jet."

I stop in the middle of the corridor to watch with raised eyebrows the nurses who are sniffing the closed door of the elevator that Lexi has just entered. I feel ashamed for them!

***

Nick has been acting strange the entire evening and this is boring me. Even the weather is not the best, the wind is strong and I think it's going to rain again soon. There has been a hurricane alert for months but nothing at all has happened; they're just tricking us and there's not even the slightest trace of the hurricane.

There are very few people around tonight, you can tell it's the middle of July, but there are still half-naked girls slobbering over Nick. They're never missing!

While I raise my eyes to heaven, he as usual is taking no notice of me and looks the other way. He is ever more on guard tonight, perhaps because I told him that I'd run into Lexi today at the hospital. He walks composed without turning either his head or his body; his eyes, on the other hand, continue to jump from one point to another in search of something. How annoying. None of the Blacks will come near me, now that Nick is here.

"Can I know what's up with you today?" I burst out, I am tired now of this silent walk.

He smiles apologetically. "Sorry, I have a lot on my mind, and I can't get rid of it." He takes my hand, kisses it softly and caresses my pendant in the form of a line on the little bracelet that he gave me for Valentine's Day, continuing to be preoccupied.

"Do you want to do the ED?"

"The Emotion Dance?" he asks surprised. Actually his reaction is quite understandable given that I have suggested to him the one thing that I've been avoiding like the plague for five months, at this point.

Nick smiles. "I invented' the ED to talk about you, not me."

"Come on, how do I know what's wrong with you at the moment?" I complain like a little girl.

308

He squeezes my hand, and very simply responds: "You just have to ask me, Jas, I am always sincere with you."

I stop suddenly, and before he can say anything else I'm already engulfed in his embrace. It was a natural thing to do, I don't know why. Perhaps I like it when he talks to me in this open and sincere way, I adore him! I feel his heart beating very hard.

"What is it?"

"You're the one who needs to tell me what's wrong, not I." I look at him, putting a lock of hair behind his ear. "What is the problem, Nick?"

"My problem has just one name: Jack."

"Ah", I tighten my lips and bow my head. I don't like this topic.

"He hasn't been seen for a week, he's certainly planning something to astound you again."

"And would that bother you if that's the case?"

"Yes."

"Why?"

"Because I am afraid that his plan is..." he pauses, a pause that is too long, I know these pauses and they never bode well. "I don't know how to express myself so that you don't misunderstand what I'm trying to say, Jas."

"Oh my God!"

It's worse than I thought.

"I haven't said anything yet."

"Your introduction has already said everything."

We're both silent for a moment. This is just the confirmation that what I was thinking was correct: we're about to have a terrible argument.

We're standing in the middle of the empty street looking at each other; he is thinking of the words to use to start speaking to me and I'm thinking about which ones to use to make him stop once he begins. All that can be heard is the Latin-American music coming from a bar at the bottom of the road. I sigh deeply. "Come on, out with it, what have I done wrong?"

As they say, best just to pull the band aid off.

"I didn't say that you have done something bad."

"Nick, talk."

"But listen to me before you attack me, okay?"

309

The more he continues with these mysterious introductions, the more I expect the worst. "Yes, yes", I cut short also because our conversation is, apparently, going to be very long.

He places himself in front of me and puts his hands on my shoulders. "Jack has had many months to study you and all those that were around you when you were in Gorizia. He is very cunning and now his plan is to win your trust by letting you do everything that I forbid you to do, Jas, do you understand? I wouldn't like him to be brain-washing you. I wouldn't like you to lose sight of our goal for your need to experiment and try new things. That's all."

That's all? I try to understand if I've understood correctly what he wants to make me understand, but I'm not really sure that I've really understood. "I don't understand. Why are you telling me this, Nick?"

"You're the one who said that you are afraid of losing yourself and I will do everything to keep you on the right track. I won't allow that lowlife to manipulate you again."

I take a deep breath and I ask him again, calmly, breathing deeply: "What have I said or done wrong to make you think like that? Can you explain that to me?" I spell out the words so as to make him understand he has to be very careful with the answer he gives me.

"You're still young, Jas, just a small distraction and you could find yourself as Jack's victim again, but that's normal because you don't have experience. All I need to know is that you won't lower your guard, you must never forget who he really is."

"Do you really think that I am a complete idiot? Do you really think this of me?" I raise my voice, annoyed.

"No, I do not think so."

"I can't believe it!" I turn around and leave, really pissed off, heading to the end of the street. He follows me. "Jas! Where are you going? What's wrong with you?"

"What's wrong with me? You're talking to me as if I was a little girl! It's not enough, you know, to just put a lollipop in my hand to brainwash me!"

"I didn't say that." He catches up to me and turns me toward him. "Jas! I didn't mean that", he tries to defend himself; it's a pity that the words say one thing and his body language another.

I explode: "I don't understand you! You were the one who convinced me to stay and work with you telling me that we must face our fears together! Except that you forgot to specify that your biggest fear is that I let myself be manipulated by John again." I go, turning my back on him once more. I cannot believe that this is really happening! I cannot believe that he could even think such a thing!

"Jas, you're misunderstanding everything!"

"I'm misunderstanding? Are you sure?" I scream, turning back to him, "The truth is that right from the start you didn't take me seriously. You don't see me as your colleague, as a member of the team, you see me like, like... I don't even know how you see me anymore!"

"Jas! You can't do this to me! I promised to stay close to you because you told me that you're afraid of losing your way again!"

"No! That's not true! Yes! Okay, it is true, but... it's not like that now! I know what I'm doing! I'm not a child any longer!" I scream trying to distance myself again.

"I didn't say that you are."

"There is no need to say it. I can see it, dammit!"

"Jas, that's enough now!"

I stop suddenly, not because he told me to, but because I really can't take it anymore. I look at him, and in his place I see Veronica telling me: *Nick will always be protective of you because it doesn't matter what age you are, he will always be eight years older than you, and you will always be his little Jas. For him you will never grow up.*

She was right. She was absolutely right.

I cover my face with my hands for a moment and then look at Nick who is coming to me to hug me, to calm me. I stop him with an outstretched hand. "Nick, the truth is that it's no good. Everything we try to do outside of our friendship becomes complicated and unbearable to manage."

"I didn't want to..." he makes a pause and puts his hands on my shoulders, "Why is it always so difficult to talk to you, Jas."

"Because I can't stand it any longer. I am trying to do my best, I'm trying to do everything not to disappoint you, but every time a new problem presents itself, or maybe I should say an old problem. If I was Veronica, you would never have talked to me like this, Nick."

"It's different," he murmurs, he knows very well what I mean.

"I know. That's why it's no good. We're not able to do a single thing together without things becoming complicated and I don't know what to do any longer. It won't work between us, Nick, nothing except the friendship."

His face becomes sad, his eyes bright. "It's not true," he whispers, "you can't know if you do not..." he squeezes his lips together and smooths my hair. "What are we talking about, Jas?" he asks softly.

I don't answer.

"I never know what is going through your head. You don't talk, you don't ask, it's impossible for me to read you and I'm afraid to bring up the matter because..."

"I was talking about John", I interrupt him suddenly. Nick closes his eyes with yet another sigh, only this one is much longer and much deeper. When they reopen, his face seems to be more relaxed. "We always start from the same point: silence. Apart from the investigations, when you go out with him and then tell me what you've seen, you never talk about Jack to me. You don't even call him by his real name, Jas. I don't know what you think of him, I don't know what you feel for him, if you're changing your mind about something, after all he saved your life, you were very close the pair of you and", he tightens his lips again, "he has kissed you too, and we both know that a kiss... changes everything."

I can't believe that he has really said that. I instantly turn red, my heart begins to beat very fast, I wish I could sink into the ground.

"I don't want to see you suffer again because of him, I couldn't bear it."

I move to avoid his gaze and more questions or embarrassing memories. I feel terribly uncomfortable, I cannot do it. After a few seconds I take courage, I stand in front of him and I begin what I have to say: "I'll tell you only once, and never again. From the moment I saw John again everything that he has said or done, every look or movement of his, even seemingly innocuous meant only one thing for me: deception. Despite all his attempts to surprise me and charm me, I can assure you that he will never have my trust. John doesn't wear his mask any longer, and when I look at him I see him for what he is: a murderer, a thief, a liar. There is nothing he can say or do to make me change my mind about him. This has nothing to do with the fact that he saved my life. I am grateful to him for this, and when you arrest him I'll tell him that. This is what I think."

Nick seems to be much more at ease now, and I actually feel better too. For once I've told him the whole truth and not a half-truth. For once my truth has not disappointed him and did not hurt him. He hugs me hard and I feel his heart beating strong on my chest. "I'm sorry, Jas. I thought..." he looks at me and smiles, "I thought the wrong thing." He hugs me again and kisses my head repeatedly.

"I'll never accept his world, Nick, I want this to be clear to you, I have made mistakes in the past, it's true, but I will never become like him."

"Are you saying that you no longer need to break the rules and cross the line?" he smiles touching the bracelet.

"Yes."

"And that you are no longer afraid of losing your way?"

"No, I'm not afraid anymore."

"I'm proud of you."

The wind blows hard and while I move his hair from his face, he moves mine behind my ear. He smiles. I thought that our argument would have lasted for hours and, instead, by talking openly and sincerely we've solved everything in a few minutes. Perhaps this story about sincerity is not so wrong.

"I'm sorry about this argument, and you're right, after all you've never given me any reason to get this paranoia in my head."

I smile satisfied, all's well that ends...

But all of a sudden I hear a female voice screaming behind me. "Buffy."

Buffy?

I turn and see a familiar-looking girl outside the same restaurant where the music is coming from. The closer she gets to me with her arms open, the clearer it becomes who it is: the Latin-American girl from the Black Cat.

I just say *Hey*, but inside I have a world of unmentionable words! I'm finished! She, wearing a white bride's veil, embraces me all happy, while Nick, confused, repeats: "Buffy?"

But why right now? Someone up there must have it in for me!

As if that wasn't enough I see more drunken people come out of the bar and head toward us. One of the brothers of the bride is explaining cheerfully who I am and where they met me; it's just a pity that none of the things they know about me is true. I try to get out of the clutches of the drunken bride before Nick discovers some other detail about Buffy, but with no success. The girl hugs me like a jellyfish. "Ooooh Buffy! This is fate!"

And Nick again who asks me intrigued: "Buffy?"

"It's a long story", I cut short. The two brothers and other people surround me as the bride explains in a loud voice very nicely: "She's the girl who speaks with the angels! God sent her here to me, it's a sign!"

"You *what*?" Nick is getting upset again.

"Okay, it wasn't such a long story after all", I try to make it sound funny, even if in the end everyone is laughing, except me.

"She spoke with mamma!" continues the girl and then looks at me with glistening eyes, "It's thanks to you that I was married today, Buffy, you were a gift from heaven!" The bride continues to provide information, and the more she talks the more Nick becomes dark in the face. The guests assail me asking about their dead, offering me money, and I don't know what to do, I really don't know how to get out of it.

"Guys, that's enough! Leave her alone now!" The bride saves me as she stands between me and the guests. "What are you making me look like? It's party time this evening, a celebration, and we have to celebrate." Turning toward me and taking my hands she says "Come inside with us, you and your friend will be my guests of honor."

"Yes, hmm, you go ahead meanwhile, okay? I'll just be two minutes", I lie. I'll never join them, ever, because in two minutes I will be dead.

"Okay, Buffy, see you inside."

Every time she calls me Buffy I shiver.

Laughing and joking, they all go back inside the restaurant, and while screams of fun and loud music come from inside, out here the third world war is about to break out. I'm afraid to turn toward him.

"What is happening here? What were they talking about?" Apparently he can't wait to look me in the face. He has placed himself in front of me and stares at me. I can see the reprimand in his eyes.

"Mah, just nonsense, Nick", I try to downplay the question laughing, "I didn't have the money to pay for my..."I remember just in time that I can't say *cocktail*, "drink, and I said that I was called Buffy and that I was a kind of medium", I laugh, thinking that by making it all sound ridiculous he can laugh, too. "I told her to get married and she really did get married, that's a beautiful thing, no? Fiestaaaa..."

"You did *what*?" Nick has no intention of laughing. "You lied, you masqueraded as someone else, conned someone and made them pay you?"

"Masquerading as someone else?" I snort, "Buffy is a character invented by a TV show! I didn't steal anyone's identity, and anyway it was only five dollars, Nick, it was only five dollars", I explain to him without telling him about the ten other people that I conned before her.

"It doesn't matter if it were five or five thousand dollars, Jas! It is still a scam! You can't do that! You live in a building that represents the law! Do you realize what you've done?"

"You're making a fuss about nothing! You're not being fair!"

"Don't talk to me about justice! You should not even mention it!" He raises his voice even more, "You don't believe in the law, but you believe in crime? I ask you to collaborate with Felix to apprehend a fraudster and a murderer and I discover that you do the same things!"

"What? Nick you're off your head! I have never killed anyone, I didn't do anything wrong! You don't even listen to me when I talk! You're making all this stupid fuss for five freaking dollars! Does that seem normal to you?"

"That's the way it starts! You falsified your documents in hospital passing yourself off as an intern, you cheated in your test in medicine, you've been accused of slander by your psychologist and last year you had a suspect acquitted."

"I didn't cheat in the medicine test and Mujo was innocent!"

"You couldn't know that!"

I cannot believe that this is really happening. He looks at me as if I was a criminal, as if I'd done who knows what.

"Why are you saying these things to me only now? You never yelled at me in all these months about the psychologists and for the test!"

"Because you're a member of the team now! You cooperate with the law! I can no longer defend you because we are no longer just Nick and Jas."

"And what are we?" I scream pissed off. He remains silent. I continue: "You always say that I can tell you everything, but I am afraid to tell you everything! Have you ever wondered why? Eh? Because every time that I'm upfront with you, you yell at me and make me feel like a piece of shit!"

He puts his hair behind his ears and with sharp and authoritarian voice says to me: "Dammit, Jas, but what do you expect from me? That I give you a round of applause? You go around telling people lies, you rob them, insult them... what you do is bad, how can't you see that?"

I remain silent, what can I ever say, I'm a bad person and Nick is slamming it in my face. "You need to start taking responsibility for your actions. Now you're going inside there, you tell them the truth and give back the money."

"What? No!"

"Jas! You have cheated and manipulated. As well as being an unlawful practice, it is also morally reprehensible. You had ulterior motives. You must apologize. It's the only right thing to do", he says in a severe voice.

"No! I don't want to do that!" His eyes become hard and cold. "As well as being deceitful, did he teach you something about murder as well? Given that Jack is an expert?"

"What the heck are you saying?" I look at him shocked. "He has nothing to do with all of this! It was just a harmless joke, I didn't say to kill herself, I said to get married, Holy God!"

"You said that you would follow the law to the letter!"

"This happened before that!"

"I will not allow you to go on doing things like that, just as I won't allow you to do what you like with Jack with the excuse of the investigations!"

Anger is mounting inside me. "You're paranoid! You're yelling at me for something that I haven't done! I haven't done anything wrong! I hate you!" I go away with tears in my eyes. He shouts behind me: "You have let yourself be influenced!"

"It's not true!"

"Stop, where are you going?"

"Far away from you! That's where I'm going! You're crazy!"

"You can't go around alone in Miami! Stop!"

"I'm eighteen years old and I can do what I want!"

"Jas!"

I walk angrily toward the Watchtower, with Nick following me at a distance. The whole time I can't get my head around it. He is accusing me of things I haven't done, that I never even thought of doing!

I never give John a thought. I've never thought of taking advantage of people, and he has never taught me anything because I haven't even listened to him! And then he gets angry with me for five damn dollars! What are five dollars? I have done nothing wrong. I didn't take her patrimony from her. I don't understand! And Mujo? He was innocent, he was innocent! And Nick tells me off as if I'd done who knows what! I don't deserve a dressing-down of that kind! My former psychologists were not real psychologists, because if they had been, I wouldn't have felt I was under interrogation every time I spoke with them! So how could they help me? I pretended to be an intern, it's true, but I didn't cheat in the medicine test, I did not cheat! Curse him and his damn law!

As I walk immersed in my thoughts, all of a sudden I see a black car come slowly alongside me. The window with tinted glass goes down and I see John. Even before I can say anything he preempts me: "Okay, before you start to insult me and start punching I want you to know that..."

"Yes, okay", I interrupt him, "Okay, here I am." I immediately go around the other side and climb into his car. He looks at me surprised. "You know, I like you when you answer questions that I don't ask you."

I look back and see Nick running worried toward us. Suddenly I panic. "Will you get going, yes or no?" I ask him urging him to hurry. John smiles, presses the accelerator and in a moment we're at the other end of the road.

The further we get from Nick, the better I feel. *He can go and get fucked! He wants to chastise me? Well, go right ahead! The next time he does it at least I'll know that I deserve it!*

"Where do you want to go?" John asks, studying me with his gaze. Obviously jumping into his car and going off with him instead of hitting and insulting him makes him suspicious.

"You're the one who always knows what I'm thinking", I say with a challenging air, "so you tell me. Where do I want to go?"

"Whoopee", he screams happily, "I like you, little girl!"

55.

And this evening as well, dinner is really very amusing. Will has not yet digested Lexi's joke of a week ago. I still can't believe that she was the old lady who had us arrested. In any case, Will has done nothing but cook to get rid of his agitation, and between one course and another he tells us about the wrong he suffered for the umpteenth time. He's too cute.

With a full stomach I go back to my room with the sole intention of sprawling on the bed and going to sleep. I close the door and, to my great surprise, between the poster of Jas and the detective Jx, I find a black arrow stuck in the door with a red envelope attached to it. I look around, then I look at the envelope, and I see that it has *for Mina* written on it.

I don't know why, but the thing is so strange that I go first to close the door of the balcony, then lock the door to the room and only then do I pull the arrow out and take the envelope in my hand. I sit down on the bed, open it and take out one of the two notes inside.

You have 10 minutes to get dressed, attach the second note to the door and go out without being noticed.

I get up from the bed, confused. Jas didn't tell me about this plan. And what if it's nothing to do with her?

While I think of what to do I'm already getting dressed and not long after the other note is attached to the door with scotch tape, I'm already in the elevator.

Perhaps, after all, I'm not all that confused about what to do next.

My heart beats madly; doing these things on the sly gives me a strange feeling of anguish.

The elevator door opens and in front of the entrance of the Watchtower I see a large and long black limousine. It's the same one that came to take Jas for her first appointment with Jack. Perhaps it's them.

I go out, looking at the limousine with wonder, the window is lowered, and Lexi's head pokes out wearing a red wig and a half-empty glass in her hand. "Holy crap," she says hiccupping, "I didn't know you were pregnant, my dear."

"But I..."

I look at my tummy, very bloated from Will's dinner. Actually I do look pregnant. I pull a face without saying anything, and then I see Ross's head stick out of the open window. He also has a red tuft on his head. "There is a country called *bad taste* and you're its queen", he says to me with his shrill voice, "Who looks after your image, a horse? Didn't your mother teach you how to dress?"

Unfortunately Ross does not know that my problem is exactly this: I have followed my mother's advice. I prefer not to comment on his provocation and ask him: "Where's Jas?"

"I wouldn't know", Lexi slurs, she does not appear to be very lucid. "Perhaps she's gone off to do something, with someone, somewhere."

"I don't understand. Why am I here?" My question is legitimate, but above all directed at Lexi, it's a pity that Ross decides to respond for her: "But of course you don't understand, you have a brain equal to your clothes", he continues to gratuitously offend me. I can't stand him.

Lexi fixes me and explains: "You're the best friend of the future first girl of my little brother Jack, so you need some sprucing up, my dear. You're not presentable at all. If I didn't know you I would pretend I didn't know you."

What on earth is she saying? Her sentence does not make sense. I don't understand when she speaks.

"Oh holy Donatella, what is that face? You're as expressive as a Chinese vase", continues Ross, who apparently only knows how to heap insults on me. She looks at me and unfortunately I cannot do anything other than shut up again. He and Lexi are not totally wrong; I'm sunburned, dressed badly and this hair doesn't help me, I feel disgusting. "I'm sorry, but I don't have the money for sprucing up."

And what I have I need for the trip to Europe that maybe I'll be lucky enough to do this year.

"Don't worry; I'll take care of you, my dear. Many years ago I was with a stylist named Stephen. He left me his entire cultural heritage as regards fashion. To tell the truth he also left me for Domenico, a very sweet person, but I'm not angry with him, because he still sends his creations to me at home", then she turns to Ross. "Shall we look for a few nice maternity wear shops, yes?"

"I am not pregnant!"

Ross thinks about that a moment and then exclaims: "Hmm, hmm, we can find the shop but I don't know if they'll let her in."

It seems that what I say is of no interest to anybody.

Lexi signals to me. "Are you getting in or not? The Jet is waiting for us."

"The Jet? What? Where are you taking me?"

Lexi turns to Ross and both of them, looking at me with great big smiles on their lips, shout "To New York, sweetie!"

56.

An hour later – From Jas's diary

I have been in the car with John at least an hour, and for a full hour we have not uttered a word. Words are of no use, everything is far too clear. Every so often I see from the corner of my eye that he is looking at me, but continues to say nothing. Something I really appreciate.

For the umpteenth time I've had the proof that there is not a single thing that Nick has taught me and shown me as he should. He continues to protect me, continues to treat me like his child, and just like every other time the only one who feels like a complete idiot is me.

I've been here for five months, and for five months Nick has shown me only the most famous part of Miami, the one you see in the television series, the tourist zone that exalts the beauty of the place. Lots of colored lights and lots of wealth: Miami Beach, Coconut Grove, Art Deco, Espanola Way; but as soon as you go into side streets, as soon as you leave the areas of the most extreme luxury, it's like waking up suddenly from the beautiful dream and finding yourself in a very different reality.

John has brought me into the more dangerous neighborhoods, the ones to avoid both day and night, like Overtown and Liberty City, north-east of the city. Immediately after that we pass through Little Haiti and Opa Locka. The names of the neighborhoods are different, but what I see from the car window is always the same: crime and decay.

On the sidewalks, groups of colored kids - some will be about my same age - turn to look as soon as we approach them with the car, and they look at us with mistrust, showing us the weapons they have under their belt.

Despite having already seen John in action and knowing with what speed and accuracy he can kill three men in a few seconds, I fear these gangs. Today, for the first time in my life I am looking at an exchange of drugs between drug dealers and supplier; exchange that takes place on the street in all tranquility, not caring to hide from prying eyes.

I also witness a bashing: two African gorillas thump another colored man until he starts to bleed and drops to the ground. When they come alongside the car, one of the two points his weapon at us.

We leave quickly and shortly after I hear a shot behind us. It is not directed at us so I can imagine where the bullet ended up.

I can't believe all this. How can they live in this way? Mostly they're Cuban immigrants who live here, people who have fled the regime, entire families forced to live in these poor and unsafe neighborhoods. Many streets have even been closed, in a desperate attempt to defend themselves from thieves, and the houses are surrounded by iron gates.

I'm afraid. Because of the place, dark, dirty and full of men and boys who make me feel like they want to do me harm for no good reason, almost as if it's a game. But I am curious to discover this world, which only a few hours ago I didn't even know existed.

As if that were not enough, another feeling won't leave me in peace: the feeling of guilt. I don't know why, but seeing the eyes of children behind the gratings - eyes full of... I don't know how to explain it, perhaps the right word is resignation – I feel a lump in my throat and try desperately to hide it from John. Without success.

"Is everything okay?" he asks me kindly, without using his usual scoffer and unpleasant tone.

"Yes", I say to him, also in a civilized way.

"Welcome to Miami."

"And there was I thinking I already was in Miami."

"You were part of the fake part of the city, tourism, full of lights, glitter and sequins. You were living in an illusion. This is the real Miami," he says, almost disconsolate, looking out the window.

"How do they live in this horror?"

"Horror?" John smiles amused. "This is the less horrible part, Jas. Do you know what the schools are like here? You have to walk a fast pace, head low, do everything you can so you don't attract attention and avoid the bullets."

"Why don't they go away?"

He smiles again, a bitter smile. "Where do you think they can go?" He becomes even more serious and continues without looking at me: "The crime rate in Miami is one of the highest in the United States: drug trafficking, prostitution, robbery, theft, extortion, murder. Many tourists die too, killed by the bands of Hispanics that control these neighborhoods", he looks at me. "Everything, here, revolves around drugs, seventy percent of the marijuana and cocaine that is destined to the American market arrives in this city."

"And where are the police in all this? Earlier they were dealing on the street as if they were doing nothing wrong, how is it possible?"

He smiles again. I see that he doesn't want to make fun of me, but explain things properly to me. "What you have to understand is that the drug dealers, thieves and murderers are not the problem, it's the police, the judges, and the politicians... All of them have one thing in common: it's called *corruption.* This is the main reason that is sending this country to ruin, and also the whole of society."

"Why have you brought me here? What did you want to do, convince me that you're the victim, that all this is normal?" I look at him and wait for a reply, but instead he stops the car in the middle of the road. I look outside. There is no-one around us, there is total emptiness, darkness. He turns toward me placing his arm along the back of my seat. I feel my heart begin to beat very fast. I'm not afraid of him, I just feel... strange. With the other hand he pulls back his blond hair and looks at me straight in the eyes. "The last time we saw each other, you said that you don't know me, that in reality you don't know who I am. It's not like that. The first step toward me you made with John, because everything that I confided to you about my mother, my self-harm, and my sense of guilt... they were not lies Jas. Today I've brought you here to take the second step, with Jack."

I say nothing. The serious expression on his face and his calm way of speaking to me takes me by surprise.

"Now it's up to you. If you want to take further steps to get to know me, you'll have to walk where I walk, Jas." He bites his lip, he seems worried, and then adds: "That's if you want to."

From the way he looks at me and waits for my answer, he is not entirely sure that it will be a yes, from me, and I like that.

Know his world. They are the same words that Nick said to me.

I don't know what to do. The only source of light in the whole area comes from the car radio that illuminates his face and emphasizes his blue eyes even more. I start to play with my hair. Strange, I usually never touch it. "What is the third step?" I ask him finally, trying to control my emotions.

57.

In the meantime – From Jx's diary

Nickolas exits the elevator, crosses through the hall and rushes toward the central corridor, the one that leads straight to the bedrooms. He arrives at Jas's room and finds a red note attached to the door that reads:

Jas called me. We're sleeping at the History Hotel tonight. Don't worry.

Mina

The door at the end of the corridor opens, and it's Patrick. He sees his friend leaning against the wall with his head down, and understands immediately that something is wrong.

58.

From Jas's diary – Miami Beach, same night

John and I, walking on the beach, barefoot, with our shoes in our hands, speaking amicably without hitting each other or insulting each other? Only an hour ago I'd have said that it would have been impossible, and instead...

This beach is frequented mostly by hawkers, jugglers, magicians, dancers, entertainers; people who, in low season, when there are not many tourists, organize their own performances.

Here too the presence of Cubans and African Americans is very strong, just like the homosexuals, moreover, who dress better than the rich people I saw at the charity gala, despite the leopard print G-strings and piercing just about everywhere.

Near a huge bonfire, there are some men playing guitars and singing, people are dancing happily, some are romancing, others chatting in Spanish, while the jugglers' show continues.

I see a man balancing a motorbike on his head, another one that sticks an entire sword down his throat, or another that opens beer bottles with his teeth isn't something you see every day.

John is smoking a cigarette as he walks next to me and says nothing, which is very odd, given how much he loves to talk.

I see some girls sitting on a log near the bonfire trying to cool off by rubbing cold bottles of beer on their neck and breast. They smile licking their lips when they see John. It is not difficult to understand what they want from him. It couldn't be more explicit. What is most embarrassing is that he seems to like it. I raise my eyes to heaven going off along the beach without saying anything.

"Hey wait, where are you going?" He asks me.

"To poke my eyes out."

"Why?" he's surprised.

I look first at him, then the two sluts. "I think that even a porno star would blush if he saw the rituals of courtship in this town."

He smiles amused. "I don't know if I get more pleasure in discovering that you're jealous of me, or that you watch porno movies."

"I don't watch anything", I clarify things and hit him with the high heels that I have in my hand.

He starts to laugh. He finds it very funny, apparently. I try to hit him again with the heels, annoyed by his attitude, but he moves and runs away from me.

"And I am not jealous of you!" I add.

"What did you think?" he asks me in a provocative tone, "Just because I've been running after you for a month doesn't mean I don't have my fans."

I stare at him with raised eyebrows.

"I'm a sought-after single guy, me."

"Yes, sought-after is the right word."

He smiles at what I just said, while I look at him seriously. Mine was not a joke.

"Well then? What is the third step? Taking a stroll on the beach?" I ask him changing the subject.

"That too. I was wondering... you haven't quarreled with your donut friend and you're using me to make him angry, are you?"

By *donut* I imagine he means Nick.

Of course he is.

I go past him without answering.

"Because if that was the case it would be fine by me, I have no objection," he points out laughing.

I turn and see another group of girls, intent on miming other suggestive scenes hoping to attract his attention.

John is a playboy. He loves to be looked at and admired; I wouldn't be surprised to see him wearing a shirt one day with his own face on it. I shake my head.

"Come on", he indicates a point on the beach and we sit down alongside one another. Behind us, the bonfire, music and laughter as a background, and in front of us the waves of the sea. Tonight the moon seems larger than usual.

"Have you ever heard the term *judicial error*?" he asks me.

"Yes", I reply, "it's when an innocent person is jailed for years before discovering that there has been a mistake, while the guilty person roams free around town. The same thing that you're doing, in a nutshell", I give him a tight little smile, challenging, while he admonishes me with his eyes.

328

"Wrong. The word *judicial error* was created for common mortals and gullible people like you", this time he's the one who smiles at me with his mouth closed and a challenging look. "The true name would be *conspiracy*. Nobody goes to prison and dies there by mistake, Jas, but to get him out of the way because someone wants it that way; and that someone, oddly enough, is always a powerful person, therefore untouchable and above suspicion."

"And so?" I ask bored.

"What do you mean *and so*? What kind of question is that, *and so*? Were you listening to me or not?"

"Of course I was listening to you and therefore I repeat: *and so*?"

"You're unbearable", he bursts out.

"You're the unbearable one, not me", I mutter.

"Anyway," he continues annoyed and returns to the subject, "serial killers, pedophiles, rapists, pimps and all those people that have got off at a legal process thanks to good lawyers and corrupt judges, and are now free, my family and I seek them out, we take them in and show them a good time just like they deserve."

"What are you? Related to Dexter?" I kid him.

"No, quite simply we arrive where the law and justice do not arrive. At least if we kill someone we have the certainty that he's guilty, unlike those judges who condemn potentially innocent people to death."

I don't understand. "Therefore, you now want me to believe that you work for the judiciary?"

He shakes his head in a sign of denial, all serious, looking at me scornfully. "But if I've been explaining to you for an hour that almost all of them are corrupt!"

"And so?" I ask again.

John raises his eyes to heaven, but I don't care. I don't understand.

"What? Again? Well then, no", he says irritated, "I don't work for the judiciary, I do justice. They are two different things." He is still trying to explain this to me when a male voice behind distracts me. "Hey Jess! Brother I'm here!"

We turn in the direction of the voice. A boy - or perhaps I should say a girl? – is running toward us.

She's strange. She has braids, a miniskirt that shows her long legs and a t-shirt that highlights her breast.

"And who's he?" I ask John, bewildered.

"It's a white boy who thinks he's a colored girl."

I nod, perplexed.

"But he's also a drug dealer, a racketeer, and recently has become an up-market prostitute", he explains to me very simply, waving to him.

"Wow, what a curriculum. Will I ever be able to talk with your delinquent friend?" I mutter, ironic.

He throws another of his nasty looks at me, as if he'd like to say that I'm a bitch. Meanwhile, his boyfriend - girlfriend? - reaches us all excited.

"Jess! White brother!"

John stands up and they greet each other interlacing their hands in a strange way.

"How's it looking?"

John raises his head without saying anything, takes the cigarette that the unknown person is wearing slipped behind his ear, and lights up. Meanwhile, the other one seems to have noticed me at last. "Hey, hey, hey, but is that a *chica*? A *chica* in flesh and blood."

He looks me up and down. His smile is huge; he takes my hand helping me to get up. "Oh, Holy God!" he cries enthusiastically and starts to turn me around on the spot to have a better look at me. "Baby, you're a real looker, let me see you. Wow, wow, wow! I'm Kate, Kitty for my friends", then his voice drops to a whisper, "and for my customers, Kit Cat," he laughs happily. "And what is your name, cutie?"

"Alright, that's enough!" John intervenes with a severe voice. Apparently he doesn't like the idea of me introducing myself to Kitty. "Do you have any news?" he asks assuming a macho pose.

Kate lets go of me, puts his hands on his hips and makes a gesture of assent. "The FBI is on your heels. I saw one of them wandering around here, a moment ago."

"I knew that already," he says calmly.

I stare. I'm also a little involved in this affair.

"I was talking about the mysterious man", explains John.

"Ah yes", once again he makes that same gesture of assent. "A picture of him is being circulated, but nobody knows who or where he is. We all know though that Boris wants him dead. I asked for info from the cops, criminals, gays and all my clients but no one knows anything, his record has disappeared from all databases. Since they took him away from the Miami airport..."

As soon I take in *mysterious man* and *airport* my heart starts beating rapidly. That's where I found my Zombie. Perhaps they're looking for him? Maybe John wants to kill him.

I get over the shock and quickly try to get into the conversation, playing it cool even if my heart doesn't want to know about slowing down.

"He has disappeared", Kate is saying gesticulating, "but at least we know that he's alive."

"How do you know?" asks John.

"Jess, it's obvious. Boris is still looking for him and he never goes looking for a corpse. No, No, no. "

"Do you think it's the usual war between Boris and his brother?"

"No, I asked. Boris Jr. doesn't know anything."

"Good."

He throws the cigarette into the sea with a serious expression. "I will be in the area for a while yet; if there's any tip-off you know how to contact me, I have to find him before he does."

"Of course, beautiful." He squares him from head to foot. "You know you get more desirable every day? Blue eyes, blond hair, perfect body", he smiles touching his chest. "Now all you need is the horse and you'll become my prince charming."

Then he turns to me. "Don't think that we colored women only like the little chocolate ones, baby, white chocolate is candy, sweet and sugar-plummy", he concludes making that gesture again.

I shake my head. Seeing John pleased by his compliments is too much for me.

Kate winks at us and goes away, leaving us alone again.

"Kate is a character", he smiles going to sit on the sand again.

I sit down too. Why are they looking for my Zombie? Maybe he is one of those who wrongly got out of jail? No. I can't even think about it. I'm trying not to get angry with him, to listen to him and finally understand something more about his work, his family, him, but it seems that my trying is going nowhere. He's too contradictory; perhaps I should stay out of the whole affair.

"Where are you?" John's voice interrupts my thoughts suddenly.

"I was thinking."

"What about?"

"You and how contradictory you are. First you give me a long speech about how you and your family do justice around the world, even though you don't work for the judicial system because justice does not exist. And there'd already be a few things to clarify here", I point out, "and immediately after I see you gabbing with Kate or whatever the devil she's called and who, from what you told me, among the many strange and illegal things that she does, also sells drugs. Do you understand that it's difficult to take you seriously?"

"If drugs sell it's because there is someone who buys them. You can't blame the drug dealers if a boy decides to take drugs of his own initiative. It would be like blaming the tobacco multinationals if someone becomes sick with lung cancer. They don't force you to smoke."

"Look, the trial of first instance took place right here in Miami which condemned the largest tobacco producer to pay the sum of one hundred and forty five billion dollars to the smokers of Florida", I specify.

"You are insufferable! Why do you always contradict me?"

"Because it's true."

"That wasn't the point. I just wanted to make an example."

"Well, you chose the wrong example."

"If you really want to know, in the end the multinational will not pay a cent!"

"We shall see!"

He continues to look angrily at me for a while, you can see on his face that he wants to knee me in the forehead. He takes a deep breath and goes on: "Drugs, sex and weapons are a market that never stops. It will never end because there is too much business behind it. That's why my family and I try not to meddle in the smuggling business. And anyway we need them because when we can't do it alone, it's thanks to the mafia, the smugglers and small dealers like Kate that we find information that's useful for our work."

"Information? Like what?" I ask him the question that I didn't ask the other time.

"Such as where and who is hiding the pedophile priest that has just been acquitted by the court. Or where he lives now and what is the new identity of the man who raped and killed four innocent women on the street. Who is the corrupt judge, the cop who killed his wife's lover saying that it was in self-defense? These are just a couple of examples, but I'd have hundreds."

"And you, what do you give in exchange?"

"To the small fish like Kate, money. But when it comes to the big fish, it's a different story. They have so much money that can buy almost everything they want. My family and I get them the *almost* that is missing."

"Such as?"

"All kinds of things. Vintage cars, paintings, stamps, knives, crosses..." he emphasizes *crosses,* looking at me to confirm my idea. "In short, anything they are unable get by buying it, I get it for them by stealing. And in exchange all I want is the information I'm looking for."

"Ah. And how do they come by this information?"

"Thanks to friends or friends of friends, or thanks to the moles or corrupt people who work for the police. There are more options than you can imagine."

"Okay", I still don't understand, "but why create all this chaos of robberies and mafia if you can simply ask the corrupt cops for the same information?"

"It's complicated. Let's say that we don't trust them, and we do everything we can so they do not know of our existence. The corrupt authorities are much more dangerous than the criminals themselves. The mafia for example has a code of honor, unlike others. If they give you their word, you can believe them."

"Do you realize that you're praising them?"

333

"I am not praising the mafia. I'm just saying how things stand, Jas."

"Yes, in fact I've understood very well how things stand, you collaborate with the traffickers and other *criminals* to capture other *criminals;* what I ask myself is who are you to decide who deserves to die and who not. What do you have, a ranking? The week's top ten?"

"We go after the people wearing a uniform or a toga that swear to do justice and then turn out to be worse than the criminals they themselves acquit for money. And the people wrongly acquitted. Guess by whom? Let's go back to the starting point."

"Okay and what if a judge has been corrupted precisely by the mafia? You said that you don't ever meddle in their business."

"You certainly don't miss a thing. When I said that we try not to get involved, I meant in their trafficking or settling of accounts, things like that do not interest us. If someone ends up becoming part of that world risking his own and his family's safety, that's not our affair. In all other cases we become involved indeed, except that they do not know. As I've already said, we try to work cleanly and without ever leaving a trace. It's one of the first rules of the manual written by..." he pauses for a moment, "the person who founded our team."

"Who is this person?"

"A person who many years ago understood what was happening and created this special team."

"Yes I get it, but what's the name of this person?"

"I'm sorry, but I can't tell you anything else because I'm going to write a book", he exclaims, clearly ironic. This is the first time he doesn't answer one of my questions.

"And what is the team called?"

For the second time he doesn't answer my question.

"And this person who created this team, has also created a book of rules", I ponder aloud.

"Yes. The rules are vital in every field; they make sure everything works properly, if you follow them. And we all treat the manual as if it were sacred."

"Wasn't it you who told me that you're made to break the rules?"

"Yes, other people's rules, not mine. Will you quit being so skeptical?"

"No. And tell me, what work did this person do prior to founding your team? He had to be with the police, or the CIA or, I don't know, the FBI... I mean, who teaches you to shoot, disguise yourself and do all those things that I've seen you do?"

I see pride in his eyes and this embarrasses me. What is he doing staring at me in this way?

"And if someone doesn't follow the manual?" I ask yet another question.

"Impossible", he smiles, still looking at me in the same way as before.

I lower my eyes. I can't help it.

"As long as my father is at the helm of everything, and as long as he chooses the members of the team, this will never happen", he points out to me. "Do you still have a few questions?"

"Yes. You said that detectives and policemen are all corrupt, right?"

"Yes." His response isn't the most convincing.

"Then how come you can't find the person from the airport? If they are all corrupt, it should be easy for Kate or someone to find this information."

He smiles, but it is a bitter smile. "Every time you speak of Nickolas you light up."

"I was not talking about Nick."

"But who are you trying to kid? I know that he is at the head of the investigations, Jas."

"It annoys you that he's not like all the others, doesn't it?"

"You can't even imagine everything that annoys me about him!"

"I don't need to imagine it, John." I look at him straight in the eye. "I know it, I see it, I feel it."

His face changes suddenly and from annoyed it turns nasty. He stands up and starts to take the very expensive watch from his wrist. "I have already warned you to wash your mouth out before you speak of me and my feelings", he says with a mongrel smile. I understand immediately what he wants to do. I stand up too and begin to retreat. "No! John! I wasn't talking about your feelings!

335

Don't even try, okay?" I point my finger at him as I say this and continue to back away.

He won't dare to do it! He cannot do this!

"I do what I want, Jas! And I've already said that my name is Jack! Jack!" he throws the watch on his shoes, and also takes off his t-shirt.

I don't know why, but seeing him bare-chested, with all those sculpted muscles, my mouth opens all by itself and I can't close it again.

He throws the shirt onto the shoes as well.

"No, no, no! I won't let you, you know! You mustn't touch..." I can't even finish the sentence. John grabs my hand and the next moment I'm lifted onto his shoulders and heading for the sea.

"Let go of me! You're touching my bottom!"

"I know, and I like it very much."

He is already in the water up to his knees and continues to hold his hand on my behind.

"Remove your hand from there immediately! John! Let go of me! Did you hear? Set me down!"

"As you like." He literally dives into the water, dragging me with him.

When I come up I'm all wet, with salt water running from my nose and ears. I hear John laughing like a madman.

From here on, the situation definitely degenerates; yelling and cursing I begin to chase him and drag him underwater trying to drown him, and he does the same with me, without worrying about how long he makes me remain underwater. I risk death!

From the beach you can hear the music at full volume, people are dancing around the bonfire, others are singing and John and I chase each other like children on the sea shore.

He looks at me with those blue eyes, splashing me with the lukewarm water, and I'm having so much fun at this point that I don't even realize that... that there is something wrong with all this. There is something now that wasn't here before.

59.

In the meantime, in New York – From Mina's diary

Here everything is fabulously beautiful! I look out the window of the limousine at the lights in the streets, the endless skyscrapers and I feel as if I know them, that I've already seen them, even though I know I've never been here. All thanks to the TV and movies, for sure. Everything here is huge and impressive. It really is a city that never sleeps.

Lexi takes us shopping in an exclusive clothing store that they have opened just for her, right in the middle of the night, to the screams of happiness from Ross. Once we're out of the building I feel as if I'm in the TV show *Sex and the City*. All three of us walk down the street dressed to the nines, with dizzying heels, very heavy makeup, unreal skirts and many bags full of clothes.

At the beginning I didn't want to accept these costly gifts from Lexi, but then she convinced me by threatening to leave me here if didn't immediately shut up and accept. It was the most beautiful threat I've ever received in my life.

Right now we're getting into the limousine again, which is white this time, to go to another shop and do more shopping.

I don't know if I'm doing the right thing. After all Lexi is a friend of Jack's. Perhaps she is a thief and perhaps she too has broken lives like he has. Maybe I'm risking my own life in this moment, but in spite of everything she inspires confidence. I'm not afraid of her. I don't think she's a bad person, just as Jack doesn't. I just hope I am not mistaken.

We get out of the limo about to plunder another clothing store.

The boys turn around to take a look at us with concupiscent eyes, and I feel perfectly at home in this situation, despite the absence of Jas. Even if I miss her a lot and I wonder what she's doing at this moment.

60.

From Jas's diary – Miami Beach, same night

A group of Hispanics have been staring at me for more than ten minutes. Their little smiles, their idiotic wisecracks in Spanish, and their vulgar gestures at me make me feel very uncomfortable and at the same time irritate me intensely. I will not give them the satisfaction of any reaction on my part, so for the whole time I pretend not to notice, looking in the opposite direction from them, but I continue to be irritated anyway.

John is on the other side of the bonfire chatting with a long-haired guy. He immediately seemed very familiar to me, except I don't know where I've seen him before. Then I have a brainwave when I see his t-shirt with *skeleton* written on it. It's Benjamina's boyfriend.

If I discover that he's had me followed by that tattooed thing, I'll kill him.

I shake my head, annoyed, when I see the group of Hispanics coming towards me. I don't know whether to get up or remain sitting on the tree trunk.

"No, no, there's no need for you to stand up, stay there, hot chick", the first one says to me as if he had read my mind. Okay, at least he helped me decide.

They continue to smile enjoying it all, I don't know for what reason. Each of the four is holding a beer in his hand. One of them kneels down in front of me, and letting me see the brown of his teeth says to me: "You're not from around here, are you?"

I don't answer, but I look for John. These here seem to be exactly the kind of sober friends that he frequents. One of the gorillas, unfortunately, obscures my view. "What's your name gorgeous?" he insists, and tries to touch my face.

All of a sudden I feel someone behind him answer: "She's called *my girlfriend*!" It's John speaking, with an icy voice.

The guy gets up and turns toward him, annoyed, but John is even more annoyed. His eyes are narrow, tiny and bad, there is not a shadow of fear on his face, on the contrary; he goes closer to the

Hispanic and, before he can say anything comments sarcastically: "Do you want to ask her a few more questions?" His voice is threatening. Everything about him is scary. He doesn't lay a finger on him; he doesn't point a weapon at him. He does nothing but speak, but it's enough to make all four retreat.

"Let's get out of here" murmurs one of them. They pretend that it's their spontaneous initiative, but the truth is that they are shitting themselves.

John sits on the trunk beside me, holding out another Mojito to me. He looks at me like someone who knows he's cool and is waiting for a thank you or some compliment any moment, which of course I'm not about to give him.

"So then?" he goes, with his usual annoying little smile.

"So then what?"

"There's nothing you feel you need to say to me?"

"Actually there is one thing: I am not your girlfriend."

"But you really would love to be, right?"

I try to remain serious, but it's very difficult. "What does it feel like flirting with a girl who doesn't want you?"

"Horrible, humiliating and very, very challenging," he confesses. Then he smiles and adds, "But it's not the case for me."

I burst laughing, this time I can't hide it. He looks at me pleased. You can see on his face that he's happy because I'm happy. I take a sip of my Mojito and continue to smile. I have learned to take his presumption with good humor.

There's just a few of us left on the beach now. Skeleton is doing some rap with two friends. Kate is dealing drugs. A tramp is collecting empty bottles and cans around the campfire and passes them to one of street artists who throws them into a corner, creating a kind of portrait or strange figure on the sand. I don't know why, but this makes me reflect again.

Each of these people, even the drug dealers and criminals like Kate and John, has found a place in this society. And me? I currently do not know how to do anything. I don't know what I'll be when I grow up and I never know which way to go. It's frustrating.

"Can I ask you a question?" John interrupts my depressing thoughts.

"That's already a question", I tell him, "Do you want to ask another one?"

He looks at me scornfully. "No. "

"Can I ask you one?"

"You've asked me three thousand today, one more..."

"Okay, then you I'll ask you two."

I see him make a strange expression that seems annoyed. "The first is: do you like your job?"

"Do you want the truth?"

"If you're capable of it."

He scowls again. "There are many things that I don't like about my job."

"For example?"

"We change identity like you others change your knickers. Except that sometimes it's not enough just to remove a wig to return to being ourselves, to feel normal. If we talk to someone we cannot do it for more than a couple of minutes and we never say anything true about ourselves. It doesn't matter who it is, because it would be risky for our cover, or because otherwise it is likely that we'll have to kill him, then. So we find ourselves only talking among ourselves, we brothers and sisters. This is sometimes monotonous." He becomes pensive and looking at a fixed point on the sand he continues: "Cover is very important to us and we cannot risk everything and everyone for a mistake made by one of us."

"What do you mean by this?"

"That each of us is trained to do almost everything and get by in the most extreme situations. We are able to enter every database and we are able to delete or manipulate all the videos or photos that concern us, getting rid of all traces of us. But if one of us is *burned,* meaning, discovered, caught in flagrante, or is captured, or stupidly gets into a dangerous situation, then the others, if they see that they are unable to help him, must look after themselves and the team. And this means abandoning him."

"What?" I ask incredulous, "That's a horrible thing! I would never do that to someone on my team, nor would I like to be abandoned by them. It's terrible!"

"On the one hand it is; however I would not want one of my brothers to risk his life because I made a mistake." He keeps his head bent. When he's not being smug he becomes almost sweet. And I can't believe I thought that.

"To do what you love," he continues, solemnly, "you must also accept what you do not love. But this is true for every job, not only mine."

"Have you never thought of doing something different?"

"Change to something different?" He smiles, "No. To find another job I'd have to change myself first of all. And I don't think this will ever happen. I'm drawn in by the thrill. I'm not made for a normal life. One where you wake up every morning to go to work, then you go home, eat, drink, sleep and then do it all over again the next day, for the rest of my days. All unexciting, all the same day after day. I would die from boredom. I need strong emotions. You're the only one who has been able to give me this without having to risk my life."

I feel embarrassed hearing him talk like this. He looks me in the eyes, far from uncomfortable.

"Did your father point you towards this work or did you choose to do it yourself?"

"Every one of us, every day, finds himself with choices to make. Whether they're important or trivial, I think that in the end it's not your head or your heart that makes you choose, it's your instinct. When you follow your instinct you don't have time to think and, in despite this, you know exactly what to choose and what to do. And I followed it."

"Instinct", I repeat in a low voice.

"Yes, as soon as you stop to reflect you mess everything up. Your head tells you what would be the right thing to do and not what you want to do. Your heart though is driven by feelings, and in the moment that you make your choice following your heart, you're totally irrational. So for me instinct remains the only truth."

Nick had made me a speech about choices too, on my birthday, but his speech was far different from John's. Nick spoke of choices made with the heart, and it was a speech that can't be faulted. But John had also said something sensible. I don't understand anything anymore. Here everyone thinks in a different way and at this point I'm in a dilemma. *How do I think?*

I'm confused.

"Jas?" John calls me back to reality.

"It's just that... I'd never thought about that."

"About what?"

"Heart, head and instinct. I didn't know there were so many options. I wondered which of the three of them I should listen to before..." I don't have time to finish the sentence before John interrupts me and starts laughing his head off.

I look at him with my eyebrows raised and can't understand this sudden burst of laughter. "What on earth has come over you?"

He's laughing so much he can't even talk. "Nothing. It's just that not only don't you know the world you live in, but you don't even know yourself, Jas."

"It's not true."

"Yes you're right, I was wrong. I wanted to say that you are so afraid of showing yourself for what you are, that you're forgetting *who you are*."

"What you say does not make sense."

"No, eh?"

"Shut up!" I'm starting to get really annoyed. I don't like being psychoanalyzed by a distorted mind like his. What does he know about me and what I am or what I'm not?

Meanwhile, he has had the good sense to stop laughing. He sips his Mojito. "When you said in front of the whole school in Gorizia that Mujo had never attacked Spela, what proof did you have?" he asks me.

"I..."

"I'll answer for you: none. You knew that it wasn't him; you felt it and you exposed yourself putting the police and the headmistress against you just to defend him. And in the end, guess what, you were right. You reacted out of instinct; when you're presented with a difficult situation, you don't run away. You address it using all the means you have at your disposal even if it's lies or manipulation because you know that you're right."

"It was just luck."

"There was no luck involved in this and you know that very well. It's just that you pretend to believe this so as not to disappoint Nickolas."

I don't know what to say, and it bothers me because it's like I'm confirming what he is saying. "If I am really so good at following my instinct as you say, then how come I didn't realize that the person I thought was John was really you?"

"The only reason you were not able to is because you were doing Vicodin", he says in a hard and angry voice, as if he had not yet digested the thing.

I am surprised.

He fixes his blond hair pulling it back, and goes on speaking in a calm way: "Do you remember that day that we were in the cube, when you fell to the ground, and even forgot who you were and where you were for a few moments?"

"Of course I remember. I was there."

"That's right and not long before you felt ill you were teaching me how to read body language. I asked you what you were able to read in me, I asked you because I seriously feared for my cover", he smiles, "and you said to me *the only thing you communicate to me is a sense of being closed, you are afraid to let yourself go.* Then you immediately denied everything and said you didn't know why you said that, that you didn't think it. But instead, you thought it and how. You knew it. Instinct made you say those things. It was the Vicodin that made you deny it."

He remembers everything. Where we were. What we did. What we said.

He talks as if it had happened yesterday. I feel odd. Why is he telling me these things? I don't even know if he really thinks that way or if he does it to manipulate me again. And yet, what he said is true. Because I was in the cube that day; I was the one who said those things, and I was the one who retracted them. And he's also right about Mujo. I knew he was innocent, I felt it.

"Jas", he whispers, "I am not here to manipulate you, deceive you or hurt you."

"Why are you here, then?"

"I won't tell you why I'm here, but why I am not. I have not come here to protect you from the world. I want to help you to get

343

to know it. I have not come here to try to change you, there is nothing wrong with you and you have no reason to hide who you are. And I have not come here to make you to do what you do not want." He seems so sincere, tender. I shake my head, and look away from him.

"I was terrified at the idea of seeing you again," he continues. "I didn't know how you would react nor if you would want to listen to me. And now that you have, you just have to say the word and I'll be gone, leaving you to your usual life. If tomorrow you decide to pack your bags and return to Slovenia I will not follow you."

"Seriously?"

"Yes, seriously, Jas", he takes a deep breath, "but until then, I'll be here. I will not leave you."

I don't know what happens to me exactly, but something in me has moved, turned, overturned and crashed. My heart begins to beat very fast. I close my eyes to try to bounce back from all this strange turn of sentiments, which does not let me breathe normally. I take a drink of my Mojito and ask him: "What was the question that you wanted to ask me before?"

John looks at me in a peculiar way. As if he is studying me. He smiles. "Why didn't you like professor Rossi?"

"That's the question?" I smile in disbelief. This was not the question that I was expecting.

"Yes. It's something that I have never understood. Why do you detest him so much?"

"I can't tell you", I smile enjoying this.

"Why?"

"I like the idea that there is something you don't understand about me."

"There are many things that I don't understand about you. But if you believe that you understand yourself, this means..."

"What the heck are you prattling on about?"

"Jack Black *understands* Jas Herzog", he does an insane dance. "From one to ten just how cool am I?" There, the fanatic has returned. I smile and shake my head. "Do you realize that you spend seventy percent of your days giving yourself compliments?"

"Hey, someone has to do it in your place."

I smile again.

"And do you realize that you spend seventy percent of your days saying *No?*" he jokes.

"I only say no to you", I point out. And getting to my feet I ask him, at last. "Shall we go?"

"Already?"

"What do you mean *already*? It's morning and it's getting late." Or should I say early?

"It's late, but it's early if you go", he whispers. "It's almost sunrise, wait just a little while longer or you'd miss a unique spectacle." He tries to convince me to stay. "Come on ask me a few more questions."

"No."

"Go on Jas."

"I'll do that tomorrow."

HIs expression changes in an instant. It becomes serious. His eyes shine, they're almost smiling. "Tomorrow?"

"Yes, tomorrow", I confirm. "That's if it's okay with you."

"Of course it is!" He's so happy. I would never have imagined I'd see him so emotional one day.

As we look into each other's eyes, the sun rises in front of us. The beach lights up. All the bright and cheerful colors that characterize the city of Miami are awakening after a long night. Everything is clearer now, more limpid.

John looks at me, the blue stone around his neck glitters and is beautiful. "Where do you want me to take you, tomorrow?" he asks me, still with that happy expression on his face.

"You mean today."

"Where do you want me to take you today?"

"I don't know, surprise me."

"But you hate surprises."

"I've made peace with surprises", I tell him. After all, surprises aren't all that bad.

He gets up off the trunk where we're sitting and stands in front of me. The light of the sun illuminates him. He is very beautiful. And the very fact that I thought it embarrasses me.

He puts his hands in his pockets, crossing his gaze with mine. "And you and I?" he whispers biting his lips. "When will we make peace, Jas?"

345

"The day before the day after."

***

I'll have slept for three hours more or less. Even though the bed in this hotel is very comfortable, I'm too agitated because of everything that happened tonight to be able to sleep. I yawn, waiting for Mina to come out of the bathroom to show me the twentieth new dress that Lexi gave her, and I start to laugh. Usually I do that because I think she's funny or ridiculous for the way she dresses herself, but this time it's different: I laugh because I'm happy for her. She's really beautiful.

Lexi has known how to choose styles that suit her figure perfectly. Now my Mina looks like a real woman. The only thing I ask myself is why Lexi has given her all these gifts. If there's one thing I've learned in life, it's that no one does anything for nothing, and here I smell a rat.

The bathroom door opens and here she is in a full dress, not too snug, a pearl necklace around her neck and an enormous hat on her head.

"How do you think I look, my love?" she asks as she looks at me over the top of pair of sunglasses and tries to stay balanced on the heels.

"You're beautiful!"

"The most beautiful thing is that I feel good in all these clothes." She looks happily at the heap of stuff on the bed next to mine. For once, she's the untidy one, not me.

"Wait, wait. And then I haven't told you the most important thing!" She runs toward my bed with the risk of breaking a leg and jumps on top of it all excited. "The when we were leaving the restaurant we met George Clooney and Matt Damon! I almost fainted from the excitement, I swear!" I feel her enthusiasm, but I can't see her face because of her hat. "But this is not the most exciting thing, Jas, it's the fact that Lexi called them by name. She knows them intimately she even introduced us too! Ross and I were holding hands and jumping up and down like idiots."

"You and Ross?" I ask astonished.

"Yes", she answers in such a simple and tranquil way that my surprise turns into terror. "The homosexual, the colored one who always insults you? *That* Ross."

"Yes."

Terror has just transformed into concern. "The monkey with the multicolor tuft of hair? Will's shopping boy? The Ross with a thousand jobs? *That* Ross?"

"*Yeee-es*", she chants.

"And what the devil was he doing there with you two?"

"Of all the things I've just told you, instead of asking me about George and Matt, you ask me about Ross?"

"Of course! Seeing that you talk about him as if he was an old friend of yours. What happened to your contempt for him?"

"It turned into *oh my God there are George and Matt in front of me!* What a shit you are, you've ruined my whole story."

"Are you going to answer me or not? What was that Ross doing with you?"

"Ross lost his head for Lexi from the first time that he saw her in jail. And she... I don't know, she has fun with him. They are on the same wavelength and she likes taking him around. She says that he is like a sister to her, and yesterday evening..." she caresses her new clothes with one hand and gesticulates with the other as she tells me enthusiastically about the relationship between Lexi and Ross, what they did yesterday evening, who they met, and how many people looked at her. She is so happy.

Maybe I should take advantage of this moment of euphoria to tell her that I don't want to go off on a trip to Europe any longer. I want to stay here in Miami.

I no longer hear her voice. She's looking at me. Apparently she has realized that I'm not listening to her very much and now she wants to know why. How do I tell her in the least painful manner possible that this year too we will not be leaving?

"Jas, I'd like to talk to you about one thing", she says displeased taking off the hat.

"To tell the truth, I have something to say to you too", my tone is even more disappointed than hers.

"Who starts first?"

"You begin", I propose, in the hope of finding the right words to give her the bad news.

"Okay, but you must promise me that you won't twist my words."

"But why does everyone worry that I might misconstrue? I don't understand, am I really so unreasonable?"

"I'm not saying this. And then, everyone who?"

"Forget it, now tell me."

"Okay. While you were being the undercover agent for Felix, and learning many new things from Jack, such as for example the fact that he's making you see the ugly side of the world in which you live, and you like it... At the same time, Lexi is making me see the beautiful side of things, and I like that. So, even if different people are making us discover different things, the important thing is that we're both happy, no?"

"Hmm... yes"

"So I thought that now that we've found that Lexi and Jack are not dangerous, and that in their own way they try to do justice, even if in reality they don't work for the judiciary... I thought... instead of going to Europe, why not take advantage of this month of vacation that we have left and each get to know the side of the things that we're most interested in, here?"

"What?"

I can't believe it! She wants to cancel our trip... because of Lexi? Yes, okay, I was going to do the same thing but, fuck, she didn't know that! It's not right! I should come before everything else!

I glare at her.

"Jas, I don't want you to think the wrong thing", she sits near me and I takes my hand.

Judah!

"You know how much I wanted to go to Europe with you, and I still want to, really, but when will we get an opportunity like this again? After all this is already a trip. Do you know how many new things we'll learn? And then next year we leave for Europe as we had planned. What do you think, my love?"

I continue to look at her askance. I'm the one that had to dump her, and not the contrary.

348

"Jas, if you tell me that you prefer to leave I'll be happy to come with you, I want you to know that. Just because I've suggested an alternative, doesn't mean that I no longer like the original plan."

61.

Jas continues to look at me with that expression of disapproval. Heck, I am sorry to see her like that because of me. I've been selfish to ask her that. I'm about to kneel at her feet and ask her to forgive me for even thinking of postponing our trip to Europe when I hear her say: "Oh alright then."

"Do you mean that?" I scream at the top of my lungs. I can't hold back my joy. I jump on the bed like a five-year-old.

"Even though the trip to Europe... I wanted to do that," she says disappointed.

I sit down again next to her trying to restrain my enthusiasm. "Yes, I know, love, but seeing how things have turned out, I think that both of us can only learn from this experience."

"Yes, you may be right. But does Felix know that you're going out with a member of the Black family?"

"Yes. However, he hasn't asked me to stop it nor be an insider, like you are. I don't know. Maybe I'm of no use to him, for now. Or perhaps he simply doesn't think I could do it."

I feel almost wounded just thinking it. But then I remember Lexi, New York and George. And all the wounds disappear in an instant. I lie on my bed with the eyes of someone in love. "Think of how many things we'll have to tell when we get back home! I have already begun to write whole pages about it in my diary."

"Wow." Her lack of enthusiasm makes me remember a very important thing.

"By the way, I had a quick look at your diary yesterday, Jas", I frown at her, "and all I saw were white pages."

"Have you looked inside my precious private diary?" she says, pretending to be indignant.

"Stop it! It was blank!"

"Yes, but you couldn't know that. Holy God, Mina. I don't know what to say. You've been through my secret diary?"

"Stop being sarcastic, Jas, I'm serious!"

"Me too. My diary..."

"Jas!" I thump her on the head with a pillow, while she continues to recite the part of a wounded nineteenth century dame. "Why haven't you written anything yet? You have to do it, okay? Especially now that we are experiencing new adventures. For you it has to be like the logbook of Star Trek."

"Come on, I was joking. Actually I still hadn't finished mine, that's why the diary you gave me is still empty", she justifies herself. "And by the way, what is Star Trek?"

"You've never seen Star Trek?" I ask amazed. She gets off the bed and goes to the window. "But where do you live? It's television series that tells the story of a crew who are exploring the universe in search of new planets, alien races..."

"Ah-ha. And did they have Darth Vader too who forbade them to take-off?" she asks looking at something or someone outside the window.

"Darth Vader? But that has nothing to do with *Star Trek,* that was *Star Wars*". The more I try to explain the huge difference between one saga and the other, the more I realize that she's not even listening. "Jas?"

She puts on her high heels and goes to the door without saying anything.

"Jas? Where are you going now?"

"To save the Jas *and Mina Enterprise.*"

"Eh?" I run to the window and I see Nick outside our hotel. He is walking nervously up and down with his head down. He seems worried, distressed. He looks sad.

And in all this, I still can't understand where Jas has seen Darth Vader.

62.

Three minutes later – From Jas's diary

I see people talking at the bar. A lady at the front desk is screaming at her husband, a child is laughing as he goes up the stairs jumping on the steps one at a time, holding his grandmother's hand, and a girl is walking up and down the hall talking on the phone in a loud voice. Everyone is gesticulating and moving their lips, but I can't hear them. The beat of my heart covers their voices as I get closer to the door of the hotel. My heart is beating fast, but I don't know the reason for it. I do not feel guilty for what happened yesterday, also because I have not done anything wrong. I am not disappointed and not even angry with Nick for how he has treated me, now that I have been able to get my head around it. So what do I feel?

I go outside and I see him standing near his motorbike with his hands in his pockets. As soon as he sees me, he looks at me and scowls. The closer I get the less I know what to say to him. Perhaps it's better to let Nick speak first and then see how things develop. I stop in front of him. "It's over!" The words come out of my mouth by themselves. I don't even know why I've said that. I'm surprised, but not as much as Nick, who looks at me with staring eyes. "What?"

"It's over." I have no control over myself now.

He continues to look at me confused. He comes to me and puts his hands on my shoulders. "What, what does *it's over* mean, Jas?"

I move away, and even though I did it slowly and gently, Nick didn't like it. Something is happening in my head. It's as if I'm putting together the pieces of the puzzle, and once I've completed the project, I've written the words as well. "There is a phrase engraved on the compass I gave you. What is it?" I ask him in a quiet voice.

Nick remains motionless. He touches the compass hanging around his neck and replies: "*I chose to love you.*"

"I chose to love you", I repeat softly, "and it's not actually a choice. It's like that, and it still is. But if it had been a choice, it would have been the only one in my life that I'd have made with my head, heart, and instinct. The only possible choice would have always been to love you, Nick. But I have realized that it is also the only choice that will prevent me from making others, in life." I have tears in my eyes.

"No, Jas, no." Nick caresses my shoulders, looking at me with bright and terrified eyes. "Jas, please..."

"Today I choose to not listen to you any more, Nick. To not do things to make you happy. To not allow you to rebuke me, judge me, mortify me any longer. But most of all to protect me from the outside world. It's over."

"I just wanted to protect you."

"But you can't! I know that you are afraid for me, but I will never be safe if I don't know what to fear."

"Please, let's sit down and talk about this calmly", he tells me adjusting my hair with a caress. His hand trembles. "Please."

We look into each other's eyes in silence, and for the first time in years I feel like we have both realized that things between us are no longer the same, even if we do everything we can to convince ourselves that nothing has changed.

"Mina and I are not going on our trip to Europe. We will be staying here in Miami until August thirty", I take a deep breath before continuing. "And up to August thirty I will continue to collaborate with Felix, telling him everything that I see and hear."

Nick closes his eyes for a moment.

"If you trust me, you will watch me go out with Jack without being afraid that something will happen to me, that I'll do something illegal, or that he will be able to manipulate me again. I want to lend a hand in these investigations. On the other hand, if you don't trust me it's your problem, because in any case I'll scrutinize Jack and you can't stop me. If in all these years you've been able to give me orders, punish me and stop me doing what I wanted, it's because I let you do it. But now it's over, Nick." I don't know how I was able to say what I said.

He trembles in front of me without saying anything. He does not try to persuade me, tell me that I'm wrong or stop me from doing what I have decided to do. At this moment he is behaving as I have always wished he would act with me: see me as an adult and not a little girl to protect. So why do I feel so weird? Because I feel that something is missing, that there is something wrong?

I have to leave. I have to go to Mina. I need her right now.

I turn and go to the revolving door of the hotel.

"Jas", Nick calls me.

I stop without turning. I don't want him to see the tears running down my face. Or perhaps I don't want to see his.

"I trust you blindly," he whispers with a broken voice.

I enter the hotel without replying. For the first time in thirteen years I have spoken to him without shouting, without quarrelling. I was serious but not angry, and he has noticed this.

One day, at the Cat's Eyes, I complained to him about the fact that we were always quarrelling, and he told me that if we quarrel it means that we care for each other and that the real problem will be when we stop doing that.

Today we have ceased.

It is not his fault that our bond hinders us, that it hurts us and makes us unhappy. Perhaps Nick is right. I am seeing Jack because it's convenient, because he makes me go where Nick has never allowed me to go. Or perhaps he is wrong, and I only want to see clearly when it comes to Jack. I only want to understand.

The two posters that Nick put up in my room flash through my mind. I don't feel like a normal student, I don't feel that I can become like Jx one day. I have simply chosen to go forward following my own road. I have decided to follow my instinct. I have decided to be myself.

63.

From the balcony of the hotel I can see Nick with tears in his eyes. He is standing still watching Jas departing.

He is probably crying. He probably hopes until the very last that she will change her mind, but this is not the case, she goes away and he is left standing alone.

He places his hands on the bike and lowers his head. Jas's words are too hard to bear.

"Nick?" It's Ginevra.

I stare wide-eyed.

Nick turns abruptly, perhaps imagining that it's Jas calling to him and instead he finds her in front of him, looking at him astounded as she sees the tears.

I go back in the room.

I find Jas there in tears too. My Jas.

64.

Nick entered the Black Cat all wet from the rain and quickly closed the door behind him. In one hand he clutched some sheets of paper and in the other was holding the cell phone to his ear. "What have you done?" he asked smiling, and shook his head as he drew near to the counter. "Jas, you're terrible, you mustn't do things like that", he paused, probably to listen to the response from the other end. "It's not true, I am not boring!" he smiled again and sat on a stool putting the papers on the counter. "Yes, yes, go, I'll call tonight. I miss you, little one." He hung up.

"When she's older you'll have your hands full," said Patrick. He was dressed elegantly, had shaved off his beard and had his hair gathered in a ponytail.

"I do already," replied Nick. He smiled again.

"I can't wait to meet her", he smiled too and took Nick's papers.

"Do you think my bar's an office? Eh? You can't stay here if you don't order anything! You have to drink and pay here!" complained Big Bob as he polished the counter with a rag. "And you've seen the notice up there", he points to a huge sign hanging on the wall behind him. *The use of cell phones is forbidden.*

"Since they invented these monstrous little boxes all I hear all day is *drin-dron-drum.*"

"Sorry, Big Bob, I'll switch it off", said Nick, exchanging guilty glances with Patrick. "Bring me a non-alcoholic beer please" he asked. Then he turned back to Patrick who was examining the sheets. "Well? What do you think?"

"It's a nice place. I like it."

"It's much more than nice. It's beautiful", he corrected him excited. "Our agency will be built right here, Watchtower Investigations!" He took the sheet from Patrick's hands and held it in the air, admiring it.

Patrick nodded happily. He looked at Nick with gratitude, honored to be part of his project.

The arrival of a young waitress interrupted the moment. Stumbling, perhaps, she ended up spilling the contents of a jug of beer all over Nick. "Oh my God, I'm so sorry!" she said upset and tried to clean the beer from Nick's with a paper towel. "Excuse me, really. I'm new..."

"Don't worry", he reassured her with a smile. "These things happen."

The girl continued to blot the stain and when the tension loosened they both burst out laughing. As soon as she had done the best she could to clean him she introduced herself, putting out her hand. "I'm Ginevra."

"Pleased to meet you Ginevra. I'm Nick", he shook her hand and looked into her blue eyes.

Patrick smiled. He immediately noticed the attraction that had clicked between the two, and moved down a couple of places in a very elegant and quiet way going to keep company with Big Bob the grumbler.

Ginevra tied her dark hair back in a ponytail and as she cleaned the beer off the counter, looked at the sheet that Nick was still holding in his hand. "And so you're an architect?"

"No, no," laughed Nick.

"He wants to be a detective, but can't even follow the rules of my bar!" remarked Big Bob. "This is not a good start", he added, before disappearing, busy with his own matters. Nick and Ginevra smiled shaking their head.

"Detective, eh? Well, maybe we shall meet again, Nick", she remarked with a smile.

"Why do you say this?"

"I want to be a forensic doctor."

"Forensic doctor?" he repeated, surprised.

"Yes, it has been my dream since I was a child. I like the idea that, thanks to me and what I'll discover, criminals will be brought to justice. I want to make my contribution. I want to make this a better world", she paused and looked at Nick embarrassed. "I know, you're thinking that I'm wishful thinking to believe I can change things, don't you?"

Nick's eyes lit up. Ginevra's words and her way of thinking impressed him a lot and the only thing he managed to say with a smile on his lips was: "No, I wasn't thinking that."

***

Black Cat, today

Nick and Ginevra are sitting in the same bar where they drank their first cup of tea together. It is raining outside, just as it was seven years ago. Big Bob is still there, but the situation between the other two is decidedly different. An awkward silence reigns between them.

Ginevra tries in every way she can to break it, but without success. "It seems like a century since the first time we met here, yet the bar seems to be the same, doesn't it?"

She looked at Nick in the hope, useless, that he would finally look her in the face and stop staring at the cup in front of him. "Yes it does", he replies quickly and disinterested.

"Veronica told me that you still haven't found my replacement."

"Many things have happened in this last year."

"I know, I heard." She continues looking at him, but Nick's gaze does not want to move away from the cup.

"She seems to be okay," she adds, trying desperately to find some kind of contact. In fact, as soon as she alludes to Jas, Nick lifts his head and finally meets her gaze. "Gin, please stop avoiding the subject. Why are we here? What did you want to talk to me about?"

The girl can't hold herself back any longer. She takes his hand looking at him with misty eyes. "I miss you."

Nick moves his hand from hers, but she goes on: "I should never have left Villa Torres. I should never have left you in that way. I was blinded by jealousy, overwhelmed by uncertainties. I am really very sorry. Please forgive me!"

"Gin..."

"No, let me finish, please. I have been holding everything inside for too long."

"Why now? Almost a year has gone by."

"I tried to forget you and move on, I tried to convince myself that I'd done the right thing... but the more time that passed the more I realized that I can't live without you, Nick. Give me another chance, please", she begs him tearfully.

"It is not a question of chance, it's about trust."

"I know that I disappointed you, that I have wounded you..."

"You're not listening to me, Gin", he interrupts her. "Trust is at the foundation of every relationship. If it's missing, everything is missing. And you did not place your trust in me." He gets up from his chair intent on leaving.

"Nick, please", she says in a desperate voice. She hugs him close. And Nick doesn't want to push her away.

"We were great together," she continues, "we were the perfect team. I was with you from the start. I believed in you from the start. We have the same ideals, we believe in the same things. You and I wanted to change the world. We can still do it, Nick!" she begs holding his face tight in her hands. "I made just one error. I'm only a human being with all the weaknesses and insecurities of a human being. I am begging you. I trust you. I have always trusted you, Nick."

Perhaps moved by the poignant atmosphere and the melancholy of his memories or simply by Ginevra's words which he so needs to hear at this moment, Nick goes to her and lays his lips on hers.

But before both let themselves fall into the kiss, a girl's shrill voice interrupts them.

"Oh, my God! But that's Nickolas! It's Nickolas Ortega Torres!"

A fan.

65.

In the meantime – From Jas's diary

The taxi stops in front of the hospital. I pay the taxi driver, get out and I see Jack, leaning against a really cool black Lamborghini. He is smoking a cigarette and looks at me with his usual sly smile.

I approach him, surprised. "Wow!" I exclaim.

"I imagine you're once again impressed by the car and not by my immortal James Dean beauty."

"The only thing you have in common with James Dean is his car."

"Ha ha, very witty, will it annoy you if I laugh tomorrow?"

"No, no, go ahead", I tell him smiling. "What are you doing around this neck of the woods?"

He opens the door and picks up a black bag and a notebook. "This", he throws me the notebook which I catch on the fly, "you have to learn this by heart. And this", he gives me the black bag; inside there is a lavender color dress and a pair of stiletto heels, "is what you've got to wear."

"Why?"

"In my work is very important to be able to act and improvise despite the stress of the moment. So I decided that today we'll crash a wedding", he says all happy, miming a strange little dance.

I give him a sideways glance. "I wouldn't even dream of it!"

"Oh, of course. Because you don't do things like that, do you?"

"No, I do not."

"I would like to remind you that last year you went to school despite the fact that it was closed, with a lot of policemen stationed outside. And just because you wanted a cappuccino."

"That's not exactly how it went."

"Ah, yes, sorry, that's true. I forgot the blackmail you did to Mujo to obtain the key to the side entrance."

I don't know how to counter, dammit! He remembers better than me all the bullshit I did in the past. I cross my arms, annoyed. "I have no intention of doing anything illegal, Jack!"

His expression changes in an instant. He's surprised and his eyes immediately begin to shimmer from happiness. "What did you call me?"

I realize only now that I called him Jack and not John any more. I lower my gaze. I feel uncomfortable. After the moment of silence, instead of commenting or making some quip that would only make me mad, he decides to act as if nothing had happened. "Anyway, you're prejudiced only because I was the one who proposed it to you and it's not right."

I smile inside. I am pleased that he didn't dwell on the question of his name.

"Lots of normal people with a normal work do it, just for fun. To scrounge something to eat, drink and why not, pick up someone as well. Why them and not us?"

What he says is true, but I don't know if I want to do it. I feel blocked by something.

"Ah, I understand where the problem is: Nickolas! If you do, daddy will get angry? He'll ground you and not let you watch TV", he kids me cheerfully.

However, he is right, I still feel the shadow of Nick behind me, and that's why I can't do it.

After all, I'm working at this moment, and Felix is hearing what we're saying through the headset, so it's not my fault if Jack wants to make me do it. And anyway it's not illegal.

I look at him, this time I'm the one with a sly smile. "What time is the wedding?"

***

"You said that we were going to a wedding! Not that we were going to the marriage of the daughter of a mafia boss", I say through clenched teeth as the boss, intrigued, comes to meet us.

Fuck! Now I can't remember anything of what I read about his life in the notebook that Jack gave me. But Jack must have guessed it: he squeezes my hand saying under his breath: "Relax, smile and let them see your boobs."

"What?!"

"Good evening", the boss greets us; he has a Sicilian accent, "are you having fun? Please pardon my frankness, but I really don't know where I've seen you before. I don't remember you."

"We are Don Mario's grandchildren. We didn't know whether to come, but then at the last moment we thought that he would have wanted it," Jack explains readily, mimicking a perfect Sicilian accent. He's a really groovy actor.

"*Aaah*, Don Mario. Good guy, Don Mario. Killed just like that from one day to the next, in such an unexpected way."

Well, from what I read in the book, it wasn't all that unexpected.

"You've grown, I wouldn't have recognized you. I wasn't able to come to the funeral, did you have received my note of condolences?" asks the boss.

He waits for me to reply, photographing every inch of my skin with his gaze.

Jack winks at me and caresses my back. He seems tranquil, as if he's sure that I'll know how to handle things.

I don't know why, but I feel better after these thoughts. I look at the boss and with a smile on my lips say to him: "Of course, we did receive it and thank you very much. And the cross was beautiful; we buried it with grandfather as you asked."

Jack looks at me with pride and he knocked a smile just perceptible.

I feel so good, relaxed and confident of being able to handle any situation.

"I was thinking," Jack intervenes, "why don't we leave aside the funeral now and concentrate on the marriage of your beautiful daughter?"

We turn to look at the bride: two hundred and eight pounds of woman, busy dancing with her husband, a skinny fellow, in the middle of the dance floor. Whoever says that all brides are beautiful has not seen this one.

"You could dance you two," suggests Jack.

"What? *No!*" I yell horrified. "I mean, no", I change my tone immediately, recalling where I am and with whom I'm speaking, "I am not a good dancer."

"Don't be modest, little sister, you won awards when you were small, remember?"

The Boss, at least four hundred pounds, leads me happily into the middle of the floor. And after embracing me and almost suffocating me between his rolls of flab, we begin to swing close to the whale bride.

Jack looks on from afar, drinks his champagne and makes fun of me, laughing like crazy.

***

Jack's near the buffet, waiting for the waiter to bring him another portion of shrimp, when a woman passes near him and touches his bottom. He moves aside in an elegant way and smiles at her. In response, I see her pull some money out from her bra and discreetly slip it into the pocket of his trousers. "At ten in the ladies restroom" she says to him with a wink and then leaves.

Jack isn't very surprised at this. As it is, he is accustomed to being courted and desired by the other sex. He watches the lady as she goes away and then takes out the money and smiles with a shake of his head.

Only a few seconds go by before another woman with a very generous neckline arrives. She studies him a little from all points of view and then caresses his pectoral muscles. "I like strong sex. Slaps, punches, spanking. If it isn't a problem for you", she inserts a business card in his trousers and goes waddling away.

I watch him, still hidden behind one of the many stone columns scattered throughout the restaurant.

Jack is dazed. Certainly, these things may also happen to him often, but not all in one evening and not so blatantly.

One minute goes by and I see the bride grab his buttocks with both hands, and so hard she almost lifts him from the ground. He turns quickly, shocked. "Your sister has told me everything," she explains and gives him a wink, fanning herself with a napkin to get some air. "Don't worry, I understand your unease", she gets closer to him, breathing in his face. "In five minutes in the ladies restroom I will be all yours", and then she goes away red in the face, continuing to wave the napkin to recover from the emotion.

Jack remains gob-smacked for a moment, then begins to look around. He has understood perfectly what is happening and who the architect of all this is: me.

Among people who are dancing, eating and singing Italian songs, he manages to make me out leaning on a column as I indicate the bridesmaids with my chin, one uglier than the next, sitting at a table nearby, who are greeting him warmly licking their lips.

He doesn't know what to do. He did not expect this, but soon realizes that the worst is yet to come. He sees the bridesmaids stand up from their chairs one by one to go to meet him, clearly with only one intention. He begins to move backwards looking around for the nearest exit, and I continue to smile and wave to him.

***

I'm lying on the table, in the midst of glasses, dirty dishes and cutlery, and I'm eating what's left of the wedding cake. I look at Jack, head down. He's messing with something at the bar of the restaurant. He has his back to me, and I must say that his lower back is not bad at all. Who knows whether it was already so nice when he was in Gorizia?

"What are you doing?" I hear someone ask at a hair's breadth from me. It's him, but how did he get from there to here so quickly? My thoughts are disconnected now too. I am really *very* drunk.

I stand up immediately, or in any case I think it's quick. I can't really tell in my condition.

Jack holds two large cups with green phosphorescent liquid inside. I take one and ask: "Is it radioactive?"

"No", he smiles, "I don't really know what I put in it, but I only know that they were spirits before got my hands on them."

"A-ha."

"I can take the first sip if you don't trust me", he proposes. He smiles again.

"*If* I don't trust you?" I smile too and drink the radioactive stuff. I must admit it's not too bad. But I didn't do so because I trust him,

I'm just thirsty. Felix by now will be pissed off like few others. I have lost both the bracelet with the imbedded GPS and audio contact with him.

Realising that, I relaxed and started to eat, drink and dance. In short... I've done exactly the opposite of what he told me. But I don't want to think of him and the consequences right now. I will think about it the day before the day after.

With a gesture, Jack throws the glasses to the ground and everything that is on the table and sits down next to me. "Have you enjoyed tonight?"

"Not as much as you enjoyed yourself with the chubby bridesmaids."

He doesn't seem to agree. "You didn't play fair, Jas."

"Oh, that's really funny coming from someone who has a degree in lies like you. Let me remind you that the whole fact of us being here was unfair, so what I did was fair in its unfairness."

Okay, I'm officially rotten drunk. I look at the cleaning women starting their work. Only after a little while do I realize that the woman is just *one*, it's not two.

He looks at me and smiles. "Fancy a game with me?"

"What game?" I ask suspicious.

"I tell you something that I like and something that I don't like, and then you do the same thing."

"That's not a game. It's called talking to you."

"I know."

"Then why do you call it a game."

"Because two people do it."

"Even when we're talking it's done by two, Jack."

"Yes it usually is, but that's not the case with us."

"What are you saying?"

"I'm saying", he pauses and puts his shiny hair in place, "that when we're together I usually talk *to you,* and not *with you*. It's different."

I have to be much drunker than I thought. I can't understand. Talk to you and talk with you... it seems like the same thing to me. I adjust the short dress I'm wearing and sit up straight on the table. "Come on, you start."

"Okay. Usually when I don't know what to do I open the fridge, I don't know why. I look inside and then I close it again without taking anything", he takes a sip of his radioactive drink and resumes: "I shower until I've used the last drop of hot water. I like to hear it slide over my skin and I like writing on the fogged up mirror when I get out of the shower even more. And I like watching the little old darlings who hang onto their purse as soon as someone comes near, for fear of being mugged."

I smile at what he has just said. I actually think they're funny too.

"Ah and I love thinking on the beach by the sea. It relaxes me a lot, I spend hours there especially if I feel sad or I need to take some important decision. On the other hand, I hate it when I have someone nearby eating crunchy food. I don't like mushrooms. I get really mad if someone damages one of my cars and I absolutely detest Nickolas."

I shake my head and raise my eyes to the heavens.

"Now it's your turn. I want to know what you like and what you hate about everyday life. Apart from me."

I burst out laughing, and after thinking about it for a few seconds, I begin to make my own list: "I shower in three minutes, on the contrary, and every so often I time myself to see if I can beat my own record. And as I've already told you... I hate dwarves. You do remember that I told you that, right?"

"Yes, go on, I'm interested", he cut in.

I leave the story of the dwarves alone and start my list again: "I hate to see the twins dressed the same way, it's like I was watching a horror movie: same t-shirt, same trousers, same bag, same hair... it's a torture for me", and as I speak I make twitchy gestures and Jack laughs amused.

"The most beautiful moment of the day for me is morning, when I have a coffee. For me it's not simply caffeine that I'm drinking but much more. I like the smell. I like the taste, the fact that it's hot. Drinking it gives me a sense of wellbeing and peace of mind. It's unbelievable how it can change the day for me. And I like Lego. When I was little, when I lived in Sempeter, I used to go and play with Stane. He had lots of pieces and I always built a house with wheels. I had this desire to travel already when I was small. I wanted to get to know the world, but at the same time I wanted to have the people I loved close to me so a house on wheels was the most suitable solution for what I wanted", I finish talking and realize I have tearful eyes.

I'd forgotten about Lego. I don't really know why I've have told him all this, seeing that one day, very probably, he'll be sure to use it against me.

66.

From Mina's diary – The month of August

Dear Diary,

I am sorry if I haven't been in touch in these last three weeks, but I've just been living the most beautiful days of my life. I know, I've often written this sentence since I arrived in Miami, but now it's different because my life has changed dramatically.

The first big news is that I've had my hair cut. Lexi took me to the most famous hairdresser in Miami - and to our great surprise we found that Ross had just been hired right there: it's incredible, I see him work everywhere - and now my hair is cut short up to my ears with some blond highlights through it. I have also learned to straighten it and curl it by myself with the irons. But that's not the only thing I learned in these past weeks, and my hair has not been the only change in me.

Lexi took me to designers, beauty salons, dentists, dermatologists, masseurs, make-up artists and I spend one hour per day in the gym surrounded by muscular instructors who help me shape my body. Now I dress in the latest fashion, I have sparkling white teeth. My skin is no longer lobster red; instead I have a perfect golden tan at last. I've got false nails, very long and all colored, I have a magic push-up that makes me look like a plus and I know how to walk on high heels without falling.

By Felix's orders I can't tell any of the members of the Watchtower that I go out with Lexi. However, he asked me to tell him should my excursions become not just limited to shopping. I felt important.

In any case the change in me is visible day after day; and from the way America and the others look at me, it's clear that something isn't right at all.

If before, when I walked down the street, people only looked at Lexi, now they also look admiringly at me, and it's a fantastic feeling!

I have acquired more self-confidence. I feel beautiful, but in all this, the most important thing is that at last I know how to behave with boys. The evening classes with Lexi and Ross have really helped me very much. Going around to bars, pubs and discos all over Florida. And speaking of that, a curious thing about the highways in Florida: there is a preferential lane for cars with more than two people on board. It makes Americans kick the habit of traveling alone. I found that initiative very interesting.

I've noticed that every place requires a different behavior, different clothes, different makeup and even a different laugh and look.

As far as boys are concerned, though, everything is still the same. They always follow the same protocol to hit on us. Same words, same penetrating glances, all shaved and perfumed with only one purpose: take you to bed.

Lexi is incredible. She uses them and turns them over as she pleases. Ross, on the other hand, goes off with a different one every night saying that he's the man of his life. But then every morning he complains that they've already split up, it's so funny.

And then there's me. No-one goes crazy about me like they do for Lexi, and I don't take men home like Ross, but to make up for that I have chatted a lot, I've received so many compliments, they buy me drinks, I've learned how to flirt and several times some nice boy has grabbed me and kissed me without permission. Something I liked very much. I really like everything.

I am so happy with everything that's happening to me here, that my mother's phone calls from Italy no longer have any effect on me. My bedroom is still rented to the German boy. At home in Italy they've cut off the electricity and water because mom hasn't paid the bills for months, and squabbling with her young boyfriend, Luke, she broke my new plasma TV, but all this has not even remotely undermined my good karma.

And while I was off improving my psychological state and my physical appearance, at the same time Jas has been probing Jack.

Eh... Jack, my infatuation for him hasn't passed unfortunately, I look at him and blush. He is really very handsome, a true tough guy in everything he says and does, a real *Bad Boy*. That bad boy that you see in movies and that your girlfriends tell you to avoid. That I too should avoid, and that I should tell Jas to avoid, but I just can't do it.

As the days pass, rather than investigate him, it seems to me that Jas is going out with him. He comes to get her downstairs from the Watchtower every day. I watch them from the small balcony and I can say that you can see the understanding between the two from a mile away. Like two magnets that attract each other, it doesn't matter if they're arguing or when they're laughing and joking. I don't know if this is a good thing or not, but the fact is that in three weeks she has failed to find any material evidence to be able to arrest him.

It seems that Jack is very careful not to leave any traces, and Jas instead is particularly careless. Every so often she forgets to turn on the GPS; she returns with the cables of various gadgets they put on her removed or damaged... this arouses a few little suspicions in me. But I avoid asking her questions because I wouldn't get any answers, anyway.

And speaking of avoiding, what has been completely ignored lately is Nick. Jas has changed in regard to him: she's elusive, she avoids being alone with him, she even avoids talking to him, not only about the investigations, but in general as well. For weeks he has watched her sneaking out of the Watchtower and go out with Jack without saying a thing. She also disappears for days and he still says nothing. No complaints, no criticism. Nothing apart from the pain stamped on his face. It's a heartbreaking thing for all of us to see him like this; his gaze is lost in space and sad as never before.

Over the years I have seen them argue, make peace, then sulk, scream and then make peace again, but this time it's different. It is the first time since I've known them that she doesn't look for him to quarrel and he doesn't look for her to make peace.

My dear Diary, I feel happy, very happy, but sometimes I wonder if my Jas is happy too. I fear that this investigation will only bring her suffering. Even if Jack has good intentions, capturing criminals, what he does is still illegal, so he has to be stopped. Nick on the other hand is a detective and it will probably he him who'll put the handcuffs on him. And she finds herself in the middle of this invisible triangle. The whole situation is confused, there is something between her and Jack, the feeling is strong and obvious but despite this she is helping Felix to nail him.

Nick is her whole world, and yet she is doing everything she can to avoid him.

If only she talked to me about what she feels, I could help her, but she doesn't. She hasn't done that since February, now that I think about it. Maybe you don't have to be a genius to understand that there is nothing more to understand.

67.

From Jas's diary – The month of August

Monday: I got my period.

Tuesday: I have my period and that idiot Jack took me diving. The underwater world is wonderful.

Wednesday: I had my first driving lesson. A disaster. And Jack did nothing but make fun of me! It must be because of my period or the driving instructor that I don't understand a fuc... thing.

Thursday: after cleaning the corridors at the hospital I went to see my Zombie and shaved his beard. Metoo looked at me puzzled and every so often climbed on my shoulder, he yelled his name and he has bitten my ear. Perhaps he was afraid that I was going to hurt his master. I brought with me to the room the cup from which I was drinking a cappuccino before finding the old man dead on the ground. Now the cup is on the nightstand and I use it as a little bowl of water for the parrot.

I had my first acting lesson with Jack. Being an actor is difficult!

Friday: Jack is a complete idiot! He says that I must not only learn to act, but also practice being my character regardless of what happens around me. Good!

His splendid idea was to have me play the part of a blind girl and take me to a really squalid place where he started playing poker with Freddy Kruger from Nightmare, while he played the part of Jack the Ripper. I thought he was doing it for me, to see if I was able to withstand the stress; after all it was a terrifying scene: weapons on the table, the waiter that served us was missing an eye, horrible baddies with yellow teeth... dreadful.

I did really well until I saw Freddy Kruger drinking his glass of beer and die shortly after and fall to the floor. I jumped off from my chair to help the poor serial killer, when I saw Jack stare at me with wide-open eyes. The next moment I found both the waiter without the eye and the other type pointing their weapons at us.

In the end Jack got rid of them with a couple of outstanding tricks and we ran away from there, but in any case I can't believe that he has once again made me witness to a murder.

When I got home I didn't tell Felix what had happened.

In any case I'm not going out anymore with Jack; I don't want to see him again.

Saturday: okay, okay. I've seen him again. But only because he made me an offer I couldn't refuse. In addition to promising not to put me ever again in situations like yesterday's as long as I'm going out with him (and while he was saying that to me I saw a little tear run down his face), he also said that he'll teach me how to really fight.

My teacher today was Koki. He taught me really a lot telling me that *the samurai limit the use of weapons to the warriors. You need to know how to fight disarmed as well.* He began to teach me Judo and Karate, but in a different and much more difficult way compared to how Nick taught me.

I don't know why I even wrote that; Nick has never taught me anything properly.

I think that Koki has a double personality, like me. When he sees a girl he goes berserk, he behaves like a sexual predator and offends thinking he's paying compliments. When it comes to combat though, he becomes very serious. He uses wise phrases and behaves like a real teacher. During combat I got hurt, I can barely walk!

When I returned home I ran straight to my room so Nick wouldn't see what I looked like. The last time, because of two bruises, he treated me the whole week as if I'd been in a war. If he could see the bruises that I have now all over my body...

Sunday: Mina is changing, both physically and personality-wise. Today she got angry with the fat intern from Arizona because he dared to interrupt her while she was talking to me. For ten minutes she yelled all sorts of things at him. And to think that all he'd said was *good morning*.

373

After I'd cleaned the corridors, I saw Lexi again wandering around the hospital. She didn't see me, I hid. I'm afraid. Perhaps she's looking for my Zombie. I immediately went to his room to see if he was still there. He was still there. And Diana's drawings stuck to the wall of her room have increased.

I lay down on the bed near the old man and hugged him. He reminds me a lot of my grandfather Nikola.

The parrot played with my hair.

Thursday: today Jack gave me a lovely surprise. He took me back to the exploded airport, but this time there was a whole incredible scenography. The road drawn, traffic lights, people made of cardboard, many cars around...

At the beginning I ran into a lot of old cardboard people and various animals. It was fun. Then Jack ruined the fun reminding me that my purpose was to avoid the obstacles, not run into them.

Pity.

The best obstacle was Koki. He stood on the road and avoided me by doing incredible leaps! I didn't know a human being was able to do that! He appeared and disappeared like a magician. After one or two... maybe ten times that I almost ran over him, I began to understand what to do so I didn't do it again.

Then it was Vladimir's turn. Of course he looked at me angrily all the time and continued to repeat *I hate you!* He sprayed water on the road, then snow (it came out from a tube, I didn't quite understand how this thing worked), then mud... and I had to try to maintain control of the vehicle. It was really, really difficult, also because Vladimir didn't make things easy for me. Today I also learned that there are cars with rear wheel drive.

Ah, and speaking of cars, for Jack every car is like a temple that should be revered. That idiot cleans the dashboard with a shaving brush!

Friday: Lexi taught me to run, jump and do somersaults on my heels. She was surprised when she discovered that I already knew how to do a lot of things. But it is logical. Each year at the Bairam I jump and dance the Kolo like a madman on heels. In these weeks I've realized that every member of Jack's team knows how to do everything. Everyone knows how to fight. They know how to drive helicopters, cars, motorbikes. They know how to act, improvise. And then they all are very well educated. They read a lot. There's always a heap of books in their cars: medicine, astronomy, psychology, together with simpler things such as gardening, cooking and crochet. They're three hundred and sixty degrees prepared.

My lessons with Koki are going well. Today we used sticks and knives. This time Jack took part as well and he almost cut me twice, I almost fainted.

Koki has made me memorize a phrase said by Wang Wei, a master of Kung Fu and Tai chi: *If I see that someone is looking at me with hatred, I do not react. I just fix him in the eyes, taking care not to convey any sensation of anger and danger. And the combat is already finished before it has even started. The enemy to beat lies within us. Martial arts do not mean violence, but self-awareness.*

I miss Nick. I'm not good with him and I feel bad without him, but unfortunately this is the only way I have to understand things. Just like our relationship.

Saturday: a lot of homeless people, very hungry and abandoned by the entire system. Jack calls them the Invisible and he's not completely wrong. For a whole night, dressed as tramps (Lexi did a perfect makeup job on me, I had dark rings under my eyes, hollow face, I looked sick and hungry... I was unrecognizable), the two of us wandered in the most out-of-the way streets of Miami.

I met some of them, I spoke with them, I ate and drank with them taking what was strictly necessary for our buffet from the garbage bins. You may think that it's disgusting, and instead it's amazing how many things, especially ones still packaged and edible, people throw in garbage cans.

We weren't there for information or to execute someone. Jack knows them. They talked to him as you do with a friend. They called him Jo and treated him like one of them. I wish I could write in this diary that the homeless people I met were poor but happy, but unfortunately it's not like that. They are poor and sad. Alone, even though they are surrounded by people. They live only a few miles from the center, but it seems an endless distance. Theirs is a world apart, perhaps because people, instead of trying to help them, turn their head the other way. They had a strange effect on me. I became sad myself. I didn't speak all the way home.

Sunday: a little while ago, I promised Nick I wouldn't do anything illegal, and despite the crazy night I've just had, I have kept that promise, also because having a good memory is not illegal, is it?

We've been to Las Vegas! Jack's entire team joined us. Or rather, I joined them.

Las Vegas is exactly as I imagined, full of lights and colorful signs, music and lots and lots of rich people who go there in the hope of becoming even richer. And poor people, on the other hand, who leave there even poorer than before.

It was only after we got to the hotel that Jack unveiled their plan. They wanted me to count the cards. I didn't even understand what they were talking about. I don't even know how to play cards. Only later I realized that counting the cards means taking advantage of my extraordinary memory and cheat. They tried to convince me that it is not illegal to do that but at the same time, however, they told me that if I got caught counting them they'd beat the life out of me. Then I realized how it all works: this is the law of the casino and not the state.

Well, the fact is that after only two hours of lessons and another hour while I stopped panicking (it wasn't easy, with Vladimir looking at me and growling in my face the whole time) I entered that casino with the others (even before that, I discover that the Black family is able to forge everything: credit cards, driver's license, documents etc.).

Each one has a fixed role: as soon as Jack and I arrive in the casino, Lexi makes a sign to us which table to sit behind. Vladimir infiltrates the guards themselves (he is far from credible with that red wig on his head and fake teeth), and from the hotel Koki checks the video-cameras focused on the tables.

I was very tense to start with. I couldn't concentrate. Panic took over when I felt all eyes on me. But Jack suddenly squeezed my hand. I thought he wanted to tell me something, and instead he remained silent.

I was amazed at two things: the first is that his eyes were able to give me courage; the second is that I didn't move my hand away as I usually do.

Seven hours later, I exit that casino with one million two hundred and thirty four dollars. I never imagined I could even say an amount like that, let alone have it in my hands. One million two hundred and thirty four dollars won playing Blackjack with Jack Black!

I was so overcome by emotion, happiness and the adrenaline in my veins that, once out of danger I instinctively hugged Jack very tight. I moved away immediately after, feeling uneasy, and he looked at me with that happy expression and that smile like... *aaaah*!

Anyway, casinos are very dangerous. Real psychological traps that you become addicted to. There are no clocks or windows, so that you don't sense how much time passes. I was in there seven hours and I thought it was only two.

Monday: Arizona yelled at me because I stole the flowers and the balloons in the maternity department and took them to my Zombie. I just wanted to make his room a little more cheerful, duh. Even if the words *A thousand felicitations and best wishes for the little one* or *best wishes mamma!* on the balloons seem a little strange next to the old man in a coma.

In the end, Diana saved the situation by making goo-goo eyes at the chief so she couldn't say no to her. That little girl is making me proud!

I have tried to find out from Will and Ben how the investigation on the airport explosion is going, but nothing doing. Will stuttered something about biscuits and Nutella, and I didn't quite understand what that had to do with my question, while Ben instead pretended not to know what I was talking about.

Today Jack, while he was teaching me free climbing, demanded a compliment from me.

In the end I did make one. I said that he is very sexy when he is silent.

Tuesday: three weeks have passed now, three weeks of workouts and also investigations. I saw Ben and the others secretly following Felix who had secretly followed me when I was out with Jack. I am not a genius when it comes to these things, but these investigations give me the shits.

Mina says that in Watchtower it's rumored that Felix should seriously retire. I've noticed that he does everything he can to keep Christoph Waltz off the *Jack case* and he is perfectly aware of it but says nothing, he smiles at him and goes to do what Felix orders him to do. I don't like this: if Waltz thinks only slightly like I do, there is a plan behind his silence that's just waiting to reveal itself.

Thursday: today (after the golf lesson) the journalists followed me and Jack. I never would have expected this. They usually only do so when I'm out with Nick. I escaped into his car, protecting myself behind the tinted windows to hide from the paparazzi. I don't know why I hid. After all, Nick knows where I am and with whom. Felix almost always keeps him informed. I don't know why I ran away.

Friday: our photo came out in the newspaper. There's me covering my face with my hands and taking off with Jack in his car. The caption: *Is Jas cheating on Nick?*

I felt very bad. I don't like the word *cheat* in any case or in any sense. I don't want to go out with Jack today. I don't feel up to it.

Saturday: I miss Nick. We see very little of each other. We speak very little. Everything that seemed too much before is too little now. In the end I wonder: how do you know when it's too much or when it isn't? How do you work out what is best for you? Know when it's too early to finish, or too late to do so...

68.

From Jx's diary – Watchtower, August

It's Sunday, the only free day the guys at Watchtower have.

Nick is sitting on the bed looking at the furniture in his room: an antique wardrobe to the right of the door, a bookshelf with about thirty books, the bedside table, a mirror, my poster with all the information that concerns me attached above it, and many framed photos of him and Jas around the room.

He closes the newspaper with the photo of Jas and Jack on the first page, gets up from the bed and goes to the door; before opening it he takes a deep breath and only then goes out into the corridor.

Opposite him he sees the open door of Jas and Mina's room. He sees the latter crawling on the floor moving clothes, shoes and other objects that belong to Jas to the other side of the red tape that divides the room in half.

69.

At the same time – From Mina's diary

I'm angry. Very angry. When I see her I'll slap her, oh, this time I really will! I feel a presence behind me. I turn and see Nick at the corner of the door looking at Jas's stuff with a sad and melancholy air. I sit down on the floor. "Nick."

It's as if he wakes up all of a sudden. He sighs: "Sorry... I... I was just going past and I saw the door open... What are you doing?" His question, simple as it is, seems very strange and complicated to me. He usually never asks me anything, unless it's about Jas.

"I'm saving my half of the room from the assault of Jas's stuff."
Well, actually this does have something to do with her.

"These clothes are alive, possessed, maybe! Each time I turn my back one of them crosses the tape on the floor! It's driving me crazy!"

He smiles at my outburst. "Do you want a hand?"

"A hand?" I repeat with raised eyebrows, "Heh heh, a hand, eh?" I repeat like a parrot. Frankly I don't see myself putting the bedroom in order with him. It's weird just even thinking about it. "It's just that I'm... I'm waiting for Jas and..." I don't need to even finish the sentence; from his expression I think he has understood that it's not a good idea to remain, for various reasons. "That's okay. I'm going to see what Veronica is doing."

"Okay."

He smiles, pretending he's fine, but you can see he's sad. I am sorry to have thrown him out like that, but I'm not accustomed to having him around, let alone talk to him of something other than Jas.

70.

Nick takes his leave of Mina and goes out closing the door of the room behind him. He stops for a few seconds, with his head down. He rubs his hands over his face and then knocks on the door of Veronica's room, next door. After a few seconds the woman opens up with an auto magazine in her hand. "Nick? Come in", she says surprised and goes towards her desk to put down the magazine. Her room is full of small wooden dwarfs scattered on the shelves, a sombrero and posters of cars hung on the walls, car magazines on the table and Spanish music in the background. Nick closes the door. "Good morning, what are you doing?"

Veronica does up the last button of her extra short shorts and turns toward him. "I'm going to see Will; there's the usual family reunion in a little while and he is too upset to make it at the moment."

"Has he spoken with his mother again?"

"Worse, mother and father together asking him questions about his work, when he'll return to England, about the new girlfriend and how they want to meet her officially on Skype", she shakes her head and opens the door, "but why are you here? Did you want to ask me something regarding the investigations?"

"No, no, I was just going past and I wanted to know what you were doing."

"Really?" she asks surprised, and quickly adds: "Come on, let's go and give Will our moral support."

They go out into the corridor and knock on his door. From inside an inarticulate grunt is heard. They enter and see him as usual sitting behind the many screens, keyboards, and other machinery scattered everywhere. He looks at them agitated scratching his beard. Veronica kneels in front of him. "How are you?"

"Frrrf, I do not know wh-wh-what to d-do", he says in a sad voice swinging around on his chair looking desperate. "I have to-told so many lies."

"They're white lies, they don't count."

Nick would like to intervene, say something, but it's practically impossible to enter into their conversation.

"Wh-wh-white lies or not, th-they are st-st-still lies."

"You don't want to disappoint the people you love, it's normal."

Nick makes a strange face; he does not support any type of lies, but he continues to say nothing so he doesn't ruin the exchange between the two.

"My father is about to become engaged", adds Veronica with a sad tone. The two men look at her surprised. "Yes, it seems he has postponed the proposed engagement because my brother Jose had an appendix operation two months ago. And 1, as you all know, I detest his new companion and I am totally opposed to this union. But do you know what I said to my father when he called me and asked for my blessing? I said yes and I gave him my best wishes."

"You lied", says Nick in a tone of disapproval, and both turn towards him.

"No-one hates lies any more than I do, Nick", replies Veronica, "but there are situations where the truth doesn't help at all because it wouldn't change things. And anyway, I might even tolerate the engagement, just as long as he doesn't marry her! Then you will indeed see me speak my mind!" She becomes enraged at the mere idea of the wedding.

"Frrrf they want me to work wiiith them, that I become a professor, that I ge-get ma-ma-married."

"You're different to them, you think in a different way, and you have different desires, Will. It's not your fault, they will understand."

"Your fa-father is still aaaa-angry because yo-yo-you did not want to work with him."

"It's true, but if I had not left him, I would have never found myself," she says showing him the tattoo that runs around her arm.

Nick looks at them in silence for a while as they console and give advice to each other, then turns around and without being heard goes out leaving them on their own. He heads to the lobby, where he sees America talking on the phone. He waves to her and goes towards the living room. Even before he opens the door he hears voices coming from inside the room. He enters and sees Ben standing beside the table with Franklin and Benjamina who are listening to him as he gives them a telling off: "And what do I discover? You've begun your pranks again!"

"They're not pranks. I act. I want to be an actor, pappy."

"If your mother could hear you!"

"Good morning", Nick greets them with a smile on his face, but the one he receives in return is Ben's angry gaze.

"Terrible day. What about you?" Ben addresses Benjamina whose lips are already trembling. "You skipped another three ballet lessons to go out with Skeleton, Holy God! If your mother finds out she'll hang me on one of those arches she builds for her VIP super-parties!"

"But I love him! I miss him!" she says sobbing, "You can't control your emotions!"

"But you can control your actions, though! Listen to me!" He sits behind the table with the gaze of someone plotting something. "Children, life is made of rights, but also responsibilities. Franklin, if you want to be an actor we'll send you to a drama school, and Benjamina, if you want to go out with Skeleton you can, I cannot forbid it. The only thing I ask is that you do not forget your duties as children; that you continue to behave in a polite way as I've taught you, and that you continue to be responsible and continue to... hide everything from your mothers!"

Benjamina bursts into tears, moved by her father's sermon, and hugs him hard, while Franklin is already on the computer searching for the best drama school to attend.

Nick moves back again, not wanting to ruin this beautiful family moment and as he leaves the living room, Pavarotti enters screaming: "Benjamin!"

"*Dad*! I am your *dad*!" Ben corrects him infuriated.

"Yes, whatever. I have to talk to you."

"What have you done and how much will it cost me?" are the last words that Nick hears before he turns the corner. He returns to the lobby and sees America behind the counter still speaking on the phone, certainly with her sister. He slowly approaches and pretends to look at the folders on the shelf, then looks at America, then looks at the folders again... America eyes him for a while; and

383

then as alarm bells ring she asks him: "Can I do something for you, boss?"

"No, no, I was waiting for you to finish the phone call."

"Why? Do you need the phone?" she asks raising one eyebrow and looking at the other four phones, some fixed and some mobile lying on the counter.

"No, no, to have a little talk."

America grips the handset and without moving she continues to stare at him trying to understand what it is he wants exactly. "What about?" she still does not understand, "Work? Today is Sunday", she points out. Nick realizes that he is definitely not wanted; he tightens his lips into a smile and adds: "I'm going to..." he takes a deep breath and goes toward the offices of the Watchtower without finishing the sentence. He feels strange, out of place everywhere, and this feeling of being unwanted destabilizes him.

He hears voices coming from Ben's office. The door is ajar so he decides to glance inside. He sees Katherine, Ben's current wife, in the middle of the room dressed all in pink, speaking with her butler and her dog. "Now watch and then tell me what you think, okay? One, two, three!" She starts dancing a funny choreography singing: *beauty, intelligence and elegance! That's what Pinky 5 is! Sisterhood is good!* And ends up on the floor doing a split.

Ambrose applauds. Naomi jumps around her as she gets up from the ground excited, and jumping up and down like her little dog, she asks: "Do you think the Pinky 5 will like it? I did all the choreography! I made it all up by myself!"

Nick watches the whole scene disconcerted then closes the door slowly leaving Katherine to her dance. As he walks towards the lobby he hears America call him: "Boss! The meeting is about to begin! Is that what you wanted to talk to me about before?"
He doesn't answer her. He returns to the living room at a fast pace and finds everyone waiting for him ready for the Sunday meeting. He doesn't have time to sit down before Will, nervous and agitated, begins to talk about the first problem as he rocks on his red chair. "I did SPRAAF of the divisions yesterday mor-morning and there we-were three jaars of Nuuutella in the pantry and today, one is-is aaalrready missing! Food, cookies, milk keep disaaapearing frrrf!"

71.

At the same time – From Mina's diary

I listen to Will's complaints and smile because I know very well where the jars of Nutella have ended up. One under Jas's bed and the other in Jas's stomach.

"Does anyone know who has taken them and wants to relieve their conscience and tell us?" asks Veronica looking at me; perhaps she has a slight suspicion regarding the identity of the thief.

"Why are you looking at me in this way?" I ask, pretending nothing is wrong, "If there is one thing I've learned in these last few months, it's that knowing something does not equate to proving it Veronica, so stop staring at me, please."

All present look at me amazed.

"Anyway", continues Veronica moving her gaze away from me, "a minimum of correctness would be welcome. At least let it be known when you take something. Isn't that right, Nick?"

I can already see that the discussion will go on for a long while. I take my lipstick and mirror from my pocket and begin to fix my makeup.

"Yes, that's right," replies Nick, "and if you take something by mistake, you must not be afraid to say so."

"Mii-mistake no way! If you ooopen the c-cuu-cupboard and take things that are not yours that's noooot a mi-miiistake!"

"Do you have any other problems to talk about, Will?" asks Nick in what seems a very bored tone.

"Yes. Pavarotti br-breaks a gl-glaaas per day, eats on the so-ssofa and does nothing but diiir-dirty it! The sofa cost two thousand dollars! DAAS!"

"Every time you mention that sofa you add one thousand dollars, old man!" responds Pavarotti rudely as he plays on his mobile phone.

"Frrrf"

"Well son, you don't eat on the sofa, there are tables for that", Ben reminds him.

"The chairs are uncomfortable, and the tables are crooked", Pavarotti replies in a very impolite way. He takes a sip of Coca Cola and when he is about to place the glass back on the table, it falls and smashes into a thousand pieces. Pavarotti looks at the ground bored. "See? I was right."

"Pavarotti! Now clean everything up!" Ben orders him, but as Pavarotti gets up from the chair he moves the table roughly and makes another two glasses fall off it. Will starts to go crazy. Benjamina watches everything as if it was something normal and Ben reprimands him for the umpteenth time.

"I'll clean it", proposes Veronica and stands up to get a broom in the kitchen.

Nick suddenly starts to speak and says: "Pavarotti will wash the dishes and help Will to clean the house until he has repaid all the damage he has caused this week."

Pavarotti just smirks when he hears Nick's sudden decision, but does not dare replicate. Veronica meanwhile begins to clean up the shards of glass under the table.

Ben turns to me and the children stating: "The red corridor is off limits for people who are not working there, okay? If I see one of the four of you again going beyond that red line it will mean only one thing: memorable punishment! Right, Nick?"

Nick nods his head scribbling something on the sheet in front of him, he seems pensive. We hear the bell of the Watchtower ring but nobody takes any notice. This really annoys America because, even if it's Sunday and therefore her day off, she has to get up and go to see who it is.

"Let's talk about security", proposes Nick lifting his gaze from the sheet. "I have printed the rules that we follow in the event of hurricanes. America will hang them on the door of each bedroom and on the board in the lobby. What you need to do is read them, learn them and follow them to the letter. Is that clear?"

All of us all nod in agreement without a word. Nick is a very calm and gentle person, but when it comes to rules and bans he becomes hard and too authoritarian.

"Veronica", Jas's penetrating voice enters the living room. She smiles and when she sees her with the broom in her hand asks, "are you cleaning or about to fly away?" She is leaning on the door, wearing a white dress, and she looks at Veronica with that nasty little smile that only she knows how to do.

Visibly annoyed, Veronica turns to Nick, but seeing that he takes no notice of her because he's too busy looking at Jas, she starts to clean the floor again with an irritated look one her face without replying to the quip. Silence falls in the room; everyone is looking at Nick waiting for him to say something, as if Jas is his business. But he doesn't speak, he looks at her dazed and that's it.

Franklin breaks the silence raising his eyes from the pc and welcomes Jas. "Hi Jas! I am going to enroll in an acting school, did you know?"

"Very good, will you remember me when you win an Oscar?"

"But of course, dear teacher!"

"If you want a few more lessons in acting, you know where to find me", she smiles, while from the other side of the table you can hear Ben cough and look at Nick frightened. Actually I can understand that, given that his last test ended up in the central police station.

America returns to the living room. We look at her, still silent. "Sorry, I didn't want to interrupt this wonderful atmosphere of terror."

"The atmosphere is not the only terrifying thing in here", responds Jas still using that provocative tone. She gives me a nod and leaves. I stand up too. "I am so sorry, guys, but I have to go. No, come to think of it I'm not sorry and I don't *have* to go, I'm going and that's that", I make sure they understand, and leave the room with total silence still reigning behind me.

72.

Mina has just left the living room and the others are looking at her astounded by her words and her unusual behavior.

"Boss, it was Ginevra ringing the doorbell. I told her you're not in, again", she says in tone of disapproval, exchanging a complicit glance with Veronica who is still cleaning the floor. "But she decided to come upstairs anyway, to say hello to Veronica and Ben", she pauses, "therefore if you are not at home, it's best that you're not in the living room either."

Nick says nothing. Pensive, he gets up from the chair, leaves the living room and goes straight toward Patrick's room, leaving the others perplexed and wondering what's going on. He knocks on the door, a few moments go by and Patrick opens it, looks at him and lets him in without asking any questions.

His room is different from all the others. There is only a wardrobe, an empty table with a chair and a bed. No photos, pictures, posters, books, TV, flowers. Nothing at all, totally bare. Nick sits on the bed, Patrick on the chair; he waits, but Nick doesn't speak. He sees that he would like to talk, but perhaps doesn't know where to begin, so he decides to help him: "Begin with one word, it will be easier."

"Kiss."

"Kiss", he repeats looking surprised.

"Yes, I kissed her", he stops briefly, "or almost."

Patrick seems confused. "You kissed her or you almost kissed her? They're two different things, Nick."

"I touched her lips," he admits distressed; he gets up from the bed and begins to walk up and down the room.

"And how does it make you feel?"

"Confused."

"And how does she feel?"

"I don't know, we were interrupted and we haven't talked about it since then."

"Why?"

"Our *almost* kiss was not the most important issue, given everything that has happened and that is still happening."

"But you're talking about it."

"What can I say?" he stops, his face serious. "That I liked it? That I'd do it again? That I'd take away that *almost*, that I feel something for her?"

"I am not the one looking for these answers, it's you, Nick."

Nick sits down again on the bed hiding his face in his hands. Patrick sees his disquiet and, sitting down in turn, rests a hand on his shoulder.

"I should not have crossed the line."

"You shouldn't have *almost* crossed it", he corrects him.

"*Between love and friendship there is just the distance of a kiss*", he says in a sad voice, "you were so right, Patrick. But unfortunately I had no other choice."

"Between you and her there has never been only friendship, my friend."

Nick fixes him. "But do you know who I am talking about?"

"I do, do you?"

73.

In the meantime – From Mina's diary

If I don't die laughing now, I'll never ever die. I'm looking at Jas who is looking at the two mobile phones on the bed trying to manage the two furies who are speaking from one telephone to the other on speakerphone: her mother and her grandmother.

"Mom, I repeat. I'll be home in a week."

"You're been coming home *in a week* for months, Jas! You've met a guy, right? You're pregnant, you want to get married!"

You can hear a moan come from the other cell phone: "I feel like I'm reliving a *déjà vu,* who knows why..."

"Grandma, that's enough!"

"Yes, mother, that's enough!" Jelena bursts out, "Stay out of it!"

"Oh don't worry, I will, especially because I have things to do, I have to prepare a layette for my granddaughter!"

"You *what*?"

"I just said enough, you two!" Jas attempts to placate them.

"That wretch of your mother said she was going on vacation in Slovenia for a few months and instead..."

"Mom, are you still going on with this story? It happened nineteen years ago! How much longer are you going to hold this grudge against me, eh? How long?"

"Till I die and even longer! I'll never forgive you! You went eight hundred miles away and left me here alone."

"I had to go my own way! *Live my life!"* Jelena shouts.

"Ah yes? Well, then you'll have nothing to the contrary if Jas too decides to live her life in Miami?"

"What? No! Jas! You can't do this to me!"

"You can and she can't? You selfish ungrateful daughter!"

I continue to hear the entertaining argument between her mother and her grandmother, but Jas takes the two phones, gets off the bed and takes them into the bathroom. She comes out and closes the door behind her as if she had just left two bombs inside and not two mobile phones, and bursts out laughing. "Your family is too funny!" I continue to laugh as I remodel my eyebrows with tweezers in front of the mirror.

"Funny is not the word I'd use, but that's how it is. Have you talked with your mother?"

"Yes, my room is still rented. I have the feeling that you'll have to put me up at your place for a while, Jas. While your mother is afraid that you'll get pregnant, get married and leave home, mine instead can't wait to become a young grandmother and get rid of me. *One thousand.* And then those idiots haven't repaired my plasma TV yet. This thing is very *bibi*. Shall we do the *JasTwentyfive* or not?"

She looks at me surprised, and takes a box from under the bed which holds vodka, orange juice and...

"Strawberries?" I exclaim.

"You can't do a *JasTwentyfive* without strawberries."

"Yes, I know, but Will can't make his cake without them either. This thing is very *bibi* too... but never mind."

"You know, Mina, this couldn't-care-less attitude of yours is starting to win me over."

"*One thousand*! I won you over before I had my couldn't-care-less attitude, sweet thing."

We hear the ringing sound of one of the cell phones coming from the bathroom and Jas's eyes pop out of her head. "Oh no, they're at it again, I'm going in there now and I'll turn everything off. I'm tired of their arguments!" she says, and rushes to the bathroom like a fury.

Her family amuses me so much. I look at my eyebrows in the mirror; they are too low, they give me a heavy look. Maybe I should go and get myself a blepharoplasty. I will ask Lexi for advice as soon as I see her.

"I have to go!" yells Jas suddenly.

I look up, and see her running around the room in search of clean clothes.

"And where are you going?" I ask intrigued.

"I don't know, somewhere with Lexi. And I mustn't say anything to anyone."

"Oh uffiiiiiii!" I snort still looking at my eyebrows bent down onto the mirror. "What about our *JasTwentyfive*? And the *Buffy* dvd?"

"Tomorrow."

"*One thousand.* Listen, have you seen my cell phone anywhere?"

"No", she answers as she grabs hers.

"*One Thousand"*, I complain again. "Who are you calling?"

"Hello, Franklin?" she whispers into the handset, "I have to sneak out of the Watchtower. Can you distract them a moment acting out one of your things?"

Oh God!

"Mah, I don't know..." she snorts bored and adds: "Faint there in front of everyone, cut an arm, make something up, no?"

74.

I follow Lexi to a parking lot full of cars. The sun is beating down on my head. I'm hot, thirsty, but above all I have so many questions that I can't wait to get some answers to. Lexi today is not herself. She walks up straight, doesn't make wisecracks or try to seduce every living being that she meets in the street, and furthermore she's not wearing a wig. I'm afraid she could be sober.

She finally stops next to a red car. She opens it, despite not having the keys, sits on one of the seats and starts looking for something inside. I stand outside watching her.

"Are you getting in or not?" she asks me, annoyed. "Do you need a leash? Do I have to pull you inside? *One thousand*!"

Well, needless to say, I don't like her tone of voice at all. "Goodbye Lexi" I say, turn on my heels and leave.

"No! Wait Jas! Where are you going?"

"Home!"

"Wait!" The sound of her heels makes me realize that she's running after me.

"I'm sorry, okay?"

I stop and turn to look at her.

"Come on, let's do the peace hug?" she opens her arms and gives me a false.

"No."

"It's just that I haven't had breakfast and I'm edgy. Please, Jas."

The more I look at her, the more I feel sorry for her: sober and her red curly hair being blown into her mouth with the wind. She pleads with me to stay looking at me with her languid blue eyes. When she doesn't drink she looks really awful. I cross my arms. "I want to know what's going on."

"Get in the car and I'll tell you."

We reach the car, and I sit in the passenger's seat. Lexi starts to fiddle around with the various cables for the ignition under the steering wheel, from the driver's seat.

"Please, tell me that this is your car", I ask her, hoping that it's not stolen.

"All the cars with a red license plate belong to my family. We leave them around just in case. I can never remember the code, dammit", she replies simply as she gets it started. "There we go!" She presses a button with a strange design on it just above the shift lever. The CD-player opens, and inside I see knives, guns and, of course, a small bottle of vodka that Lexi takes out and drains in a second.

"Ah, I feel better already. Remember, breakfast is the most important meal of the day."

What on earth can you do after a scene like that? I know what you can do, just pretend that you have not heard anything and go to the next question. "Are all your cars equipped like that?"

"Yes. This is a real gun", she shows me taking the weapon in her hand, "and this instead", she takes another, "is full of tranquilizers. We use it for Vladi when has one of his funky moments."

Call them funky...

She puts her hands on the steering wheel and we start.

"Tell me what's going on here, Lexi."

"Jack." She sighs. "He has decided to do something very very stupid."

"And what's that got to do with me?"

"He wants you to watch while he does it."

"While he does *what*?" I still don't understand.

"The very stupid thing", she cuts short. She looks at me and smiles. "When we get to the Jet I have to blindfold you. You must not know where we're going. It's for your safety, Pet."

Safety? I hope she won't be flying the Jet while I watch Jack doing the very stupid thing. Maybe I should have let Felix know I was going somewhere with her.

***

She kept me blindfolded the entire trip. I don't understand why considering I couldn't see any landmarks, among the clouds.

After about two hours we landed, I don't know where, and Lexi took me to a kind of van, I believe, where she dressed me and put a headset on me.

She got ready too, and I had to wait for her blindfolded all the time. She is strangely silent and I haven't succeeded in getting anything out of her or where Jack is, nor what the very stupid thing is that he wants to do. This not knowing makes me nervous.

After another hour of travel time in silence in the van, we finally stop.

"Now listen to me carefully", Lexi says to me. "Vladi will be in there too. If you see him, pretend you don't know him. You must ignore him, understand?"

"I have to do what I usually do, in a few words?"

"Yes."

"And where's Jack?"

"You will see him."

"Do I ignore him too if I meet him?"

She is silent for a few seconds. I don't know what she is doing since I'm still blindfolded.

"Listen, I have to tell you another thing that is very important", her voice becomes serious: I can hear her take a deep breath before starting to speak again: "If something should go wrong, anything, you don't know us. Ignore us completely, listen to what you're told to do in the headset and run. Let us do the rest."

I can't hold back a smirk. For the entire journey, Lexi remained silent and now that she has begun to talk she has repeated the word *ignore* ten times. I don't understand what she has brought me here for. To watch Jack while he does a stupid thing and ignore him at the same time? It makes no sense. "Okay", is all I say making the same smirk as before.

"It's a serious thing, Jas."

I think she must have noticed it. "Yes, I understood that. You asked me to ignore all of you, not to defuse a bomb. What's the problem? And anyway, it wouldn't be the first time I see him do something dumb."

I hear her get out of the van and shortly after she opens the door for me. "Now you can pull off the blindfold."

At last! I couldn't live in that darkness any longer!

I take it off. Initially, I see everything dark, but it's normal, I think, after four hours of darkness. Immediately after I realize that it's not my eyes which aren't right. "It's all dark in here."

"Yes."

"Why the devil did you make me keep the blindfold on then?"

"What does that matter?" she asks annoyed, "It's always darkness, no? Here." She says *here*, but how do I take hold of anything if I can't see anything? I continue with my grimaces and hold out my hands to try to take the mysterious object and finally touch a piece of plastic. From the shape I can understand that they're spectacles. I put them on immediately. "It's a pair of night vision glasses," I exclaim with joy. I see Lexi before me in a sexy pose leaning on the door. The glasses color everything in various shades of red. Even the inside of the van. Rock on!

"But now, we do the make-up." She makes me remove the glasses and while I'm plunged into darkness I feel her fiddling with brushes and sticks on my face. "Come on, Pet."

I put the viewer on again and get out with a smile stamped on my lips. As she wiggles toward the elevator, I look around amazed: there are a lot of cars, vans and motorcycles in the parking lot.

"These glasses are really cool!" I remark all excited. "Will you give them to me?" I ask as I get into the elevator, but she pays no attention to me.

It is very cold here. I was certain that we would go up, and instead we descend a few floors, always in darkness. "is it possible to know why we have no light?"

"We have disconnected the electricity, but only for a few minutes, just to run a test."

"A test of what?"

"A test of darkness?" she answers as if I was a slow learner.

The door opens. Light enters the elevator, blinding me. I take off my glasses, upset for a moment, and when I get used to the light all I do is stand there with my mouth open because of what I see appear before me. In front of us, along the wall of the hallway, there is a huge mirror. I see our reflected image. The right word to describe us is *stunning*. Black leather shirt and pants; wig of long black hair and magnificent heavy makeup. It is unbelievable that Lexi has been able to do such beautiful make-up just looking through the visor. It's all very tight, with a plunging neckline and bare midriff – which I usually avoid -, fake piercing on the nose, lower lip and ear. And yet I really like the look of myself very much.

"Life is never hard for beauties like us."

I turn to Lexi and see her lick the mirror and caress her breasts. I'm not surprised at anything she does anymore. When she stops acting like a slut, she adds nonchalantly: "Put the glasses in the back of your pants and follow me."

I do that, leaving the mirror with difficulty, I have to admit.

The hallway is very narrow, dirty, full of cracks and the lights on the ceiling flash occasionally. I begin to hear shouts, it sounds like men rooting for someone. And once we arrive in front of a steel door with the notice *Taking photos and videos inside is forbidden*, whistles and laughter are added to the shouting.

Lexi takes a huge breath before knocking. The door is opened, and we find ourselves facing one of those heavies with a stupid face that you see in third-rate movies. Except that that heavy is Vladimir. Dark glasses, bald, prosthesis on his nose. He is unrecognizable. He looks us up and down as if he doesn't know us. "Watchword?" His cold voice with a Russian accent has remained the same, though.

"Svetlana", answers Lexi, pronouncing the word very slowly.

He moves from our sight without even looking at us and it's only once I'm through the door that I notice that there's a metal detector on the other side. Seeing I haven't let either Nick or Felix know about my destination and my companion, it's consoling to know that at least no one is armed in this place.

I follow Lexi and look around me. There are a lot of people, mostly men who are looking at a ring sitting in the middle of this huge underground bunker. It is surrounded by a metal net and inside it there are two guys belting the crap out of each other. Due to our dark clothing we don't go unnoticed to the eyes of those present, but other than smile and admire us they do nothing else. I'm prepared for a few vulgar words, a grope on my behind or any other attitude worthy of a place like this, but oddly I don't have to deal with anything of that kind. It's all, how can I say, clean.

"Oh, *fuck*", I scream disgusted. "Is that blood I can see pouring down from the ring?"

Lexi shrugs as if it's something normal and goes ahead. I knew it was too good to be true. As usual as soon as I say something with conviction, something happens immediately after that contradicts me.

The smell of blood is sickening. Two colored types run toward one of the boxers lying on the ground, motionless. They lift him up and carry him away while a girl dressed like me and Lexi cleans the floor of the ring with a mop.

"Lexi?" I grab her arm and turn her towards me, angry. "Tell me that it's not what I think!"

She looks at me without even understanding what I'm alluding to. "Okay, it's not what you think", she answers, to make me happy.

"Tell me that man isn't dead", I point to the ring, to make her understand. She looks at me as if she was doing me a favor and answers me: "Okay, he's not dead."

"I cannot believe that you have brought me here", I yell again, pissed off, "What is it? One of those clandestine clubs where the first rule is *there are no rules*?"

"No, the slogan says", she takes a flyer stuck in the middle of her boobs and reads: "*I don't hit to hurt, I hit to kill.*"

"What? Lexi! When you said that Jack is about to do something very stupid..." I don't even finish the sentence when I hear a voice boom throughout the bunker. "And now a big round of applause for the new fearless competitor who is about to climb into the ring, his name is Jake Sparrow!" The presenter in the center of the ring shouts into the microphone indicating, in a corner, Jack.

"You were talking about *this* stupid thing", I finish the sentence is disbelief.

He is not masked, he's simply Jack, bare chest and black trousers. He bows to the delirious crowd. Made up mostly of women. I can't explain where all those screaming girls suddenly sprang from, but one of them doesn't waste any time in squashing her boobs flat against the metal net, calling on his name. And of course that imbecile Jack stands there looking at her all pleased. As

398

soon as he sees me, however, he stares wide-eyed and with a huge smile moves closer to the net.

I really don't know where to look, because wherever my eyes fall I find something embarrassing in front of me. Jack is very muscular: he has very developed pectorals, strong arms, sculptured abdominals... I can't take it.

He looks at me like one who knows he has a model's physique. "Do you like my build that rivals marble?" he asks, cocky.

"I've seen better", I lie. I look away and clean the drool from my mouth.

"But if I look as if I've been sculpted by a sculptor," he continues to praise himself.

"Yes, by a drunken sculptor."

He smiles amused and then begins to look at me from head to foot. Focusing, however, only on my breasts. I shake my head; I'm accustomed to his *chivalry* now. Meanwhile I notice that Lexi has disappeared and a great many people who are trying to touch and speak with Jack have almost overwhelmed me.

"Have you got a minute?" I ask him.

"Yes, only one."

"Have you gone mad by any chance? What does all this mean? Do you want to get killed?"

He leans on the rope of the ring giving me a satisfied little smile. "Ah, so you care if I live or die?"

"Of course I care, especially because I have not yet decided if I prefer to see you in a cell or a coffin."

He smiles again. "If you like, I'll tell you where I prefer to see you", he says in a mischievous tone staring at my breasts again.

"Shut up."

"Come on, give me a good luck kiss." He puts his plump lips to the net waiting for the kiss while I look at him with raised eyebrows. "Will you quit being an idiot? I ask you, you've read their slogan, right? There's blood everywhere on the ground and they just took away a man who was half dead! You promised that you would never get me involved in situations like this ever again! And what's more I don't want to be the one who has to clean your blood off the ring! It's dangerous! Get down immediately." I say all in one breath. I'm angry and agitated and... worried? I'm worried about Jack?

I start to feel hot. I don't like this feeling of being protective of him. I would not have expected it from me. Especially because he's no longer John the disabled person.

He is still leaning on the net and looks at me in silence, but his blue eyes say everything. He's happy with my reaction, and this bothers me. And it also bugs me when he stares at me too long like this, because I don't know what's going through his mind. I move my gaze from him, embarrassed.

"Don't worry, I know what I'm doing", he reassures me with a calm and relaxed voice.

"Actually I'm not worried." I am not credible.

"It'll be child's play."

The presenter stops us. "And here we are ready to present his opponent. One of our old acquaintances, back after a year's absence, directly from Russia... here is *The Russian*."

Everyone turns to the ring to wait for *The Russian* from Russia – what imagination.

I certainly was not expecting to see a small skinny boy get into the ring, but I am somewhat surprised when I realize that *The Russian* is a cross between Big Foot and the abominable snowman. His shoulders are enormous. He must be high at least six feet six tall. Jack, in comparison, looks like a hobbit.

"Hmm", is the only comment he is able to make once he's seen him, while all around us delirium is raging.

"It was nice to meet you, Jack," I say.

"Now you tell me?"

The Russian begins to emit strange noises, similar to Bruce Banner before he turned into Hulk, and lashes out at the audience that, instead of escaping, roots for him and praises him.

"How do you think you'll get out of this alive?" I ask curious.

"I have my methods", he responds trying to look cool. "Excuse me, but I have to go now." He turns to the gorilla that in the meantime is screaming and looking at the ceiling. This makes me think that I made a big mistake not telling anyone where I am.

"Ah, Jas" Jack calls me again.

"Yes?"

"You're beautiful," he says softly, looking into my eyes and I don't know why, but my heart begins to beat very fast and I blush. I shake my head to bounce back from this unexpected embarrassment and I turn to go and join Lexi, who is three feet away from me staring at Vladimir on the other side of the room and biting her nails. Here we have another unexpected reaction. Why is she nervous? I didn't know she knew this state of mind too.

I cross my arms and join her, looking at her with a serious face.

She sees me out of the corner of her eye; I know she sees me, but she pretends she doesn't and this, as she is usually says, is *very bibi*. I tap her on the shoulder. "Lexi!"

She moves away quickly, shrugging her shoulders, and not from fright. This is a clear sign that she's blaming me for something. Now the question is .. what?

"You think it's my fault, don't you?" I say.

"What? No! I don't know what you're talking about? Fault... for what?" She looks at me wide-eyed, I have never seen her so serious before now. "Lexi, your *body* is contradicting your words."

She looks down, another proof that what I'm saying is true.

"What's happening, Lexi?"

She snorts and then points to a man a few yards away from us. "That guy there is called Boris."

Boris. A distinguished looking man, dignified and a reassuring gaze. At last I'm looking at the person who perhaps is searching for my Zombie.

"He is a dangerous criminal and is very well known here in Miami," continues Lexi. "And that one there", she indicates another man to me, on the other side of the ring, "is Boris Jr., his younger brother, but above all his number one enemy."

I take a good look at him and he seems harmless: a man with black hair and a goatee, quite thin. I imagined them to be different.

"They spend their days doing spiteful things to each other to show which of the two of them is the most powerful, in any field. Jack has made an agreement with Boris Jr.: If he manages to beat the Russian, who is his brother's fighter, Boris Jr. will give the cross back to him."

"Which cross?" I ask.

"You know which cross I'm talking about, Jas."

401

I momentarily shiver. I feel a huge stone fall onto my heart and I can't even breathe. The headmistress's cross! She's talking about that cross!

"And if he doesn't beat him?" I ask frightened. "Lexi?"

She looks at Jack on the ring and says nothing. "Has that Russian ever been beaten?" I ask her.

I don't like the way she hesitates. She looks at me. "No." she replies under her breath.

"Jack!" I rushed down to the metal net screaming his name. "Jack!"

There is too much noise inside the bunker: too many voices, too many shouts, everyone calling his name or the Russian's. He can't hear me. But I have to try to stop him, and tell him that it doesn't matter about the cross, that I don't want it any more. I am worried for him again, I admit it, but the only thing I want at this moment is see him get down from that ring.

I call him again a couple of times, in vain, when I hear the sound of the bell boom in the bunker, the combat has now begun. I return to Lexi and take her by the shoulders. "Why didn't he tell me this beforehand? Why?"

"I asked him not to."

I am beginning to feel sick. I try to take control of myself but it is difficult. I turn to look first at Boris and then his brother. They are challenging each other with glances not giving a damn about Jack and the Russian who are perhaps about to kill each other. I don't know what to do!

Boris Jr. has the headmistress's cross, and his brother, as well as wanting to get rid of my Zombie wants to get rid of Jack as well.

The lights are lowered and in the midst of the screams and the total delirium of the spectators the first blows start to fly between the two. The Russian pounces on Jack and he quickly jumps and does incredible acrobatics to avoid his blows. At the same time he makes fun of him with wisecracks about his enormous stature. Nice tactic, it tires him and makes him edgy at the same time. After all, he's doing quite well; between one jump and another he hits him laughing in his face and in doing so he makes us laugh too. A couple of times the Russian seizes him and smacks him against the net, Jack gets up immediately and goes on the counterattack.

I'm starting to enjoy it and I'm a little more tranquil seeing that they're not using any type of weapon in this fight.

The Russian is exhausted and his face is bloodied, while Jack doesn't have even a scratch. I'm amazed. I see Lexi jumping up and down and cheering while she's drinking a beer, surrounded by guys who don't know whether to watch her or the encounter. Boris instead is visibly upset, and I'm surprised when I see the Russian look at him scared after receiving Jack's last blow straight in the stomach and finding himself against the net. Boris Jr. rejoices shouting Sparrow's name. Jack, between moves acts like a clown and continues to take the piss and then turns to me and smiles. Even if he doesn't speak I can hear him say with his eyes *look how cool I am!*

Apparently I was worried for nothing and Jack really knows what he is doing. He's winning. Lexi looks at me happy. "I knew from the start that he'd win, I'm never wrong!"

But wasn't she shitting herself earlier? I look at her with raised eyebrows. Once again she sees me out of the corner of her eye. I know she sees me, but just pretends she doesn't. What a hypocrite.

All of a sudden I see Jack fly toward the net in front of me and the Russian magically recovering his strength. People are shouting. This huge din is giving me a headache.

Even though the audience is urging him to get up, Jack is still on the ground. Lexi and I look at each other concerned but Jack finally gets up again, albeit with difficulty. He is holding his right arm, he seems disoriented; the Russian approaches him angrily and gives him such a hard punch that it sends him bouncing to the other side of the net.

Drops of sweat slide down his body, he's having trouble breathing; he closes and reopens his eyes as if he is seeing everything blurry, and he gets up, still with difficulty. There is something wrong.

He starts to look around again, disoriented, and covers his ears with his hands as if the noise and screams were bothering him, while his right arm becomes redder and redder.

I turn pale. "They've poisoned him. They have poisoned him!"

"What? Are you sure?"

"Yes, Lexi! Dammit! He has been poisoned or drugged, he has all the symptoms, you must pull him out of there or it will kill him!" I scream terrified, as the Russian, limping, approaches Jack once more.

Lexi looks at Vladimir petrified, and in a loud voice just says: "Cyrus!"

Jack is on the ground again, visibly disoriented, while the Russian approaches and begins to kick him in the stomach.

"No! We must help him!" I scream desperate.

Jack tries to protect himself as best he can.

"You know what you have to do", I hear the voice of a man speak in my earpiece.

"Who is it talking?" I ask, but do not receive any reply.

Lexi seizes me by the shoulders. "Jas, do you remember what I told you in case something went wrong?"

"Yes, yes." I don't understand what that's got to do with things at this moment.

"Do it!" she orders me. "We'll find you! Koki, lead her toward the secondary exit!" she says loudly touching her ear.

"What? No!" I look around me shocked. A lot of people are yelling; the Russian is massacring Jack, who is now immobile, on the ground; Boris smiles satisfied as he feels up a woman; his brother stares at him angry; Lexi runs toward Vladimir; Koki repeats in my ear that I must get out of there taking the stairs... I'm confused, I no longer understand anything!

Jack is in the ring with blood on his face and everyone is abandoning him!

In a moment - I don't know how it happens – I'm on the ring intent on launching a hard kick on the back of the mountain that is bashing Jack.

Grandma has always said that the area of the kidneys is very sensitive and vulnerable to blows, especially if they are caused by stiletto heels. And in fact the Russian falls to the ground bending over from the pain.

Silence descends.

I look around and tremble: the men below the ring are looking at me surprised. Lexi and Vladimir are in front of the door, standing stock still, shocked and their eyes wide. Jack tries to understand if it's really me standing in front of him. And the Russian is... very, very mad.

The moment of silence ends, and between applause, shouts and audience approval I realize that I'm in deep shit. I don't know what to do or how to get around. I would never be able to beat the Russian, and he goes to the net called by Boris.

"Jas, get out of here..." Jack can hardly talk; he is sitting on the ground.

"No!"

"Listen to me, woman! This is not the time to be a heroine; you must get out of here now! If something happens to you I..." he coughs, and I see the blood on his hand.

The Russian is still talking with Boris.

I kneel in front of Jack as he continues to plead with me. "Jas, please go, I'll be alright. Leave me here."

"No."

"I beg you..." he fails to finish the sentence. He is no longer able to keep his eyes open. His face is very pale. I embrace him, whispering in the ear with a trembling voice. "No, I'm not leaving you."

I feel a strange burning inside my chest. I can't breathe nor let him go.

"You cheated, Boris! You cheated!" I hear Boris Jr. protesting behind me. He is holding a weapon and is pointing it at his brother. Apparently the metal detector is not for everyone.

"Who are you?" the Russian asks coming to meet me. I stand up and look at him pretending not to be afraid of him, even if my head hardly comes up to his knees.

"His substitute", I reply. The audience around us goes berserk, yelling and clapping.

"I don't fight with girls."

"Nor do I."

He smiles. A smartass smile. An evil smile that means *I'm laughing about the pain that I'm about to give you.* He starts to go around in a circle inside the ring.

Jack continues to repeat my name, while the Russian smiles, licking his lips in an obscene manner and looking at my boobs. It seems that the two Boris like the exchange too, since they're standing there silent staring at me, without shooting at each other.

"I can't wait to get my hands on you, Dark Lady."

"No..." I hear Jack protesting. "Cyrus! Come and get her!"

I look around me scared: I would never have thought that I'd want to see Vladimir, and instead that's exactly how it is. I hope he changes his mind and comes to help us. Just as I never thought that one day I'd be defending Jack, but here I am: in a clandestine bunker, alone, watching the Russian approach in a threatening way. I put myself in combat position, even though I know very well that I am powerless against him, and then... darkness.

I am not quite sure if I'm simply dead or just unconscious, I only know that I don't see anything except darkness.

Suddenly I hear a loud shot, and immediately after the screams of girls, glasses and bottles breaking on the ground and the voices of two men insulting each other in Russian a few steps away from me.

I don't understand anything anymore.

I kneel on the ground trying to find Jack. I cry out his name in the dark when I remember the night vision glasses slipped into the back of my pants. I take them and quickly put them on. The first things I see are the frightened and disoriented people around the ring; they don't understand what has happened either. Then the two Boris still insulting each other and looking for each other in the darkness. I turn and see the Russian lying on the ground motionless. I'm looking for Jack when I find Vladimir standing in front of me. He looks at me from behind his night viewers and growls at me angrily as he loads Jack onto his shoulders. "Follow me", he tells me before turning, leaving the ring, and running through the frightened people with Jack on his shoulders toward the door. Of course I do follow him, trying not to run into someone or stumble.

Once outside, Vladimir blocks the door with a kind of steel bar in between the two handles, and still in the dark we begin to run along the corridor, when the light suddenly turns on automatically opening the door of the elevator a few meters away from us. I'm blinded, but I go forward anyway removing the viewer.

We get into the elevator. Vladimir rests Jack on the ground. He's now unconscious with blood running from his nose.

"You wanted to abandon him! You're all bastards!" I begin to strike him with all the strength that I have. I'm furious. What kind of people are they?

After snarling at me, Vladimir opens the hatch of the elevator, above our heads.

"You're not a team, you're a pack!" I continue to yell at him, sitting down on the floor next to Jack and putting his head on my knees.

Vladimir pulls a black bag down from the opening above our heads, opens it and starts to pull out all kinds of weapon.

I hear gunshots come from the floor above. I turn pale again.

"Lexi has already left with the van. Koki is on the roof. Boris' men are rushing up the stairs armed with 38 caliber Kalashnikovs, they'll arrive a few seconds after you. Be prepared", I hear the voice I heard earlier speak in to earpiece.

In a few seconds, Vladimir put on a bulletproof vest and picks up the weapons he has recovered from the duffel bag. He throws a flak jacket to me and says: "You just stay there, and don't move."

"*You just stay there*? What am I, a dog?" I scream angrily.

He looks at me as if I really am an animal to be put down. The elevator door opens. He gets out. He goes a few feet forward and then turns pointing the weapons at the door next to the elevator. Behind him there is a helicopter: the wind of the propellers is so strong that it ruffles my black wig. I'm putting on the bulletproof vest when I hear the next door open, and all I see after that is Vladimir open fire and begin shooting with a machine gun. Instinctively I clasp Jack in my arms and close my eyes while the deafening noise of weapons echoes everywhere.

"Jas!" I hear Lexi's voice in the earpiece, "when I say *go*, stand up and run toward the helicopter, Vladimir will cover you."

"And Jack?" I ask worried.

"Jas, trust me, we won't leave him here."

"Again. You forgot to say *again*!" I correct her annoyed, despite the unreal situation I find myself in. She says nothing. I don't know what to do. When Lexi said that Vladimir will cover me perhaps she wanted to say that he'll cover me with bullets.

Why on earth should he help me? He hates me. I look at him. His jacket is full of holes. His arms and legs are bleeding, but he continues to shoot at someone in front of him.

"Go!" I hear Lexi scream into the earpiece. "Jas!"

I rest Jack's head on the ground and get up. I don't know what to do. The shootout is still going on and I don't trust Vladimir at all. Jack is on the ground, poisoned and bleeding, while Lexi continues to scream: "Jas, *one thousand.* We won't leave him here, run!"

I begin to run as fast as I can, while bullets are flying all around me, also hitting the helicopter and the strange pipes that are poking out from the roof. I only just manage to climb inside, panting. My legs are trembling from the fear and the adrenaline. I look back immediately toward the elevator, except that before I see Jack I see another scene similar to the ones you see in Rambo movies: heaps of people dead on the ground, blood everywhere and only one person in front of them that is killing them all.

Then, suddenly, there is silence.

I can't even metabolize the scene before I see another: still with his weapon pointing toward the door, Vladimir is approaching the elevator, he puts Jack on his shoulders and moves backwards coming toward us. I can't breathe, I'm afraid that someone can still arrive and shoot at us, but fortunately that doesn't happen. Vladimir places Jack next to me, he too gets in quickly, and the next second the helicopter is already taking flight with Koki in command.

I look at Jack, trying to figure out how to help him. Vladimir comes to us also. Through the earpiece he gives information to someone about how he is, as he bandages the wounds on his body. The situation does not seem to be all that serious until I see blood coming from Jack's nose and ears. I am overwhelmed by panic. "Koki! Jack is bleeding a lot, it's very serious!" I scream desperately talking through the earpiece.

"He's dying!" Vladimir bursts out fiercely, "He is dying!" He rushes toward the seat of the helicopter, puts on the belt and with his hands grasping the handle he begins to kick with his legs.

I watch him completely shocked, and he seems to want to stop, restrain himself from doing something. "It's all your fault! I hate

408

you! I hate you!" he snarls like something crazy as he looks at me. He's like an animal. Now I know what he's trying to resist doing: kill me with his very hands.

"Vladimir put your handcuffs on", Koki intervenes worried.

"I hate her! Jack is going to die now!"

"He won't die. Put your handcuffs on immediately", he orders him.

He looks at me still full of blind rage and actually cuffs his wrists and puts himself in the corner of the helicopter. But I don't have the time to be scared now! I open the first aid box in the helicopter; I take some gauze to quickly clean the blood from Jack's face then stand up and join Koki. "I need a phone! I have to call my grandmother."

"What?" he asks me as he pushes blinking buttons. "No, I can't give it to you; we'll soon be home and we'll give him some medical attention."

"Koki! Don't make me angry! Jack isn't well. We have to find out what kind of poison or drug we have to deal with before it's too late! He may die, do you understand this or not?"

At that exact moment, Vladimir starts to yell again and throw himself around like an animal trying take off the handcuffs so he can get to Jack. I am afraid.

"No Vladi, everything will be fine, he won't die! He was just joking." Koki turns toward me, angry. "Don't ever say that word again in front of him. Here", he gives me a cell phone.

There is no time to think about this absurd situation that I am experiencing. I take the cell phone, dial my grandmother's number, and after just one ring she answers me all perky. "If you're calling me it's because you love me."

"Grandma! It's me!"

"What do I need to know?" her tone of voice becomes serious in an instant, she knows that there is something wrong, she knows me too well.

"Jack is... he has been p-poisoned, he's bleeding, I don't know what poison it is, or maybe it's a drug, I don't know what to do, grandma", I say confusedly. Not worrying about the fact that she doesn't even know who is Jack.

"When was he poisoned and where is he bleeding from?"

"About twenty minutes ago. Ears and nose. He's in a cold sweat. He's bad, grandma!" I don't know why, but the more I describe his physical condition the more I panic.

Vladimir starts again with his hysterics and, between his screams and the deafening noise of the helicopter I can't hear what grandma is saying to me. "Hello grandma? Vladimir, for Christ's sake!" I protest exasperated. "Will you close your damn mouth once and for all?" But yelling at him like that just makes the situation worse.

He starts to pull the handcuffed hand again as hard as he can. He has almost removed it.

Gripped by the panic of the moment, I grab the first weapon that I can put my hands on and shoot him in the leg.

Koki turns toward me with his mouth wide open, while Vladimir looks at me incredulous, and before he faints, or dies perhaps, he mumbles: "Filthy piece of shi..."

"Did you fire at him? Did you really shoot him? How did you know that was a stun gun?" Koki asks me astonished.

"I don't know", I inform him, and go back to talking on the cell phone. "Grandma, can you hear me now? What did you say?"

"Boomslang."

"Wh-what? What is it?"

"It's a very poisonous African snake. It is a deadly killer, Jas. It kills in forty eight hours and the victim dies in a terrifying way."

"No, there were no snakes there. I... No!" I stutter scared. I stand up and go to Jack, kneeling beside him.

"The blood is no longer able to coagulate", grandma continues to give me information, "the victim begins to lose blood, but that's nothing compared to what is happening internally. Hemorrhages of the heart, lungs, kidneys and stomach", the more she talks the worse I feel. I look at Jack, unconscious, and covered with blood. I can no longer breathe. "Jack will bleed to death if you don't find an antidote immediately."

"And where can we find it?"

"It's available in Johannesburg."

"What?"

"I'll call you back." She hangs up leaving me sick to my stomach and even more terrified than before. I think I'm in shock. I look at a fixed point of the helicopter without saying anything. I can't even move, and Koki continues to ask me what my grandmother said. *Only bad things, that's what she said.*

"Jas! Where is Jas?" It's Jack speaking.

My heart begins to pound as soon as I hear his voice. I go to him and to my horror I see that he is bleeding from his eyes too, as he continues to ask for me. I slowly take his hands. "Jack, I'm here, I'm here."

"Jas." I can barely hear him speak through the earpiece. A smile appears on his bloodied face. "You're here. I can't see you." He closes and reopens his eyes with difficulty.

I take a dressing and try to clean it as well I can.

"I'm in a bad way, aren't I?"

"Just a little", I lie. To tell the truth, he's in a very bad way.

"Look what I have to do to have you notice me", he says under his breath, and smiles. I continued to look at him terrified.

"I promised you that I wouldn't get you involved again", he coughs.

"It doesn't matter. It doesn't matter, Jack!" I clasp his hand tightly. Why did you do it? I don't care about the cross."

"I did it for you. I want to make it up to you."

Tears fill my eyes suddenly. "You'll be alright, Jack. Grandma is going to call me now and she'll find a solution, you'll see", I try to reassure him, even though the tremor in my voice contradicts my own words. I feel so bad, so much at fault. After all, it is my fault if he is in this condition. I'm the one who told him I wanted that cross back.

"Jas." Jack stops my hand as I clean his face.

"Yes?"

"If I die", he pauses, squeezing my hand. I'm going to weep. "I want to be sure", he coughs, "that you will never ever get over the sadness."

I smile. Even in this difficult situation he doesn't stop being a jerk. Then he closes his eyes and doesn't talk anymore.

"Jack! Jack, please talk to me! Don't leave me!"

"Never", he replies in a whisper without opening his eyes, blood still running from them. "I will not leave you."

"Listen, you asked me why I hate professor Rossi, right?"

411

"Yes."

"At school, I memorize everything. In many cases I don't even know what I'm studying, I don't understand anything and I still get great marks", I begin to relate to him. "Nobody ever noticed, except professor Rossi. In the first year of high school I realized that I have a prodigious memory and that in fact I didn't understand math. So one day he called me to the blackboard and changed the letters of a geometric problem, and..." I'm speaking in a nervous worried way. "And that was enough to confuse me. I wasn't capable of solving the problem, understand? He did that on purpose", I continue to speak in a muddled way, I don't know if he understands what I mean. "From then on I started to make his life unbearable and got bad marks on purpose."

Jack smiles. "Now I know everything about you."

"Yes, now you do", I tell him and I smile along with him.

Suddenly the phone starts ringing. It's the most beautiful sound I've ever heard in my life. "Hello? Grandma!" I reply with my heart in my throat.

"I've found the person who has the antidote. I'll give you the address now, they're already waiting for you; you just need to say that I sent you."

"Thank you grandma!" I hang up immediately and scream: "Koki! We have the antidote!"

I look at Jack to give him the good news, but he has his eyes closed and the first drops of blood are starting to run from his mouth.

I throw the phone on the ground, terrified. "Jack? Jack, look at me! I beg you, don't die, hold on just a little longer, don't leave me Jack!"

75.

Luxury apartment in Manhattan. Cyrus, a colored man, stood looking out of the panoramic window. He was pensive. Inside the room Koki came in with papers in his hand. "Cyrus."

"Any news?"

"Unfortunately, no," the Japanese man replied disappointed, "her parents' house, Mina's house and their phones are protected from white noise. Interceptions of any type are practically impossible, but we already knew that." He put the sheets of paper on the table and continued: "Nickolas's team is very tight and no-one lets anything out. What happens in their team stays in their team."

"You could always go to her school", proposed Lexi as she entered the room. "They know everything about everyone there. I can go dressed as a sexy prof."

"No, it's too dangerous", Koki warned her. "If Jas has talked, they're not waiting for anything else. I don't want to fall into their trap."

"If she has talked, we'll soon find out", whispered Cyrus continuing to look outside. Lexi approached him intrigued. "What do you mean by that?"

Without warning the door opened abruptly and Vladimir entered infuriated. "Where's Jack?" He went to the table and slammed his fists on it. "He's gone to her, hasn't he? He's gone back to Italy!"

"What? *One thousand*!" exclaimed Lexi.

"I couldn't stop him," said Cyrus in a serious tone, turning toward the others.

"He's been under the spell of that crazy girl on stiletto heels for months, now!" protested Vladimir continuing to thump the table and shouting: "Is this all we do? Stand and watch? Have you forgotten who his best friend is? Hey? Have you forgotten Cyrus?"

"No, I have not forgotten. How could I?"

"Then why? Why do you allow him to risk his life and endanger all of us for some stranger, why?"

Cyrus's face turned nasty. "Because ever since Jas came into his life, it's as if Jack has been reborn, he's well!" he explained his reasons raising his voice. They all remained in silence. "He doesn't drink anymore! He's not on drugs! He doesn't frequent fleshpots, he doesn't get into unnecessary fights, he has stopped self-harming. She is his medicine! And as long as that's the way it is, you will support Jack!" he said angrily pointing his finger at him. "We all will!"

"She doesn't want to be with Jack! By now she'll already have told Nickolas everything, and he'll do everything he can to find us!" yelled Vladimir, continuing to make his point, when the telephone began to ring. The colored man went to the handset and before he answered, he turned to Vladimir "Now we're going to see if you are right or not. It's the call I was expecting." He picked up the phone and put it on speaker. "You've decided to collaborate, at last."

"Jas is in Miami, at Watchtower & Co.", replied a male voice on the other end of the phone.

"Has she talked?" asked Cyrus. Everyone in the room was waiting tensely for the response.

"No," replied the man. Lexi and Koki couldn't hold back a smile.

"She has had a head trauma and... seems to have a temporary loss of memory."

"If she's in Miami, why haven't any of my people seen her there?'"

"She hasn't been out of the building in two weeks."

"Thanks for the information you've given me."

"I didn't do it for you, Cyrus!" the man on the other end burst out angrily. "I'm just keeping my side of the agreement, something which I hope you will do too."

"We won't tell him anything", Cyrus reassured him.

The man on the other end hung up and silence descended. Lexi in the meantime poured herself a Martini, sat on the table and, smiling, took the glass to her lips. "She hasn't talked, the thing is becoming interesting! Cin Cin, boys."

"This is the beginning of the end." commented Vladimir, unhappy.

"She is very *one thousand*, but I like her," admitted Lexi, earning a dirty look from Vladimir. "What? It's always just us five; it's nice to know new people for more than a second, no?"

"By now, Jack will have heard the glad tidings", commented Cyrus.

The phone rang again.

"Here it is - it's him", said Cyrus and lifted up the handset putting it on speaker again. "Hello, Jack?"

"Let's go to Miami!" said Jack's voice before hanging up.

Koki sniggered, leafing through a number of *Playboy*. "Empires have been destroyed because of a beautiful, young girl."

Vladimir took the magazine from him rudely and threw it to the ground. "We will still have problems because of him."

"We will still have *many problems*", added Cyrus and started to laugh loudly rocking on his chair. "But we'll deal with them one by one." He continued laughing like a madman with Lexi following suit, while Vladimir began clenching his fists and repeat: "I hate her! I hate her!"

76.

I have watched him sleeping all night, all morning and all afternoon, sitting on the chair next to his bed. The sun is setting behind me, turning the room and everything in it into magic.

Jack is simply beautiful.

I feel my tired eyes rest on him, and I look at him asleep between the white sheets with the red reflection of the sun; looks like an angel... but this doesn't mean anything. As we know, so did Lucifer.

He opens his eyes slowly. He is still weak, but is far better than he was seventeen hours ago. He opens and closes his eyes until he can see everything well. He sees me sitting here, on the chair, looking at him. Behind me is the huge panoramic window which overlooks the sea. I sit composed adjusting the pink dress that Lexi has loaned me. "Good day", I greet him with a serious tone.

"Good day? Why is the sun setting if it's day." Jack makes a wisecrack and smiles, but doesn't get the same reaction from me. I look at him and say nothing, not showing any kind of emotion. He realizes right away that I'm acting strange, but decides to pretend it's nothing. He peeks under the blanket with a worried face and then, looking at me with relief, says: "Thank heavens I still have my underpants on and you haven't taken advantage of me!" He smiles at his smart remark, again. He has just woken up after a long and painful night and yet he's already in a good mood and full of energy.

I, on the other hand, don't feel like smiling. I stand up from the armchair. "You have to take those pills on the nightstand once a day. With a couple of days of rest you'll be fine. Grandma said to go to see your doctor anyway, as soon as you're feeling better."

"Your grandmother is too *cool*! I don't know how she did it but please thank her from me; you two have saved my life. Thanks Jas." His blue eyes glisten as he speaks. I shake my head.

"Well," I say as I go to the door. "If you show me the way out, I'd go home, now."

He sits in the middle of the bed and looks at me confused. I can see that he is trying to understand the reason for my reaction. "Okay. It's just that..." he tries to get out of bed, but doesn't succeed; he is still too weak to do so by himself. I don't want to help him. "I thought... we could have a coffee together."

"No, thanks, but... I don't feel like it."

"Please, I'll have it ready in a moment," he says, while he awkwardly tries to stand, pretending to feel good. With only his underpants on he starts slowly toward the minibar of his huge bedroom. I feel uncomfortable. I don't want him to make that coffee for me. I just want to go back home. I'm about to tell him to forget it, that I have to go, when I see him put some familiar cups on the counter. I take a better look and am lost for words: they're the cups that I gave him in February. Suddenly memories come flooding back. Mujo giving me the cups, the knife and other knickknacks for saving him from the prison. Then comes John, and then the image of me shocked after seeing his arms full of cuts and wounds, him weeping, and then...

I start to breathe quickly, I feel hot, then cold, then hot again, until the only thing that I can feel is anger.

He smiles. "Yes, they're exactly the cups that you think," he says, as if it would please me.

"First you gave me just one and then you said *no, let's make it two, in case you have special guests one day*", he smiles again, "This is the first time since then that I have special guests." He looks at me with those glistening eyes as my face turns red like the scenery behind me.

"You're definitely thinking about..."

"Stop it!" I interrupt him irritably.

"Doing what?" he asks with that annoying tone of someone who has no idea what he's saying.

"Telling me what I am or am not thinking! You can't get into my head so you can't know, and even if you knew, there is no need to tell me because I know what I'm thinking, since I'm the one who is thinking!" I'm not sure what I said exactly, but I'm certainly right.

"Okay, okay, calm down Jas."

"No! I won't *calm down*!"

417

"I just wanted to surprise you", he looks at me baffled as I restrain myself from throwing myself on top of him and squeezing my hands around his neck. *He doesn't understand a shit! I don't want his stupid surprises!*

I take a sigh deep. "I want to go home!"

He closes his eyes and lowers his head for a moment, leaving the coffee machine turned on with all the coffee dripping down the bench near the two cups. Then he raises his head, and I see that look again.

"And stop looking at me that way, Jack!"

"Which way?"

"The wrong way! If I helped you yesterday it's because I felt guilty and not because... not for the reason you think, I want that to be clear!"

"But I didn't say anything to you!"

"Talking is not necessary!"

"I'll put something on and", he pauses and looks at me in the eyes with a sad expression, "and I'll walk with you to the exit."

"Good!"

He goes to the closet slowly for fear of falling and, with great difficulty, he gets dressed as I look at him immobile without helping him. I feel guilty, after all it's my fault if he's in this state, I shouldn't have asked him for the cross back, but it is also thanks to me if he's alive now, so...

He puts on a t-shirt and half-dead comes to stand in front of me. "If you still have a moment for me, I would like to introduce you to someone", he uses his sad tone hoping to soften me.

"If he's on the way...", I agree, but I have not been softened.

"Yes, he's on the way." Of course, he's not happy that it has ended like this, his wonderful surprise.

We go out into the corridor; it's very bright, very luxurious, disproportionately long, and wide enough to be able to go around it in a car.

Every so often we encounter a few doors, some tables and several statues along the way, but they're the paintings of inestimable value hanging on the wall that attract my attention. I come to the conclusion that they have been stolen from someone as usual. Who knows how many people have died for all the things that are on show here. Jack continues to walk slowly with his hand resting against the wall so as not to fall.

"Now that you've got rid of Boris's man and you've wiped out half of his body guards, what will happen? Will he start looking for us?" my question is legitimate even if, judging by the face he makes, maybe he doesn't think the same way.

"No one will look for you and will not even look for me since they don't know who I am and that at this point I should be dead already."

"Listen, I'm going to tell Nick about this, I don't feel safe, now!"

As soon as I mention Nick his expression changes, he stops and clenches his fists against the wall without looking at me. "We deleted all the videos, all the photos, everything that could be connected to us. You're not in any danger, Jas!"

He looks at me irritated. "And anyway, Nickolas couldn't do a damn thing, seeing that Boris has diplomatic immunity!"

"What?" I ask aghast, "but he's a criminal!"

"Strange how these things happen, eh?" he says in a sarcastic tone and opens the door on his right. I enter and I'm flabbergasted. In front of me is a huge library on two levels, all in wood, with a huge number of books of various shapes and sizes. It reminds me very much of Isobel's, only it's ten times larger. In the middle of the room, a very long table, and behind it a colored man with gray hair looks at me with a very serious expression. We approach him, and once in front of him, Jack exclaims all proud: "Jas, let me introduce you to my father."

"Yes, you're the spitting image of him", I can't help myself after hearing the umpteenth load of crap. Jack looks at me with eyes wide, unable to believe my surly attitude.

"Excuse her", says the white man to his black father. "Today she's a little shit!"

I just glare at him and say nothing. His father continues to stare at me very serious and then holds out his hand. "Nice to meet you at last, my name is Cyrus." When he says his name, I'm stunned for a moment. I've been hearing about him since last year. The father who is a magician, who had to do a show, *what a load of bullshit!*

My blood pressure goes up thinking back to the past, and even more thinking about yesterday, when he wanted to leave me and Jack in that clandestine bunker.

"Your silence says it all", I don't like the tone of voice he uses in addressing me.

"No offense, but you do not know me well enough to be able to interpret my silence", the more I say to him the more Jack glares at me. In the meantime Cyrus starts to play with a domino, putting the blocks in a row, one behind the other. "You're a complicated girl in many respects," he continues, still using that annoying tone, "but you are simple in your reasoning. Your head is a killer machine able to accumulate all kinds of information. You have demonstrated your knowledge and skills in various fields, and I'm impressed. You must always have everything and everyone under control; this is true for the people that surround you, but above all for yourself. Letting yourself go to emotions for you means losing control, and this frightens you because there is a part of you that you don't know, the black part, the part which is hidden deep inside you, because those few times that it has risen to the surface you haven't been able to control it and this frightens you. Some people are afraid of the dark, some are afraid of loneliness or rats. You are afraid of yourself", he finally takes a breath, leaves the domino and leans back in the chair asking me: "Do you think I know you well enough?"

I fix him like an idiot not knowing how to react. He has taken me by surprise, and few people are able to do that. Both Cyrus and Jack look at me serious, waiting for a reaction, and this makes me strangely anxious. I take a deep breath trying to regain control of myself and the situation, just as Cyrus said. I look at him for a moment; his hands, his face and stature, my eyes move rapidly up and down his body, and then I begin to speak like a machine too. "In the past you played the guitar, quite well. You've been a boxer. A professional. You have problems moving your left arm, you often have headaches. You're diabetic. You wear a wedding ring but you're divorced, or widowed. You're wearing the Alcoholics Anonymous badge around your neck, but you still drink in secret and you look at me straight in the eyes even though you are blind."

This time it's Jack who is staring at me with an idiotic look on his face and his mouth open. It is clear that he was not expecting such a precise analysis. Unlike him, Cyrus studies me, or better, he keeps his face turned to me without seeing me, since he's blind, and with a half-smile on his lips asks me: "Have you finished?"

"No", I answer and continue, "You are a man full of rancor that has decided to form a team, or should we say a herd, a sect of people with abnormal qualities, different from the others, calling them *special* instead of *freaks*, to convince them that you love them and that what they are doing is right. I'm not saying that you don't feel anything for them, but you certainly love your work if to continue doing it you are willing to sacrifice those people you define as *your children*. So then, do I know you well enough, sir?" After my question silence falls and immediately after something happens that I would never have expected: Cyrus starts to laugh aloud like a madman. I'm stunned!

It is an overreaction, and far from fitting for the man who only a few seconds ago was looking at me all serious, passing himself off as normal.

"Apart from work and the love for my children, it was all correct!" he says, still laughing. He gets up and opens his arms to hug me. I look at him still amazed and I don't move an inch; as if I want that man there to hug me!

"Are you drinking?" I hear Lexi's angry voice arrive from the end of the room. I turn and see her coming towards us with her usual unsteady gait, fixing her red hair. "Are you drinking alcohol? I mean, are you kidding, daddy? Drinking is bad for you! How many times do I have to tell you? *One thousand*! You risk doing *bibi* to, that thing there, to an organ, I mean!" She rebukes him as she drinks her glass of Martini. "Where's Vladi?" she asks looking around disoriented.

"He is still sleeping", I hear Koki suddenly speaking one inch from me! He frightened the life out of me; where did he spring from? He sits on the table and smiles at me. "After the horse dose tranquilizer that you have fired at him, he will wake up towards the end of 2017."

"I should tie one of those little bells for cats around your neck, that way you can't creep up on me", I'm very careful to say it in a serious way, to make him understand I'm not joking at all, but it seems that Koki didn't understand anyway, seeing how he smiles at me amused, doing strange contortions on the table. Then he stops, takes a calendar from the drawer and starts to drool over the pictures of naked women.

"What do thing you'll be when you grow up, Jas?" Cyrus asks me in a very low voice.

"I don't know, but I know what I want to do now: go home."

"It just so happens that I represent a group of very, very powerful people, who have a great desire to clean up the world. It is an important organization and we need capable people like you", while he speaks he looks like one of those guys you hear in trailers of horror films. "You could join us, Jas."

"And be abandoned at the moment of need? No thanks."

"There are rules to follow, but my team is the best."

Evidently he doesn't listen to me when I talk.

"And you, with your fantastic memory would be added value to this great family. But what I'm saying? You're already part of the family."

"No thanks."

Jack continues to study me. Cyrus smiles and says to me. "The things which you pretend are not important to you are, in reality, the ones which are the most important." His trailer-like voice becomes deeper and deeper. "Do you like classical music?"

I don't answer. He gets up from the chair, takes the stick for the blind and goes to the shelf with the CD player "Listen to this song."

He turns on the CD player. I don't listen to the song: I'm more interested in understanding what the hell I'm still doing here.

Lexi is lying on the table staring at the ceiling and smiling all happy: her fairy-tale world must be really wonderful. Koki continues to slobber over the dirty pictures in the calendar. Jack looks at the ground all thoughtful. Cyrus, on the other hand, is dancing. He moves around the enormous room in time to the music, throwing the stick into the air and catching it with such ease it seems impossible that he's blind. Then turns to me and looks at me straight in the eyes.

How the hell does he do that?

"Do you like it?" he asks me.

"Yes, yes", I short cut.

"The song is called *lick my lovely little ass*", he explains to me and starts to laugh aloud with Lexi following suit, who in my opinion is only laughing because he is, without even knowing why, while I wonder if that's really the name of the song or if he's taking the piss. Cyrus's laughter makes me shudder: who knows what it feels like to be schizophrenic?

"Mozart went mad and wrote these songs using very, very vulgar words. You're shocked, aren't you?"

I don't answer.

He sits down again on the chair looking at Jack, who is still staring at the floor, all gloomy and sad. It almost seems like he can see him. Then he looks at me and says: "I like stealing the sachets of sugar at bars; I take them home and fill my sugar bowl."

And what on earth should I say after hearing such a thing?

He's amused, he is expecting something from me, that I say or do something... I could give him a round of applause; I wouldn't seem anymore out of it than he is. "Do you believe in God?" here he goes again, from one extreme to another. A second earlier he's laughing and talking about asses and sugar bowls and the next second he becomes serious and asks me about God.

Okay, I've had enough of this. "Well, I have to go."

"I'll accompany her", at last Jack decides to speak after minutes of absolute silence.

"Son", Cyrus calls to him in a distressed voice from gone with the wind, "only seventeen hours ago you were close to death. Are you sure you want to go out?"

"Yes, I'm absolutely fine."

"Goodbye", I say to everyone, and go to the door quickly.

"Jas?" calls Cyrus. I turn almost terrified, not knowing which of the two personalities I'm about to hear now. "We did not want to abandon him, we would have pulled him out of there, we were prepared for this, but if it hadn't been for you, we'd never have found the antidote in time. Thank you for saving the life of my son."

Okay, this time he seems normal and sincere. I prefer not to say anything and just smile politely.

"We're going, see you later guys."

"Have fun you two, and don't do anything I wouldn't do", Lexi screams at us, then turns to Cyrus, and they both burst out laughing. "There is nothing I wouldn't do" she adds and burst into psychopathic laughter, not healthy at all. I look at them one last time before disappearing behind the door; after all when will I get to come across crazies like them again? I don't have time to take two steps before I feel a grasp on my arm. I turn around. Jack is looking at me all serious. "Can you tell me what's wrong with you today?" he asks.

"Of course I can tell you", I say this very calmly, and pull my arm back. "This is the last time that we'll see each other, Jack."

HIs expression changes suddenly. "No! I do not agree!"

"I didn't ask you if you agree or not!"

"Well, you should have!" he tells at me.

"No, I should not. I am not interested in your opinion."

"Well, you should!"

"Stop this!"

"Why? Why do you want to leave?"

"I agreed to get to know a part of your world, and I have, but now I've had enough, I'm going home."

"But there is still one week left!"

"What I wanted to know I've learned, I don't need anything else!"

"And you just go away like this? Enough, finished, the end, goodbye?"

"You said that all I had to do was tell you. I'm telling you."

"No! You say one thing but you think another! I saw you yesterday! You put yourself in front of me, to protect me, you risked..."

"Jack, stop it! I said no!" I repeat raising my voice. I can't take this debate any longer, I've had enough of the entire situation, I just want to return home.

He remains silent hanging his head. He rests on the wall slowly, closes and reopens his eyes with difficulty, his forehead is covered in sweat; he's not well. I go over to him to hold him up. "Jack?"

"Well I tell you what," he whispers, "It's better if I don't tell you!" He sits on the ground with his head propped against the wall.

I feel ill seeing him suffer in this way. I kneel in front of him worried. "Do you want me to call..."

"It's finished!" he says in a loud voice without looking at me. I stare at him in surprise, mostly because they are the same words that I said to Nick three weeks ago. "Get out of my house!" he looks at me with malice and bitterness, his blue eyes make me afraid. He hits his hand against the floor and repeats. "Did you hear me? Get out!"

I snap to my feet, scared and angry at the same time, while he continues to look at me with threatening eyes despite his discomfort.

"Jas, I'll say it one last time! Get out of my house!"

"You can't order me to do something that I want to do anyway!"

"Get out of my sight!" his lips tremble from his agitation.

I turn and go.

All along the road, as I pass luxurious villas and shining cars, I repeat only one thing: Jack *is a thief! Jack is a liar! A killer! Now I know what Nick was trying to tell me three weeks ago, I've been so stupid! Instead of sitting down and listening to his advice I eliminated him from my life! I feel so bad! I need to talk with him, Ii need to apologize to him... I need my compass!*

***

Shortly after

The elevator door opens and I find myself in front of the African girl with a head full of braids who looks at me condescendingly before I open my mouth.

I rush to the counter. "Where's Nick?"

She looks me up and down curling her lips. "On the roof."

"On the roof? Doing what?"

"Getting into the helicopter which is on the roof."

I hurtle to the offices of the Watchtower and climb up the stairs to the roof. I absolutely must speak with Nick, he can't leave like that, I need him! I open the door and I see the helicopter that is already taking off. I call him: "Niiiick! Niiiick!"

He's inside the helicopter talking to a man; I keep calling him but unfortunately he can neither see me nor hear my screams. Curse!

I run back down the stairs, passing through the lobby and I meet America coming out of Veronica's bedroom carrying some sheets. "I left the clean towels on Mina's bed, I would have put your towels on your bed, but since I couldn't find your bed in that disaster..." she says ironic, continuing to look at me from under her eyebrows. I run quickly into my bedroom, open the door, and there's nobody there!

Nobody except Highlander. As soon as he sees me, he begins to wag his tail and show me his teeth with his head outside the aquarium. I remain here, standing between my half of the room and Mina's just wondering: *where have they all gone?*

77.

How on earth did I lose my cell phone? I've been forced to write a note to Jas in haste and leave it on my bed telling her where I'm going before running to this bar. I lift my head and see a large poster that says *the use of cell phones is forbidden.* Now that I think about it, perhaps it's just as well that I didn't bring it.

This place reminds me a lot of the Cat's Eyes. I thought long and hard about why and then I thought that perhaps the name *Black Cat* could have something to do with it.

The candles on the tables make the bar really nice and the mini stage to the right looks very much like the one we have in the cube at school, where Rodrigo presents and the Olsen twins dance. And what's more the owner is wearing a shirt with *Big Bob* written on it. Bob, like Susy's ex.

Oh God! *Cat's Eyes*, the cube at the school, Susy's ex, am I getting homesick by any chance? I sit at the counter next to Ross. "Hi, Ross, why have we run into each other in this place?" I ask him curious.

He barely looks at me. "Apparently, they let anyone in here."

This comment is definitely addressed to me.

"Didn't you see the sign outside, Mina, it said *animals not allowed.*"

"Ooh I can see that you know how to read", I retort.

"Excuse me, waiter?" he calls with his rasping voice, waving his little hand without even answering me. The waiter who, given the t-shirt, I guess is called Big Bob, comes over immediately asking: "Can I help you?"

"Yes, I want you to tell the elderly lady sitting next to me that we are here because I have a job interview as a singer with Skeleton in person."

I imagine that the old lady of whom he speaks is I. The waiter does not seem to be a very patient person; in fact he places his enormous hands on the counter and looks at him annoyed. "Why don't you tell her yourself?"

"Because *M* and I interact only when *L*'s there, otherwise we ignore each other and keep ourselves at the proper *D*, as in Distaaaance!" he says the word *distance* in a really unpleasant way.

Big Bob frowns. "Listen to me, *D* head! I don't have time to waste with these little games, understand?! And even if I did..." he goes close to Ross's face, furious, "I do not like to speak with people!"

"And you work in a bar?" Ross begins to laugh, "Ku-ku?" he laughs again, turning around to see if anyone is listening to this dangerous conversation between him and Big Bob. Just the very name had to suggest that you don't mess with him too much, but Ross continues: "And then, let me say, brother, couldn't you wear a t-shirt that's mooore, how can I say, leeess..." he looks at him with an expression of disgust on his face; I really fear for his safety. "This shirt is abusing my refined eyes. It's really uuuuuuugly."

From this point on I don't know exactly how things went, considering the speed with which Big Bob acted; but the fact is that, a second later, the big black man is dragging Ross by his ear to the door of the bar, literally kicking him in the butt.

I found myself laughing to myself sitting at the counter with a single desire: to see the scene again in slow motion. *I should start bringing the video-camera with me, dammit!*

I take a look at the luxurious watch on my wrist, it's getting late, but where the heck is my Jas?

"Hello, Mina, do you have a minute?" I hear a voice calling me. Okay, I don't know where she is, but to make up for it I know where Jack is. He sits down on the revolving stool next to mine. *On the stool. Next to me. Oh my Goooood!*

I swallow the saliva that I no longer have, looking at his pecs squeezed inside the pale blue vest and my eyes are unable to climb up further than his neck. Damn me! I shake my head to come to my senses and finally look at him in the face and it's even worse. I get lost in the color of his eyes that recalls the sea on sunny days.

"Are you alright'" he asks me.

No I'm not alright! I give myself a pinch under the table making a grimace of pain while Jack looks at me bewildered. "Yes, I'm perfectly, perfect. Hmm, now what did you want to spread me eeeeeh, hm sp spe speak to me about." Okay, now I've really gone way too far. I'm entering phase three of Will's claptrap and I can't allow that. I start to look at a fixed point, the only point that can't make me go out of my head: the blue stone at his neck.

Why isn't Jas with him?

"What did you", I stop a moment so I don't make more mistakes, "Tell me, Jack."

He takes a deep breath and then I think he looks me in the eyes, I don't exactly know, I'm staring at the pendant.

"I did everything I could for her."

I imagine that *for her,* he means Jas.

"I have risked my life to save hers, I have humiliated myself to get her attention, I have organized breakfasts, dinners, the Batman car!" The more he speaks the more his tone of voice becomes angry. "I have really tried, but now it's finished! I've run out of ideas! Why doesn't she want me? Why?" he asks me yelling in my face.

I turn pale.

"And you know what the funniest thing is, Mina? That in reality she wants me but she doesn't want me because she cannot forgive me! Do you understand? She's a lunatic! But she's *my* lunatic!"

He's the one who seems to be a lunatic, he gestures with his hands and gets angry, I don't know how to react. "Is this what... you wanted .. to tell me?"

"Why does she do this? She's not logical."

"Jack, I'm sorry, but I will not speak for her. If you want to know what she thinks, you'll have to ask her yourself", I say calmly, hoping that he doesn't get angry with me too, "don't involve me, please." Also because I don't know anything. I don't even know where she is right now and why she hasn't come even though I left her a note.

I think he looks at me again in the eyes. "Please, Mina, give me some advice. Just. Some. Fucking. Advice!"

I feel terribly uneasy. I don't know what to do or what to say, how can I give him advice on a situation when I don't even know what the story is? And then it is so strange for me seeing him speak in this serious way. He still reminds me too much of the disabled person John.

He lowers his head, he looks so sad. "Jas is my damn kryptonite that works in reverse", he says touching the pendant around his neck. "When she's, aaah!" he screams nervously, "she pisses me off with that shitty character she has. She does nothing but order me around, she's never satisfied, she's always complaining, competing with me, and always has a wisecrack ready to slam me as soon as the opportunity arises! She never gives me a compliment, never, she thinks she's superior, the piece of shit, she only knows how to say no, she's more demanding than a job in the mines, sometimes I wonder whether she is the vendetta for my crimes at a karmic level! And what's more she's a lunatic! First she smiles and looks at you with those fantastic dark eyes like a blond angel and the next moment she turns into the little girl of the exorcist! But not the old film in black and white, no, no, no, the remake, the one where you see the demonic expression of the little possessed girl! There are some days that I would like to set her on fire! Aaaah!"

I don't have a mirror, but it's not difficult to imagine my expression at this moment, especially after hearing that he has a recurring desire to set my Jas on fire. I know it's only a figure of speech, but coming from him it's a bad figure of speech.

"But when she's not there..."he continues with a more tranquil voice, "when she's not there I feel bad, I feel all alone, I feel empty, I feel like half a person. Her absence slowly destroys me, carrying away all my forces; it makes me weak, vulnerable and the suffering that I feel is worse than a wound from a firearm. I'm not able to, to breathe if she is not by my side. To be happy, to feel good, you must have reasons to be like that, my reason told me today that she is about to return to Slovenia."

I'm about to cry. He is so sweet and sensitive, so tender. My lip is trembling and I try to hide it with my hand. I can't say anything, his words are so romantic, I feel that my mascara is going to run down my face. I knew that Jack had come back for her, I knew from the outset, but I had no idea that such deep feelings tied him to her.

"I'm really fucked", he whispers and smiles as he gets up from the swivel chair. "I fell in love with her imperfections", he continues to laugh.

My eyes fill with tears again. What a magnificent sentence *I fell in love with her imperfections!* It's so beautiful! How I wish that someone, one day, will say that to me too.

"Oooh sorry, Mina, I'm terribly late, I know!" chirps Lexi justifying herself as she jumps out from behind me. "But I have an explanation! I was looking for my white miniskirt. I wanted to be in tone with the Yacht I'm taking you to tonight, but I couldn't find it anywhere. Only later I remembered that it was not at home, but at the store: I forgot to buy it, *one thousand*!" she starts to laugh loudly making everyone in the bar turn towards us. And, there you go, the men are already approaching her, excited.

"Anyway. Tonight a fabulous evening awaits us! There'll be plenty of muscular boys wearing thongs who can't wait to awaken the naughty girls who are sleeping in us!" she says in a very provocative way. Then she looks at Jack, asking him with a sad face: 'How are you, little brother?"

"Like ten minutes ago..." he answers all sad from his stool. He drinks the beer that in the meantime Big Bob has brought to him; I feel so sorry for him.

"Anyway, we don't need to go on the Yacht now."

"Of course we do, little brother," says Lexi and grabs my arm leading me away. "We're going." Then she looks at me in a strange way. "You know why Ross is outside caressing his backside, don't you? I'm five percent sure that he was talking to me about a try out, or maybe it was just out without the try in front? I'm confused..."

I am about to tell her about the funny story of Big Bob kicking Ross's ass, but I feel the need to give priority to another person. I stop suddenly. "Jack!"

He turns and looks at me with that sad and abandoned air.

"Have you have tried to simply say: *I'm sorry, Jas*?"

He looks at me with raised eyebrows as if to say *is that all?* This is proof once again that males don't understand a thing!

78.

The morning after – From Jas's diary

I woke up hearing Buffy on TV yelling at Spike, telling him that he is a vampire without a soul, a killer, and that she does not love him, while he tries to convince her otherwise. I open my eyes and the first thing I do is look for Mina, but she's not there.

"Good morning to no-one", I say as I look at her bed still intact and on it the clean towels that America brought yesterday evening. I take the phone trying to call her again, but nothing, she's unreachable. I really do not understand.

I get out of the bed, rush to Nick's room and burst inside without even knocking, but he's not there either.

I don't know why, but I thought it was Sunday today, and instead it's not evidently, if he's not there.

I go out again into the corridor and stop. To my left I see Nick's empty bed and on my right is Nina's empty bed. I can't move.

I feel an enormous weight on my chest, I am breathing with difficulty, and I feel lost and terribly alone. I am having clear symptoms of a panic attack.

I dress quickly, write a message to Mina leaving it on her bed, turn off the TV and go out hurriedly.

79.

Nickolas leaves Ben's office very thoughtful. He is holding some sheets of paper in his hand looking at them one by one as he goes to the counter where America is at work.

"Call the lab and ask if the analyses are ready please, send these by fax, and please call the court and tell them that our super witness is ready, and find out if everything is confirmed for today."

"Yes, boss", she says as she writes everything in the diary.

"Is Jas already up?"

"Already? It's three o'clock in the afternoon," America points out.

"That was not my question."

"Yes, she is *already* up and went out ten minutes ago."

"She went out? Where has she gone?"

"I don't know, boss."

"Didn't she ask for me?"

"No, that wasn't her question."

Nick turns pensive. He is about to return to the office when he suddenly stops. "And what was her question?"

"If three times three still makes nine, boss."

433

80.

Two hours later – From Jas's diary

Has an epidemic broken out, or what? I can't find anyone any more. Mina has disappeared for two days. Nick is always away. The chief isn't around. Metoo hasn't been seen, and even Diana who was always hanging around before, isn't here today. At least Zombie is here with me. Even though it would be unlikely that he'd go anywhere since he's in a coma.

I should go and clean the hallways; after all today is my last day of torture here, but I can't get up from this bed. I don't know what's wrong with me, perhaps I've got some strange influenza after all the time I've spent here in the hospital.

I have no energy, I have no appetite, I have strange cramps in the stomach and my heart should calm down a bit. I'm sick. I hug my Zombie and sing the homonymous song of the Cranberries. "At least you haven't disappeared like all the others." I look at him and answer the question that he didn't ask me. "*What's happened*, you ask?" After all, all I need is to talk. It doesn't matter if my interlocutor is in a coma. "It so happens that Nick and I..." I don't even know where to begin. "Jas and Nick, Nick and Jas. I like to say our names, put them together. Our compass has stopped, it is broken. Or perhaps it is only going around the world in an unexpected way. It's all so complicated, grandpa." I hug him and feel so good in his arms. He reminds me a lot of my real grandfather. I miss him, my grandfather. "I can't find Mina, I need her, but I can't find her. I don't know where she is. And Jack is..." I don't know why, but my eyes are filling with tears. "He has the same sense of humor as me, the same way of doing things, he understands me immediately. Sometimes when I talk to him it's as if I'm standing in front of the mirror. He has always known how to talk to me, both as John and as Jack. However he is still a ruthless murderer, a thief, a liar. There can never be a future between us. He is the wrong one. And the worst thing is that I knew that right from the start and despite this..."

434

I can't control the tears and it's strange, because I don't cry easily. I sit on the bed trying to regain my composure. After all I'm not actually crying, I'm just wiping away tears that are falling down my face by themselves. I adjust the blanket on grandfather, take the mop and go to finish cleaning the corridor without even putting my *cleaning lady's* uniform back on, as Diana calls it.

I must distract myself, the silence is making me hear my thoughts and this just complicates things. I get quickly into the elevator and descend to the fourth floor, the door opens and I see Diana herself running to me with her arms wide. "Jaaaaas! You've come! You're here! I knew that you would come!"

I drop the mop and the broom on the ground while she jumps on me, all happy. It's no use explaining that I have no idea what the little girl is talking about, but I'm happy someone was expecting me. I exchange the hug trying to have a quick look around to see what I've missed.

"Come on Jas. We have to hurry, the show is about to begin! The black man is about to arrive!"

Or perhaps what I *have not* missed: her birthday party. I should have realized that already from her little yellow dress and the shaven head which is shinier than usual.

She grabs my hand dragging me to the door of her room, I look inside: lots of balloons, party hats, whistles, and other small bald children, but, above all, a lot of adults made up of parents and doctors, sitting uncomfortably on the micro-chairs for children. It's like seeing so many Gullivers seated on Lilliputian stools.

I remain at the entrance to the room and, with a fast move like Lupin III I sneak a small gift package sitting on top of a huge package that Tim is holding in his hand. It's strange for me to see him here and not hear Arizona's usual cries telling him to go back to the laboratory.

"Arizona!" screams Diana excitedly, attracting the attention of all present. "Jas is here!"

They greet me with love and affection, and all I can do is wave the gift to make them understand that I have not forgotten her birthday, seeing I seem to be the one most wanted at this party, and not the black man.

Arizona gets up from the small chair, comes to the entrance door and puts a little colored hat on my head saying, "Hello, Jas", her tone is somewhat surprised. "Diana, go back to your place. The show is about to begin."

"Alright, come on Jas". Diana pulls my arm, but I have no intention of sitting on those uncomfortable chairs for dwarves. I hate dwarves!

"I'll watch from here, okay? So if there is some latecomer, first I'll rebuke him and then I'll send him straight to you. What do you think?"

She looks at me pulling her lips into a very funny grimace. "Just as well you're here to take care of these details." She takes the gift from my hands thanking me all happy, and runs to sit on her red mini-chair in front of a mini-stage.

"I was afraid that you wouldn't be coming", murmurs the Chief to me.

"Woman of little faith."

"Today is your last day of punishment and I thought that you would have taken off as soon as you finished cleaning the corridors."

"You offend me."

I don't know why, but from the way she looks at me, my words are not very convincing. "You and I have to talk, Jas."

"We are already talking."

"You're not funny."

"It wasn't my intention."

"Jas!"

"Yes, that's my name."

"Shame on you!"

"Is that it?"

Her gaze is much more expressive than usual. Perhaps for the first time in seven months I see an ounce of anger in her eyes, instead of the usual easy little tear that regularly appears on her face when things don't go as she wants. She should thank me, instead of going off in such a rude way.

I see the nurse Pamela arriving too, with her gift for Diana, together with the fat intern and the twins from Beverly Hills 90210, Brenda and Brandon.

"Hello, Jas!" Pamela greets me. "It's great to see you here. Diana was worried that you'd forget."

"No, really?"

"I swear."

Pam takes the door handle and is about to enter, when I see Diana turn in our direction and look at us through the glass. I block the door immediately and turn toward the interns pretending to reproach them for being late. I'm not really talking at all. I'm opening my mouth at random waving my hands.

Diana is happy with my performance, while the interns are looking at me shocked and Pam is already pulling a thermometer from the pocket of her coat to make sure that I'm okay.

I shake my head and start to laugh. In their eyes I must indeed look as if I'm crazy.

"Where have you left Steve and Donna?", I ask Brandon and Brenda, who of course don't get the joke, as usual, and continue to look at me as if I've got a few screws loose.

They enter. Pam remains outside with me. "Why aren't you going in?" I ask.

"Oh well, I prefer to stay here to keep you company."

"Okay." She stares at me in a strange way. It's probably because I acted like a lunatic before. "What's up?"

"Excuse me," she shakes her head embarrassed and then looks at me again, "it's just that you look so incredibly like my sister. She was full of life too and had a special way about her just as you do."

"*Was*?"

"Yes, she was", she says and I don't ask anything else. For sure her sister will have died of cancer too or some other illness, and since today is a day of celebration, it doesn't seem right to investigate any further.

Finally everyone has gone to their places and silence has slowly fallen. What I really needed was a little show so as not to think about my problems: I'm happy I came because I wouldn't have liked to disappoint Diana.

I hear music behind the mini stage and to my great surprise, holding a guitar, someone I know appears on the stage.

"Skeleton?" I say in surprise.

437

Pam looks at me even more surprised than I am. "Do you know Skeleton? You're full of surprises, Jas."

"Yes, I've seen him around. What do you know about him?"

"He's a very famous rapper here in Miami, but he's also a little strange, like all artists are I suppose. Every so often he leaves the scene and hides in some seedy bar for months."

I have to admit that it is strange for me to see a man all tattooed and tatty walk up and down the room playing the guitar for sick children. The melody seems familiar to me. I need a couple of seconds, but then I remember: it's called *The Cat Came Back*. Diana hums it often in Zombie's room while she's drawing.

"Why does he call himself the black man?" I ask Pam.

"Who?"

"Skeleton."

"What?" she smiles. "Skeleton doesn't call himself that."

"Then who is the black man?"

"Him." She indicates a point in the room.

I stare. On the stage, near Skeleton, without a mask, without any disguise or wig, is Jack.

I instinctively take a step backwards. I can't believe it. He is everywhere. He's a nightmare that follows me and I can't get rid of it. I turn my back and I don't know whether to run to the right or the left. My head begins to hurt. I am about to lose control.

"He's wonderful," says Pamela. I continue to watch the show without realizing that I am going mad. "He's called Jeremy Black. He has been coming here for years to do shows for the sick children."

What? What I've just heard shocks me and calms me at the same time. I know, it's contradictory, but it happens. "For years?" I ask, visibly amazed.

"Yes, and he is also our greatest benefactor. The only one, to tell the truth", she speaks to me as she continues to look at him with admiration through the window. "His lawyer, Ms. White, comes every year see what our hospital needs and then he..." she pauses and comes closer to me, "I shouldn't tell you but", she whispers, "today he has given us a check for one million two hundred and thirty four thousand dollars. It is an amount that has literally..."

438

In an instant everything around me becomes silent and the only sound I hear in my head is *one million two hundred and thirty four thousand dollars.* Stunned and in shock I look inside the room: Diana is swaying happily holding her yellow teddy in her hand, the other children are singing, the nurses and parents are applauding and they are all looking at the same person: Jack. He is singing, dancing, laughing with them, he makes funny faces trying to entertain the sick children and is doing all this for them, just for them and not to make impression on me. Now I know where the Las Vegas money ended up. He didn't want to tell me.

"We can finally buy the modern ambulances with all the equipment..." Pamela continues to fill me with information that I still don't listen to, because the only thing I need in this moment is to be heard. I have to find Mina. I must absolutely talk to her.

While I'm running along the corridor, confused, scared and with my heart almost jumping out of my chest, I still have the image of Jack in my head, who is singing a song to Diana with a sweet empathic expression...

"Old Mister Johnson had troubles of his own
He had a yellow cat which wouldn't leave its home
He tried and he tried to give the cat away
He gave it to a man goin' far, far away.
But the cat came back the very next day
The cat came back; we thought he was a goner
But the cat came back, it just couldn't stay away"

81.

In the meantime – From Mina's diary

My God, I feel so ill. I have my eyes closed and yet I see the darkness spinning around me, I am nauseous and I'm also afraid that I've wet the bed. What the devil happened tonight?

I can't remember, nor do I know where I am or what time it is. I hear voices coming from the other room; some giggles of drunken people and I also feel the saliva running down my face, ugh. *Oh my God I feel so ill.*

I open my eyes slowly, it's dark in here, my head continues to spin, maybe I should drink a little water. I see the window in front of me, I could get to it in three steps but these steps represent miles for me right now. I sit up; my body feels heavy, as if I'm dragging a ton on my shoulders. I realize I have only my underpants on. I struggle to reach the window which is so far away, I open the drapes and the sunlight blinds me! I rub my eyes... I'm on a yacht! But when did I get on it? I see the sea around me and now that I know where I am, I feel as if I'm really about to throw up, seeing that I suffer from sea sickness.

"Close that drape!" I hear a male voice behind me. I quickly cover what little breast I have and turn slowly also because I couldn't do it any faster given my state, though I can't imagine that my state could get any worse. I am looking at the most terrifying scene of my life.

I begin to breathe quickly, my eyes fill with tears, my legs begin to shake.

I fall to the ground: the table in front of me is covered with marijuana and white residues of cocaine, wrinkled money, empty bottles of alcoholic beverages and clothes everywhere. I think I have touched the bottom already seeing this scene, but it's not the case, the worst is in the bed!

A naked colored man is sleeping on the ground, on the side where I slept; he has my bra in his hands and there is another man close to my pillow, not just naked, but also with a familiar face.

Vladimir! The only thing that covers him is his hand tattooed black.

I'm kneeling on the ground with eyes filled with tears; I tremble with shame, asking myself how I ended up in their bed. I feel dirty, I cannot believe that I've really done this!

I don't know where I find the strength to stand up, I look for my clothes on the floor sobbing. I can't see anything from the tears that are streaming down my face. I approach the bed to get my skirt, when I see Vladimir wake up and open his eyes.

The discomfort, the shame and the feeling of filth can be seen on my face, but his is even worse. He fixes me with arrogance, with satisfaction, and smiles at the evident shame that I feel in this moment, making a terribly vulgar gesture with his hand to show me what I did last night. I run away like a thief, I feel the Scarlet Letter on me, I disgust myself!

I escape along the corridor of the yacht, almost falling several times because I'm sick, I'm still drugged and dazed from the evening before. I can't believe it! I will never get over all this, never!

Patrick has said that after a traumatic experience the mind tends to protect you, so why hasn't mine protected me? *I want to forget!*

Along the never-ending corridors I see people sleeping on the floor, glasses scattered everywhere and on the bow it's even worse: people half-naked on the deck chairs doing terrible filthy things.

Panic takes over, I don't know what to do, nor how to get out of here, I'm in the middle of the sea, how do I get off? I sit on the ground in a corner hiding my head between my hands in shame! I want my Jas! Where is my Jas?

"Mina, is that you? What are you doing there on the ground, *one thousand*!"

I raise my head and see Lexi smiling at me all happy. I throw myself at her. "You're bad! Bad!" I scream pushing her with all my strength, "You brought me on this kind of floating brothel, you got me drunk, drugged me made me have sex with two men in the midst of pounds of cocaine!"

"It's not clear to me what the negative part in all of this is, but you're a woman now, these things happen."

441

"Not to me!" I yell with tears in my eyes. I cover my face with my hands again, full of shame, I can't breathe. "I don't even know if I used any protection, I could be pregnant or even worse get some disease! Damn you!"

"Come on, calm down now, I can guarantee you that Vladimir is as healthy as a fish and that other one, well, whoever he is, I'm sure that he took take care of his big black snake."

I look at her shocked as she comes to me with prudence putting her hand on my shoulder. "Let's do the peace hug?"

"I want to go home. I want to go to Jas!"

"But why? Aren't you enjoying yourself with me anymore?" she hugs me. "Come on, now let's make a nice breakfast; that way you'll calm down, and then I'll take you to the hairdresser and if you like we'll go and do a little shopping? What do you think?"

I'm drugged, drunk, my head is spinning, I see everything blurry, but in reality I've never seen more clearly than this in my life. I move from her quickly looking at her with my eyes wide open. "It was your plan from the very start. How didn't I... figure that out earlier? New clothes, massages, discos. It was all part of a precise plan! To make me remain in Miami! It was like that, wasn't it?"

Lexi doesn't even blink, she takes a glass from the hands of a half dead man lying on the sunbed and smiles saying, "Well, that could be one way of reading it..."

"It is the only way to read it! You have used me to keep Jas here! You're... let me get off! I want to get off!"

I push her and make her purse fall to the ground. The contents spill out. I lean on the railing so as not to fall, I feel sick, and then I see my cell phone. I thought I'd lost it and instead she stole it. I look at her, shocked by this discovery. Made fun of and humiliated to the very end!

I take it and run away along the jetty trying to dial Jas's number, I need her, I have to speak to her and tell her what they did to me, what they've done to us! They have tricked me, used me, they have turned me into a piece of trash, they drugged me! I'm going to have a panic attack, I feel lost and trapped, I need help!

The number you called... the message service answers. How do I call her, now? How do I warn her about these false manipulators? My legs are trembling, my breathing is becoming labored, I sit down on the ground. Tears roll down my face, I am crying aloud, everyone can hear me but I don't care. I look at Miami from here, wonder where my Jas is, how I'll be able to find her, wondering where I am, how I will be able to find myself again, whatever there is left of me...

82.

I feel lonely. The first time that I took refuge in this bar was because I was looking for solitude, I was looking for a quiet place to think away from everyone, it was what I wanted. This time it's different, I'm alone but not of my choice. I don't know where Mina is and I don't know if I want to know where Nick is. What do I say to him? Where do I begin? For the second time in less than a year I'm like my wardrobe: a mess. Inside are scattered new clothes, old ones, the ones that I had thrown away last year, others that were too tight, the one that are too big and still others are impossible to imagine myself wearing. My closet is about to explode. Perhaps I would do well to just set fire to them.

"Hey Bob, my minibar is empty!"

"I don't care about your minibar", he replies resting on the counter, "You've drained three glasses of spirits and two beers! Sponge! Throw up in my bar and I swear that I'll send you flying outside! I'll send you to the moon!"

"Hey! It was you who brought me all those drinks! First you get me drunk and then you threaten me? Throw me another *servesa* and then I'm going."

"I'm not bringing you any more to drink! Did you read the sign up there or not?"

I look in the direction of his finger, near the sign *no smoking, mobile phones forbidden* and *no yelling* there is a new prohibition: *getting drunks drunk prohibited*. But that doesn't make sense! Big Bob looks at me with his arms crossed.

"Aren't you giving me anything to drink because I'm black?"

"You're not black."

"Then why aren't I?"

"Do you really want me to kick every centimeter of your white ass?"

"See! This is racism!" I turn toward the other people in the bar. "You all heard it, right? He said *white ass*! Don't you feel offended?" only now I realize that they're all black in here and

444

they're giving me dirty looks. I bow my head turning around to the counter. Big Bob seems sick of me. "What do I have to do to get rid of you once and for all?"

"Give me a *JasTwentyfive*." At the exact moment that I say this, his face is transformed from irritated to *if I get hold of you...* He takes off his apron without saying anything and heads quickly to the little door of the counter. It's not difficult to guess what he wants to do. I shoot down off the stool in an instant saying, "Okay, okay, okay, I was kidding, I was kidding!" I run off immediately. As I run toward the exit looking behind me for fear of being caught by Big Bob, I end up colliding with someone. "Excuse me, excuse me", I say looking for Big Bob, and fortunately I see that a customer called him to order.

"Jas?" I just have to hear his voice to recognize it. I turn and see Jack in front of me, so beautiful. He looks at me with his eyes lit up, surprised to see me. Beside him, Skeleton, guitar in hand, also looks at me, but I don't know what he sees exactly, pothead that he is. I don't move a fraction of an inch, I cannot; it's as if I'm paralyzed, or perhaps I just don't want to leave. I look at him, he looks at me. Silence, embarrassment, we look like two proper idiots.

I feel a strange rumbling come out of Skeleton's mouth, even a pothead realizes that behind our silence hides a world of words. "I'll leave the scene now."

"Thanks for today, Skeleton", Jack thanks him, but without taking his eyes from me.

"I have to thank you, Jeremy. Are you staying?"

"No," he replies with a sad voice, tightening his kips. Skeleton goes and my heart is about to roll along behind him because of a whole series of emotions that I'm feeling at this moment.

"I didn't follow you, I didn't know you were here", Jack says in a low voice, with his head down. I feel sorry for him because he is convinced that I don't believe him, just as I didn't believe him the day I met him in the elevator at the hospital, but this time it's different. I believe him. "What were you thanking him for?" I ask, pretending not to know.

"For nothing", he slowly raises his head, "nothing important." He doesn't want to tell me. He could act cool like he usually does, and instead has chosen to downplay the thing, saying that it's nothing.

Skeleton gets up on the stage and starts to sing a song with the guitar while Jack and I continue to look at each other without saying anything. This time he's the one who's embarrassed; he doesn't know how to act with me nor what to say to me; for the first time he has no idea what I'm thinking.

"Can I have a little attention please!" I hear Skeleton say into the microphone. "Today was a very significant day for me. Today, for the first time, instead of doing rap, I sang English songs!"

I am not quite sure that I've understood what he's saying, but he seems proud of himself. "So for this reason, tonight I decided to sing some more English songs, in English, for all the English people present today!" He starts to applaud and whistle all happy as everyone looks at him incredulous: no-one is English! I smile, while Skeleton starts to sing the song *Sorry seems to be the hardest word.*

On Jack's face instead there's not a hint of a smile. He is looking to the floor with his head lowered, he's sad, quiet, thoughtful and even if I don't talk to him he's there in front of me waiting for what I intend to say or do.

"Do you want to dance?" I propose suddenly. He lifts his head, surprised by my question and then gives me a sad smile, of disillusion, and then moves back a step. "You're cruel", his voice trembles, you can clearly see in his face that he is suffering, "we both know that you don't want to dance with me."

To see him so fragile and weak makes my heartbeat accelerate again, I feel hot with a huge need to have physical contact with him. I slowly go to him, take his hands and put them behind my back, while I place my hands around his neck. Surprise, dismay, terror, all these expressions show across his face as he asks me in a broken voice: "Why? Why are you doing this?" he holds me tight in his arms, the same embrace that he gave me in Gorizia after saving my life. I can feel his heart beating against my chest, and his breathing becoming faster. I close my eyes for a moment taking a deep breath and then I ask him: "When did I tell you that I hate dwarves, Jack?" After my question, I turn to stone. He holds me to him, he doesn't want to let me go, but I feel that he stopped breathing for a moment. I realize only now that I am afraid. If he doesn't answer my question, or if he doesn't reply exactly to my question, he will tear my heart from my chest, because it will mean that for the second time I was wrong about him, and that he has lied to me again. I'm about to pull away from him, his silence already says it all, when I feel him hold me to him even tighter and he whispers to me: "You never told me."

I close my eyes and what I feel is indescribable. For months I've felt as if I were attached to a breathing machine that helped to keep me alive, but now at last I feel like I can breathe alone.

Jack puts his hands on my shoulders pushing me from him. His beautiful blue eyes are filled with tears. "It probably won't mean anything to you, but I need to tell you one thing before you go away forever", he takes a deep breath, his lips tremble. "I don't know if I can do it", he touches his chest with his hand. "I see myself as a very strong person but, before you, when I look at you, my legs tremble. I feel like a child, I feel as if I'm John. I have never lied to you, Jas, I have always been sincere with you and... I'm sorry. You have helped me so much and I've ruined everything. I am sorry for what I did and for what I have not done, I am sorry for everything, Jas."

There are those who follow their heart, those who follow their head, others their instinct... I definitely do the latter when suddenly I throw myself in his arms. He is taken aback only for a second, after which no more words are spoken. We begin to kiss each other with passion unable to move away from each other. A warm thrill runs through me, I need to touch him, breathe his smell, feel his hot tongue touch my... this is the first time in my life that I'm not afraid of losing control.

***

A month ago

It was one in the morning. Mina was asleep. I opened the door and sneaked along the corridor trying to not make any noise. I took the handle and slowly opened the door of his bedroom.

Patrick was already waiting for me sitting behind the desk.

"Hey, goldilocks", I called him in a soft voice closing the door behind me.

"Hey, grandma duck", he greeted me with a smile without adding anything else, even if his green eyes said more than they would have liked. I smiled too sitting down on the chair next to him. "So?" I asked him trying to be serious.

"So what?" he pretended not to understand.

We continued to look at each other with these unmistakable little smiles on our faces without commenting. I like these mental games that I have with him. I got comfortable, as he began to put this kind of electrode on me at heart level, on my temples and on my neck. As usual everything started to itch as soon as he turned on the lie detector. How annoying! He placed his thumbs on my wrists and without wasting any time we began to chatter. "Is your name Jas Herzog?" he asked with a calm but decisive tone of voice.

"Yes." My heart beat was quiet, relaxed, the level of perspiration as well, the machine showed that I told the truth. I looked Patrick straight in the eye without any problem.

"Is your name Jas Herzog" he repeated the question in a slightly more abrupt tone. I continued to breathe calmly. I felt his fingers grasp my wrists, I just had to tell him the truth, and without taking my eyes from him I replied: "No. "

He studied the monitor that marked my heart beat and blood pressure, but I didn't, I continued to gaze at him without fear because I had told him the truth: My name is not Jas Herzog! Patrick seemed satisfied. "The lie detector says that it's true."

"Because it is true!"

He smiled; I read in his eyes that he was proud of me. "What is your name?"

"Grandma Duck." This time I smiled, but despite this, the lie detector confirmed my words. Patrick let go of my wrists and leaned back on the chair. "You're ready!"

I jumped to my feet, with all the cables still stuck to the body and hugged him hard letting out a cry of happiness.

"And just as well this room is sound proofed, Jas."

"I am so happy!" I moved away from him knowing how sensitive he is to physical contact and I sat back on the chair all excited. "After all these months of study and sleepless nights I finally have visible results!" I couldn't help praising myself.

Patrick gave me a smile as he carefully began to take the wires from my body, being careful where and how he touched me. I thought how this made him feel uncomfortable, even if he tried to hide it. But his gaze confirmed how well he understood my thoughts.

"You were right, everything is in the head", I changed the topic so as not to embarrass him any further, but I knew he understood this too.

"Yes, everything is in the head", he confirmed, playing along with me. "If first you convince yourself that what you think is true, you will convince everyone else as well, grandma duck", he smiled as he said it.

"So have we finished? No more nocturnal lessons?" I asked him upset. He said nothing, just tightened his lips in a half-smile, but from the way he looked at me I understood that he too was sorry that our clandestine meetings were finished. The only thing I could say was, "Thanks, Patrick, for everything. I feel much surer of myself now."

"Don't mention it", he pulled his lips again. I saw that he was trying not to move too much nor reveal his state of mind with his gaze. The mere fact that he was controlling himself said it all. He looked at me, and as usual he knew that I knew what he was doing.

Perhaps the silence between us was a sign. Maybe I should have told him what I'd discovered. I only had to look at him to make him understand; he leaned against the back of the chair and said simply: "I'm listening."

"I think there is a spy in Watchtower", I explained without beating around the bush.

"Why do you suspect this?"

"Two days ago, when I got Franklin involved in the disastrous prank I played on John, I did it in a moment of madness because he had filled my balcony with garden dwarves. And you know how much I hate dwarfs."

"Yes, I know. But I can't see the connection, Jas."

"I never told John that I hate dwarfs."

449

"Are you sure?" he asked, his face serious, even though he already knew my answer.

"Absolutely sure. You know that I have a memory like an elephant, but despite this, last night I stayed up until five in the morning on the balcony to think and rethink whether or not I was wrong. I told him many things about myself when we were in Gorizia, but not this, Patrick. He couldn't know that. And then today when I returned from the breakfast/dinner and I heard Felix say that the entire Watchtower is protected with white noise I had further confirmation. If it wasn't bugs, then it was real life spies who told John about the dwarfs."

"Why didn't you tell Nick?"

"How do you know that...?" I interrupted myself, realizing that I was going to ask him a stupid question. "Because I'm not sure of it and I don't want to make him suspicious without first having the proof."

"Without having the proof?" he repeated surprised, "you've really taken this investigation seriously."

"Yes, I decided to seriously get to know your world and I do not want to make mistakes, nor make things difficult for Nick."

"Now that you've confided this to me, what do you expect from me?"

"The usual", I said getting up from the chair, "Look, watch and smile."

He smiled looking at me with those beautiful green eyes of his. *He is so beautiful and fascinating in the way he acts and looks that sometimes I just want to...*

"Jas." Fortunately he interrupted my impure thoughts. I left the door handle and turned to him. "Yes?"

"I'm proud of you."

I smiled embarrassed. I opened the door and said in a low voice: "Everything I know, you taught me, Patrick."

83.

From Mina's diary – The day before the day after

I get out of the elevator passing close to Veronica and America without even greeting them and run toward my bedroom. I open the door but my Jas isn't there. Damn! My eyes are swollen from crying, I feel lonely, I feel dirty, I'm going crazy! I look at my bed and I see a note near the towels.

I am at the hospital; today is my last day at work... where the hell have you disappeared to? I need you! Jas

Feel like a huge stone on my heart, Jas needs me, but she still doesn't know what I've just discovered: that they have manipulated and used me for all these weeks just to get to her. I feel sick. I hate Lexi.

I put my mobile phone on charge and rush to the door. I have to tell her about their dirty plan.

I go past Veronica and America again without saying hello and as fast as I can I push the button to call the elevator, fixing my skirt that has gone up too far. I can't wait to reach the hospital, I can't stand it anymore. I must get if off my chest.

As always happens when you're in a hurry time goes very slowly and it seems to me that I've been waiting for the elevator for a century, when I hear Veronica chuckle in Spanish behind me. I've had enough now! I turn and bark: "Was that addressed to me, by any chance? If you need to tell me something, say it to me in my face and in my own language, please! I'm tired of people that do things behind my back!"

Both Veronica that America look at each other confused; they did not expect a reaction like this from me, while I'm waiting for only one wrong word from Veronica jump on top of her.

"I apologise."

And instead, loser that I am, she says the right thing.

"I did not realize that I was speaking in Spanish. And yes, I was addressing you. I was saying to America that you are becoming a perfect copy of Jas. Poisonous, aggressive and rude."

"Was it better to become like you? Cold, viperous and false?"

451

America raises her eyebrows turning toward Veronica who is looking at me calmly. "Cold, viperous and false", she says, "so that's how you see me? How come?"

"And you even dare to ask me that? Since I arrived in Miami you've done nothing but size me up, you barely say hello to me, you criticize my Jas and do everything you can to convince everyone that she is a lunatic! And you're false, since you pretend so hard to make out you're Ginevra's friend while behind her back you can't wait to take her ex-boyfriend to bed, even though she's still in love with him! That's why!"

"It seems you're the one who needed to tell me to my face what you thought, not me."

"No! You must tell me too! What have you got against me and Jas! What have we done to offend you?"

"What I think of Jas is no secret, but if you want I'll repeat it. I don't like her because she's a spoilt little girl, immature, selfish, accustomed to having everyone get her out of trouble, while she spends her time ignoring advice and rules and enjoys self-destructing! When I say that she needs a good psychologist it's because I really think that, and not because I want to seduce Nick. And speaking of Nick, I think that Jas has ruined his life. He and Ginevra, my best friend, could have worked together and be happily married at this point, but that didn't happen because Nick gave up everything for Jas. He has always chosen her, putting her in first place before everyone. Jas instead does nothing but treat him badly, hurt him, disappoint him, she is thankless and does not deserve his faith or his love!" She approaches me with arms crossed. "And I am not in love with Nick; I'm homosexual, in case you didn't know."

If I didn't already have a lot of problems of my own, I would be shocked right now, but seeing everything that has happened, I limit myself to looking at her with my mouth open wondering how I hadn't realized it earlier.

To be wrong on everything and everyone is unbelievable.

In front of my silence, Veronica leans on the counter and continues with the calmest of voices: "As for you, on the other hand, I think you're a good person, honest and sincere, but you are losing all these values as time goes by because Jas is ruining you, just as she ruins everything she touches, you just have to look at you." She looks me up and down as if I were a tramp, even if in reality I'm wearing designer clothes and very expensive jewelry.

"It wasn't Jas who changed me, it was just me who wanted it and did it, okay? She didn't dress me like this! I did it alone, she wasn't even there..." I stop talking. I close my eyes for a moment, and in an instant images of me slide by, trying on clothes, make-up, hairdressers, massages, parties, limousines, the night with Vladimir, marijuana, alcohol... they didn't use me, or manipulate or exploit me, they didn't use me, because I went looking for this all by myself. Everything I've done, even the drugs, I did because I just wanted to. I let myself be bought.

I'd wanted this all my life, I wanted to be noticed, I wanted to be admired, become beautiful and escape anonymity, and now that I've obtained this...

Veronica and America are looking at me in a strange way, I can't even stand up; they are surprised at me, at what I've done. I turn and staring into space, without a goodbye, I go down the corridor. The only thing I would like at this moment is to hide under the sheets and feel ashamed of myself in silence.

***

Four years ago

It was a very hot summer. I arrived tired at the top of a small Italian mountain pushing my rusted bike. I sat down on the green lawn and looked at the house on the tree for a long time, admiring all its detail. I had wanted to come here for a long time, but I never found the right way to get here.

"*Kdo si ti?*" I heard a female voice behind me. I turned and saw a girl with dark eyes and dark hair who was looking at me in a threatening manner. She had her arms crossed and a bag on the ground near her.

"Excuse me", I said frightened, "I don't understand Slovenian."

"I asked you who you are."

"I am... my name is Mina."

"What are you doing here? Didn't you know that this is private property?"

"I'm sorry." I stood up from the ground grabbing my bike as quickly as I could. "I didn't know, I didn't mean any harm. Now I'm going, excuse me." With my heart in my throat I tried to climb onto the bike, but, clumsy as always, I fell awkwardly onto the ground scratching my hand. "I never get it right! Not even once!" Still on the ground I began to blaspheme and hit the bike angrily. "Dammit!"

"Falling off the bike does not mean never getting anything right", the girl pointed out as she came near me.

"Falling off the bike is just the latest in a series of things that aren't right that happen to me every day," I explained in a sad tone, my voice trembling because of the umpteenth bad impression.

"How you fall is not important", she said holding out her hand to me, "it's how you get up."

I looked at her for a few seconds and then grabbed her hand.

"Come here", she said to me. She sat down on the ground and took a bottle from inside the bag. "It just so happens that I brought a bottle of vodka with me, so I can disinfect the wound for you."

"How come you go around with a bottle of vodka in your bag?" I asked intrigued.

"I'm fourteen and I've never got drunk, yet. So I thought I'd take advantage of Nick's absence and do it today, will you join me?"

I continued to look at her puzzled. "I have a lot of problems, that's true, but drinking isn't the answer."

"Yes, but drinking helps you forget the question."

"Nice one", I smiled at the quip stop despite the burning of the vodka that I felt on the wound.

"Come on, come on", she began to insist, "I'll help you climb up to the house."

"Really? I've been looking at the Gorizia castle for so many years and I have always wondered whose it was. It's a dream for me to be able to go up to it." As I jumped up and down around the house happily, the girl looked at me with cunning eyes. "My name is Jas", she introduced herself offering me her hand again.

454

Hours passed, darkness fell and Jas and I were still on the *Cat's Eyes* telling each other about our lives, laughing, joking as we discovered that we were on the same wavelength, while the bottle of vodka became increasingly empty.

"My mother is so..."I couldn't even finish the sentence; I lay down on the wooden floor of the house and began to laugh with my leg lifted upwards.

"I can't wait to meet her, an adult who thinks she is a teenager."

"And I can't wait to meet Nick, a teenager who thinks he's an adult instead."

"Nick is no longer a teenager; he's almost twenty-two now."

We both continued to laugh, both of us having a great time.

I complained laughing: "I am so drunk. How do I get home, can you tell me? Where did I put the bike?"

"If you want, I'll accompany you."

"But you're in a worse state than me, Jas!"

"Let's do this, I lean on you, and you lean on me, we'll be a crutch to each other."

"You're totally crazy," I smiled.

"It's fun to be like that, where did you say you go to school?"

"This is the third time you've asked me."

"No, first I asked the other two Minas", she began to laugh and clap her hands, "I'm asking this because I think I'll enroll in your school in September, that way we'll see each other every day and we'll be close and closer."

From lying down, I quickly sat up looking at Jas with raised eyebrows. "Would you do that for me?"

"No I wouldn't. I'll do it in September. Listen, do you want to become my best friend? I'm serious."

"You're drunk."

"Yes, but I'm also serious."

"But you don't even know me."

"You're sincere, good and honest, you look after your mother, so you're also responsible and reliable. You remind me very much of Nick, he takes care of his grandmother Isobel as well. And he takes care of me too", she smiled. "Only that he's not funny like you, he's boring, but shhhh", she puts her finger on my mouth, "he mustn't hear me, otherwise he gets angry."

455

I said nothing more. I looked pensively toward the castle of Gorizia from the little balcony. My eyes were glistening.

"What's the matter?" asked Jas, noticing it.

"Nobody has ever done anything for me," I replied, hanging my head down, "my father left me, my mother does not know how to take care of herself, let alone me, at school a lot of people make fun of me because of my surname, Gallina, which means hen, my classmates think I'm a whiner and kids... never mind. No one respects me." I lifted my head and looked at her. "And then you arrive, so beautiful, friendly and intelligent, and tell me that you want to enroll in my school just to be close to me. You pay me compliments, you ask me if I want to be your best friend... I'm scared that this is just a beautiful dream, I'm afraid to wake up and realize that nothing has changed and that I'm still alone."

"Will you stop feeling sorry for yourself?!" she said in an annoyed voice, "you're not alone, I'm not a hologram, and I'm not going anywhere without you!"

I gaped at her, disoriented by this attitude which was so... unique. I smiled, as she added: "You're my best friend and best friends don't abandon each other. So that's enough paranoia, get off your butt and let's go before Nick finds us!"

***

The day before the day after

I've been here waiting for two hours now. I don't know where she is, I don't know when she'll come back, but I'll be here as long as it takes. I won't go without saying goodbye to her; I will not leave a shabby note on the nightstand with some predictable words.

On the building on the other side of the road the enormous billboard with the question *Do you give in?!* is still hanging there.

As I read it over and over again, I think what a cruel blow of fate it is to find myself facing it. I see a taxi stop in front of the Watchtower and feel my heart stop too. The door opens and Jas gets out. Her smile is the only ray of light in the midst of this darkness that I feel in my soul.

"My looooove! I've searched everywhere for you in these last few days, but I couldn't find you! Where were you?" she asks in a loud voice all radiant as she pays for the taxi, "I need to speak to you, something has happened..." She closes the door of the taxi and comes up the stairs, but the closer she gets the more her smiling face becomes serious. She stops half-way up the stairs looking at the suitcases on the floor beside me. We are both silent, I look at her, she looks at the luggage. I would like so much to be able to skip this part and find myself directly in my bed in Gorizia.

"What's going on?" she asks me in a serious voice.

"*Twentytwo.*" It's enough just to use our code to make her understand that I am leaving, that I'm going away. My eyes are full of tears.

"Why?" she asks me. I take a deep breath and go down the stairs stopping in front of her. If I look at her it hurts, but not as much as the way she looks at me.

"For more than six months", I begin to speak with a trembling voice, "I have done no more than watch without asking questions..."

"Mina..."

"Don't interrupt me, please", I ask her. Jas lowers her head.

"I know you, and if you didn't come to speak to me, it's not because you didn't want to, but because you didn't know what to say to me, this I know."

She nods her head without saying anything.

"I need to ask you just one question, Jas, you can tell me everything else when you feel like doing it, that's not a problem, I'll keep waiting, but I have to ask you one now, I need to know."

"Okay", she replies with a worried face as she tries to hold back tears.

"If I hadn't asked you to stay in Miami, would you have remained just the same? It is very important for me that you tell me the truth, I need to know, even if it will hurt", I tell her with tears in my eyes. Never in my life have I been more afraid of a reply than at this moment. Everything depends on what she answers, what has been, what it is, what it will be. She does not even realize it but she is about to decide my future and her silence is killing me with every second that passes.

457

She raises her head looking at me with eyes full of tears. "When we were in the hotel" she pauses. But in that pause I lose ten years of life, "I was thinking how to tell you that I wanted to stay in Miami."

I close my eyes with an enormous sigh, the tears begin to roll down my face. They are tears of joy. I hug her hard.

"I wanted to stay ", she continues to repeat in a broken voice, "If you had said no I don't know what I would have done, but knowing me, selfish as I am, I would have stayed just the same, not giving a damn about our trip to Europe because I wanted so much to get to know Jack's world." She's like a little girl with so much need to be understood. "No, that's not true", she corrects herself, "I wanted to get to know Jack."

"Thanks, Jas, thank you for telling me the truth."

"Always."

"I have to go away from here to sort things out, I'm going back to Italy, but..."

"I'll come with you!"

"No, for you to sort things out you have to stay here, Jas."

"No, I don't want to," she shakes her head confused. I put my hands on her shoulders "Jas, your *Enterprise* has not finished its journey yet."

"I don't want to do it without you."

"Listen to me, the day we met you said that you wanted to enroll in my school so you could be near me and now I'm going home to stay close to you. I know that seems to be contradictory but..."

Jas embraces me tightly, full of emotion, without letting me finish the sentence. "I love you."

"Me too, Jas."

"And if I make the wrong choice?"

"Whatever your choice is, you have to make it alone. Don't be influenced by anyone or anything. And if it's the wrong one, I'll be your crutch", I smile, hugging her tight again, "I only hope that he moves closer to your world, and not you to his, Jas", I whisper to her before I leave.

They say that when you return from a trip, you come back different from when you left. I don't know if I'm returning or fleeing toward home, but what I said to Jas is true: to clear my mind and see the person I have become, accept *who* I have become, I have to leave here.

I feel that I am no longer the Mina of Gorizia, I feel the strong change within me, but I'm not even the Mina of Miami. I need to find a balance, and I'll only find that being alone with myself for a few days.

As far as my Jas is concerned, on the other hand, she knows, she has always known it. She knows who she is, she knows what she wants to do and who she wants to be with, but as they taught me at the Watchtower, knowing is not enough.

84.

Two minutes before – From Jx's diary

"Hurricane Warning! The disturbance is officially a hurricane that will hit within twenty-four hours! The mayor has declared a state of emergency! Evacuation is mandatory! Follow orders and take shelter in safer areas in the hinterland, do not venture outside for any reason! A tsunami could cause damage of unpredictable extent"

On television they're announcing the news of the approach of the hurricane that has been announcing its arrival for months. Ben's sons get up from their chairs at the dining room table, worried, and go quickly to the lobby where America is already waiting for them with a serious look on her face and a sheet with all the instructions to follow in her hand. Nickolas leaves his office at a fast pace. "Is Jas back?" he asks the woman worried.

"Yes."

"Where is she?"

She looks at the screen in front of her and answers: "Still out front of the Watchtower. She's saying goodbye to Mina."

"Why? Where is she going?"

"I thought you knew, boss. Mina is returning to Italy."

Nick rushes to the elevator completely disoriented and alarmed by the news. Why is Mina going home days earlier?

Something must have happened, he thinks. After a few seconds he reaches the first floor, gets out of the elevator and goes into the street, but Mina and Jas are no longer there. The siren begins to sound, alerting all the inhabitants of the arrival of the hurricane. People are preparing to evacuate the area, worried, and among them also Nick, desperate in the middle of the road, but for different reasons.

Before the arrival of a hurricane the weather is always spectacular, with a lovely breeze, a clear sky and a peaceful sea. The classic calm before the storm.

85.

Miami Hospital, evening – From Jas's diary

I wake up with a hallucinating headache, I open my eyes and I see Metoo on top of me, having fun pulling my hair with his beak. Annoyed, I look straight into his small sly little eyes and he lets go of my hair and turns his head the other way pretending he wasn't diong a thing. Incredible, taken for a sucker by a parrot.

I grab his beak. "Will you stop annoying me? I'm fed up with you!"

As soon as I let go of him, he flies over to Zombie screaming loudly "metoooooo, metooooo..."

"Good evening, Jas", I hear Diana's voice come from under the bed. I take a good look and I see her lying on the ground doing her usual little drawings which have overrun the walls of this room in recent weeks.

"How long did I sleep?" I ask her seeing darkness from the window.

"A lot, you looked like you were in a coma like Zombie. Do you feel better now?"

"No."

"Do you want me to do a little drawing for you?"

"No."

"Do you know why they say that a cat has nine lives? Because it is strong and resistant. It's able to survive almost everything, it is unlikely to give up." She's very close to my face now and she looks at me with her big dark eyes, smiling at me as if she felt the sadness I feel at this moment. "Did you know that?"

"No", I reply with a sulk on my face.

"No! No, no, no, no, nooooooo..." the parrot begins again, screaming his head off.

"Did you hear, Jas? Metoo said *no!* He said a new word!" She jumps up and down the room trying to capture it.

"And it was about time."

On the internet I've read that this type of parrot learns I don't know how many words, but Metoo has done nothing but repeat only two: me too and k.o.

He lands on my head starting to pull my hair. "Will you stop pulling my hair, once and for all?" I hit him with my hand and make him fly away again.

"No, no, no, nooooooooooooooooooo..."

"He loves you," says Diana between one cough and another.

"Nice way to show it."

What with the parrot that is annoying me and Diana's presence, I must admit I feel a little better. At least I'm not thinking about Mina's departure and the heap of questions that she has left unanswered before she climbed aboard that taxi. Diana starts to cough again, I look at her; she is right next to my bed looking at me with a huge smile squeezing the yellow toy. "While you were asleep, they said that a hurricane is on the way. We're not in danger, but just the same we have to stay away from the windows", she explains to me.

What a load of nonsense, they've been frightening us with this hurricane for months and nothing happens. And then this morning the sun was shining, it was a lovely day, before becoming horribly ugly.

"Look, I'm wearing the bracelet with the kittens that you gave me for my birthday. Did you see? Look..." She shows me the bracelet putting it up close to my nose. At least I know what was in the package that I stole from Tim, the Chinese guy that worked in the laboratory. I am so depressed, one minute I'm happy and two I'm sad, it sucks.

"Are you listening to me?" she asks.

"No", I say in a sick girl's voice as I hug my Zombie.

"Just say no, Jas, and he begins to say yes."

I stare with wide eyes and turn toward the door. Leaning against the wall I see Jack. He comes in with his hands in his pocket and smiles when he sees me embracing the old man. I stand up immediately from the bed, embarrassed. "Jack? What are you doing here?"

"The black man! The black man! You came to see me again as you promised me." Diana flings herself on him hugging him very

462

hard. I'm speechless as I watch him cuddle the little girl with a different expression from usual: gentle, protective, and her totally mad about him. I smile involuntarily, but I'm not even aware that I like what I see.

"Koooooooo..." Metoo starts screaming again and flies around the room. Jack looks at him amused, then looks at the old man, then at the parrot again, then looks around and while he is busy snooping I quickly hide the cup that I stole at the airport under the pillow before he sees it. I don't want him to connect my grandfather to that day in any way.

"What's a parrot doing here?" he asks amused.

"It's called Metoo", Diana immediately starts to fill him with information, "and he's Zombie's and he's..." she doesn't have time to finish the sentence before I'm already dashing to Jack distracting him with a kiss. I don't want him to hear, given that I haven't understood yet if it's my Zombie that he and Boris are looking for.

If at the beginning my kiss only serves to distract him, it soon turns into a real and desired kiss. I close my eyes and all I need is to feel his lips on mine, touch him, feel him mine, he's like a magnet: I can't get unstuck from him.

"You two are an item! You're a couple." Diana exults jumping around us between coughs. I detach myself from Jack suddenly, embarrassed and annoyed by the word *couple*.

"No! No, no, no, noooo, kooooo..."

"Metoo has already replied for me."

"But you kissed him", Diana specifies.

"So what? I don't go with everyone I kiss you know."

"What, sorry?" Jack blurts out dazed, he grabs my hand with force and turns me toward him holding me tightly against his body. "Who else have you kissed, apart from me?"

"It's none of your business", I smile in a provocative way.

"As soon as I find out I'm telling you now that I'll kill him!"

"You'd kill a man just because he kissed me?"

"I would do it even for a cigarette if needs be, let alone if he touches my things."

"*Your things?*"

"You're so beautiful when you quarrel," says Diana coughing, and watching us with dreamy eyes, "I am so happy that you are, that you are not together! Did you know that cats choose who to love and that cats grumble even when they're happy?"

"Did you hear, you're always complaining", he says to me and holds me even closer, trying to kiss me.

"I am not a cat."

"I love you", whispers Diana behind us. She is so sweet, smiling and hugging the toy, it seems that Jack and I together bring her immense happiness and I can't explain to myself why.

Jack kneels in front of her. "We love you too, little one", he caresses her bald head and starts playing with her yellow cat. I feel strange; Jack has called her *little one.* It's been months since Nick said that to me, I realize only now.

"What shall we do now?" asks Diana bouncing around him.

"First I'll sing you a song, then we'll do a drawing of the three of us together, and then", he turns to me. "I've prepared a surprise for Jas."

"What surprise?" I ask Jack surprised. Jack and Diana exchange complicit glances, and secret information in the ear. The only thing that comes to me to say is: "This isn't fair!"

***

"I don't understand this obsession of yours to blindfold people!" I say frustrated as I try to find a comfortable position on an uncomfortable floor.

"What are you talking about?"

"You and your family Jack! It's the second time I find myself blindfolded in less than three days!"

"Stop complaining!"

"Can I know where you've brought me? On a boat? I'm going to throw up! And besides, why do I have to be barefoot?"

"You're a ball-breaker, Jas. Why did God give you the gift of speech?" he whispers. I am about to answer him back rudely when I feel him take the blindfold and he removes it from my eyes. I am afraid to open them, the last time I did that I found myself in a dark garage and don't need to recall what happened after that. I open only one eye first and see Jack in front of me beaming idiotically at me and then I open the second and... I gape, as has often happened in recent months.

I'm on the roof of the tallest skyscraper in Miami, in a sort of cage, hanging far above the ground thanks to a construction in iron. I get to my feet keeping close to the bars of the cage. Below us is a huge swimming pool. I can't close my mouth from the amazement I feel. We're over the whole of Miami, we're looking at it from above, it's like flying.

The people below us are going crazy, they're running along the road, many are putting planks of wood at the windows, there's a lot of confusion, shouting, squabbling; I look at the palm trees and think that the wind will uproot them from the ground from one moment to the next. It is magnificent.

From here the colored lights of the skyscrapers seem to form beautiful, huge designs while on the other side the sea is rough and dark clouds are coming toward us. I like this contrast of light and shadow, my heart is starting to beat faster and faster, I can't believe that this is happening really. "Jack it's beautiful!" is the only thing I can say.

He embraces me from behind and gives me a kiss on the neck. "In a few minutes the most severe storm of the season will begin, Jas. When the sirens begin to sound and everyone is hiding in their house scared of the hurricane, you and I will be here, seeing live what nature is capable of doing."

"We'll be electrocuted live, you mean?"

"No", he smiles and kisses me again on the neck "this cage is made of iron, it will protect us from the lightning, you won't get a shock."

"You're... incredible", I admit as I continue to watch the landscape as it becomes ever more threatening as it appears before us. I sigh, enchanted.

"Jas, today is my birthday."

"What?" I turn toward him, surprise, "I didn't know."

"I know, how could you?"

"And how old are you?"

"Twenty-two."

"You're twenty-two?"

"Yes, why do you ask me that in this surprised tone? Look, I'm only four more than you, eh."

"Yes yes, okay, but... I didn't give you a present", I say displeased. I managed to get one for Diana at the last second, but here, closed in a sort of cage covered with glass in the middle of the sky I'd say that my chances of success are very low.

"I know what I want as a gift", he smiles putting his hands on my hips. If he dares ask me what I think he wants to ask me I swear I'll knee him in the middle of his legs.

"I want to commit myself to you, Jas."

"Eh? What do you mean?"

"Make a serious commitment with you. I want us to become a couple, Jas."

"No, no, no", I repeat terrified. Perhaps I preferred that he asked me something else. "We can't, it's too soon, no, no, no!"

"Too soon? We've known each other for almost a year."

"No, that's not true. *You've* known me for almost a year. I've known you for scarcely a month. And then there are things about you, your work that I don't like and that I don't want to be involved in, no, no, no", the more I say the more I hear the noise of my nails clutching at mirrors.

"What things? Tell me what they are, I can change, you can change me."

"Yes, with someone else."

"Jas, stop joking, I'm serious. What don't you like about me?"

"Your work. In the sense that I understand and support what you do, but I don't like how you do it. All those dead people, all that blood, I don't know if I'd be able to stand seeing you take human lives again, Jack."

"That's not a problem, if that's what you want I will not do it again. My brothers will do it."

And he thinks this is a solution?

"Jack", I try to explain "in any case, you told me yourself that you couldn't ever change your job because you're the first who isn't able to change."

"It's true, nobody changes their nature, but we can learn to manage it. I didn't have a good reason for doing that before, but

466

now I do." He pulls me to him looking at me straight in the eyes. "It's you."

He's so sweet and sincere, I don't know what to say or what to do, I don't know if I'm ready to be with him. Nor do I know if I am ready to have a boyfriend.

"Please, give me a chance. I'll do whatever you want and how you want it. I can do it!" His blue eyes are so intense; I've never seen them like that before. It might be because of the atmosphere, or for the grayness around us, I don't know, but the more I look at him, the more I think how beautiful he is.

"Listen", he takes my face with both hands. "If you want something, you find a way, and if you don't want something, you find an excuse. Now it depends on you. What do you want, Jas? What do you want?"

He waits for my answer, but there's not always a simple answer to a simple question. I remain silent, and the more seconds pass, the more his head drops and his gaze becomes sad. I can't look at him in this state. If he is suffering, I feel bad too, dammit!

"Okay."

Now I've said it!

"Continue to do your work, arrest who you want and how you want, but I don't want to see them die at your hands, Jack. Do you understand? If you can avoid killing anyone for at least one hundred days, *if* you can do that, I'll give you a chance."

"As a real couple, though?"

"Yes."

Now I've said this too.

"As a real couple. But you mustn't cheat..."

Suddenly a loud clap of thunder makes me jump with fear. I have never heard anything like that in my life. I turn toward the sea, toward Miami and for the umpteenth time I am lost for words. While I was occupied clarifying our future relationship with Jack, the scenario has changed behind me, giving life to an unprecedented spectacle.

The wind has become very strong, I hear it howling through the glass and steel that protects us, the sea has become a dark gray color, the waves are high, violent, the first rain batters the glass of the cage and the thunder is becoming louder and louder.

467

Miami with the lights off is no longer the same, the streets are deserted, no cars, no people, looking at everything from up here is like witnessing an apocalypse. The lightning flashes are different too, it's as if they're alive, angry, the colors are not what I usually see on the ground, but a mix of blue, green and yellow, an indescribable beauty.

"For me you're all of this, Jas", he whispers hugging me from behind, "flashes, thunder, lightning strikes, wind, hurricanes... fascinating and frightening at the same time."

I turn toward him. There is one thing that I forgot to do, I'm so distracted by all this wonder that surrounds me. "Happy birthday Jack."

"It's the most wonderful birthday of my life."

I remember that there is another thing that I forgot to do. "I don't think I've thanked you yet for saving my life, twice."

"No, you haven't", he replies smiling.

"One day I will."

"I'm not in a hurry, I'll wait."

"Jack", just by saying his name my heart begins to beat fast, "thank you for all of this", I look at the cage, then the hurricane that is devastating the city, and then again at him. "I don't know how you do it."

"Now I'll explain it to you, and listen to me very carefully, woman."

I smile, I already know that he's about to come out with some of his bullshit: "There is only one boy that's good for someone like you and it's the one you're looking at right now, so get used to it."

"Of course, and what have you got that others don't have?"

"The question is not what I have", he caresses my face gently, "but what the two of us have, that you don't have with others, Jas."

I blush. I can't describe what I feel. I like what he says, how he says it, I like... him. "Jack..."

He kisses me and stops me from finishing the sentence. He kisses me again and holds my face tight in his hands as if there were no tomorrow. Needless to say my heart is going crazy. The emotions that this boy can make me feel are incredible. I detach myself from him and look at him. His eyes are bright with tears, worried. This is not the reaction I was expecting. "What's wrong, Jack?" I ask him baffled.

He kisses me again and without letting go of my face he whispers: "I have to tell you something very important, Jas."

86.

The day after – From Jx's diary

It's breakfast time in the Watchtower. Ben and his sons have just got up, gone to the kitchen and are sitting at the table which Veronica and America have just set.

Patrick looks out the window: after the passage of the hurricane the entire town has gone to work to clean up the streets, reopen the bars and take tourists back to their hotels.

On the radio they are listing the number of injured and the damage that the hurricane has caused.

Will places the tray with coffee on the table, followed by America who brings bread and jam. Everyone sits in their place, all in silence, still sleepy and tired from the night just passed. Will, giving Pavarotti a threatening look as a warning to be careful not to break or spill anything, takes a sip of his coffee, opens the newspaper, takes a look and the next instant spits his coffee out all over Pavarotti under the amazed eyes of all present.

87.

The taxi stops in front of the Watchtower. I look at the building from the car window. It seems different to me, perhaps because I'm different from the last time I was here. There inside, however, nothing has changed, the people are exactly what they say they are, they work honestly, they fight for what they believe, don't waste time with cheating, lies and manipulation. Inside there it's like that and I should follow their example, but I can't. I feel an enormous weight stifling my chest, the weight of not being able to speak, to explain. They wouldn't understand. Nick couldn't, I know him. The profound disappointment which he would feel in discovering the truth would be devastating for him. I have to do the right thing, but how do I do the right thing, if I know that it's wrong while I do it?

I get out of the taxi. I go up the stairs and reach the elevator. I am about to do the scan of the retina to have the door open for me, when I feel someone grasp my arm. I turn around in surprise and see Patrick in front of me. He moves me away from the elevator with a very serious face and looking at the surveillance camera above us, whispers worried: "We don't have much time."

"Time for what?" I ask, amazed by his abnormal behavior.

He just opens the newspaper in front of my face. There is a headline in large letters with the words: *Jas has betrayed Nickolas Ortega Torres!* with a big picture below it of me and Jack kissing inside the iron cage of yesterday evening.

I think I'm losing my senses standing on my feet.

"Everyone knows, I wanted you to know before you went upstairs", he says unhappily.

I am not able to react, my breathing becomes shorter and shorter, I feel dizzy, I look at the newspaper and my sight becomes more and more blurred. Perhaps it's just a nightmare, please, let it be a nightmare, now I'll wake up and I'll discover it's only a nightmare.

"Jas!" Patrick calls me raising his voice.

Yes, I'm called Jas, I'm the one who has ended up on the tabloid, the one that has disappointed Nick, the one who has betrayed him. I don't think I have ever felt the sensations that I'm feeling at the moment ever before in my life: fear, tension, I feel lost. I begin to step back, I'm going to run away, I can't look Nick in the face, I'm not that strong. Patrick looks at me surprised, I have just disappointed him as well, he knows what I am about to do, there is no need to read my body language, my expression says it all. "I can't do it, I cannot... cannot face him and..."I can't breathe, I collapse to the ground, I don't feel well. Patrick kneels down quickly trying to help me, as I cover my face with my hands. I don't want him to see me in this state. I'm about to crumple.

"Breathe deeply and try to calm down", he tells me pressing my head to his chest.

"I can't leave, but I can't stay either. I never know where I should be, never!" I scream slamming my fists on the ground.

"Jas, it's normal to find yourself at a crossroads. That's life. You just need to assess whether the person you are fleeing from is more important to you than the one you are staying for. And you'll find the place to put yourself."

There is no need for him to say any more. My heart is still beating very hard, I am trembling, I have tears in my eyes, but in spite of everything I find the strength to stand up. Patrick is right. I am about to do an enormously stupid thing. Nick doesn't deserve it.

"Where is he?" I ask him with my voice still trembling.

"In his room."

"How is he?"

"You can imagine."

I close my eyes for a moment. His *you can imagine* in reality means *you can't even imagine*. He only wants to save me the pain for these few remaining seconds before I see him. I go to the elevator and scan the retina. "He waited up for you all night, Jas. He was worried. He didn't know where you were during the hurricane."

That's great. Now he knows where I was. Things are going from bad to worse; I feel terrible. "What... how can I tell him,

Patrick? What do I say to him?" I can't even speak without stammering.

The elevator door opens; I get inside once again feeling an enormous weight on my chest not allowing me to breathe. I look at Patrick hoping for another piece of his precious advice, an illuminating phrase, anything. Instead the only thing he says to me before the door closes is: "Try with the truth, Jas."

Only after the door closes, I whisper: "I cannot."

I look at myself in the mirror of the elevator. Eyes filled with tears, face repentant, humiliated in front of all Miami, branded as a traitor, I pity myself. How did I reduce myself to this state? Why am I allowing it?

The door opens and in the lobby I find all the rest of the team around the counter looking at me like I was a beggar. Ben lowers his eyes; America raises her eyebrows and then starts messing around with cards; Will, disoriented and embarrassed, tries to look elsewhere; Veronica has the newspaper in her hand and fixes me furious.

I say nothing, the newspapers and the TV hanging on the wall already say it all. I lower my gaze and go past them feeling like a piece of shit, judged and mortified with only the force of their gaze. I have not betrayed Nick, I did not do so. If only I had a chance to explain, perhaps they would understand, or at least in part, enough to know that I have not betrayed Nick.

The closer I get to his room the worse I feel, I am shaking, I'm afraid that I will not stand up to the stress of the situation, I'm afraid I'll have a psychological breakdown. What will happen now? He will yell at me, he'll give me a real dressing down, he will think that Jack has manipulated me or perhaps that I've manipulated him not telling him anything, maybe he'll throw me out of the Watchtower or insist that I take him to Jack to arrest him. I really feel ill. I rest against the wall breathing deeply, I must calm down, I must calm down, I must calm down...

I need some minutes to regain my composure, and before I am overcome by another panic attack, I pluck up courage and knock at his door.

Silence.

It is the worst sound I could hear at this time. I knock again. What goes through my mind is incomprehensible and contradictory: on the one hand I feel sick because he doesn't answer me and on the other hand I feel relieved. I came to speak to him; it's not my fault if he's not there. But what am I saying? I give myself a blow on the head and open the door. The room is dark, but the little that I can see thanks to the light coming from the entry, is enough to make me feel bad. Nick is sitting on the bed, shoulders bent, head down, he doesn't even turn to see who has entered. My heart is going crazy, I don't know what to do, what to say, where to start, just to see him there mute and motionless causes pain in my chest.

"Is it my fault?" he asks me in a broken voice, ending the silence. "Did I make a mistake? Is it because I worked all day and have not been as close to you as you wanted? Have I disregarded you? Or is it because I haven't fully understood you? Is it because of Borak? Do you think he attacked you because of me? Do you want to get your revenge, is that what it is? Do you want to... do you want to punish me?"

I keep thinking they're questions, what he says. His fears. Instead I realize that it's not fear but hope. I look at him with tears in my eyes, I am unable to say anything, I can't, my voice has disappeared. Nick is making all my emotional side come out, a side that I don't even know I have. I don't know how to handle it, I feel powerless. "No... it's not like that" is the only thing I manage to say.

"Tell me that it's just an adventure, an escapade, a crush that will last a few days, I need to hear that, Jas", he begs me.

All I would like is to have him yell at me, tell me *I told you so*, castigate me. And instead, I have to look at him sitting on the bed like a wounded animal. Tears begin to fall on my face. I am going to hurt him even more. "I cannot," I reply.

He puts his hands in his hair, and in a low voice asks me: "Do you love him?"

"I... I don't know."

"You don't know", he says. "You don't know if you love a ruthless murderer, a black soul like Jack", he says with contempt. "He has been good at manipulating you."

"No, that's not how it is, you're wrong. Jack is not... there are things that you don't know, not only about him. If I could exp..."

"No, please, don't do that", he interrupts me. "Don't protect him in front of me. Not in my home, I could not tolerate it."

"I am not protecting him, Nick."

"No? So tell me, tell me how this could happen. You said that when you looked at him you saw him for what it is: a murderer. What has changed, Jas? What happened in the meantime?"

I would like to tell him everything, but I can't.

He takes a deep breath and asks me: "H long has this relationship been going on?"

"We don't have a relationship."

"And what do you have?"

"I don't know."

He looks at me and his gaze kills me: sad, disappointed, I can't tolerate it. "What do you think you'll do, now? How did you think you'd manage the whole situation?"

"I don't know! It happened all of a sudden, so many things, so much information all at the same time and I don't know what to do, I don't know how to move. I know that everything seems so wrong, but I swear to you Nick, I have not lost my way!" I've never ever found myself in so much difficulty before now, this constant burning sensation that I feel inside my chest, my head spinning, I'm afraid I won't make it.

"And me? What do I do now? What do you expect from me, Jas?"

I don't know what I expect, but I don't know if I should tell him. I don't know how he might react. If he will understand. "I want... I want you to leave these investigations. I want you to forget Jack and everything that concerns him. This is what I want. I want everything to go back as it was as before", I finish the sentence and I stop living. His disappointed eyes fill with tears in a second, he is trembling. He gets to his feet, gripping the tabloid in his hands.

"Please don't look at me like that."

"When did you recover your memory? At the gala?"

He has understood that I lied to him. He has realized that I was not honest with him regarding my memory and that Felix was right about me. I close my eyes for a moment, guilty and sorry for what I've done.

"You never lost it, you're memory, did you? You've protected him from the start, isn't that right?" his voice falters. He's standing in front of me without moving, his gaze lost in the space of someone who already knows the answer. I would never have wanted to do this to him, he is everything to me. Patrick says that it's all in the head, months and months of lessons at night to learn how to lie, but the only truth is that the truth hurts. The truth does not let you live better.

I lift my head and looking at him in the eyes I say to him: "I recovered it at the gala, on my birthday." They say that the greatest enemy of a lie is not the truth, but a new lie.

"I have not protected Jack."

They were wrong. Nick's gaze has changed, despite the pain and disappointment that he is feeling right now, he is better now, and the worst thing is that I do not regret lying to him.

"That's where everything began. From your birthday on you became even more elusive, strange", he says through his tears. "I knew it. I already felt that night that something would change, but I was hoping that if I didn't say it aloud, it not would happen."

"No. Nick, no, please, believe me. My birthday has nothing to do with it, it would have happened anyway. I... I beg you, trust me, please."

"Trust", he looks at me straight in the eyes. "I think that even today you don't know what trust is, Jas. You don't know what it means to give it, because you've never given it to anyone. You don't know what it means to earn it, because I gave it to you without you asking me from the first moment I saw you. And you don't know what it means to lose it, because despite what I see", he throws the tabloid to the ground, "despite what I feel, in spite of all that you do to me, the disappointment and suffering that you inflict on me, I am still here, in front of you, to fight for you, to protect you before everyone, while you protect Jack. I am ready to bear everything and listen to everything you say, Jas, because despite everything I trust in you, and I know that in the end you will do the right thing. This is trust", his words weigh like a boulder. He is weeping, and I cry too seeing him in this state because of me.

"Don't talk to me like this, please!" I scream sobbing. "I'm not protecting Jack! I trust in you! I would do anything for you!"

"If you trusted in me you would not be afraid to talk to me, Jas. And I wouldn't have had to learn all this crap from the tabloid press. You never trust anyone and I'm afraid that one day, precisely because of this lack of trust toward your neighbor, you'll end up getting very badly hurt." He goes toward the door, but I stop him, grabbing him by the arm. "Nick, don't go" I beg him, but he frees himself from my grip without looking at me.

"Every time I wanted to talk to you, you interrupted me and sent me away saying that you wanted to be alone. This time I want to be alone. I need time to think. Think of what to do about you and Jack. Think of what to say to my colleagues, to your parents. What to say to myself, about you."

"Don't leave me, please don't leave me!"

"I'm not leaving you. You'll be the one to do that. I am a detective. Jack is a criminal. The more you're in his world, the less you'll be in mine." He goes out leaving me alone crying a deluge of tears.

I feel bad for having made him cry, to have disappointed him, for having lied to him. I did not want to make him suffer, he means everything to me. I don't know why all this is happening to us and I don't know what I need to do to save our relationship, even though I was hoping to the very end that there would not be any need to.

Devastated to my very soul, I went to my room. Opposite me is the building with the billboard on top of it.

Do you give up?!

Yes... I surrender.

88.

Isobel watched them quarreling on the balcony of Villa Torres. He was a man now, she a beautiful teenager, both grown, and they would grow some more, but unfortunately she would not be able to see it happen, she could not be beside him. Overcome with emotion, she wiped away the tears and with a thin voice called them from her bed. "I need you to listen to me, my children."

The two children stopped arguing immediately, Jas ran to the grandmother's bed, grasping her hand firmly, while Nick approached slowly. Isobel was even weaker than usual and this hurt him.

"I have made some irreparable mistakes during my life, because of my pride", she explained with difficulty. "I have not spoken with my daughter for twelve years, and nor with my best friend for two decades. Trivial quarrels, useless, nothing that a chat and a hug couldn't repair", a cough interrupted her, the cough that had not given her any respite for days, now. Nickolas handed her a handkerchief as Jas held her hand tight with a worried face.

"Before I leave this lying and corrupt world..."

"Grandma, please, don't talk in this way, you won't go, not yet."

"Of course I will go, Nick, and I can't wait," she said with an annoyed voice, trying to sound tough. Jas and Nick exchanged glances; they didn't know how to react after these words from her.

"I was saying, before I go, I want to have security, the certainty that the misfortunes which happened to me don't also happen to you two."

"Nothing will happen, grandma", Nick sought to reassure her, "We won't let it."

"Be quiet, please", she coughed again. "Nothing will happen because I will stop it from happening. As my last wish before I die I want a promise, a pact that you will make here, in front of me, now."

"What pact, grandma?" asked Jas curious, pushing her blond hair behind her ear.

"Give me the knife", she pointed toward the small crystal table in the center of the room. Nickolas took it to her and without explanation and before the two had time to react, the woman had already made a small cut on their index fingers putting their fingers one above the other.

"That burns!" whimpered Jas looking at the bloodied finger.

"Grandma, I don't understand," said Nick.

"Quiet", she ordered holding their fingers tightly between her hands. "Nickolas, from her eighteenth birthday on, regardless of where you will be, or what you are doing, you'll have to get on a plane and go to her."

"The smell of blood is making me vomit, I don't feel well, grandma", Jas complained Jas holding her nose with the other hand, disgusted.

"Do you want me to get you a glass..." began Nick, addressing Jas.

"That's enough you two! I was speaking! You are very rude!"

"Excuse grandmother, but the blood is making me..." she dared not continue as she saw Isobel's serious and upset face.

"I was explaining to you", she sighed deeply; "that you have to go to her and give her your best wishes personally, do you understand? Personally."

"Alright grandma, but I don't understand the meaning of all this."

"I understand it", broke in Jas but then quickly plugged her mouth, remembering that she could not speak. Isobel smiled and the held her hand even tighter. "You are my pride, Jas, you always have been, little one, I see much of me in you", she whispered and with a nod of the head gave her permission to speak.

"If one day we have a really bad quarrel" Jas explained to him. "And neither one of us wants to take the first step, you will necessarily have to do it for my birthday and that way we can make peace."

"Why is it always me who has to take the first step?"

"Easy, because I refuse to do it, Nick."

479

"Then we can also not make this pact, because in the end I would come to you just the same."

"Instead you will do it, and I want you to also have a physical contact."

"Is it alright if I give him a slap, grandma?" suggested Jas and smiled.

"I have a better idea: you will kiss each other."

"What?" asked Nick, shocked and in complete disagreement, "No!"

"This is my last wish Nick. Is it so hard to carry it out? Can you look me in the eye and tell me that you do not want to do it?"

"Grandma, I didn't mean that, but..."

"A kiss on the lips has never killed anybody. Promise me", she tightened her hand around their fingers.

"I promise you," Jas replied happily, with no problem. Nick looked at her shaking his head and with a less enthusiastic tone said: "I promise you too, grandma."

"Good. Also because, if you don't do it, you will see that only unpleasant things will happen between you, and you will soon regret not having kept the pact with your poor sick grandmother." She coughed again. "Nick, can you go and get me a glass of water please", it sounded more like an order than a request.

"Of course, grandma."

Isobel let go of their fingers, and as soon as Nick went out of the room, took Jas by the hand and looked at her with misty eyes. "Little one, when your eighteenth birthday arrives, Nick will feel uncomfortable, perhaps he will hesitate for a moment, so I ask you please make things easy for him, don't talk too much, but just kiss each other and that's all. I know that it can seem like a stupid request, but one day you will both understand."

"To me it doesn't seem stupid at all," she replied shrugging her shoulders, "but wouldn't Ginevra get angry?" she asked doubtfully, looking at the blood on her finger with a strange air. Isobel smiled.

"Before you come of age, Ginevra will already be out of the picture, little one" she said with the tone of someone who couldn't wait for that to happen. Jas looked at her feeling odd.

"Thank you for everything, Jas. For what you have done for me and Nick from the first moment you came into our lives", she coughed again, she was losing strength, "you are a gift from heaven. Nick loves you so much, little one, and would give his life for you."

"I would too, for him."

"I know. Please, keep him safe, he is strong but at the same time so fragile. Please, protect him..."

***

Today

Nick and his entire team, including America, come out of Ben's office after a two-hour chat about what to do and how better to address the issue with Felix. After the publication of the photos of Jas and Jack together, he has already announced his arrival at the Watchtower.

The guys go to the lobby and find a box on the counter. Ben and Veronica go quickly to it and look inside; Nick picks up the note beside the box.

I didn't want to protect Jack, I wanted to protect you.

He recognizes Jas's handwriting. He looks up and sees the surprised faces of Ben and the others: inside the box there is all the proof necessary to arrest both Jack and his whole family. Glasses, tablecloths, hair, cutlery, all kept in plastic bags. All cataloged by date, with names below, and finally Jas's red diary. Nick opens it; certain pages are missing, which she has torn out.

He closes it pensive. The others look at Nick, agitated and impatient to know what his decision will be.

"Nick, I know that you are friends, but Felix cannot stop you doing it now", Ben hopes to persuade his friend.

Nick, without looking at him, responds in a hard and authoritarian tone. "I want an arrest warrant."

A smile appears on the faces of Ben and Veronica who are eager to take the case back again, while Nick, worried, runs to Jas's bedroom.

The door is open, but there is no trace of her. Ben's voice comes from the lobby. "An arrest warrant for Vladimir, Koki, Lexi and Jack Black, accused of multiple voluntary and intentional homicide, armed robbery, fraud in public deeds, aggravated fraud..."

***

Jas is in the hospital. She is walking down the corridors, still in tears, despondent because of what she has done and for all the consequences that this gesture will bring. Her body feels heavy, her head hurts, she is holding a bottle of vodka and at a slow pace she moves along the corridors of the hospital not giving a damn about anyone and anything.

She sees Arizona in the distance, also with her shoulders curved, head hanging; also in a bad mood. As soon as she sees Jas she stares and goes up to her looking at the bottle of vodka. She stops in front of her dismayed. "It's always difficult to express what you feel in moments like these and it's even more difficult to understand why it happened", she pauses and dries her tears.

Jas looks at her confused; she doesn't understand why she is saying all this. She thinks that perhaps she has read the tabloid newspaper, but why would the chief care if she has betrayed her "boyfriend" or not.

"Diana was very religious and we thought we'd..."

"Was? Why was? What is she now, an atheist?" asks Jas startled. She is afraid to even think about anything bad that concerns Diana. Arizona realizes that the bottle which Jas is holding in her hand is not for Diana and begins to weep upset. "It happened this morning. She had been coughing for several days, her physical condition was worsening and...", before she can finish the sentence, Jas is already running to Diana's room.

She sees Pamela in tears changing the sheets; the interns are putting her pastels in a box. Diana is no longer there and Jas can't take the blow.

Her scream of pain can be heard all over the hospital and with her head in her hands she starts to sob, venting all the sorrow and anger she is feeling inside. Arizona and Pam run to her and hug her tight, as one of Diana's drawings falls off the wall at Jas's feet. On the drawing it's her with her shaven head holding Jas's hand on one side and Jack's on the other, as they walk on a rainbow.

***

Nick's black jeep, sirens blazing, is approaching the Black family's villa. Jack looks out the picture window with his hands in his pockets, serious. Behind him: Cyrus, Vladimir, Lexi and Koki, unsettled.

"Are you sure?" Cyrus asks him yet again.

"Yes."

Jack's response triggers a raging attack from Vladimir who grabs a chair and hurls it against the picture window a few inches from Jack. Then he goes off snarling, but it is a different snarl from usual, it is a snarl of pain. The others remain silent, displeased, as the jeep arrives at the villa.

"Go," says Jack raising his voice, but without turning around.

With heads bent and in clear disagreement with what Jack wants to do, they leave, without saying goodbye to each other. Jack looks at the trashy newspaper on the table that shows him and Jas kissing. Then he turns again to the picture window while Nickolas comes up the stairs to get him. The door opens with a crash. "Jack Black. You are under arrest" he says with the gun toward him.

Meanwhile Ben comes up the stairs in search of the other components of the Black family. Gunfire can be heard and a helicopter taking off and then silence again. Jack turns to Nick, calm. He has no intention of escaping. "You're late, Nickolas", he says with the same calm. Nick recites his rights to him and he smiles, even more when he puts the handcuffs on his wrists.

They leave the villa. Jack raises his head, looks at the gray sky above him and stops. "You've finally managed to get me. Are you happy?" he asks Nick as the first drops of rain begin to fall on his face.

"Where are your accomplices, Jack?" he asks him as he takes him to the jeep.

"There is nobody here," he answers sadly and lowers his head as he gets into the vehicle. "There's just me."

***

Interrogation Room.

Patrick is seated composed on the chair; he is calm and relaxed, while opposite him on the other side of the table Jack is even more calm and relaxed. He still has the handcuffs on his wrists, legs on the table and he is singing the Metallica song *Nothing else matters* as he rocks his chairs.

"Lovely song," says Patrick looking him in the eyes.

"Metallica are the best."

"I don't know if you remember me, we've already met. I have to admit that it has been an honor for me to be given the run around by you."

"Bravo!" says Jack enthusiastically ceasing to rock on the chair. "That's the right spirit Patrick, see the positives and just make a joke of it."

"It's not a matter of seeing the positive side, but to see things for what they are, and not for what they should be."

"Oscar Wilde."

He knows who wrote the phrase that Patrick has just recited.

"He's the best," observes Patrick.

Jack leans on the table looking at him slyly. "And tell me, Patrick, how are the things for what they are, when you look at me? A ruthless murderer, a professional killer, death's assistant... eh?"

"No," he replies and then continues, speaking slowly. "I see a fragile guy, a guy who until recently did not know how to tell the difference between a punch and a caress. A rich boy but terribly poor without the people he loves."

After Patrick's words silence falls. The smile disappears from Jack's face; he lowers his head looking at the handcuffs around his wrists.

"Right now, though", he continues, "I see a boy alone, closed in a cold room with a stranger, no friends, no family, no girlfriend, betrayed by everyone. You have no-one left any more. They have abandoned you to your fate. How does it feel?"

Jack's eyes are tearful. He looks at the mirror behind Patrick; he knows that Nick and the others in the team are watching the interrogation. Then he looks Patrick straight in the eye without hiding the sadness and suffering that he is feeling at this moment, as a tear runs down his face. Even the Watchtower team is not indifferent to his pain, when suddenly Patrick starts to applaud. The sound echoes through the room. He shows the hint of a smile looking Jack straight in the eye. On the other side of the mirror the guys look at each other edgy.

"Jack, what I see is what it should be. It's what you want me to see. Why not stop acting and tell me how things really are?"

Jack's devastated expression turns into a smile, his blue eyes get small and he starts to swing on the chair again. "You're great! You're wasted here, why don't you come and work for us?"

"I'm fine where I am."

"Really?" he smiles and looks toward the mirror for a moment, then turns back toward Patrick. "Have you ever read *Macbeth*?"

"Yes, I have read it."

"In that book good appears only in vendetta", he pauses and smiles, "eight years have passed. Eight years of pursuits, investigations, interceptions, and nothing. Doesn't that seem strange to you, Patrick?" he looks at him, he knows that he is hitting where it hurts. He is talking about a matter that none of his team ever dares take up with him. "To see her agonize in your arms and not be able to do anything to save her must have left a great mark on you, Patrick. Where do you find the strength to go forward knowing that he is still free somewhere out there?" he continues. "When I met him a few months ago he told me that he chose Emily as a hostage just because she was the prettiest."

Patrick snaps up from the chair and rests his hands on the table in front of Jack. He stares at him with wide-open eyes, angry, and starts to breathe deeply.

"Yes, Patrick, I know who you're looking for and know where to find him." Jack also stands up from the chair. "Join us, I will tell you where he is. And once you have him in your hands, no one is going to try to stop you while you open him in half."

The door is flung open and Nick enters the room, angry and worried at the same time.

485

"Something you cannot do with the fairy godmother of justice at your side", says Jack referring to Nick.

"Are you okay?" asks Nick approaching Patrick and putting a hand on his shoulder.

"Yes."

Patrick's *yes* is not the most convincing. He looks at Jack again and goes from the room without saying anything, but before closing the door behind him he hears him say: "Think about it, Patrick."

Nickolas sits opposite him, shocked by what he has just heard. He can't help asking himself how Jas can like a person as bad and rude as Jack. But he's there for work, not for personal matters, so he opens the file, while Jack continues to swing on the chair." The cuffs you've put on my wrists are ugly and are too tight for me, I want the complaint form."

"You're calm and smiling for someone who is risking life imprisonment."

"What life imprisonment? I have faith in the justice system", he continues to mock him.

"Where are your accomplices?"

"By accomplices do you also mean Jas?"

"She has never been an accomplice of yours", Nick immediately makes clear. "She is your victim. She has been from the start."

"That's exactly the difference between me and you, Nickolas. You see her as a victim the whole time, as someone weak, a little girl who does not know how to protect herself, but she's not like that. She is not a victim, she's a survivor." He sits up straight on the chair. "If she falls she knows very well how to pick herself up, just as she knows how to make her own choices. She is an adult now and she no longer needs you and your advice. Get used to it.", he says with a sure and arrogant tone of voice, but Nick doesn't turn a hair.

"I've read all the nonsense that you've told her. You have filled her head with scare stories, corruption, manipulation, murderers... you don't realize what disastrous consequences your stories could have on her."

"How can my words hurt her? It's not the knowing that hurts, but ignorance. Do you have the courage to tell me that everything I have said is not true?"

"I don't deny that there have been cases where..."

"Cases?" he interrupts him abruptly. "There have been cases in the small states like Slovenia where she was born, but not here! Here we are talking about constant injustice!"

"And you're the one who will bring justice to the world, Jack? And how? Killing and putting people to death yourself? And what if those people were innocent?"

"They are not."

"And what if some madman wanted to imitate your gestures? Do justice by himself? What would happen, Jack?"

"It won't happen. That's the reason nobody knows about us."

"Knew, that no-one *knew* about you, you mean", he corrects him.

"No, I wanted to say exactly what I said. And when I do something it's because I know that it's right to do it. And Jas shares my opinion."

"If she takes your stories too seriously and something happens to her because of you, I will hold you directly responsible."

"The only thing that will happen, Nickolas, is that Jas will pack her bags and come away with me."

"You're not going anywhere", he says without an ounce of concern. "You're here thanks to her."

"I am here because I chose to be here. And I'll be with Jas because she has chosen to be with me", Jack continues to provoke.

Nick closes the file in front of him and gets up. "Maybe you've managed to upset Patrick by touching his weaknesses in a cold and disrespectful way, but you'll never do it with me. Jas has already made her choice, I have faith in her and I know she won't disappoint me."

"Cursed bastard!" he screams infuriated banging his hands on the table. "You're ruining her, can't you see? For years she has thought she has a split personality because of you", he stands up agitated.

Ben enters the room. He grips his arm as he continues to scream at Nick. "And it's not like that at all; she does not have two personalities. She has only one, which is great, but she has to hide it because she does not want to disappoint you, you son of a bitch!" he offends in no uncertain terms. "She is afraid. I look at her and I see she is terrified that you might see who she really is, because the more time that passes the less you like what she is becoming!"

"Ben, take him away", says Nick quietly and calmly, but Jack, despite being handcuffed, agile as he is, jumps onto the table and then onto the ground placing himself a couple of inches from Nick's face.

"Jas has always wanted more from life and she has always acted on instinct, breaking your damned rules, always. The truth is that she is much more like me than you'd care to admit. And if you despise me, deep down you also despise Jas. And she knows this."

"You'll never put us one against the other, Jack", he says with conviction, without moving an inch.

Ben takes Jack by the arm.

"I'm not trying to separate you from her, you're doing that very well by yourself."

The door opens suddenly and Veronica enters agitated. "Nick! We have a problem. The evidence has disappeared from the archive. The DNA tests, the analyses, the recordings... there's nothing left. The box has disappeared!"

Jack smiles and turns toward Nick. "Oops", he says shrugging his shoulders.

"How is that possible? When did you realize it had happened?" Nick asks shocked. He starts toward the door and finds Felix in front of him. He opens his eyes surprised. "Felix?"

The man looks first at Jack, then the others, but says nothing.

"I would have let you know as soon as I found a spare minute", Nick begins to justify himself. "I know, you told me to stay away from the case, but it was Jas who gave us the evidence that..."

"We need to talk" interrupts the man with an irritated voice.

"Ooh, you've upset granddad, Nickolas", intervenes Jack.

"That's enough!" Felix raises his voice annoyed. "Take off the handcuffs."

"What?" Veronica says in surprise.

"What are you saying, Felix?" asks Nick.

"Wait for me outside, Jack."

"Well goodbye then, Nickolas. And congratulations on the uniform, it looks great on you," he jokes and goes out with a smile.

"Ben! Don't take your eyes off him! He must not leave here, is that clear?"

"Don't worry, Nick!"

Both Ben and Veronica, still in shock, leave closing the door behind them.

Felix starts walking up and down the room, unhappy. Nick stares at him with his arms crossed. He is about to explode. "I did everything I could to stop this day arriving."

"What are you talking about, Felix? What does all this mean?"

"It's not in my nature to beat around the bush, so I'll tell you everything in one breath", he leans on the table with his head down. "Everything that you read in Jas's diary is true."

"How do you know about the diary?"

"Jack Black", he continues to talk ignoring his question, "is one of the rare members of the CIA's secret organization called *The Nobodies*. Their task is to be everywhere, but not be anywhere. They intervene only where the situation requires it, where justice loses all meaning or becomes synonymous with conspiracy. They say that they maintain the balance in the world."

"Are you serious?" he asks shocked. "How long have you known this?"

"I've known for forty years, Nickolas", he whispers unhappily.

"What?"

"I haven't told you before this, not because it's about the CIA, but because I gave my word to the founder of *The Nobodies* that I would have protected you as long as I could. I want you to know that..."

"Who is he?" interrupts Nick approaching him threateningly. "Who is the founder?"

"Nick."

"Felix, tell me!"

The man passes his hands over his face and with bright eyes just pronounces a name. "Isobel."

***

489

Diana's many drawings are attached to the walls of the room.

On the bed is the man in a coma, still without identity, and on the ground near the bed is Jas, sleeping huddled with the empty bottle of vodka in her hand. The parrot Metoo walks around her, worried, he sees that his friend is not well; she doesn't rebuke him when he pulls at her hair, nor does she want to play with the red ball with him.

He goes near her face again and caresses it with his little gray head. He squawks in her ear.

"Hey, little guy", whispers Jas. She is very drunk; she can't keep her eyes open. She looks at the parrot for a while and says in a low voice: "I love you".

"Meeetooo", he begins to scream close to her ear and opens his wings, happy that Jas has spoken.

She moves the bottle of vodka, sits up on the floor and looks around. For a little while she looks at Diana's drawings hanging on the wall. On one there is God who is returning money to her that he owed her; in another Diana and Jas hiding the parrot from Arizona; in yet another, Diana with her parents.

Jas's eyes fill with years again. Metoo takes flight and lands on her shoulder. Once again he caresses her face with his little head and, when he sees the tears roll down her face, starts to repeat nervously: "Noo. No. No. No. No. Noooo..."

"I am so... sad." She can hardly speak. The alcohol prevents her from formulating sentences longer than this. "I want to go back... home."

She hears the door of the room close. She gets up slowly, too drunk to do otherwise. She looks toward the door but there's nobody there. She closes her eyes for a moment, tired, sad. She gets to her feet leaning on the bed and lies down close to her Zombie. The parrot follows her bringing the red ball.

"I really wish you would wake up" she says looking at the old man in a coma, "that you spoke to me and told me where to put myself and what should I do." She takes a deep breath. "I wanted to know Nick and Jack's world so much that I ended up destroying both of them. I also destroyed my own. I want my Mina."

Metoo tries to console her by bringing her his favorite toy, the red ball. She caresses him.

89.

At the same time – From Jas's diary

I caress him, and suddenly feel my fingers wet. I look at them and I see that are dirty with blood. I sit up quickly on the bed looking at Metoo worried, and notice with a fright that his eyes are bleeding.

Gripped by panic and with my head that won't stop spinning, I take him in my arms and began to clean him, trying to understand why he is bleeding. What's wrong? He seemed to be fine, in spite of everything. I rest him on the bed when I see with terror that even my Zombie is losing blood from his eyes, nose and ears. Just the nauseating smell of blood is making my stomach turn. I don't understand. Why are they both bleeding? But suddenly everything becomes clear: Boris! He has found what he was looking for and he has killed him with the same poison that he used with Jack. He could have poisoned me too, but fortunately he did not see me because I was lying under the bed. Shocked, I run outside to seek help, I call Arizona and Pamela, they can help them.

"Jas! What's happening?" Arizona asks me worried as she runs toward me.

"The old man in a coma is sick, he's bleeding! And the parrot as well, you must help them! They've been poisoned with the Boomslang, a snake, it's poisonous." I try to give her a brief summary. I realize that I'm talking confused but I'm unable to do any differently at this moment.

"The parrot? Poisoned?" she repeats disconcerted and worried. We start running toward Zombie's room, but before we get there I see two familiar figures getting into the elevator. Boris and the Russian! So he is still alive? Vladimir didn't kill him! I leave Arizona and run to the stairs to try to catch up to them, enough dead people, enough injustice! He might have diplomatic immunity, but now I have had enough. I'll be the one to stop him!

I hardly make it to the basement, my head is still spinning, my step is precarious. I see them climb into a black van, similar to the one Lexi was in when she came to pick me up a few days ago. What do I do now? How do I stop those bastards?

As I run behind their van I see a yellow Ferrari with a red license plate parked near the sidewalk. And Lexi's words come back to me when she said that all the cars with a red license plate were theirs. I run across to the other side of the road, pick up a huge stone under a palm tree and launch it at the car window!

90.

Two minutes before – From Jx's diary

After hearing Jas call out to her, Arizona runs to the room where the man in a coma is lying. Very concerned she flings open the door, goes in and stares wide-eyed. To her enormous astonishment she finds the man in his bed, motionless, but above all looking to be in good health.

There is no trace of the blood Jas was talking about, even the parrot isn't there, but something is there, something much more terrifying: an empty bottle of vodka on the floor with a half empty container of *Vicodin* on the bed.

"Oh my God! No!" she takes the container and goes quickly from the room in search of Jas. But she is longer there.

***

In the meantime

"You didn't tell me a thing! You used my sense of gratitude to manipulate me!" yells Nick slamming his hand on the table.

"I had to do it! I promised Isobel, she knew that you would never have understood..."

"Understand? Go around killing people! But who does he think he is?" he asks furious, "Everyone is entitled to have a legal process! This is barbaric and I can't believe that my grandmother Isobel was the twisted mind behind all this! She created a clan of assassins." Nick continues to raise his voice.

In the other room, behind the mirror, his entire team is listening to the argument, totally incredulous and in shock at the discovery that Isobel worked for the CIA.

Patrick finally learns that the spy Jas spoke about is Felix; he was the one who told Jack about the dwarfs and all the rest, while Veronica lowers her head, overcome by feelings of guilt; without knowing it she provided a lot of information that helped Felix protect the Black family.

"Nickolas, let me explain, I beg you! I knew, it's true, but I never shared the choice she made! I work for the FBI, she worked for the CIA, it was complicated. I couldn't arrest her, but I couldn't watch what she was doing either, that's why I left! I haven't spoken with her for more than twenty years! I have protected the Blacks, that's true, but she asked me to do that before she died! Please, believe me. I am not their accomplice. I am on your side."

"No! It's not true!"

"Nick," sighs Felix vainly trying to make him reason.

"I trusted you!"

"I wanted to tell you everything, about Isobel, about *The Nobodies*, I really wanted to. But at the right time and in the right way! I just wanted to protect you!"

"Protect me? From what? From the truth? I wanted to know! I..." and at that moment something clicks inside his head. He stops breathing and all he can say with terror is: "Oh my God, Jas." he turns to Felix who continues to look at him mortified. "What does she know? What does she know, Felix?"

The man doesn't reply, he doesn't have the courage. Nick takes the note that Jas wrote to him from his pocket and reads it again.

I didn't want to protect Jack, wanted to protect you.

He crushes the note in his hands, he realizes what has happened.

"That was why I wanted to send her away from here, Nick; if she had gone back to Slovenia, Jack would not have searched for her any more, that was the agreement..."

But Nick doesn't listen to him; he opens the door and goes into the hallway. The rest of his team comes out of the other room, their gazes are unmistakable, sorry for Nick, shocked at what they have learned and angry with Felix.

Nick enters the other room furious, where Jack is sitting behind the table with the handcuffs still on his wrists. He grasps his arm roughly. "What does Jas know? Did you tell her about Isobel and Felix? Did you tell her?"

"Everything", he answers with a smile, "from yesterday evening she and I have no more secrets."

The two men look into each other's eyes, except one has the gaze of a winner and the other full of remorse and guilt. He lets him go pushing him against the chair and goes out into the hallway.

"Nick, please, let's sit down and..." tries Felix.

"If I don't quit speaking to you," he interrupts him, "it's only because you saved my life twelve years ago, not letting me drown along with my parents! But that's also all you will have from me after stabbing me in the back!"

"Guys", America's voice comes from the end of the corridor, "we have a problem."

"Not now," says Ben trying to make her realize that it's not the right time.

"But it's serious!" insists the woman.

"Call us when it becomes very serious", Ben cuts her short.

America crosses her arms and, annoyed, says in one breath: "They called from the hospital; Jas has escaped into the street, drunk, and drugged, in a state of confusion and most likely is hallucinating! Is that serious enough for you, sir?"

"What?" Nick goes to her with eyes staring, the boys follow him.

"It seems she launched an alert saying that a man in a coma was bleeding because he'd been bitten by a snake called Boomslang", she reads from her notes. Jack's face turns serious in an instant, but Nick continues to not understand.

"Man in a coma? Boomslang? What are you talking about? America, call the hospital chief now! Will, track down Jas via the GPS in her bracelet, Veronica..."

"Yes, I know," says the girl and goes off quickly still with her head down.

"But what is happening, I don't understand?" Nick, miserable, runs his hands through his hair. Ben looks inside the room where Jack had been sitting earlier and asks terrified: "Where's Jack?"

The only sound is the door slamming at the end of the corridor. All that remains of Jack are the handcuffs thrown on the ground.

91.

I see the van stop at the gas station. I stop too, but at a safe distance. I don't know what to do, how to act, the only thing I know is that I don't want to lose sight of them. The Russian is filling up the tank; he looks around suspiciously, while Boris is sitting on the front seat. All I can see is his hair. I push the yellow button of the manual gearbox like I saw Lexi do; the CD player opens and I see the two guns inside: one loaded with sedatives, the other with real bullets.

I take them. I feel a strange sensation inside of me. I rest my head on the back of the seat and begin to take deep breaths of the air coming through the broken window. What on earth am I doing? Drunk, full of *Vicodin,* with a stolen car, armed and chasing criminals...

I hear the engine of the van start; right now I don't have time to think about what is right and what is wrong, I'll think about that later. I will think about it the day before the day after.

I take off too and start following them again. At the beginning I drive slowly, trying to mingle with the other cars, but shortly after the black van accelerates, and starts to go faster. I'm struggling to keep up, given my own physical conditions.

They have poisoned my grandfather. They have poisoned my parrot. Someone must stop these criminals. I drive faster, I decide to get behind them and then we'll see. I am about to overtake a white car when another gray car comes alongside mine. The tinted window is lowered and Jack's blond head pokes out. "What was the first rule?" he screams at me enraged, "Do. Not. Touch. My. Car!"

"Jack! Oh my God, Jack! How are you? You're angry with me? And Nick?" I don't even know which question to ask first.

"And what was the second rule?"

"What?" I ask confused, "There wasn't a second rule."

"Right! Well done! There was only one rule, ONE! And you have broken it!"

"Jack, stop it! I need the antidote!" I yell to him out of the window. He looks at me angrily while I, on the other hand, am so happy to see him. "Boris has found the old man."

"Stop immediately!" he orders me. "You must get out of my car!"

"Jack! But do you listen to me when I speak?"

"Is the window broken? The window of my Ferrari 458 Italia Spyder convertible is broken!"

Now I've had enough! I turn the steering wheel to my left bumping into him and purposely damaging both the cars.

"Nooooo! What are you doing, woman! My... aaahhhhhhh!"

"Will you listen to me now or not? Fuck!" And as I thump my hands on the steering wheel in rage the sunroof of the car opens. "Jack! I'm telling you that Boris has found the old man! He has poisoned him!"

"Which old man?"

"The old man of the airport you were looking for! He found him in hospital and has poisoned him! I need the antidote!"

"What? No, Jas, no! It's not possible!"

"Yes it is, I'm telling you! I want you to stop him!! But without killing him!"

"But who?"

"Fuck, what are you, stupid? See the black van?" all agitated I gesture at the van in front of us where you can clearly see Boris and the Russian. "The Russian isn't dead! You must stop them!"

92.

At the same time – From Jx's diary

Jack looks in front of him, but doesn't see any black van on the road. Boris isn't there and the Russian can't be because he was killed. He turns to Jas, who continues to ask him for help, she's worried with eyes staring. Jack turns pales in an instant. He realizes that there *really* is something wrong and that she's not putting on an act.

"Jas, pull over", he says in a serious tone, but careful not to frighten her.

"Okay, but don't lose sight of it. Okay?"

"Alright. But now, darling, please pull over."

"Okay!" Jas puts on the indicator and pulls to the side of the road. When she sees Jack stop too, a few meters from her, she gets out of the car, confused, and runs to him screaming. "What are you doing? You have to go after them! You'll lose sight of them like this, Jack!"

"Darling, come here." He holds her tight in his arms. "Everything will be fine."

"But... have you let the others know? Will they get them?"

"Jas, did you start on Vicodin again?" he asks without replying to her questions. She is disconcerted for a moment.

"What does that have to do with anything right now?" She strikes him, incensed by his question and the fact that he is still there.

"You said you'd stopped. You said..."

"Jack! There's no time for this bullshit! You must warn your brothers! You need to tell them to... to get him!"

"Yes, I've warned them, I've warned them, okay. But now, please, answer me."

Jas breaks away from his embrace. She doesn't like the way he's holding her, she doesn't like the tone of voice he's using to speak to her and she doesn't like the way he's looking at her either. She feels that he is lying. She steps back.

"Jas, like I said, don't worry, my brothers will take care of Boris, but now you come with me, please."

"You promised you would never lie to me ever again!" she yells angrily at him. "You promised me, Jack!"

"Sweetheart", worried, Jack grabs her by the arm. "You have to trust me. I'll explain everything along the way."

"You're a bastard!" she screams, disappointed and angry, letting fly a couple of punches and knees him in the lower parts, then runs toward the car leaving him bent to the ground in pain.

Cursing, Jack tries to get back on his feet to reach Jas and stop her, but she's now already going out onto the road with his car. "Jas, stop!"

She passes in front of him with the sports car. Jack can see a lot of anger and resentment in her eyes, a lot of pain. He is getting up to go toward his car when he sees Jas point the gun at his tires and fire.

"Nooooo! Fuck! Damn you!"

Jas goes off in pursuit of her imaginary van, as Jack kneels desperate beside the punctured tires and realizes that they have been hit by the tranquilizer darts. "She shot a tranquilizer at the tires? She has put them to sleep!" He puts his hands in his hair, and swearing, takes the mobile phone. "Cyrus! I need help! I want the whole team here!"

***

Jas is driving as fast as she can. She is sad and disappointed because Jack has tried to trick her. Particularly disappointed to discover he continues to lie to her. The road becomes busier with more traffic, but she is still able to see the van in the distance. Her driving is becoming more and more daring: she weaves between one car and another, often risking losing control of the vehicle and causing an accident.

A white motorbike appears behind her.

"Jas! What the hell are you doing, do you want to kill yourself? Slow down!"

"Veronica", Jas murmurs annoyed. She bawls from the car window. "I see you have transformed your broom into a bike."

"Stop immediately! You don't even have a driver's license! Have you gone mad?!"

"You'd like that wouldn't you?" she gets even angrier hearing herself constantly being called crazy, and presses on the accelerator, overtaking the bike.

Veronica, unable to do anything else, talks into the headset. "Dammit! Will, can you hear me?"

"Yes."

"We are approaching a crossroads. How long before the red?"

"E-eleven seconds!" responds Will readily.

"Good! Warn Nick that when Jas stops at the traffic lights I'm going to slap her. She has almost had three accidents in less than a minute! Spoilt drunken little girl that she is..."

Jas, meanwhile, sees the black van cross the intersection. She accelerates, she doesn't want to lose sight of it. Before she is able to reach it, the lights turn red but she has no intention of slowing down.

"No! Jas, no! Don't do it, you'll end up killing yourself!" screams Veronica trying in vain to reach her and prevent her from doing something ridiculous, but it is too late.

Jas doesn't take her foot off the accelerator and runs through the red, narrowly avoiding impact with the other vehicles without even realizing it. And as she goes forward along the road, there is chaos happening behind her. More than fifteen cars, in order to avoid her, are involved in a chain collision.

Flames, smoke. Veronica, still standing at the traffic lights, looks on all that's happening appalled, as does agent Christoph Waltz, who has seen the whole thing from the other side of the intersection.

"Will," Veronica calls again.

"I kn-knooow", he answers shocked. He has seen everything too, on the road safety video-cameras.

"Call an ambulance! I'll stay here to give first aid to the wounded! Where is Nick?"

"He is a-approaching from the other side of the bri-bridge."

"Contact him immediately. And tell him that Jas is totally out of control."

Will is in his usual position: sitting on the torn red chair behind several monitors and computers from where he monitors the traffic, traffic lights, and all the movements that his colleagues are making, Jas included.

In the meantime, in the lobby of the Watchtower, America and Ben's sons are watching TV and listening to the radio, completely shocked.

"Will, a helicopter is following Jas. They are filming her with the cameras, but they don't know yet who the mad person at the wheel is", America informs him through the headset.

"Roger", he says as he too tunes into the police radio. The voice of agent Waltz reaches him immediately. *"This is agent Christoph Waltz. This unit is following the vehicle, I'm asking for assistance. I repeat."*

"Ben!" he calls, still into the headset.

"I'm listening, Will", Ben responds promptly.

"Waltz is following Jas. He has asked for assistance and asked for checkpoints on the bridge."

"Damn!"

Ben, driving his jeep, is hurtling along at a hundred and fifty miles an hour. He turns toward Felix sitting beside him, still mortified by what has happened. Ben knows that he is perhaps the only one who will be able to keep Christoph under control.

"I'll take care of agent Waltz. Tell Nick to hurry up!" says Felix, as if he had read his mind.

In the meantime, Patrick is in the Watchtower, in his bedroom, agitated and pensive after hearing Jack's words. He doesn't know what to do. He needs time to reflect. He must know. But he also knows that in this moment Jas needs his help, so he decides to put aside his thirst for revenge for now and help his team. He brushes the tears from his eyes, gets off the bed and heads straight toward Jas's room. The door is open. He is looking for something; he just has to understand what and where to find it. Mina's side, clean and tidy, or Jas's half in a huge mess.

But this is not the place to look, too obvious and exposed, he knows her well now. Memories spring back to his mind, the small details that hide a big meaning.

Jas isn't here. She has been in the bathroom for three hours! How many times has he heard Mina say this in the last few months?

He opens the bathroom door. It's clean and tidy. On one side is Mina's sink, on the other side there's Jas's. He looks around, touches the body wash, the toothbrush, the towels. He opens Jas's medicine cabinet. Inside only towels and creams. He kneels down to take a better look, and then, with his hand, knocks on the bottom of the cabinet. He discovers a false floor.

He opens it and is aghast: *Vicodin*, various vials of who knows what medicines, bags of drips, needles... his eyes widen and he covers his face with his hand.

How hadn't he noticed before that she was still doing *Vicodin*? How had Jas managed to dupe him? Another hard blow hits him: Jas's words begin to resound in his head.

Everything I know you taught me, Patrick.

***

Mina is at home, in Italy. She is walking up and down the room while her mother, her toy boy Luca, and the new German roommate are sitting around the dining room table with heads bent.

"And I don't care if you thought that I'd be back in September, October or November. This house is mine and I can come back when I want," she yells at her mother. "So I'm giving you ten minutes to clear my room of everything that is not mine, clean it and polish it, after which we'll talk about the hygiene of the house, the roster for the bathroom and the division of the food that's in the refrigerator! I'd had enough! You follow the rules and if you don't like it get out! And from next month onwards the maintenance check that my father sends you, you'll give it to me. Is that clear? That's *my* money and I'll do what the hell I want to with it!"

They all look at her shocked and don't dare open their mouth. The German doesn't understand anything and looks around saying *Ja* shaking his head.

502

"What are you still doing here? Quick, move it!"

They jump up from their chairs run to empty her bedroom that in recent months has been rented to the German.

Mina slips off her high heels, lies down on the couch and turns on the TV. She feels tired, angry with her mother and she can't wait to go to bed. She presses the keys on the remote control at random, shakes her head when she sees that she's watching a TV from the '80s in black and white, given that they broke the other.

She looks towards the door and shouts, "And I expect you to buy the plasma TV for me again!"

The frightened voices of the three can be heard coming from the bedroom as they quarrel with each other and accuse each other of wrongdoings.

Mina continues to change channels. It's a strange thing for her, after more than four months, to watch the Italian programs again. Suddenly the news draws her attention. The journalist is speaking about a pursuit, there are two helicopters flying overhead filming a Ferrari, the police are chasing it. A link shows the road accidents caused by this blond girl without any identity.

A word captures her attention: *Miami*.

She opens her eyes wide and turns up the volume on the TV. She has a strange presentiment. The Ferrari is crossing a bridge when it stops abruptly, it can't continue because there is a road block on the other side. It can't make a U-turn because the police cars are close behind, also blocking that escape route.

The situation is tense. Nobody goes close to the vehicle. When suddenly the door opens, the blond girl gets out and turns toward the helicopter with a gun in her hand.

Mina gets up from the sofa completely in shock. "Oh fucking he.."

93.

I am surrounded, unjustly! Boris and the Russian are inside the black van in front of me, two criminals that kill as if it's normal and all the cops are looking at me? I can't believe it! Jack was right, they are all corrupt. They know who is in that van, they can see them, and yet they pretend not to only because Boris has diplomatic immunity.

I take the gun and get out of the car. Everything is focused on me: the weapons of the policemen, the lenses of the video-cameras and the journalists' cameras. I point my gun at the black van. I go a little closer. Boris looks at me and smiles with a satisfied look on his face. I don't know if he has recognized me, nor if he knows that the police are following me and not him, but from his expression you can see that he's not worried.

"It's Agent Christoph Waltz speaking. I order you to throw down that weapon slowly and put your hands up," Waltz says into the loudspeaker, but I don't have time to listen to him.

I go even closer to the van shouting: "Come out you bastards!"

Boris and the Russian continue to stare at me with that mocking smile on their lips, I can't tolerate it. "Come out!" I repeat but they do not seem to be afraid of me.

I feel everyone's eyes on me, more and more horrified.

My head begins to spin and I have blurred vision. The door of the van opens and the pair get out armed to the teeth. I instinctively step back, I didn't expect this, and the police instead of pointing their weapons at Boris, who is pointing a machine gun at me, are still concentrating on me, talking to me with the loudspeaker, trying to convince me to throw my little pistol to the ground.

"Are you blind?! Don't you see?'! They're the bad guys! You should arrest the two of them not me, I don't want to harm anyone, for fuck's sake!"

"I have diplomatic immunity," says Boris. "You don't. And even if I'm arrested, in a few hours I'd already be out looking for you and your family", he threatens me, laughing, I can't tolerate it.

I look around me disoriented. I don't understand. The journalists are taking pictures only of me, they're only filming me. I don't understand, I do not understand.

Boris and the Russian approach, laughing. They're weird, like drug addicts, I don't have the courage to shoot, but not even to flee. I go further backwards.

"Put down that weapon and put your hands where I can see them. This is the last warning!" screams Waltz again. I feel trapped.

"Stop! Don't shoot! Don't shoot", I hear a familiar voice. I turn and see my Nick. My Nick. He rushes up to me looking worried, while telling the others not to shoot or get closer to me. I am still clasping the gun, pointed at Boris and the Russian, but I know now that Nick will resolve everything. Nick will arrest them. He stops a few feet away from me, ignoring Boris who is smiling even more behind him. "Jas, I'm here. I'm here!" He raises his hands and approaches as if to reassure me that he does not want to hurt me and looks at me worried. He comes closer to me like you do with someone who is off their head. I don't like it, I don't like this gaze of his, no, I don't like it. "Why are you looking at me in that way?! Don't look at me like that!"

"Please. Give me... give me the gun, Jas", he asks me again with that irritating tone, while Boris laughs behind him and makes fun of me by repeating what Nick said a few months ago: *Jas has some unresolved problems..."*

"Shut up!" I scream at Boris, but he doesn't listen to me. "They poisoned my old man and the parrot, they are armed, they want to kill me!" I try to explain to Nick, even if the situation is more than evident.

"Who? Who wants to kill you, Jas?"

"Them! Don-don't you see?! What are you, are you blind too?! He has poisoned my Zombie!"

Nick looks over his shoulder and then looks at me worried. "Jas, if they're pointing their guns at you it's because you're holding one in your hand. So please, give it to me, give me the gun and you'll see that we'll work everything out," his hand is outstretched and his face is very worried. He wants my gun, not giving a damn about Boris and the Russian who are making fun of me behind him and pointing their weapons at me. "Jas, please..."

"No! I won't give it to you until you disarm Boris and the Russian!"

94.

Jas trembles, she points the gun at someone behind Nick.

He turns slowly, again. There is no one there except a couple of cars abandoned by citizens who have fled in fear, and Jas's yellow Ferrari, the policemen in the distance, also armed, and many untimely journalists with their gazed fixed on them from afar.

Jas continues to point the gun scared. Nick's expression, from concerned becomes terrified: he realizes that she has really intense hallucinations. He doesn't dare move closer to her so as not to bother her, when suddenly he sees Jack jumping along the roofs of the cars in the midst of the crowd, until he reaches the police, then do a somersault in the air and stop at a few yards from her.

"Jas! My love!"

She doesn't greet him or look at him. She tightens the gun in her hands and scrutinizes every movement that comes from Boris and the Russian who, in her head, are walking up and down behind Nick laughing and making fun of her.

"Get out of here!" Nick says to him through clenched teeth.

"And if I don't? Will you shoot me?" answers Jack, addressing him provokingly.

But it's Jas who shoots, at her imaginary enemies, hitting the Ferrari; and in doing so she frightens everyone around. Jack stares at her and mouths *my car* without any sound coming from his lips.

"No!" Nick screams to the agents. "Don't shoot, no! She hasn't hurt anybody!" He tries to prevent the intervention of the marksmen, as Ben and Veronica appear among the crowd. They speak with the police, explaining to them that Nick will deal with the situation.

"They wanted to take you out, Nick!" cries Jas, more and more frightened and nervous. "They wanted to shoot you! Jack, tell him about Boris. You know him. Tell him about the man from the airport!"

Nick looks at him, hoping that he can explain where the hallucinations are coming from.

"My love, listen to me", Jack tries to reason with her, ignoring Nick. "The man that Boris is searching for is not your friend in a coma in the hospital, he has nothing to do with it. He is all right. You're having hallucinations."

"What?! Keep back! Stay back," Jas shouts, still talking to Boris.

"Oh, fuck!" exclaims Jack.

"Which man are you talking about, Jack? Who are all these people?"

"It's not true! You're all liars!" Jas continues to respond to Boris' provocations which are in her head.

"I told her... I took her to Boris and I have..."Jack fails to finish the sentence, perhaps only now he actually realizes that Nick was right and everything that he told her was perhaps too much for her. He runs his hands through his hair.

"Boris *who,* Jack*?!*" Nick yells at him. Then he seems to realize. "Don't tell me that..." he pauses, terrified. "Tell me that you haven't done this, I beg you. Tell me that it's not the Boris I think, Jack!"

Jack doesn't reply. He looks at his Jas, disoriented, frightened, as she continues to retreat further and further getting dangerously close to the parapet of the bridge. He feels terribly guilty for everything that is happening.

"Stop it! Stop it! It's not true! Nick is not corrupt, he's not! Stay back!" Jas keeps screaming and presses the trigger, but this time she hits an agent who falls to the ground wounded.

This is enough for pandemonium to explode.

"Noooo!" Nick says and stands there petrified for a moment. The flashing lights, Waltz approaching them, journalists running away frightened, the helicopters flying overhead recording everything and his Jas, frightened and terribly alone, with the gun in her hand.

He suddenly recovers from the shock; he must react and manage the situation. "Will! Code nine," he says into the headset, and then turns toward Jack who has already pointed his gun at Waltz, intending to shoot at him if he gets even one step closer to Jas.

"Don't even try it, Jack!" Nick intimates.

Jack stops, and without objecting lowers his gaze and the weapon, when another shot comes from the gun Jas is holding. This time in the air. "This is my last warning and then I swear that I'll plant a bullet in your head", she says threateningly "looking" at Boris.

"Waltz", Felix's voice comes from a megaphone in the middle of the crowd. "It's Felix, wait two more minutes then you're free to intervene if necessary."

Waltz does not seem to agree with his decision, but because of the respect and high esteem that he has for Felix, he stops.

"Jas, listen to me", Nick speaks to her, but she does not seem to listen to him. "Jas, can you hear me?"

Still no reaction. He approaches her slowly so he can remove the weapon from her hands, but she immediately turns toward him, pointing the gun at him. "Move away or I'll kill you! I swear I will!"

At this point she doesn't recognize even Nick.

The situation is degenerating. Nick moves a couple of steps back and then kneels down looking her in the eyes; around them the sirens stop, the two helicopters depart, the journalists are silent. Will is implementing code nine.

"Jas", he says in a broken voice, "if you cannot hear me, I hope you can at least hear this", he tears the necklace from his neck and opens the compass. Across the entire bridge sweet melody of the song *Bang Bang* can be heard, coming from the pendant which Jas gave him for his birthday almost a year ago.

Something inside her changes; she closes her eyes for a moment and when she opens them again she sees Nick kneeling in front of her, with tears in his eyes and the compass in his hand.

Jas is breathless, she looks at the necklace and listens to it play in silence. In silence like everyone around them, including Jack.

"Nick", she says scared.

"Jas, do you trust me?"

"Yes, I trust you blindly."

"Then give me that weapon, please", tears fall down his face. "I beg you."

"They will kill us." She turns to Boris again, terrified. "They will kill you, Nick. How will I be able to live without you? Boris will kill us, and he has diplomatic immunity, and they are all corrupt and he will be free, judicial error!" She is confused and disconnected. Nick is trembling.

"They are all corrupt, tell them, Jack! Where is Jack? He has run away again! He is a liar, he lied to me!"

Jack is there a few steps away from her, but it is as though he's not there. His eyes are shining. He is impotent in front of what he himself has created. He turns his head to the other side clenching his fists without reacting.

"They won't kill you, trust me, I beg you."

"I am not afraid to die. I'm afraid to live without you, Nick", her lips tremble. Nick is still kneeling in front of her. He is trembling too. "Jas, despite what you see, despite what you feel, despite the pain and disappointment that I'm causing you at this moment, I beg you. Trust me."

She bursts into tears, desperate. In her head she knows that if she lets go of that weapon, Boris and the Russian will shoot at both of them. Nick is weeping as he looks at her helpless. And then, Jas puts the gun on the ground, slowly, her hand is shaking, she closes her eyes, she knows that she is about to die because Boris is about to shoot at her; but what she feels is not a bullet straight into her heart, it's Nick's strong hand that grabs her and pulls her tightly to him in a fierce embrace. He lets himself go and weeps in liberation.

From here, the whole atmosphere changes and chaos breaks out once more. Ben and Veronica are trying to stop the journalists and the police who want to fling themselves upon them.

Felix stops Waltz. The helicopters are flying over the area again. While there, in the center of the bridge, Nick continues to hold Jas tight in his arms.

Doctors go quickly to the agent that Jas wounded, led by Arizona who injects something into his arm and puts an oxygen mask on his face. Nick doesn't leave her even for a moment, nor does he allow anyone to come near her except Arizona. He caresses her hair and watches her recover slowly until she opens her eyes.

He gently brushes her face. "I lost myself", she whispers with tears in her eyes. "I lost myself again."

"And I've found you, Jas. I told you that I would find you and brought you back to me, I told you that." He smiles and kisses her on the forehead, while she continues to look at him and caress his face... The compass is still on the ground beside them.

As everyone runs around, pushing and shoving to get to the middle of the bridge, a sad boy goes away, all alone, full of remorse and with his head bent. That boy is Jack.

***

An hour later

Ben enters the hospital waiting room and goes to Nick who is pacing back and forth in front of the chief's door. He's worried.

"I think things went like this", he tries to connect the pieces of the puzzle, showing Nick some documents. "Both the man in coma and the super witness that we were protecting at the Watchtower, were involved in the explosion at the Miami airport. What I believe is that, because of a series of misunderstandings, Jas thought that Boris was looking for the man in a coma", he explains.

Nick is about to ask him a question when Arizona comes out of the room and slowly closes the door behind her. He approaches her immediately looking concerned. The others get up from the sofas in the waiting room and join him.

"Tell me, please, what happened to her? What caused the hallucinations? Will she be okay?"

"First of all, I would like to apologize for not taking your calls. Unfortunately, a regrettable incident kept me away from the office and..."

"Don't worry. Tell me how Jas is, please", Nick cut short.

"Do you know anything about her medical history?"

"What do you need to know?"

"Serious illnesses, hospitalizations, surgeries she has had... the use of any painkillers?"

At the word painkiller, Patrick doesn't turn a hair even though inside him, considering the things that have happened to Jas and what Jack said to him about Emily's murder, he is experiencing intense emotions.

"When she was six she had her tonsils out. At twelve she broke a leg jumping from a tree, and last year she suffered a head trauma after a blow to the head, but there were no consequences", Nick lists, sure of what he says. This time Patrick lowers his gaze for a moment.

"Can this information help you?" asks Nick.

"I fear that there have been some consequences, unfortunately."

"What? What are you talking about?" he asks concerned.

"I suspect that the intracranial hematoma has never completely healed, and is provoking chronic pain that she can only put up with by using *Vicodin* and she has become hooked on it."

"Hooked? There must be a mistake. I'd know if what you're saying is correct."

Arizona lowers her head. "I'm sorry. Her hallucinations were caused by mix of *Vicodin* and alcohol. It is very dangerous", she looks at him apologetically. "We can wait for the tests if you like, but..."

"Yes, I want to. There has to be a mistake. That's not the reason for her hallucinations", he says convinced.

Arizona bites her lip for a moment. She looks around and then moves towards Nick. "A few months ago, when you brought her here for a cut on her hand", she takes a deep breath, "she already had traces of *Vicodin* in her blood. I wanted to tell you but... she prevented me. I'm mortified."

Nicks expression turns dark. Ben joins him quickly, worried, and the others look at each other incredulous. All except Patrick.

"Now you have to explain how a little girl of eighteen was able to stop you from telling me about it."

"She blackmailed me", she sounds more and more embarrassed, she can longer stay silent; at this point she just can't. She decides to explain everything before the man challenges her again. "She found the injured man in the bathroom at the airport the day of the explosion."

They all look at her shocked. Even Patrick stares, they were there that day.

"I know, I lied, but I was afraid. She was underage and... she should not have even been there, much less go..."

"Do you realize what she has done?! All because of your negligence!"

"You wouldn't be here if it wasn't for my negligence!" she screams with tears in her eyes. "If Jas hadn't found the man, you three would have gone into that airport and you'd be dead!" She gives vent to her feelings, looking at Nick, Ben and Patrick. She herself is amazed that she reacted in this way. All remain silent, thoughtful.

"I don't know what the consequences of my actions will be," continues Arizona. "But I know what will happen to Jas if you don't give her adequate assistance."

Nick puts his hands in his hair looking at his companions. He feels ill; it's as if he's going through the worst nightmare of his life. He turns to the chief and in a much calmer voice than before asks her: "How... how can I help her to... to get better?" he stammers.

"I can put you in contact with the chief of a clinic which specializes in the recovery and detoxification of..."

"What?!" he stops her abruptly. "Detoxification?! She is not a drug addict! She doesn't need a place like that! Tell me what I can give her, which medications. Anything, but at home!" he raises his voice again.

"Nick..." He hears the voice of Ginevra. Nick looks at her surprised. "Gin! What are you doing here?" he asks her. She greets the others with just a nod of the head and then turns to Arizona. "You can go, I'll talk to him", she smiles at her gently. "Thanks for everything."

The chief smiles bitterly, upset by everything that is happening, and returns to her office.

Nick quickly begins to explain the situation to her, furious. "She wanted her to be closed away in an awful... I can't even say it. She is not an addict!"

"Jas has an addiction, Nick. She needs help; something serious and qualified."

"I can give her that! She doesn't need to be closed in a psychiatric clinic. I can speak to her, try to make her reason, I can help her quit."

"No, it's not that simple," insists Ginevra calmly. "It's not just a mistake, all the things she has done, or a one-off over indulgence. She has abused it, Nick. Do you think that a couple of vitamins and a little chat can solve her problem? You'd be wrong. You don't realize just how serious this is and the risk that she's running." She tries to explain it to him in the simplest possible way, but he does not seem to want to listen. "She is not a drug addict."

"No? And are you a doctor? Because I am and I know what I'm saying. If you really want to help her, you can't do it alone", she says with regret, realizing how devastating this situation is for him.

"Nick", Veronica goes to him with a sad face and puts a hand on his shoulder. She sincerely feels bad for him and for Jas, but he moves brusquely away from her.

"Are you happy now?!" he barks at her. "You were right, Jas should be shut away!"

"Nick, I'm not..." she can't continue with what she wants to say, her trembling voice won't let her.

Will goes to her and takes her hand, while Nick sets off down the corridor. "Will, call Mina!" he orders. "Tell her that we have to talk."

"Nick!" Patrick goes after him worried, along with Ben.

"What do I do now?! What do I say to her parents'! How do I pull her out of trouble? Waltz can't wait to arrest her! The press will eat her alive!"

"Everything she's done, she's done under the influence of *Vicodin*", intervenes Ben. "That's temporary insanity, so she would not be totally responsible. Now it depends on how much alcohol she drank before leaving the hospital. An excessive alcohol reading would complicate her position", Ben reflects aloud. Nick looks even more worried than before.

"But in any case we will find a solution. They're children," he adds trying to reassure him.

Patrick puts a hand on his shoulder and says nothing.

"Temporary insanity", says Nick leaning against the wall. "Why didn't she tell me anything? Why didn't she tell me?" he continues to torment himself with questions, unaware that the only person who can give him the answers right now is precisely Patrick, his best friend, who chooses to remain silent.

514

***

In the meantime

Police are monitoring the hospital entrance, the elevator and the stairs. Waltz wants to be sure that nobody can enter or exit the building without his knowledge.

Lexi, disguised as the lawyer Ms. White, parks her flaming red car in front of the entrance, opens the door and gets out with a slow and sensual motion. She fixes her dark hair and goes towards the agents wiggling her hips. "Good evening, agents," she says in a breathy voice, looking at them like a cat.

In the meantime Koki, with bare hands and no security ropes, is climbing up the building directly to the fifth floor. Fast and agile, he manages to reach it in a very short time. He enters from a window left ajar, silently, without being noticed by anyone, takes the papers, files and photos from his black bag and starts to arrange them on the shelves.

Lexi enters the building. She knocks on the door of the chief's office and enters.

"Miss White?" Arizona says surprised as soon as she sees her. "Sorry, did we have an appointment?"

"We do now", she closes the door behind her and turns to the hospital chief. "They're Jas's tests you're holding, is that right?"

"I'm sorry but I can't give you this kind of infor..."

"Sit down, please," she interrupts her and goes to sit on Arizona's big chair, leaving the latter taken aback by her behavior. "Well," continues Lexi and opens the file she has brought with her. "Cutting edge equipment, new ambulances, pro-bono clinic", she looks up at Arizona, "those are only three of a series of improvements that the money of my client, Jeremy Black, who is also your only benefactor in this moment, has been able to purchase over the years." She closes the file and rests against the back of the chair. "Now, in order to continue this wonderful and valuable collaboration that you have, my client would need a *small* favor."

"How small?" asks Arizona, her voice unsteady. She realizes that the smell of blackmail is in the air.

With a smile on her lips, Lexi takes off her spectacles. "Smaller than one million two hundred and thirty four dollars."

Koki is already in the hospital lab tampering with the computers, changing the surveillance video, dates, recordings, times...

***

Shortly after

Nicholas's full team, plus Waltz, is gathered in the waiting room. They are waiting patiently for Arizona to arrive. Nick already knows what the outcome of the tests will be. He looks at Waltz, concerned. Very coolly he approaches him and asks in a low voice: "What are you still doing here?"

Ben and the others look at him warily.

"I will not let you take that brazen girl anywhere, is that clear? She has caused too much trouble lately and Christoph has seen everything with his own eyes."

To anyone watching them from a distance, it looks like he's talking to Nick about something pleasant. He is smiling and slapping him on the shoulder as if he was a friend he wants to help.

Nick moves away from him, annoyed. "Nobody was thinking of running away with her. And Jas has always paid for her mistakes."

"Mistakes?" Waltz smiles amused and goes close to Nick's ear. "She struck a disabled person and closed a minor in the trunk of a car. I was not allowed to investigate what happened after that and why she did it, but what I'm sure of is that this time she won't get away with it." He puts a hand on his shoulder again. "What happened today was not a mistake. She was armed, she fired at an agent, stole a car, caused a traffic accident injuring many civilians, she was driving without a license and, very soon, medical tests will confirm my suspicion that her alcohol reading was at least two or three times over the limit. And you know what that means don't you?"

"Nick, is everything okay here?" Ben intervenes, standing beside his friend in a tough pose as he looks Waltz up and down.

"Of course it is," says agent Waltz. "Waltz would dare to say that it's more than fine." He looks at everyone and smiles. "You guys are not real detectives. It is only thanks to the support you have from Felix and his good name that you collaborate with the FBI and have an agency. If it were not for him, no one would take you seriously. You wouldn't even have been able to open the Watchtower, seeing you're... what? Eighteen years old?"

"What's your problem?" Ben asks him, edgy, standing in front of him. His hand is shaking he wants to hit him so much.

"You people are my problem. Go and parade in front of photographers and journalists somewhere else! We are agents, not models."

The situation is tense. Veronica and Patrick rise from their chairs and go closer to Ben for fear that he'll do something stupid, while Waltz continues to fix his eyes on them and smile. Everything seems to point to the worst, but suddenly the elevator door opens and two black men get out: Cyrus and Felix.

The first, with dark glasses and a stick for the blind, smiles as he approaches the boys in an easy-going way. Felix, instead, doesn't seem comfortable and when he faces Nick he lowers his gaze.

"Sir!" Waltz rushes quickly to Felix. "There was no need for you to come, the situation is perfectly under control", he reassures him.

"Under control?!" Cyrus interrupts in a rough authoritarian voice. "A crazy criminal has escaped and you dare to speak of control?!"

Nick and his team look at each other bewildered. They know nothing about the criminal on the run, and don't even know who the colored man is with the white stick in his hand, but from the look of Felix, only one thing is certain: they must be quiet.

"Excuse me, but what are you talking about?" asks Waltz.

"What's your name?"

"I'm agent Christoph Waltz, sir, and..."

"Be quiet!" Cyrus interrupts him, hitting him with his white stick. "When I ask *one* question I expect only *one* reply", he explains, as if they were at the army barracks. "A dangerous", he pauses to reflect, "man by the name of Otto Who invented a wonderful chemical mixture commonly called hallucinogen, and thought it a good idea to try it out on some of his patients, before trying to poison all the citizens of Miami", he says as if he was telling a fairy tale and then suddenly his face becomes serious again. "Unfortunately, there are two complications. The first is that the lunatic has escaped", he shrugs his shoulders like children do, "and the second is that Jas was in the wrong place at the wrong time and he poisoned her with this very powerful mixture. We all know what happened after that, poor little victim."

"Victim?" repeated Waltz taken aback. It not is difficult to read from his face that he doesn't believe a word of what Cyrus has just told him. In all this, Felix is still silent. Waltz looks at them with mistrust.

"I have Jas's tests", Arizona's frightened voice breaks into the discussion. She looks at a point somewhere on the floor and hands the clinical record to Nick as if she can't wait to get rid of it. Nick takes it and after a few seconds opens his eyes and stares, incredulous. Ben and Veronica who are peeking at it beside him stare too.

"Traces of chemicals in the blood," he reads in a loud voice. "Ethyl-test negative."

He raises his head and looks at Arizona who does not move her gaze from the floor, as she goes away at a fast pace along the corridor.

"Excuse me", intervenes Waltz, visibly annoyed by the latest news they have received, "I don't want to seem rude, but you haven't shown me your badge", he turns to Cyrus who without any problem takes the badge from his pocket and shows it to him. Waltz takes it in his hand, turns it and looks at it for a few seconds and then still with a diffident voice says: "Claus Moore, eh? How come I wasn't informed of this... mysterious operation?"

"Simply because we didn't consider it necessary."

Waltz, irritated by his response, returns the badge to him. "You don't mind if..."

"Absolutely not," he replies without even hearing the entire question. "The hospital is full of evidence. Videos, photos..." he smiles, knowing that Otto Who does not exist, but that he is readily interpreted by Vladimir with a black wig on his the head. "And in the lab I'm sure you will find the poison we're talking about. It was a great pleasure to meet you, Mr. Waltz."

"For me, too", and in reality his face says the opposite. Both Cyrus and Felix get into the elevator, the latter still without saying a word.

"Ah", Cyrus stops the elevator door before it closes. "Ms. Herzog's lawyer will be coming here. Of course there is no need for me to tell you that she is exonerated from all charges, given the circumstances."

"Oh, of course", murmurs Waltz through clenched teeth.

The door of the elevator hasn't even closed before Waltz rushes along the corridor gesturing to his men to follow him, determined to check whether the evidence which Cyrus was talking about really does exist.

Nick and the boys stand there open-mouthed, still unable to believe everything that has just happened: false evidence, corrupt people. All this in so little time. It is a shock for them, but given recent events, they decide to stay out of it and not investigate any further.

***

In the elevator, Felix turns to Cyrus, worried: "You didn't fool Waltz. I told you it wouldn't work."

"Knowing is not proving, Felix. You should know that", he smiles.

There is silence. Cyrus, with the stick for the blind, pushes the red stop button and stops the elevator. "How much longer is this war between us going to continue, brother?" you can hear the sadness in the tone of his voice, perhaps for the first time after more than twenty years.

"Nick is the only reason I'm here today and the reason I agreed to help Jack in these months", he says completely ignoring his brother's question, and pushes the red button to restart the elevator.

The door opens, but before Felix manages to get out, Cyrus grips his arm. "F, please!"

519

Felix brusquely shakes himself free from his hold without even turning around, and the only thing he is able to say is: "You were the one who started this when you took away the woman that I loved from me."

The door closes and the two brothers are once again separated.

Felix is leaving the elevator when he hears hysterical laughter coming from the inside. He turns, looks at the door for a moment and goes away.

On the other side, Cyrus is sitting on the floor. He is laughing at the top of his lungs; he removes the dark glasses.

A sorrowful tear runs down his face.

***

It is deep night in Miami. Olivia Fox, one of the most ruthless gossip journalists in America, slips into the hospital, and disguised as a nurse furtively takes a couple of photos as she hides in the room where Jas is sleeping and then runs toward the elevator. Happy with this scoop, she hides the camera in her bag and pushes the white button to go down to the basement, when a strong hand tightens around her neck and slams her against the wall.

It's Jack's hand. Angry, he looks at the journalist straight in the eye as she suffocates. "You're all a bunch of damned vultures," he says through his clenched teeth.

Olivia is now close to passing out. Her face turns blue. Jack lets her go and pushed her violently on the ground. He takes the camera from her bag and breaks it against the wall smashing it into a thousand pieces.

The woman, terrified, desperately tries to catch her breath; the red imprint of Jack's hand is still on her neck. He kneels down next to her pulling her hair fiercely. "Next time", he whispers in her ear, "there will not be a next time, is that understood?" He doesn't wait for her answer because it's obvious. Without adding anything more he gets up, leaving the frightened woman on the floor, and goes toward the room where Jas is hospitalized. He takes off the black wig and glasses, tosses them into the rubbish bin and stops in front of the glass that divides the corridor from Jas's room. He looks at her with tears in his eyes. Her face is pale with dark circles under her eyes and she's full of tubes and needles inserted everywhere.

Beside her, Nick, sitting on a chair, is holding her hand and is sleeping with his head resting on her bed. Jack looks at them as if he's watching TV. Immobile, with his gaze fixed on them, waiting for the next scene.

"Good evening", he hears a female voice behind him. He turns around and sees a very beautiful dark-haired girl, who is looking at him with sweet blue eyes. He doesn't know that the girl is called Ginevra.

"You're the guy who came to Ben's wedding, right?"

"Yes, I am", he cuts short.

Ginevra understands that the blond boy has no desire to talk. She also goes to the window and for a few seconds they look together, in silence, at the pair in the room. Jack was looking at Jas. Ginevra was looking at Nickolas. Both of them sad and melancholy.

"Nick and Jas", she whispers without even realizing it, and a bitter smile crosses her face. "All the rest of us are just third wheels", and with bright eyes continues to look at them.

Jack stares at her for a moment. He puts his hands in his pockets and goes away down the corridor.

***

A year ago, Villa Torres

"Gin, please, stop!" Nick continued to repeat chasing her down the stairs.

"No! No! I can't stand it any longer, it's driving me crazy, Nick!"

"I can't understand you! Where are all these doubts coming from? Why don't you trust me?!"

"I don't know!" she screams and she stops, putting her suitcase on the ground. "You, you depend on her, Nick, and you don't even realize it! Regardless of where we are and what we're doing, as soon as she calls you jump and run to Jas immediately!"

"What's wrong with that? I would do it for you too, Gin." He put his hands gently on her shoulders. "Help me to understand, please, I don't want to lose you, I really don't."

"Your relationship is.... *too much* for me. The way you... the way you look at each other, touch each other, how you know one another, I can't bear it!" Her voice was broken by her sobbing, she couldn't stop the tears. Nick pulled her to him and then looking into her eyes said to her "I've known her since she was five years old, she's like a sister to me, how do you see her as a threat? Please see reason, don't ruin everything because you're afraid." Try as he might, he couldn't reassure her. She took a deep breath and lowered her head.

"Ginevra?"

"Why are we still here, Nick?" she asks looking around her, "Why don't you pack your bags, why don't we leave for Miami? Everything has been ready for months now, they're all just waiting for you, but you're not there. Why?" She stared at him, her eyes filled with hope, she was waiting for a response that denied her fears, her insecurities, but she received exactly the opposite. Nick remained silent; what he desired more than anything else in the world was to reassure her, give her the answers she wanted, convince her to remain, but all he managed to do was lower his head take a step backwards.

"You don't leave because you don't want leave Jas", said Ginevra with a bitter smile, "You can't tear yourself away from her."

"That doesn't mean a thing," he whispered, "it has nothing to do with our relationship."

"This", Ginevra stated showing him the engagement ring she wore on her ring finger, "this means something, though, Nick. It should represent the love and the union between two people." She took off the ring and gave it back to him. "Then why do I feel like the third wheel?"

She said nothing else, picked up her suitcase and went out the front door weeping without saying goodbye to anyone.

In the living room the boys were sitting in silence, embarrassed by what they had just heard, feeling sorry for Nick. Veronica stood up quickly from the table and ran after Ginevra, while Patrick and

Will went to their friend, sitting devastated on the stairs with the ring in his hand.

"Courage, my friend", Patrick consoled him putting a hand on his shoulder. "I am with you always and in any case."

"Me too frrf drasssssssssssss."

***

Miami, today

There is not much to say in these cases, and it's perhaps the only time in life where words are really superfluous, where the right words do not exist, because the excruciating pain that a parent feels in the loss of a child is indescribable and there is no phrase or gesture that will make him feel better... it's terrible at the beginning, but in the end you find that it becomes even worse...

Arizona embraces Diana's mother in tears; there are a lot of people around them including interns, hospital doctors and the young friends of the little girl accompanied by their parents.

Jack kneels; he takes a handful of earth and throws it on the small white coffin. He gets up slowly looking at the photo of Diana; under the photo are the yellow cat, her inseparable cuddly toy, and many little drawings she had done in recent months. Amongst those drawings there is also a portrait of him and Jas kissing inside a heart. He clenches his fists and goes angrily toward his motor bike.

***

A few days later

"No, no and no!" barks Ben angrily. He takes an empty basket and turns to his sons who are looking at him annoyed.

"I don't want phones, video games or computers on the table! So now you're going to put everything in this basket and you can have it all back only after dinner!" he tries to act tough, but he doesn't manage do it as he'd like to. For days now, too many thoughts and concerns are running through his mind after the discovery about Isobel and her team.

The three of them get up from their chairs snorting, they take their electronic devices and put them in the basket and sit down again without comment seeing that America is arriving with dinner. It looks like the usual quiet family evening, when suddenly the noise of a helicopter can be heard from outside and the more the seconds pass the more the noise becomes deafening. Ben gets up and goes to the picture window to see what is happening when it is suddenly smashed and Jack appears in the middle of the kitchen. He gets up from the ground slowly and looks around with a furious gaze; it is not difficult to realize who he is looking for. A red light enters the room: Vladimir is pointing his weapon at Ben from the helicopter.

"Hey guys! Is everything okay?" Nick's voice can be heard coming from the corridor, he opens the door but hasn't time to realize what is happening before Jack attacks him. "Where is she?!" he screams angrily pointing a gun on him. Nick does not reply, he looks around, he sees Ben's children huddled frightened in a corner, America on the other side of the room, scared, with the dish of pasta upside down on the ground, Vladimir in the helicopter pointing his weapon toward Ben and the latter showing him with a look that he has a gun in his holster. Veronica is hiding behind the living room door, also armed.

Only after assessing the situation, Nick turns to Jack: "What's this, Jack?" his voice is challenging, "You're so good at manipulating, bribing and blackmailing all around you, and you can't find her?"

"Where is she?!" he asks again through his teeth. His finger moves nervously on the trigger.

"I'll never tell you", he answers in a hard tone. "You've done enough damage already! You have to leave her alone!"

"I will when she tells me to! Now tell me where she is Nickolas!"

"No!" he has no intention of revealing where Jas is, but unfortunately Jack is as obstinate as he is and will never leave the building without that information. He tightens his blue eyes and without taking his eyes off, turns his arm and points the gun at little Franklin to the amazement and concern of all present, all except Nick.

"Tell me she where is or I swear I'll shoot him straight in the head!" His hand is shaking, it's like he's on drugs or drunk. Ben stands in front of his weapon raising his hands in a sign of surrender, there is no need for words, his terrified eyes say everything. Veronica decides to come out of hiding and points hers weapon at Jack, but from the helicopter in flight Vladimir changes his target, ready to shoot at her if she even dares make a move.

"Nickolas!" shouts Jack firing a shot two millimeters from Franklin, who is increasingly pale.

"No, no, no!" America despairs. She runs to the children and takes them in her arms, covering them with her body. "They're just kids! They have nothing to do with this, don't shoot, please!" She begs him, her eyes bright with tears protecting them as if they were her own children.

"You've got to tell me! Where is Jas?! Where is she?!"

"In the Miami psychiatric clinic", reveals Ben. He can no longer stand the tension seeing his children in danger; he looks at Nick with a sorry air, but not repentant for what he has done.

"You have locked her in a psychiatric clinic?! You've..." Jack can't even finish the sentence from the shock and anger of the moment. "You don't realize what you've done!" He looks at him, his eyes turning nasty. Nick lowers his gaze. "It's for her own good", he whispers.

"For her own good?! For her own good?!" he repeats approaching him in a threatening way with the gun in his hand. Veronica is ready to shoot; Vladimir is also ready to do the same from the helicopter.

"Have you ever been in there, Nickolas?! Eh?!" he goes forward and stops right in front of his face. Nick doesn't move.

"Well, I have! I've been there and..." once again he does not continue the sentence. Jack's eyes fill with tears and in a broken voice he adds: "Jas does not deserve this. You shouldn't have done this to her." Then he immediately starts to run. He jumps out of the broken window and clings to the ladder hanging from the helicopter. Vladimir continues to point the weapon at Nick until they disappear behind the Watchtower with their helicopter. Once out of danger, Ben runs to his terrified children, taking them and America in a strong embrace. Benjamina is wailing in his arms and Pavarotti for the first time in years embraces him calling him daddy.

Nick is standing motionless looking at the floor, his head hanging.

Veronica approaches him, her face serious. "What the hell came over you, Nick?!"

"He wouldn't have fired", he responds confidently and runs out of the room into the corridor, leaving everyone there with their mouths open.

Little Franklin turns toward his father. "Was that a joke? A test? Eh, daddy?"

"Yes", he answers him kissing him on the head, "it was just a joke, son."

***

Shortly after

The black helicopter lands in the parking lot in front of the psychiatric clinic. Shortly after, the entry door is literally kicked open by Vladimir, and once open he goes in snarling with the gun in his hand.

He goes to the counter, scaring to death the doctors and nurses. Behind him you see pointed Japanese stars arrive like rockets and fly straight toward the video cameras putting them out of use in a second. Only after that Koki enters the room, with a black hat on his head, followed by Lexi, dressed like a masochistic nurse. She goes to the counter and asks the terrified doctor in a provocative and sensual voice: "Excuse me, handsome man, can you kindly tell me where I can find Jas Herzog."

The doctor, terrified by Vladimir's presence, shivers glued to the wall unable to articulate anything that makes sense.

Jack bursts into the room, his eyes are small, nasty, and he walks nervously like someone who has neither the time nor desire to wait for the answer he is looking for. Pushing off the frightened people he finds in his way, he goes to the doctor and punches him

526

fiercely in the face making him fall to the ground. "Which room is Jas in?! Tell me where she is!" Jack is no longer in control of himself, it has been days since he saw her, heard from her, he doesn't know how she is, he feels as if he's going mad. A nurse goes quickly behind the counter and even though her hand is trembling with fear manages to press a couple of keys on the computer and then with her voice broken by sobs says: "Fifth floor, room seventeen."

Jack doesn't need to hear any more. He turns around and goes fast along the corridor with his heart in his mouth; behind him, are his brothers covering his back. Koki continues to launch star spikes and break every camera hanging on the ceiling. Vladimir points his weapon at anyone who dares move along his path; Lexi instead parades between the frightened people as if she was on a catwalk and every so often strikes someone with the whip she has in her hand. Jack arrives in front of room number seventeen, takes a deep breath and opens it slowly. To his right, Will and Patrick get up from their chairs as soon as they see him, not in the least surprised. Jack rushes toward Jas's bed.

She is sleeping, her face is still so pale, like last time he saw her, she looks thin. He takes her hand gently. "My love", he whispers. Trembling like a leaf as he caresses her hand and her head, he feels fragile, weak seeing her in this state. He feels like John again.

Delicately, he removes the drip, takes her in his arms and before leaving the room with her, turns to Patrick who looks at him in the eyes: sincere, suffering, repentant, in love.

All he does is nod his head, Jack thanks him with the same nod and he goes, followed by Koki and Vladimir.

As he holds her up along the corridor, Jas opens her eyes slowly, she doesn't feel well, her head is exploding, but despite the pain and confusion, she recognizes Jack and caresses his face saying, "Jack, leave me, here." She can barely speak, but her words are clear. "I need help, leave me", she repeats in a low voice.

He looks at her with bright eyes and kisses her hand. "No, I will not leave you! I will not abandon you, Jas!"

Jas caresses his face again, she would tell him so many other things but she can't do it, she feels tired, her eyelids are becoming heavy and it's not long before she becomes unconscious once more as Jack looks on in tears.

Patrick leaves the room and watches them move away, he knows Jack well by now, he has had the chance to study him in all these months, he knows where he is taking her and that it is the best choice for her. Lexi is behind him; she enters the room in silence and sees Will sitting on the chair stammering something, all alone and agitated after what has happened. She takes the whip and hits it on the floor hard making him jump in fright.

As soon as he sees her he starts to stutter even more, scratching his beard and hair, she smiles, throws the whip to the ground, and literally jumps on top of him, pushing him against the wall and giving him an aggressive tongue kiss. Then she moves away from him, looks at him straight in the eyes and slaps him hard screaming: "How dare you! *One Thousand*!" then goes away offended and angry, leaving Will dazed.

The four boys leave the clinic and head toward the helicopter.

A short distance away, Nick, Ben and Veronica are watching them from inside their jeep.

"Nick, we're ready!" Ben says as he loads his gun. Veronica does the same, eager to intervene. He sits there in silence, gripping the steering wheel with both hands, and watches Jack board the helicopter with Jas in his arms.

"Nick!" Ben opens the door impatiently; he doesn't want to lose the person who only half an hour ago threatened one of his children with a gun, but Nick does nothing. He doesn't get out of the vehicle and with his gaze fixed on the helicopter turns to his two teammates and all he says is: "No."

They both look at him shocked; they can't believe what they just heard.

"Let them go," he adds with tears in his eyes.

***

In Serbia, Danica, Jas's scrawny little grandmother, is running up hurriedly up the stairs of the hospital. "What do we have?!" she asks the intern behind her brusquely.

"Eeh... a helicopter is arriving with a... an emergency," stammers the boy, scared by the impetuosity of the hospital chief, trying hard to keep up with her. "Breathing difficult, cold sweat, it seems she had a drug withdrawal crisis and has been sedated because she was too ill and..."

"How on earth are you talking?!" the elderly woman interrupts scandalized as she goes up the stairs in a sprightly fashion, despite her age, leaving the boy behind. "An intern cannot express himself in this inadequate manner! You're fired!"

"But?"

"No *but*! Is it possible that at sixty years of age I have to find myself working with these dyslexic imbeciles and..." she opens the door to the roof and sees a white helicopter landing, "And furthermore this is not our helicopter! Who are these people?!"

"I, I don't..."

"You're so dyslexic and impaired that you're not even able to stutter!" Danica keeps criticizing him as she goes to the helicopter and sees a blond boy getting out. She is about to rebuke him too when she sees him take a girl in his arms, but soon realizes that she is not just any girl, but *the girl*: her grand-daughter Jas.

Danica stares wide-eyed and rushes toward them, the intern's confused words immediately become clear. "Emergency stretcher and fast! Stethoscope, oxygen, I want an antibiotic solution drip prepared..."

The scared intern immediately brings the stretcher... Jack is still holding her in his arms, he doesn't want to let her go, and as Danica gives him a filthy look her blue eyes have become even more severe than usual. Jack notices that but he says nothing, gently laying Jas's unconscious body on the stretcher and caressing her head with tears running down his face.

Danica still says nothing and before going away with Jas to give her all the help she needs, she gives Jack one last icy glare. She has neither accused nor thanked him, she can't do anything because she doesn't know exactly what has happened, but in the depths of her heart she does not like Jack at all.

***

We all tell lies. That is the one and only truth. We all act like "beautiful" people, we say that we prefer to hear the truth, but it's not true, because that is exactly what we're afraid of.

There are many reasons why we lie: so as not to offend someone or to try to get off scot-free when we make a mistake. We often lie to be right, not to jeopardize ourselves. Sometimes we tell lies unknowingly... some people lie for fun, or as a joke; sometimes for fear of being judged by others, or in order not to hurt the person we love because they wouldn't understand what we're doing and why we're doing it; because we're insecure, to avoid unnecessary arguments that lead to nothing other than unsettle the people involved. There are people who tell them to be nice or to do harm, or because they are bullied, those who lie to themselves, those who lie for their own gain, or when they are ashamed of the truth.

We lie to protect others or ourselves, or others from ourselves; a person who lies to someone who is ill to give him strength so he doesn't stop fighting, those who tell lies bigger than themselves, or out of fear of what might happen by telling the truth...

My conclusion is this: even though telling the truth sometimes makes you feel better, the lie makes you live better.

I far prefer a lie, beautiful or ugly as it may be, as long as it lets me live the only life I have been given in peace and serenity.

***

Two months later

Go along the main road and after the small convenience store where Nikolas usually bought the *zele* - a typical Serbian cake - for Jas, turn to the left. Proceed along the narrow dirt street for about twenty yards, and on your left you'll see a small white house, with an old rusty bike leaning on the wall, flowers at the window, a few pear trees around, and clothes hanging on the rope pulled from one side of the garden to the other. You can hear sound of the pigs coming from the yard and the radio on the terrace playing Balkan music as Danica throws the hen's feed over the green lawn, and they all run to eat.

The sun is hidden behind the clouds; it's starting to get cold outside. She feels a presence behind her; she turns around and sees her granddaughter at the front door: no make-up, wearing a tracksuit, her hair pulled back and suitcase in hand. She goes to her.

"Are you ready to leave?" asks Danica.

"Yes."

"Do you know where you are going?"

"Yes."

Danica can see the sadness in the eyes of her granddaughter; in two months she has been able to heal her body and her mind, but not her heart; that is still deeply wounded. She caresses her face. "Granddaughter of mine, the most important relationship you can have in your life is the relationship that you established with yourself, always remember that. Grandparents and parents will die sooner or later, loves will end, friendships very probably won't last, but you will have yourself for your whole life."

Jas's eyes are misty, she lowers her head, but the grandmother immediately lifts it with both hands. "You have to learn to love yourself and respect yourself first of all. Promise me that you will not do yourself any more harm, others will take care of that."

Jas smiles and hugs her small but great and wise grandmother very hard; she hasn't left yet but even so she feels she is already missing her. "I love you and I adore you, grandma."

"I love you too, my darling granddaughter."

She accompanies her to the gate and as she watches her leave her heart begins to tighten in her breast... in reality she does not see Jas, but her daughter Jelena, as she disappears along the dirt road carrying her suitcase.

95.

I've lied, stolen, done drugs. I'm sorry... I'm sorry for the people that I've hurt and disappointed, but above all I am sorry for what I did to myself.

I am tired of having to fight, argue, I'm tired of suffering, I just need a little peace, a little serenity, and there is only one place where I can find it.

I'm going to people who give me advice, but don't forbid, who rebuke me but do not judge, I'm going to those who leave me to myself, but do not abandon me, I'm going to the only people who teach me without giving me lessons.

I'm the last to get off the plane. I don't know why, but I chose to do it this way. I walk along the corridor and after showing my passport at document control I get my suitcase. It's easy to find, it's the only one in the luggage section. I start towards the exit, my heart is beating very fast, my legs are trembling with emotion, who knows if they're still there waiting for me? I'm terribly late, I turn the corner and I see them. I can't hold back the tears; they stream down my face as I run to meet them.

I don't say anything. I just put down the suitcase, embrace them, and let myself go in a liberating flood of tears.

Mina and Patrick. My crutches.

96.

A month later, December – From Mina's diary

Nothing has changed at the school in Gorizia. Rodrigo is dragging his red trolley along the corridor, trying to sell his mini Christmas trees to the students. Susy is taking pictures of the big fir tree set up in the cube, decorated by the first grade children. Chanel has just come out of the editor's office, all agitated as usual. And Mujo is carrying a large heavy parcel to the Principal's office, swearing in Bosnian.

I go down the stairs and see the Olsen twins arguing, and start to fight and push each other; this makes me really mad. I go across to them, the noise of my heels echoes all along the corridor. "Now I've had enough of you two!" I shout as I separate them. They look at me wide-eyed.

"I would like to remind you that last year Jas and Ja..." I stop just in time, "Jas and John injured themselves because of your shitty behavior! If I see you pushing each other in the corridor ever again, I'll kick your butts! Have I been clear?"

"Hi, Mina!" Chanel interrupts, coming towards us at a fast pace. Tim and Tom, meanwhile, have taken advantage of my distraction to run away, frightened.

"Hello", I greet her disappointed and go to the bathroom.

"Is Jas in her office?" she asks me, starting to follow me.

"Yes, but keep away from the bathroom because I have to talk to her."

"Well, I must ask you to give me a..."

"Chanel!" I interrupt her, raising my voice. I put myself in front of the bathroom door to prevent her from entering and ask: "Which part of the sentence *keep away from the bathroom because I have to talk to her* don't you understand?!"

Chanel lifts her hands in sign of surrender and answers annoyed: "Okay, okay." As she goes along the corridor, she sends some offended looks my way. Before I enter the bathroom I hear her complain to Susy: "Since she came back from Miami she's become a dictator!"

I shake my head, ignoring her comments, and go into the bathroom. There's not a soul there. I open the door of Jas's office and see her sitting on the bowl looking at the new poster that she has hung on the wall.

Surprised, I exclaim: "Wow, Iron man?"

She looks at me pretending to brush the slobber from her mouth and says to me, "Robert Downie Junior, grrrrr..."

"And what happened to James Marsters, grrrr?"

"Vampires don't do it for me anymore."

"Then why did you choose an old man as a vampire?"

Jas starts to laugh and starts throwing pieces of the old poster of Spike at me.

"I already told you that even my mother finds them younger, didn't I?"

The bell rings. Why does lunch time pass so quickly? Jas gets off the toilet bowl and starts toward the exit, holding a piece of the torn poster in her hand. I follow her, thinking of how to tackle the topic and instead of turning toward corridor B, she goes toward the cube.

"Jas?"

"I don't feel like going to class."

"Jas?"

She stops in the middle of the corridor and lowers her head; she already knows what I want to speak to her about. "Wait and see, he'll call you, give him time to..." I don't know how complete the sentence to reassure her, "I know that sounds like the usual platitude, but give things time and you'll see that it will all work out."

She smiles and gives me a nod, but her gaze is still sad. She turns and goes toward the cube without a word.

97.

At the same time – From Jas's diary

I've gone outside into the cube. The Christmas tree is so high, this year, that I don't think they will be able to close the opening in the roof.

I don't want to go to class. I don't even want to sit here in the cube all alone, let alone go back home and look at Nick's empty villa all day.

How strange, me not knowing where to put myself, I think, ironic

"Jaaaaaaas, Jaaaaaaas..." I hear someone calling my name, I look around me disoriented, I recognize this voice, but I can't believe that it's really him. "Jaaaaaaas!"

I lift my head and I see him enter from the opening of the cube. Metoo.

He is beautiful, more beautiful than I remembered. He flies around in a circle and continues to cry out my name.

"Metoo! Metoo, do you remember me?!"

"No, no, no, no, Jaaaaaaaaaas, I, I loooove you!"

I look at him with tears in my eyes, his words warm my heart; it feels like I'm seeing a piece of Miami flying around me. But how can he be here?

Suddenly he flies behind me, I turn and... I see Jack.

98.

At the same time – From Jx's diary

Jack walks quickly toward Jas and before she can say or do something, he takes her head in his hands and gives her a kiss full of passion. He unwillingly pulls away from her and meets her intense dark eyes. "One hundred days have gone by, Jas", he says, reminding her of their pact as he gazes at her with a determined look, but inside him his heart is beating furiously. "Are you my girlfriend, now?" he nervously caresses her head; his eyes are becoming bright with tears. "It's not difficult, yes or no, Jas?!" he asks, increasingly agitated and scared by her response, he can't take it any longer, it is clear from his face that he is going crazy. "Yes or no?! Tell me! Tell me, Jas!"

"Yes! Yes!" Her answer resounds all around the cube. Jack, as astonished as she is by what he has just heard, grabs her again and begins to kiss her, unable to stop himself any longer, with the parrot darting around them shouting: "Metoooooo, no, no, no, no Jaaaas I loooove youuu, kooooo!"

***

At the same time

Mujo drags the parcel as far as the Principal's office. "This paco too much of weight I carried", he complains.

"Who sent it?" asks Principal De Filippi who, curious, searches for some note or card of the sender on the parcel.

"Paaa, no I don't know who sends, but I know who brought this one paco. I brought, alone like magician!" he complains.

As she continues to look for the sender, the Principal thanks him.

"*Djabe tebi thanks ka mene kicma boluses! You Picka materina...*" he swears in Bosnian and goes off in a huff.

536

The Principal takes the scissors, opens the huge parcel and the next instant she collapses to the ground, putting her hand on her heart. Then she shouts, "Jill! Jiiiill!"

Jill opens the door and to her great surprise she sees the Principal kneeling on the ground, shocked, unable to even speak. With her finger she continues to indicate to her to look inside the huge box, still keeping her hand on her heart. Concerned, Jill approaches and looks inside. She stares wide-eyed.

Inside the box is the crucifix stolen a year ago.

Summary

❧ J.H.Project ❧

Official website: www.jhprojectbooks.com
E-mail: jay.acca@yahoo.it
Facebook: www.facebook.com/JHProjectBook
Twitter: @JayHProject
Instagram: j.h.project

Printed in Great Britain
by Amazon